DOCTOR SPEKTOR®

MASTER OF THE OCCULT

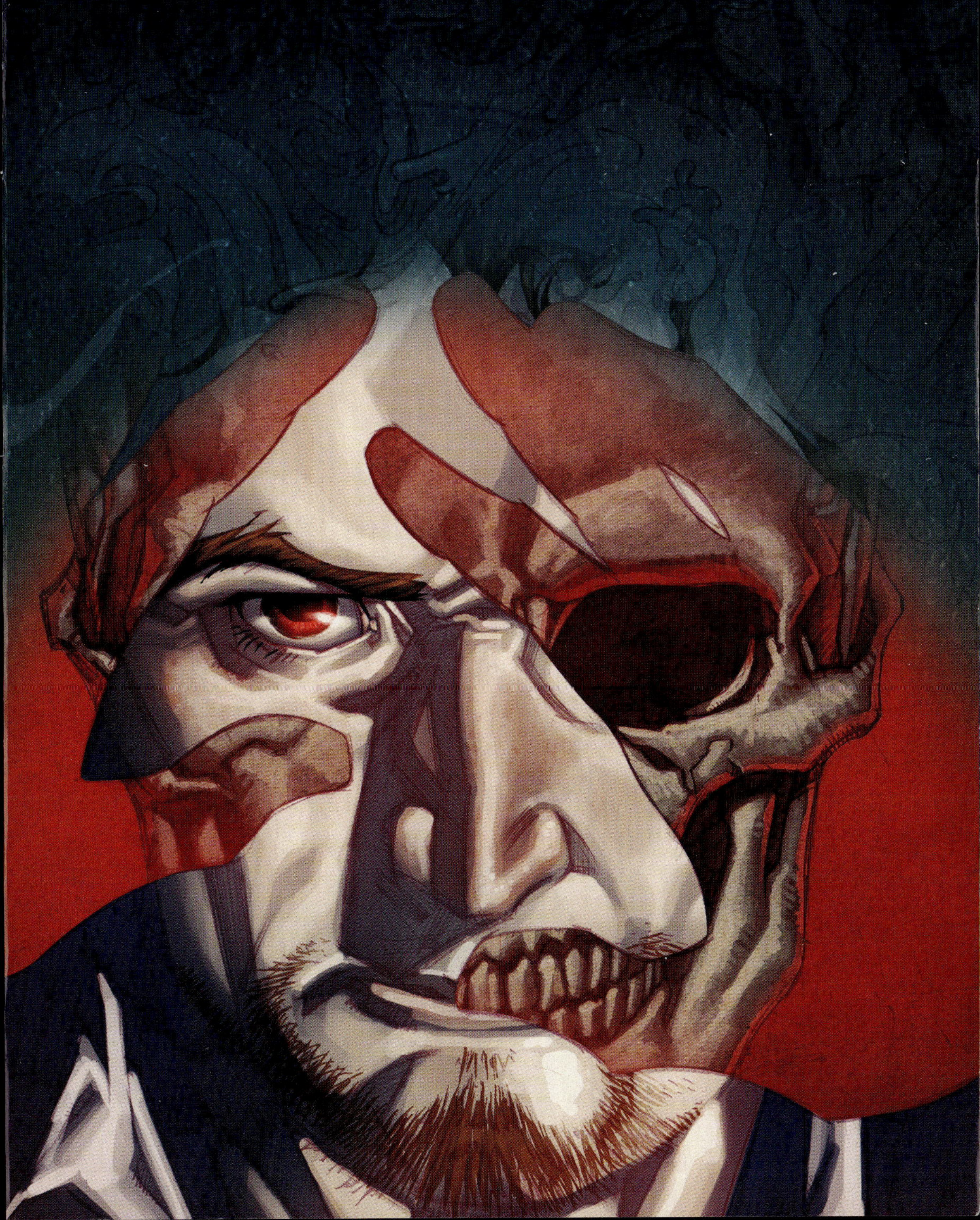

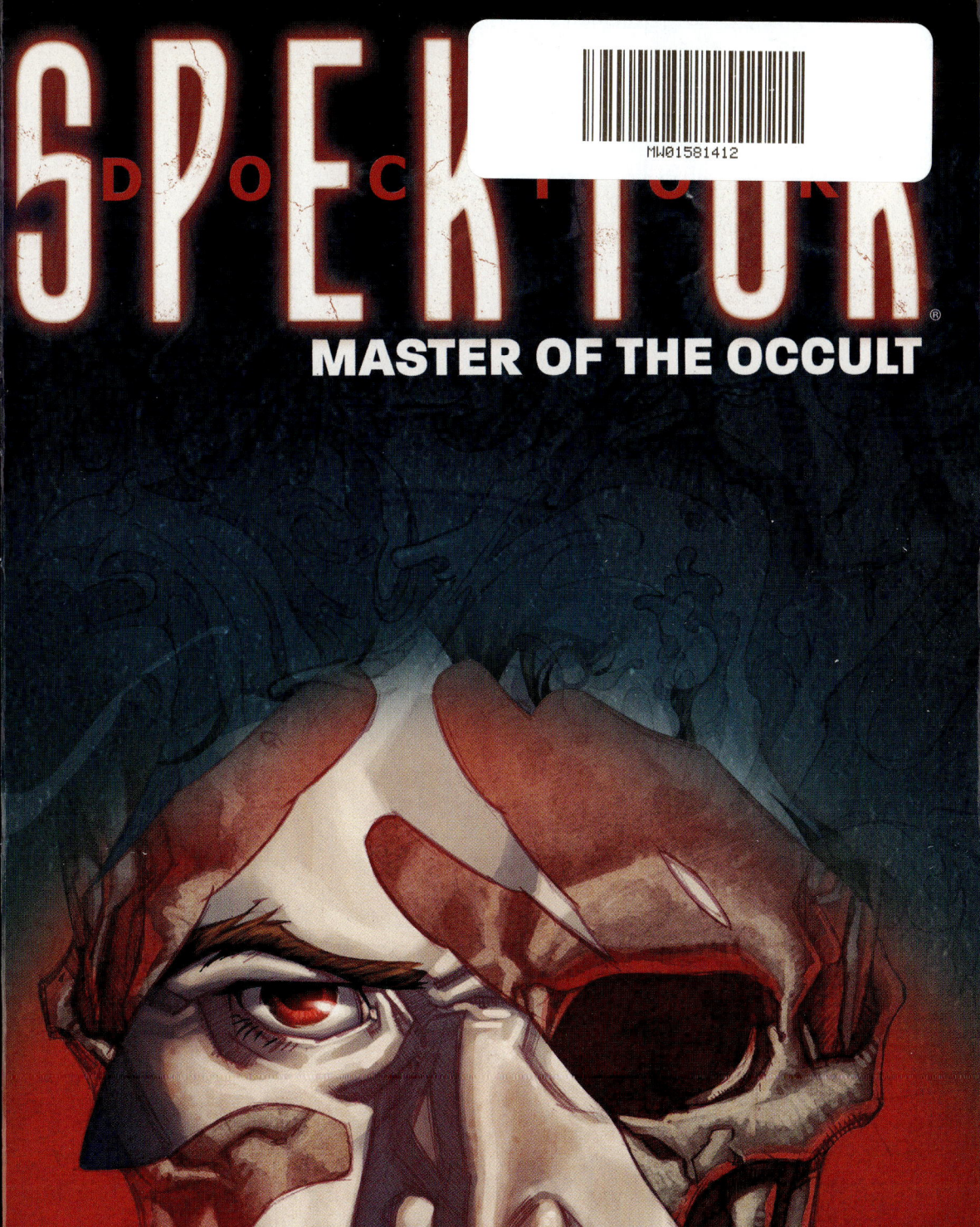

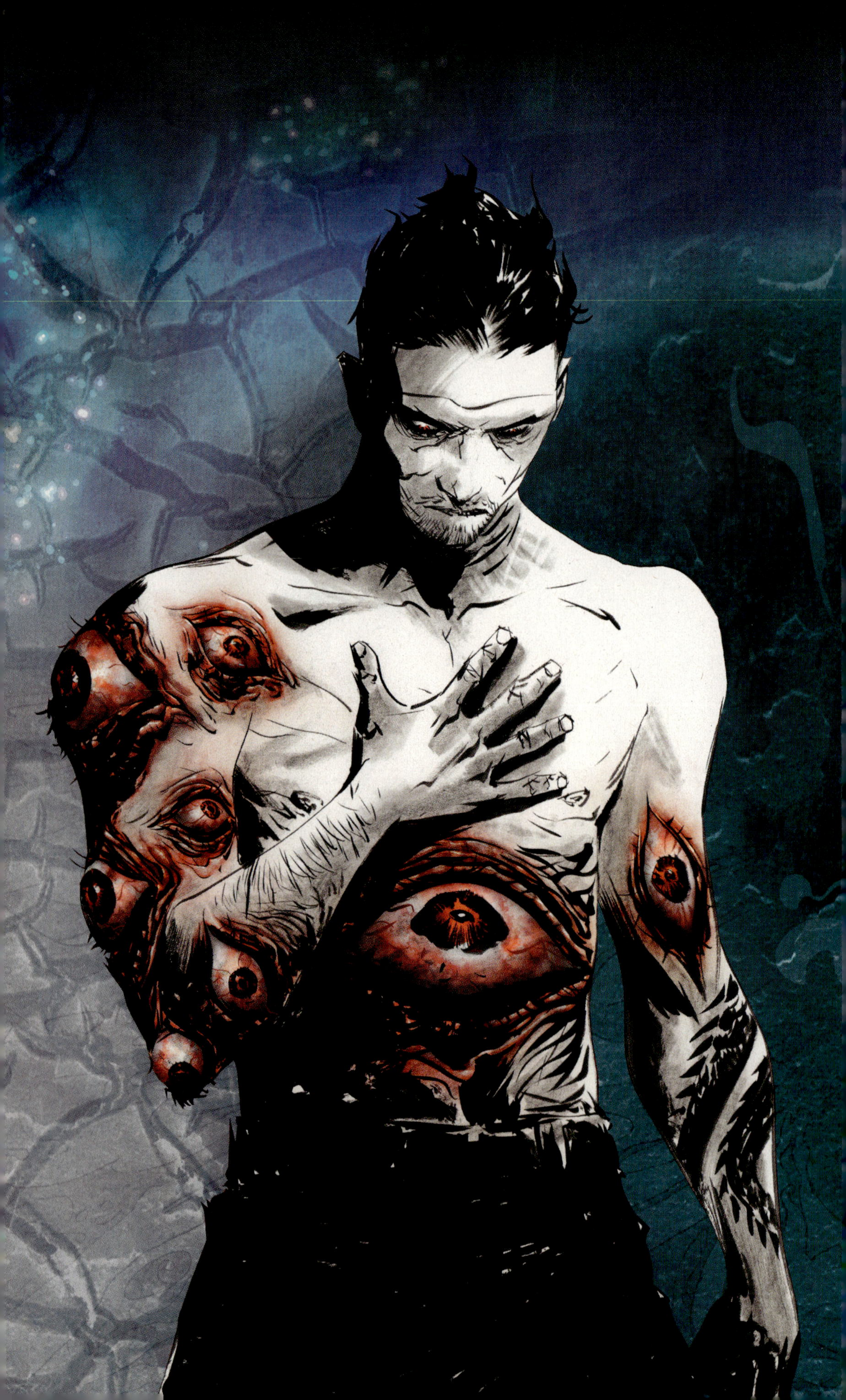

DOCTOR SPEKTOR
MASTER OF THE OCCULT

WRITTEN BY
MARK WAID

ART BY
NEIL EDWARDS
ROBERTO CASTRO

COLORS BY
JORDAN BOYD
LUIGI ANDERSON
MAURÎCIO WALLACE

LETTERS BY
MARSHALL DILLON

COLLECTION COVER BY
CHRISTIAN WARD

COLLECTION DESIGN BY
KATIE HIDALGO

SPECIAL THANKS TO **TOM ENGLEMAN, BEN CAWOOD, NICOLE BLAKE,** AND **COLIN MCLAUGHLIN**

PACKAGED AND EDITED BY **NATE COSBY**
OF COSBY AND SONS PRODUCTIONS

THIS VOLUME COLLECTS ISSUES 1-4 OF DOCTOR SPEKTOR: MASTER OF THE OCCULT BY DYNAMITE ENTERTAINMENT.

DYNAMITE

Nick Barrucci, CEO / Publisher
Juan Collado, President / COO
Rich Young, Director Business Development
Keith Davidsen, Marketing Manager

Joe Rybandt, Senior Editor
Hannah Elder, Associate Editor
Molly Mahan, Associate Editor

Jason Ullmeyer, Design Director
Katie Hidalgo, Graphic Designer
Chris Caniano, Digital Associate
Rachel Kilbury, Digital Assistant

Visit us online at www.DYNAMITE.com
Follow us on Twitter @dynamitecomics
Like us on Facebook /Dynamitecomics
Watch us on YouTube /Dynamitecomics

ISBN-10: 1-60690-561-9 ISBN-13: 978-1-60690-561-6 First Printing 10 9 8 7 6 5 4 3 2 1

DOCTOR SPEKTOR: MASTER OF THE OCCULT®, VOL. 1. This volume collects material originally published in Doctor Spektor: Master of the Occult #1-4. Published by Dynamite Entertainment. 113 Gaither Dr., STE 205, Mt. Laurel, NJ 08054. DOCTOR SPEKTOR: MASTER OF THE OCCULT is ® and Copyright © 2014 by Random House, Inc. Under license to Classic Media, LLC. All rights reserved. DYNAMITE, DYNAMITE ENTERTAINMENT and its logo are © & ® 2014 Dynamite. All rights reserved. All names, characters, events, and locales in this publication are entirely fictional. Any resemblance to actual persons (living or dead), events or places, without satiric intent, is coincidental. No portion of this book may be reproduced by any means (digital or print) without the written permission of Dynamite Entertainment except for review purposes. The scanning, uploading and distribution of this book via the Internet or via any other means without the permission of the publisher is illegal and punishable by law. Please purchase only authorized electronic editions, and do not participate in or encourage electronic piracy of copyrighted materials. Printed in Canada

For information regarding press, media rights, foreign rights, licensing, promotions, and advertising e-mail: marketing@dynamite.com

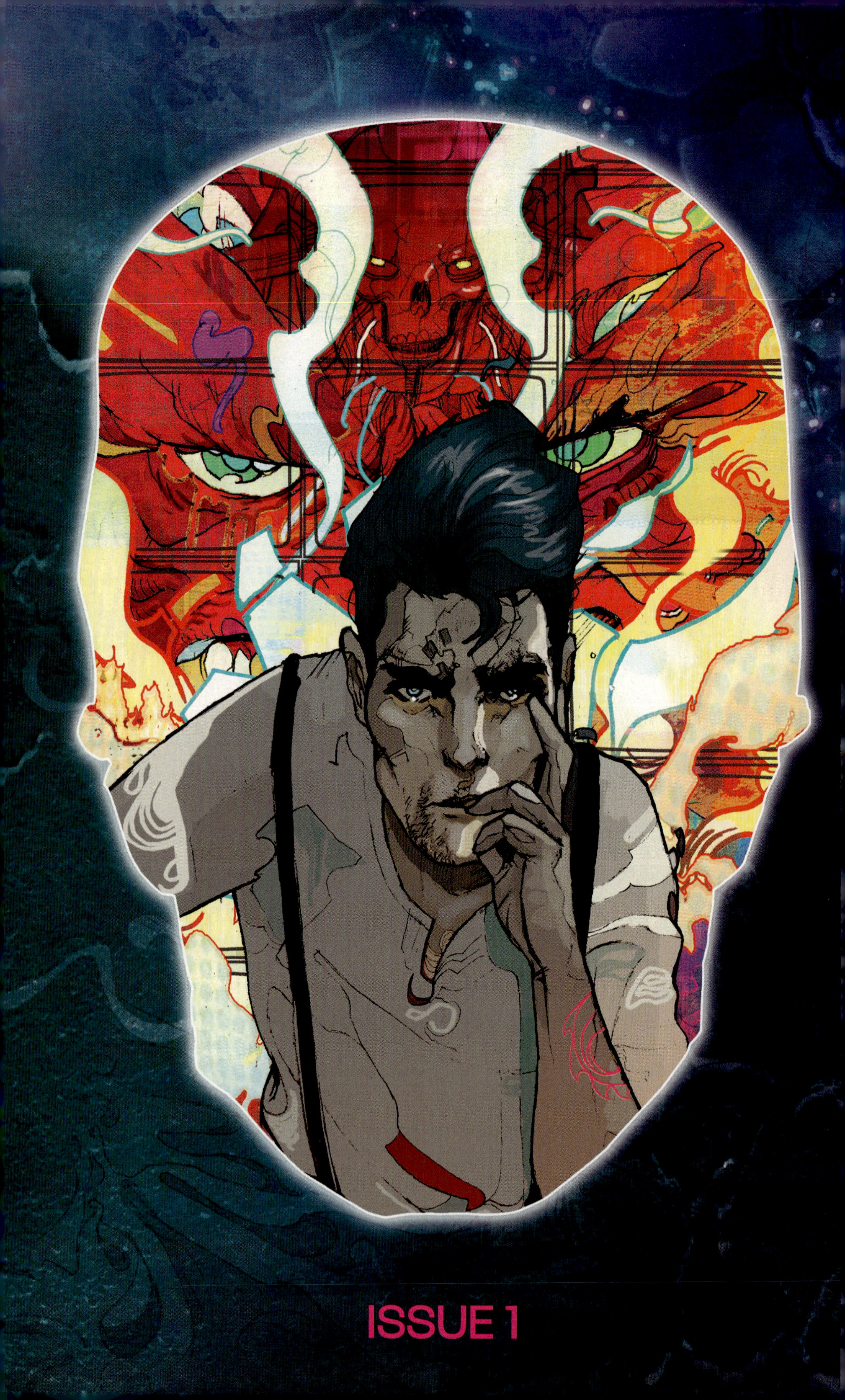
ISSUE 1

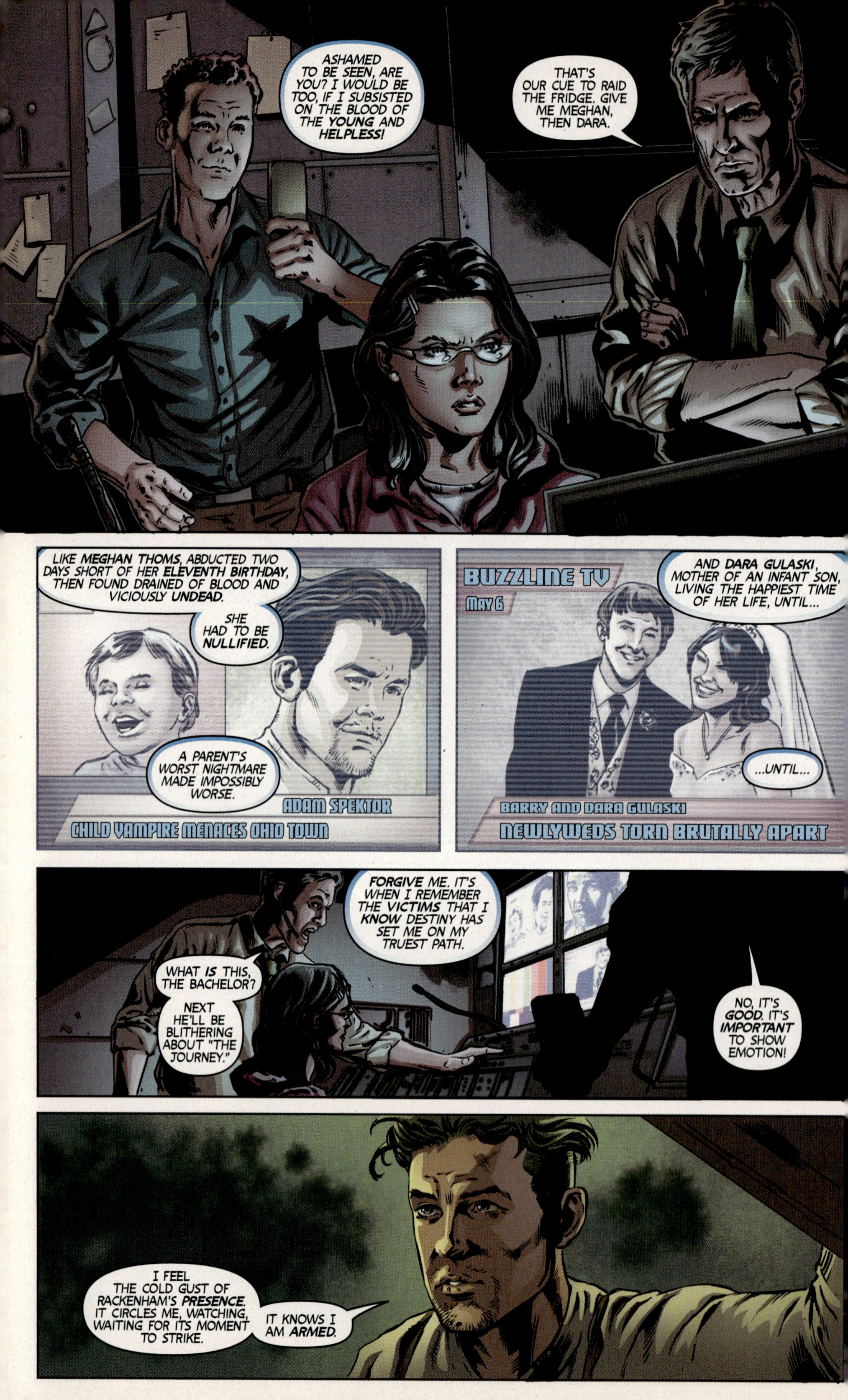
ASHAMED TO BE SEEN, ARE YOU? I WOULD BE TOO, IF I SUBSISTED ON THE BLOOD OF THE YOUNG AND HELPLESS!
THAT'S OUR CUE TO RAID THE FRIDGE. GIVE ME MEGHAN, THEN DARA.
LIKE MEGHAN THOMS, ABDUCTED TWO DAYS SHORT OF HER ELEVENTH BIRTHDAY, THEN FOUND DRAINED OF BLOOD AND VICIOUSLY UNDEAD.
SHE HAD TO BE NULLIFIED.
A PARENT'S WORST NIGHTMARE MADE IMPOSSIBLY WORSE.
ADAM SPEKTOR
CHILD VAMPIRE MENACES OHIO TOWN
BUZZLINE TV
MAY 6
AND DARA GULASKI, MOTHER OF AN INFANT SON, LIVING THE HAPPIEST TIME OF HER LIFE, UNTIL...
...UNTIL...
BARRY AND DARA GULASKI
NEWLYWEDS TORN BRUTALLY APART
FORGIVE ME. IT'S WHEN I REMEMBER THE VICTIMS THAT I KNOW DESTINY HAS SET ME ON MY TRUEST PATH.
WHAT IS THIS, THE BACHELOR?
NEXT HE'LL BE BLITHERING ABOUT "THE JOURNEY."
NO, IT'S GOOD. IT'S IMPORTANT TO SHOW EMOTION!
I FEEL THE COLD GUST OF RACKENHAM'S PRESENCE. IT CIRCLES ME, WATCHING, WAITING FOR ITS MOMENT TO STRIKE.
IT KNOWS I AM ARMED.

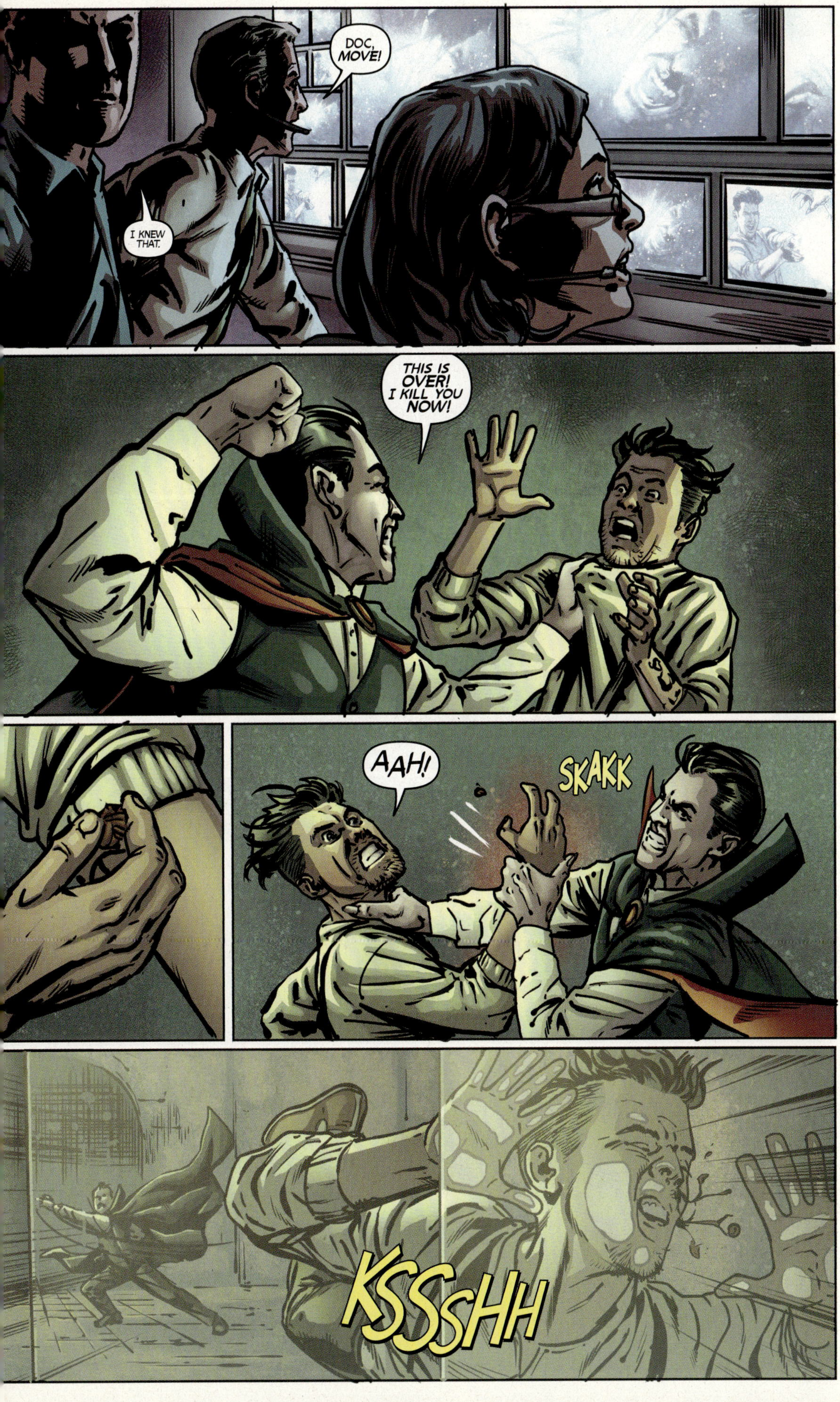
DOC, MOVE!
I KNEW THAT.
THIS IS OVER! I KILL YOU NOW!
AAH!
SKAKK
KSSSHH

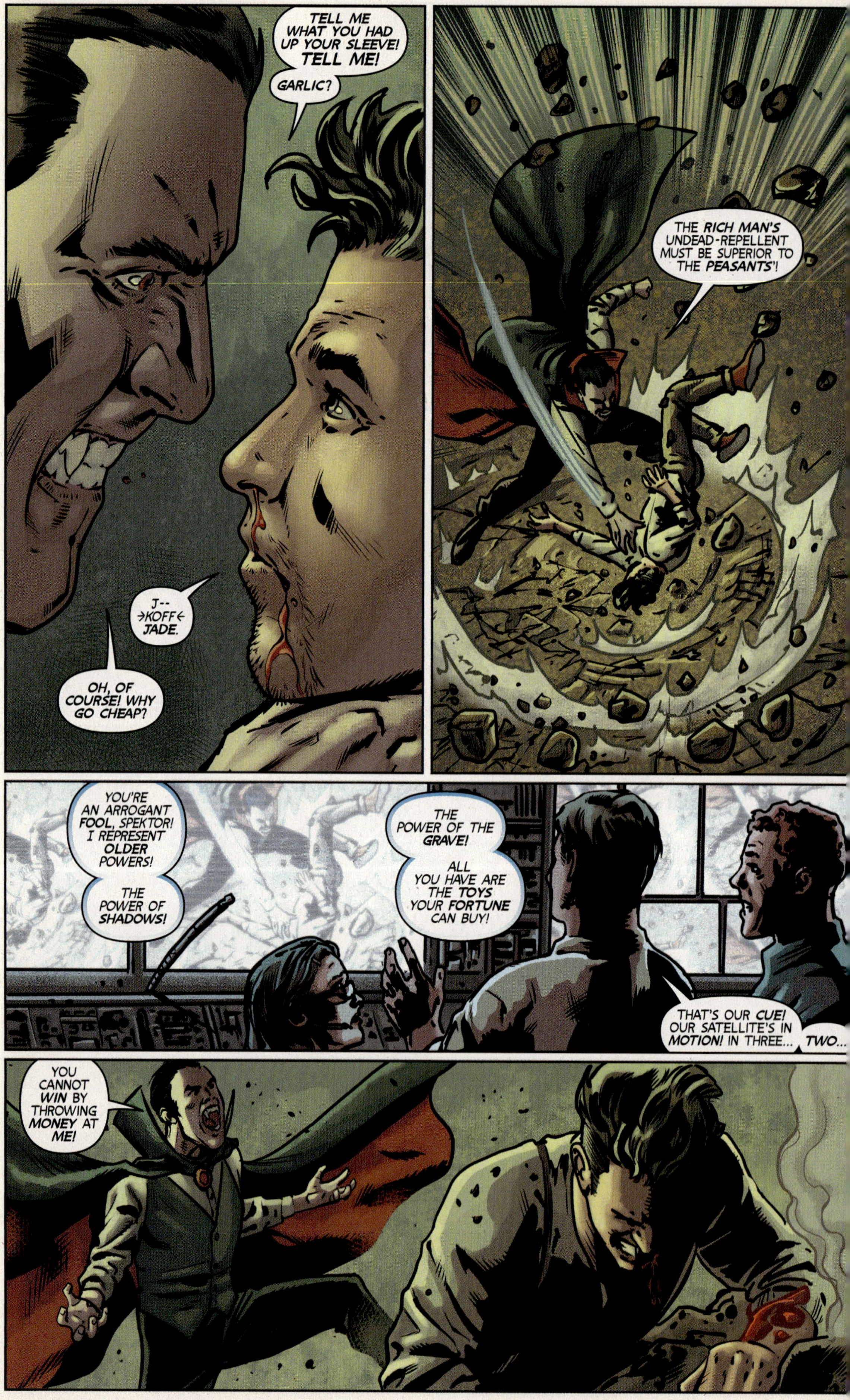
TELL ME WHAT YOU HAD UP YOUR SLEEVE! TELL ME!
GARLIC?
J-- ≻KOFF≺ JADE.
OH, OF COURSE! WHY GO CHEAP?
THE RICH MAN'S UNDEAD-REPELLENT MUST BE SUPERIOR TO THE PEASANTS'!
YOU'RE AN ARROGANT FOOL, SPEKTOR! I REPRESENT OLDER POWERS!
THE POWER OF SHADOWS!
THE POWER OF THE GRAVE!
ALL YOU HAVE ARE THE TOYS YOUR FORTUNE CAN BUY!
THAT'S OUR CUE! OUR SATELLITE'S IN MOTION! IN THREE... TWO...
YOU CANNOT WIN BY THROWING MONEY AT ME!

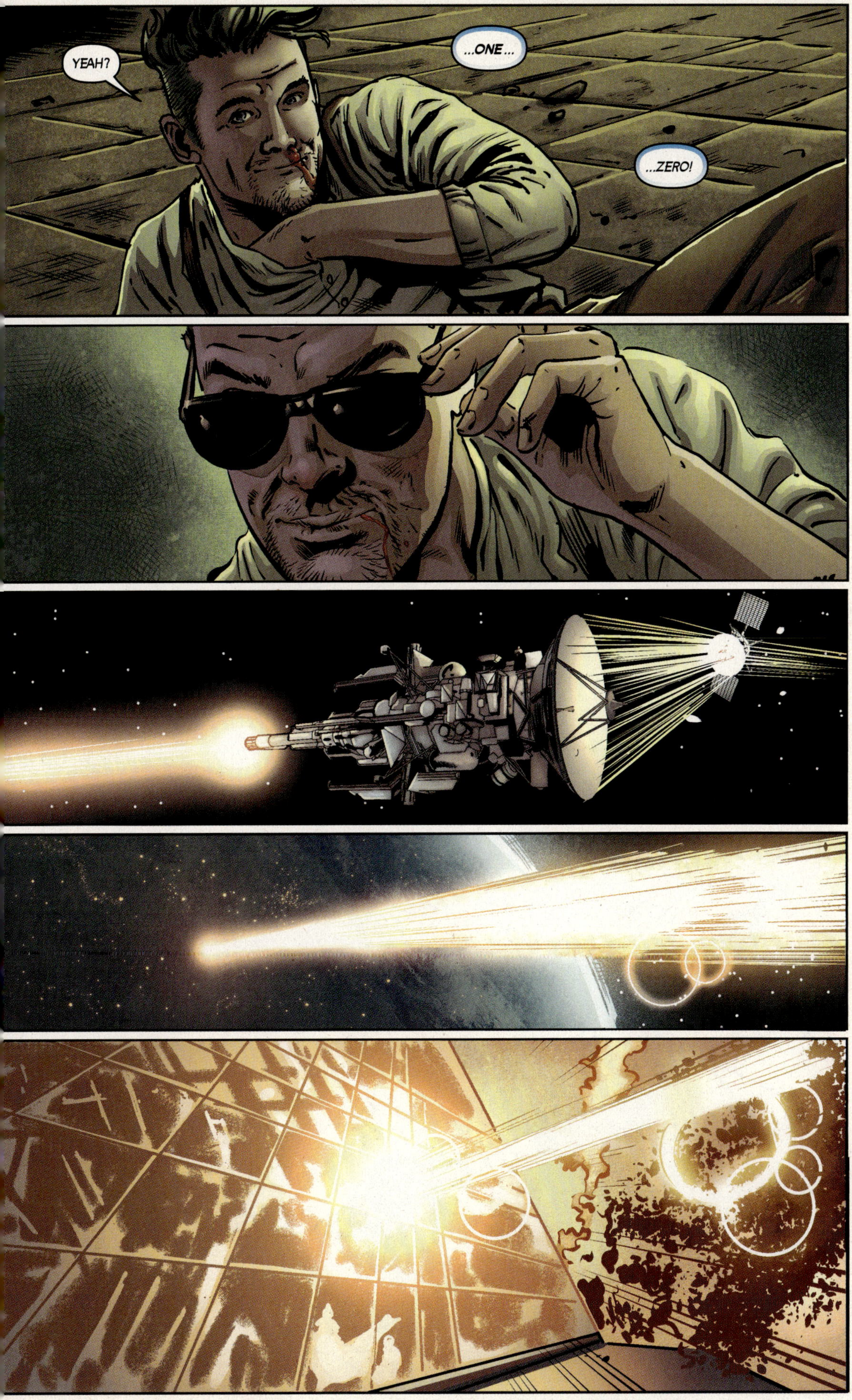
YEAH?
...ONE...
...ZERO!

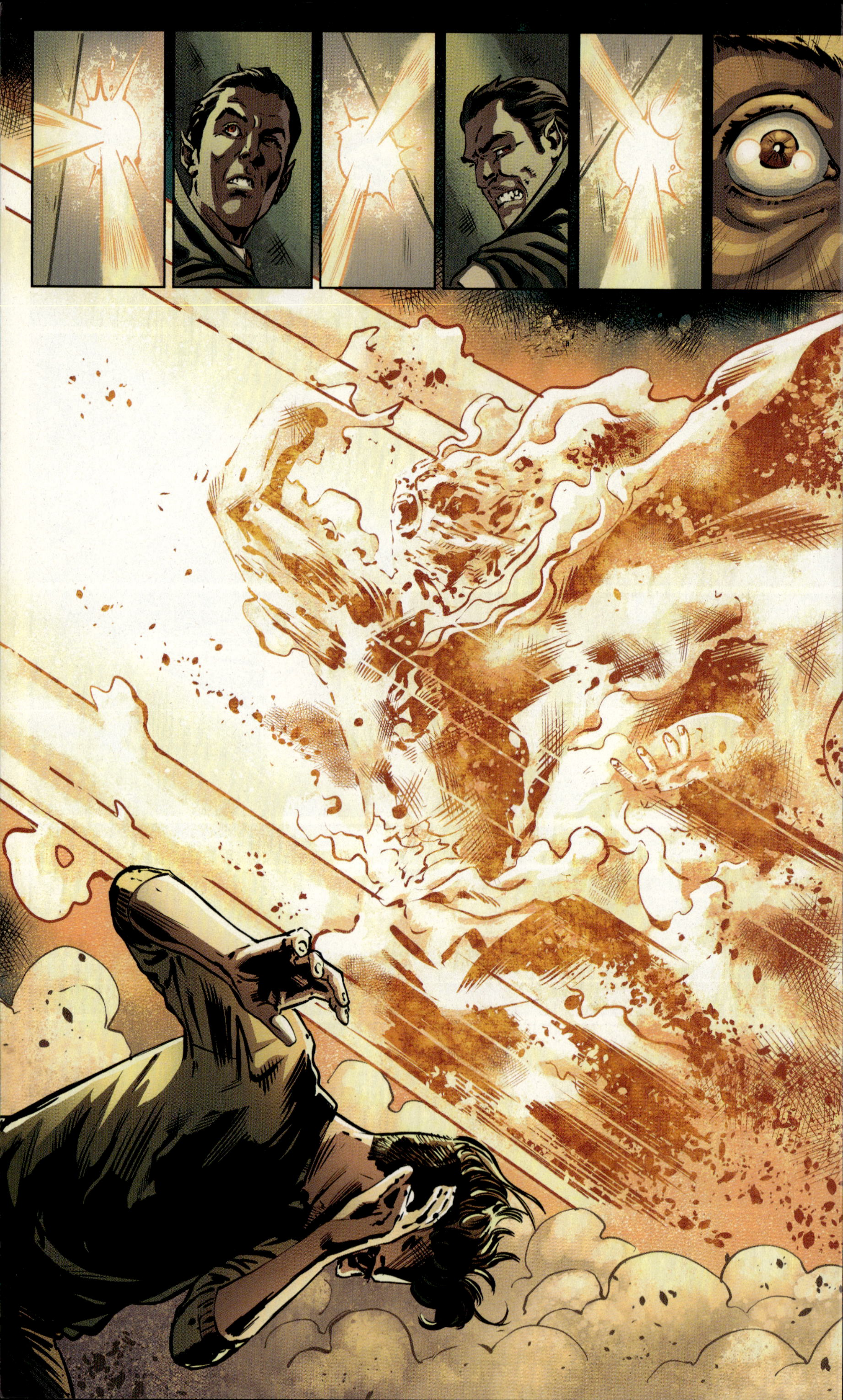

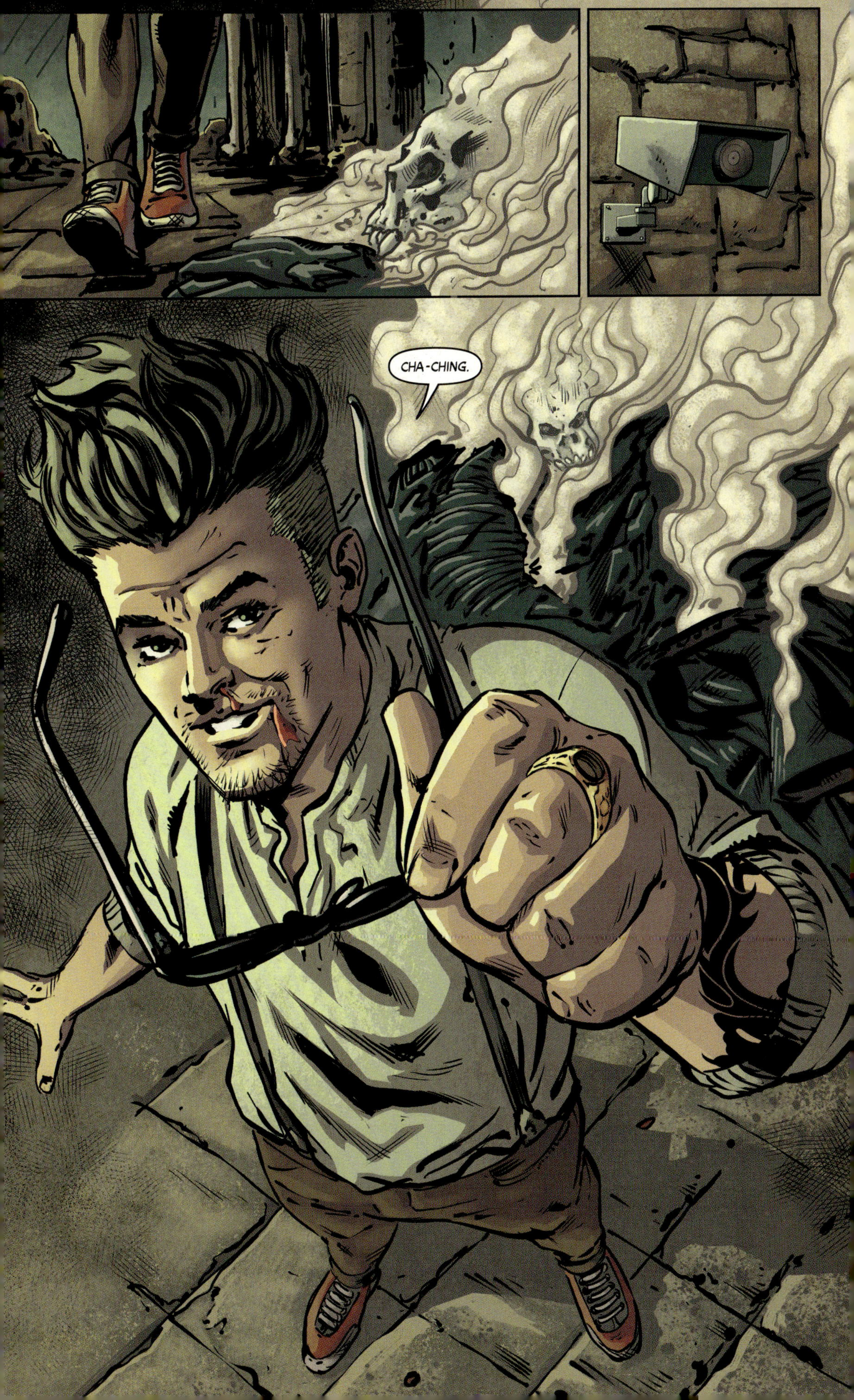
CHA-CHING.

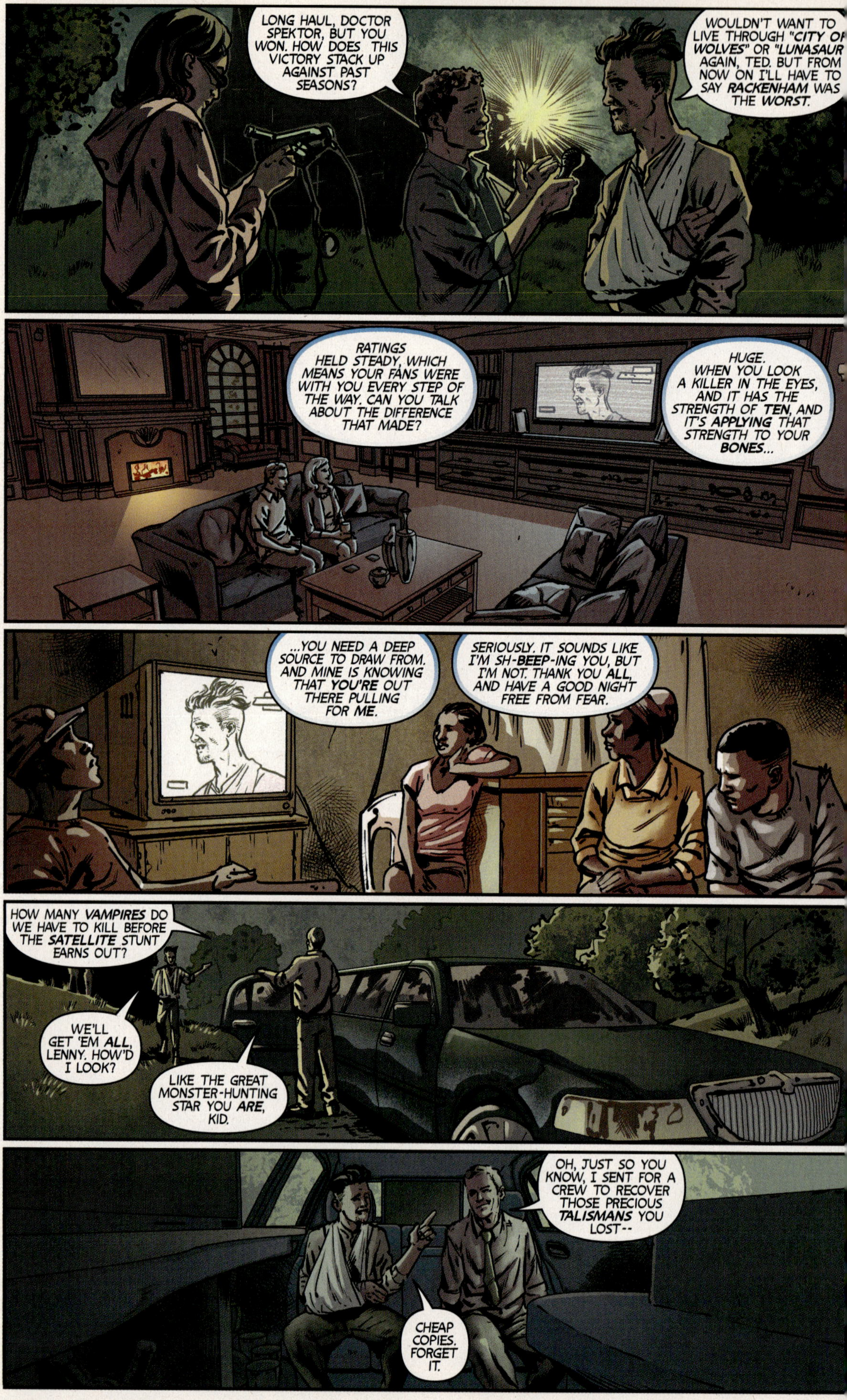
LONG HAUL, DOCTOR SPEKTOR, BUT YOU WON. HOW DOES THIS VICTORY STACK UP AGAINST PAST SEASONS?
WOULDN'T WANT TO LIVE THROUGH "CITY OF WOLVES" OR "LUNASAUR" AGAIN, TED. BUT FROM NOW ON I'LL HAVE TO SAY RACKENHAM WAS THE WORST.
RATINGS HELD STEADY, WHICH MEANS YOUR FANS WERE WITH YOU EVERY STEP OF THE WAY. CAN YOU TALK ABOUT THE DIFFERENCE THAT MADE?
HUGE. WHEN YOU LOOK A KILLER IN THE EYES, AND IT HAS THE STRENGTH OF TEN, AND IT'S APPLYING THAT STRENGTH TO YOUR BONES...
...YOU NEED A DEEP SOURCE TO DRAW FROM. AND MINE IS KNOWING THAT YOU'RE OUT THERE PULLING FOR ME.
SERIOUSLY. IT SOUNDS LIKE I'M SH-BEEP-ING YOU, BUT I'M NOT. THANK YOU ALL, AND HAVE A GOOD NIGHT FREE FROM FEAR.
HOW MANY VAMPIRES DO WE HAVE TO KILL BEFORE THE SATELLITE STUNT EARNS OUT?
WE'LL GET 'EM ALL, LENNY. HOW'D I LOOK?
LIKE THE GREAT MONSTER-HUNTING STAR YOU ARE, KID.
OH, JUST SO YOU KNOW, I SENT FOR A CREW TO RECOVER THOSE PRECIOUS TALISMANS YOU LOST--
CHEAP COPIES. FORGET IT.

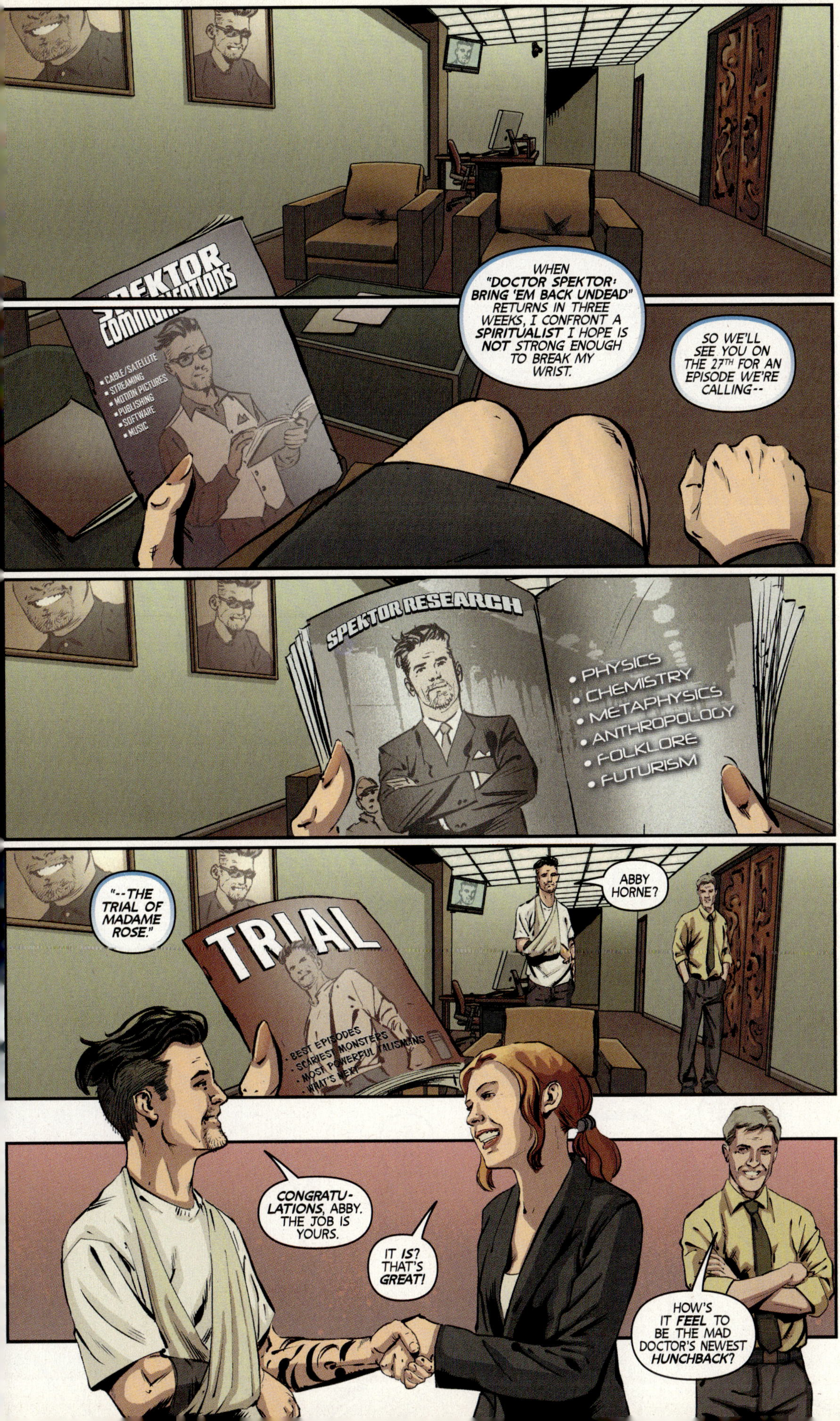

WHEN "DOCTOR SPEKTOR: BRING 'EM BACK UNDEAD" RETURNS IN THREE WEEKS, I CONFRONT A SPIRITUALIST I HOPE IS NOT STRONG ENOUGH TO BREAK MY WRIST.
SO WE'LL SEE YOU ON THE 27TH FOR AN EPISODE WE'RE CALLING--
CABLE/SATELLITE
STREAMING
MOTION PICTURES
PUBLISHING
SOFTWARE
MUSIC
SPEKTOR RESEARCH
PHYSICS
CHEMISTRY
METAPHYSICS
ANTHROPOLOGY
FOLKLORE
FUTURISM
"--THE TRIAL OF MADAME ROSE."
TRIAL
BEST EPISODES
SCARIEST MONSTERS
MOST POWERFUL TALISMANS
WHAT'S NEXT
ABBY HORNE?
CONGRATU-LATIONS, ABBY. THE JOB IS YOURS.
IT IS? THAT'S GREAT!
HOW'S IT FEEL TO BE THE MAD DOCTOR'S NEWEST HUNCHBACK?

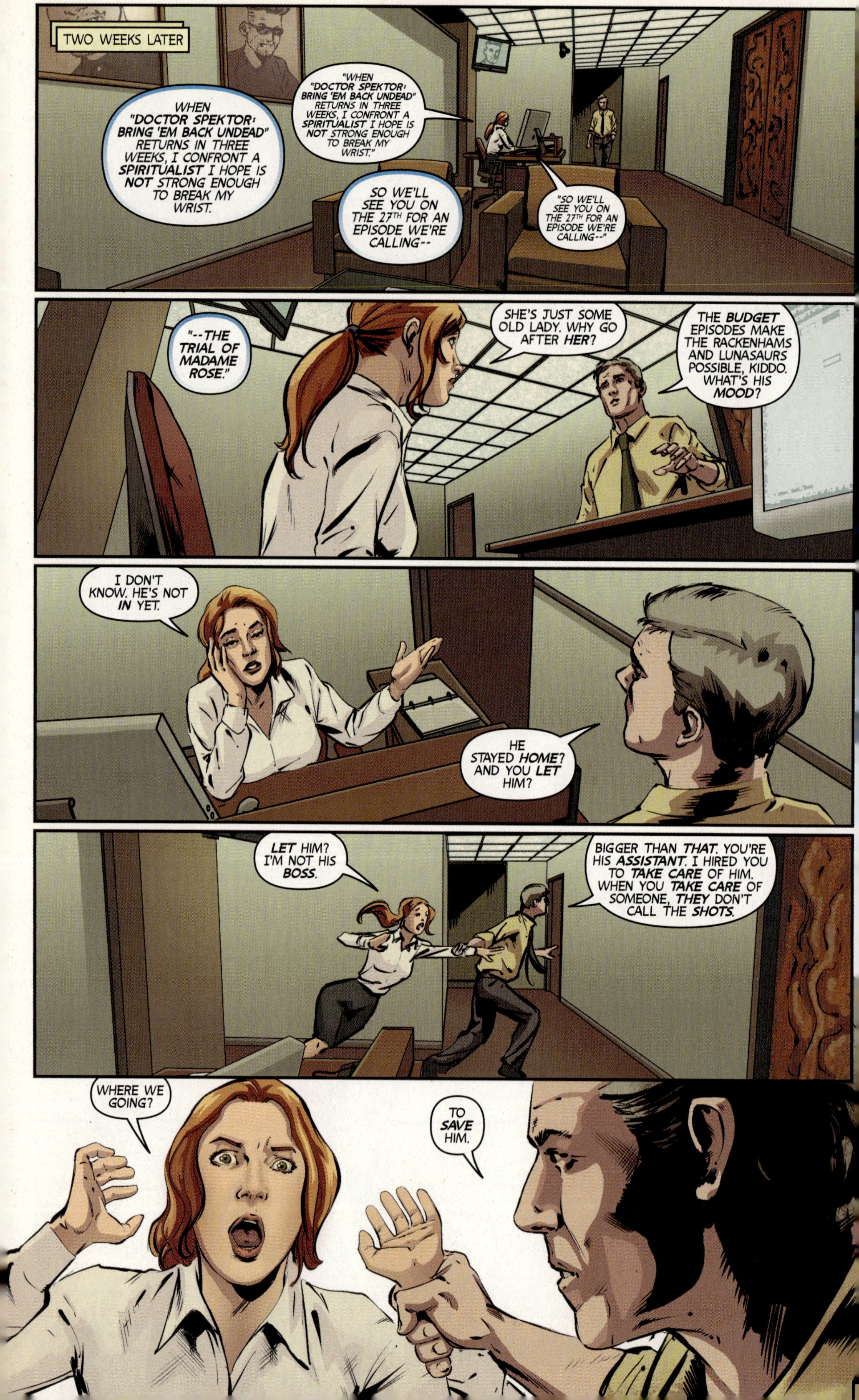
TWO WEEKS LATER
WHEN "DOCTOR SPEKTOR: BRING 'EM BACK UNDEAD" RETURNS IN THREE WEEKS, I CONFRONT A SPIRITUALIST I HOPE IS NOT STRONG ENOUGH TO BREAK MY WRIST.
"WHEN "DOCTOR SPEKTOR: BRING 'EM BACK UNDEAD" RETURNS IN THREE WEEKS, I CONFRONT A SPIRITUALIST I HOPE IS NOT STRONG ENOUGH TO BREAK MY WRIST."
SO WE'LL SEE YOU ON THE 27TH FOR AN EPISODE WE'RE CALLING--
"SO WE'LL SEE YOU ON THE 27TH FOR AN EPISODE WE'RE CALLING--"
"--THE TRIAL OF MADAME ROSE."
SHE'S JUST SOME OLD LADY. WHY GO AFTER HER?
THE BUDGET EPISODES MAKE THE RACKENHAMS AND LUNASAURS POSSIBLE, KIDDO. WHAT'S HIS MOOD?
I DON'T KNOW. HE'S NOT IN YET.
HE STAYED HOME? AND YOU LET HIM?
LET HIM? I'M NOT HIS BOSS.
BIGGER THAN THAT. YOU'RE HIS ASSISTANT. I HIRED YOU TO TAKE CARE OF HIM. WHEN YOU TAKE CARE OF SOMEONE, THEY DON'T CALL THE SHOTS.
WHERE WE GOING?
TO SAVE HIM.

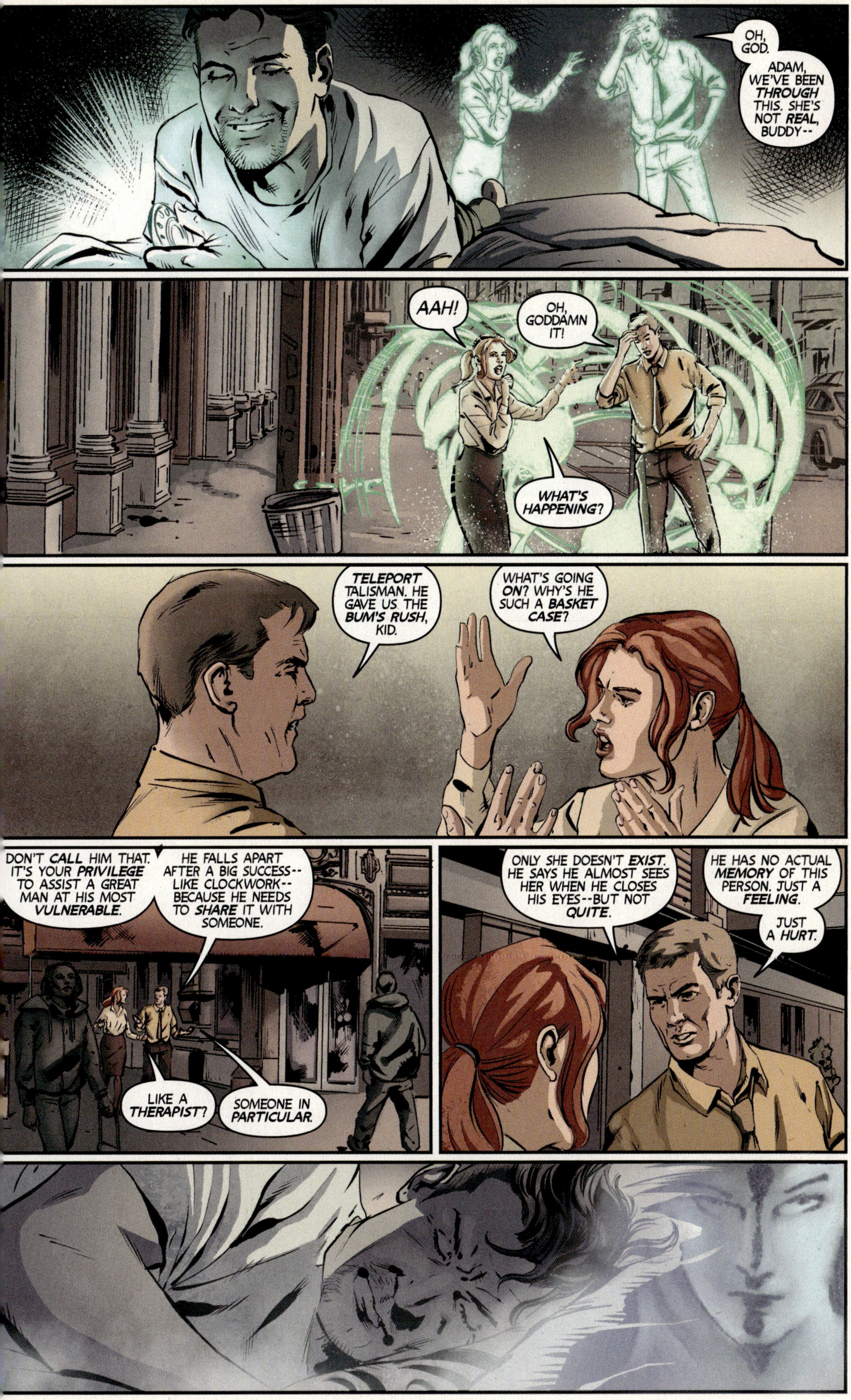
OH, GOD. ADAM, WE'VE BEEN THROUGH THIS. SHE'S NOT REAL, BUDDY--
AAH!
OH, GODDAMN IT!
WHAT'S HAPPENING?
TELEPORT TALISMAN. HE GAVE US THE BUM'S RUSH, KID.
WHAT'S GOING ON? WHY'S HE SUCH A BASKET CASE?
DON'T CALL HIM THAT. IT'S YOUR PRIVILEGE TO ASSIST A GREAT MAN AT HIS MOST VULNERABLE.
HE FALLS APART AFTER A BIG SUCCESS-- LIKE CLOCKWORK-- BECAUSE HE NEEDS TO SHARE IT WITH SOMEONE.
LIKE A THERAPIST?
SOMEONE IN PARTICULAR.
ONLY SHE DOESN'T EXIST. HE SAYS HE ALMOST SEES HER WHEN HE CLOSES HIS EYES--BUT NOT QUITE.
HE HAS NO ACTUAL MEMORY OF THIS PERSON. JUST A FEELING.
JUST A HURT.

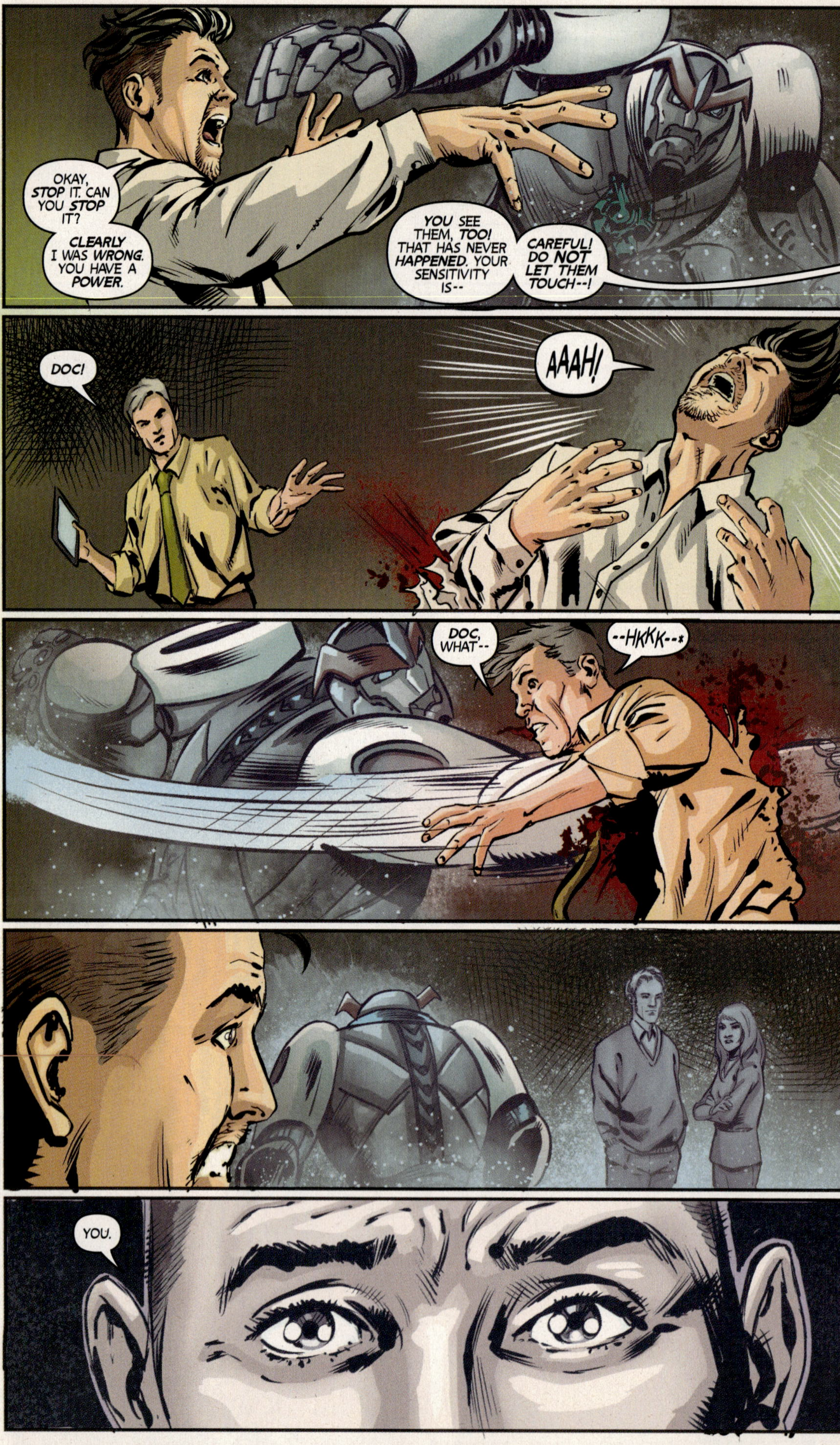
OKAY, STOP IT. CAN YOU STOP IT?
CLEARLY I WAS WRONG. YOU HAVE A POWER.
YOU SEE THEM, TOO! THAT HAS NEVER HAPPENED. YOUR SENSITIVITY IS--
CAREFUL! DO NOT LET THEM TOUCH--!
DOC!
AAAH!
DOC, WHAT--
--HKKK--*
YOU.

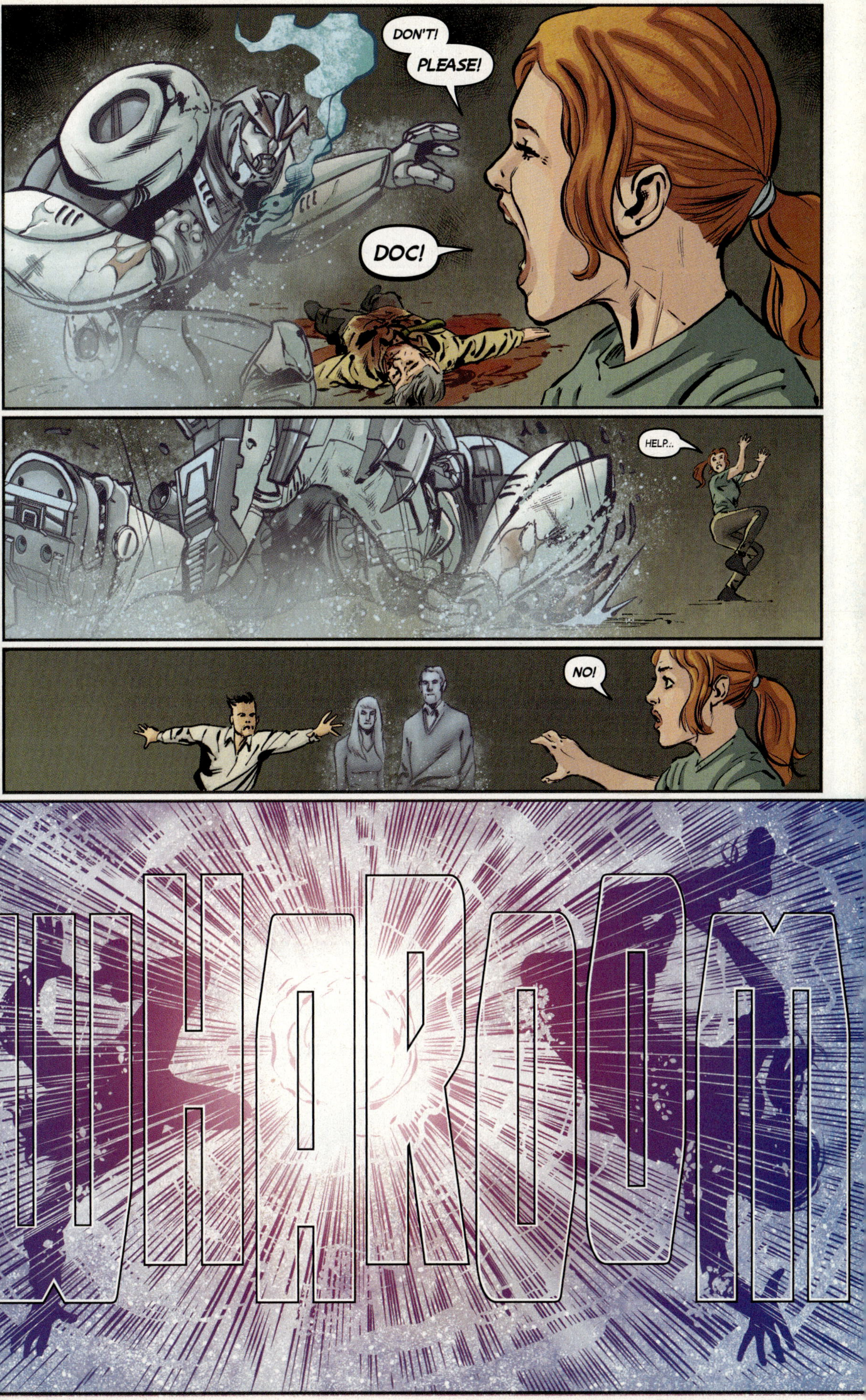
DON'T!
PLEASE!
DOC!
HELP...
NO!
WHAROOM

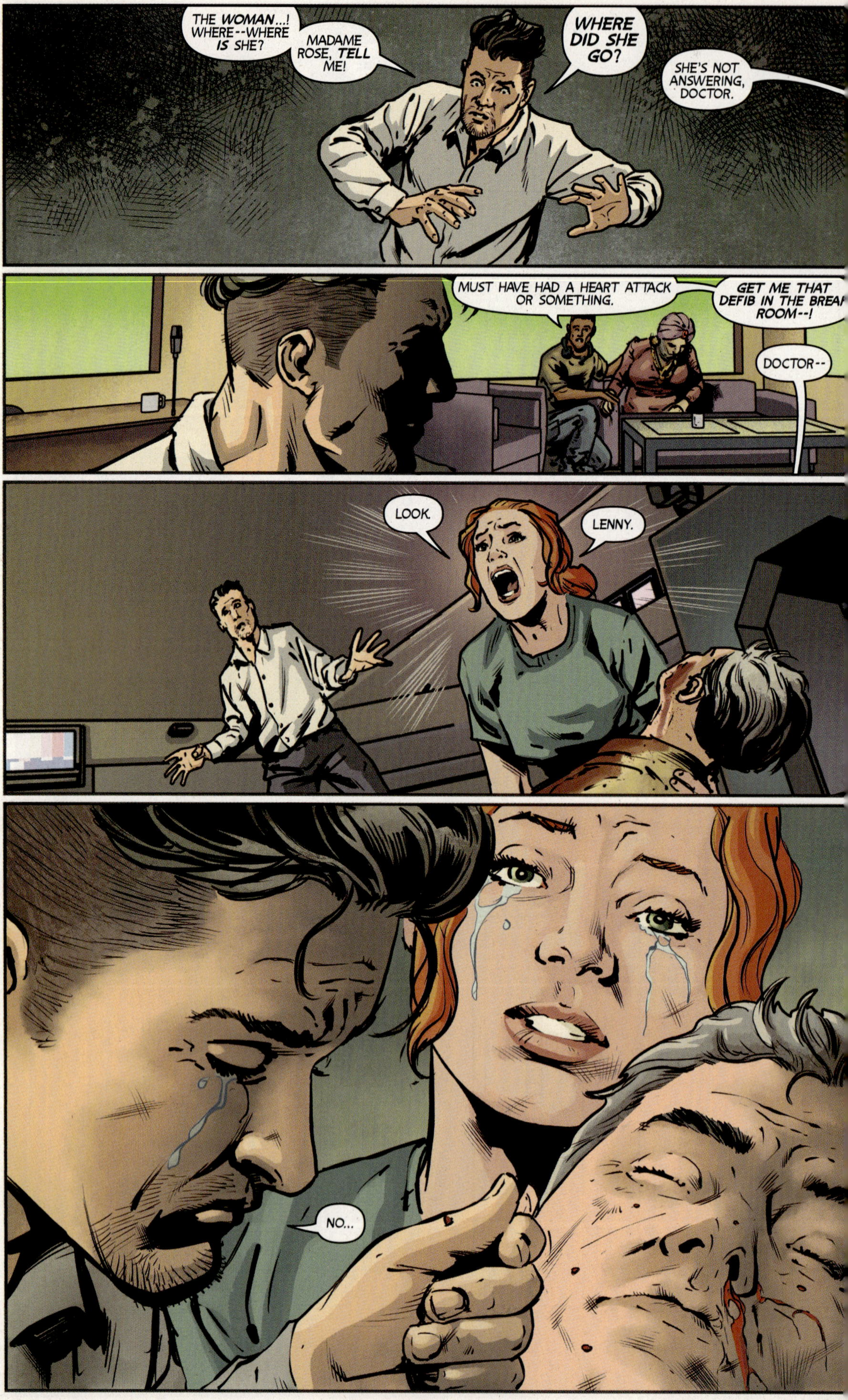
THE WOMAN...! WHERE--WHERE IS SHE?
MADAME ROSE, TELL ME!
WHERE DID SHE GO?
SHE'S NOT ANSWERING, DOCTOR.
MUST HAVE HAD A HEART ATTACK OR SOMETHING.
GET ME THAT DEFIB IN THE BREAK ROOM--!
DOCTOR--
LOOK.
LENNY.
NO...

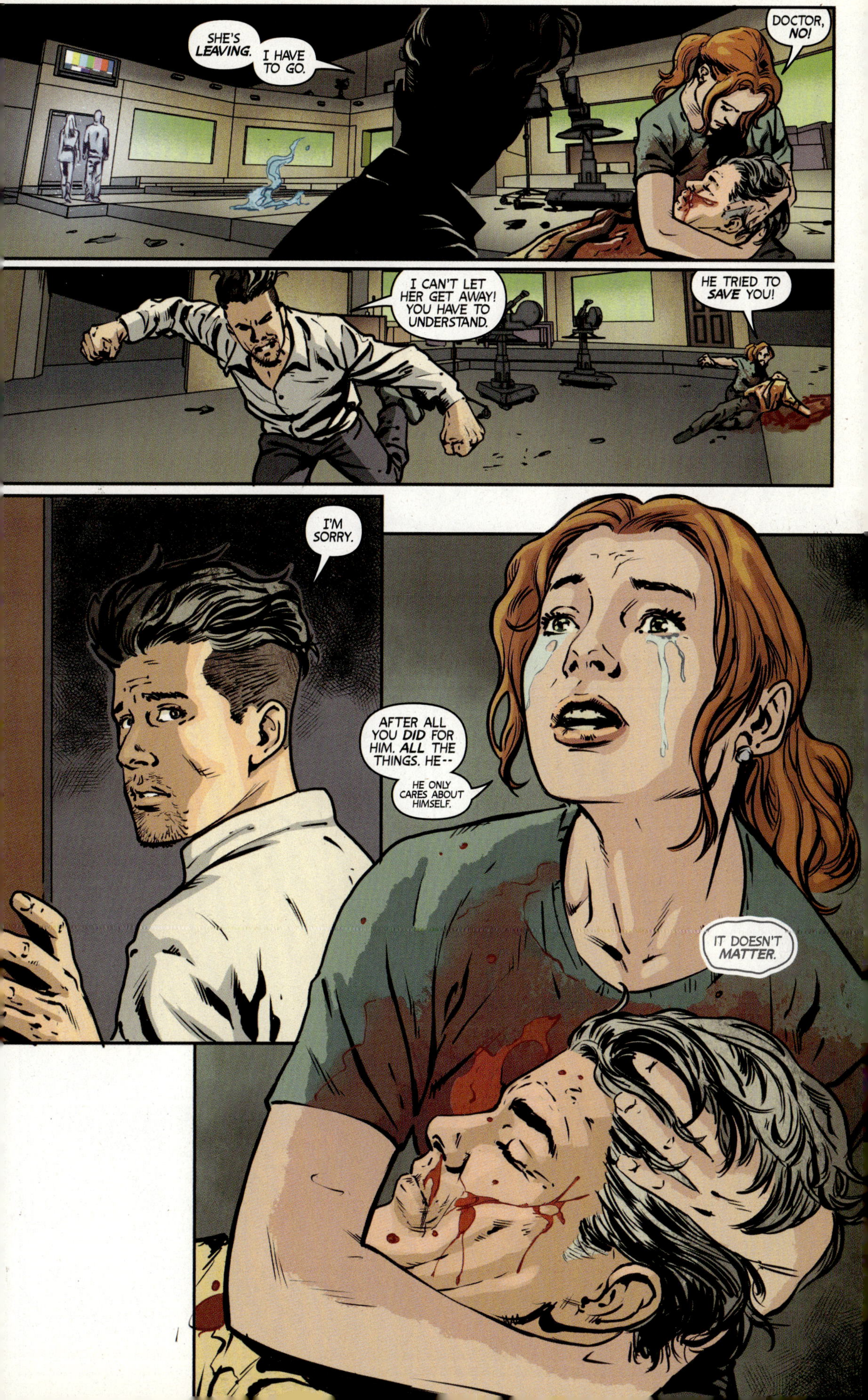
SHE'S LEAVING.
I HAVE TO GO.
DOCTOR, NO!
I CAN'T LET HER GET AWAY! YOU HAVE TO UNDERSTAND.
HE TRIED TO SAVE YOU!
I'M SORRY.
AFTER ALL YOU DID FOR HIM. ALL THE THINGS. HE--
HE ONLY CARES ABOUT HIMSELF.
IT DOESN'T MATTER.

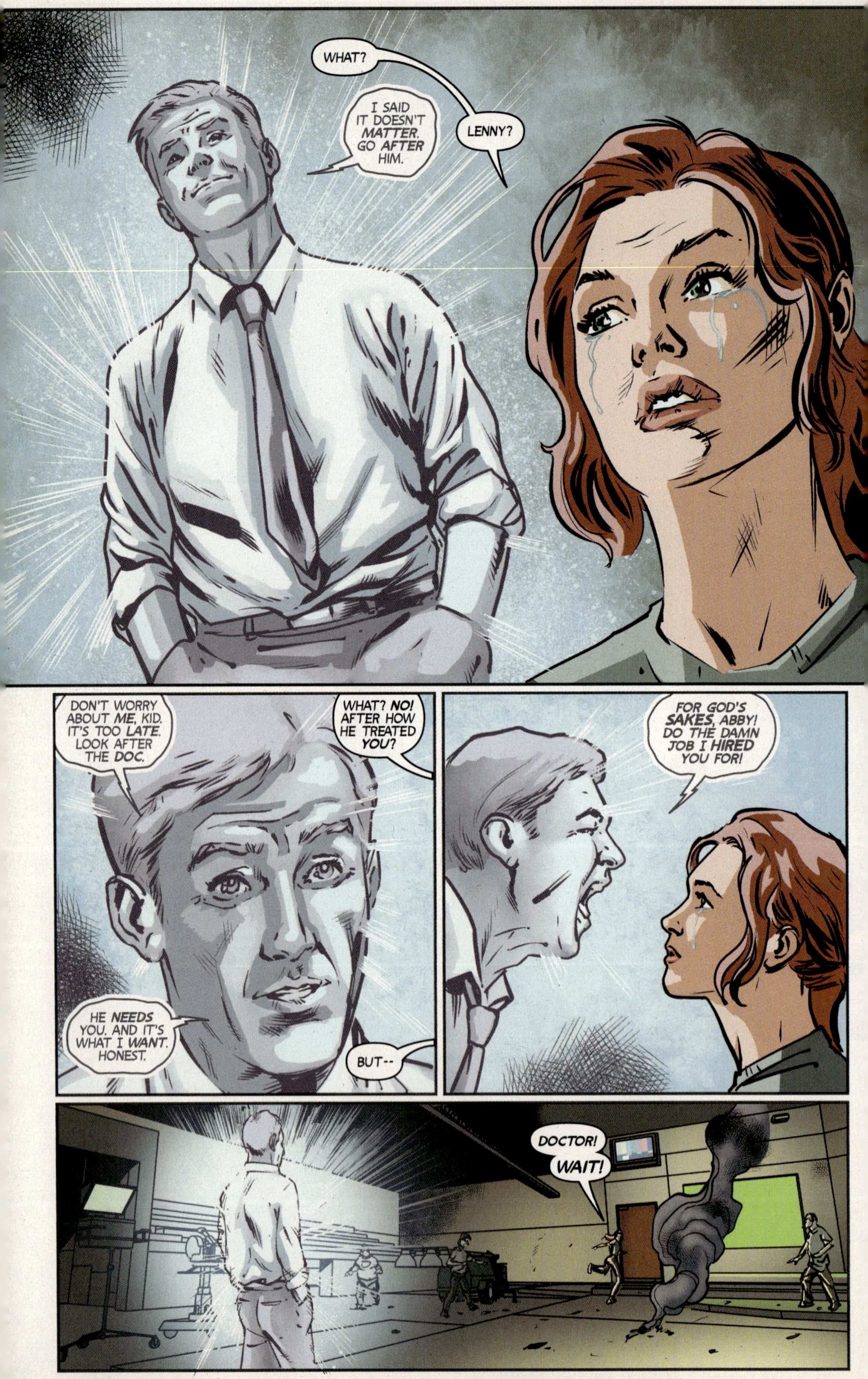
WHAT?
I SAID IT DOESN'T MATTER. GO AFTER HIM.
LENNY?
DON'T WORRY ABOUT ME, KID. IT'S TOO LATE. LOOK AFTER THE DOC.
WHAT? NO! AFTER HOW HE TREATED YOU?
HE NEEDS YOU. AND IT'S WHAT I WANT. HONEST.
BUT--
FOR GOD'S SAKES, ABBY! DO THE DAMN JOB I HIRED YOU FOR!
DOCTOR!
WAIT!

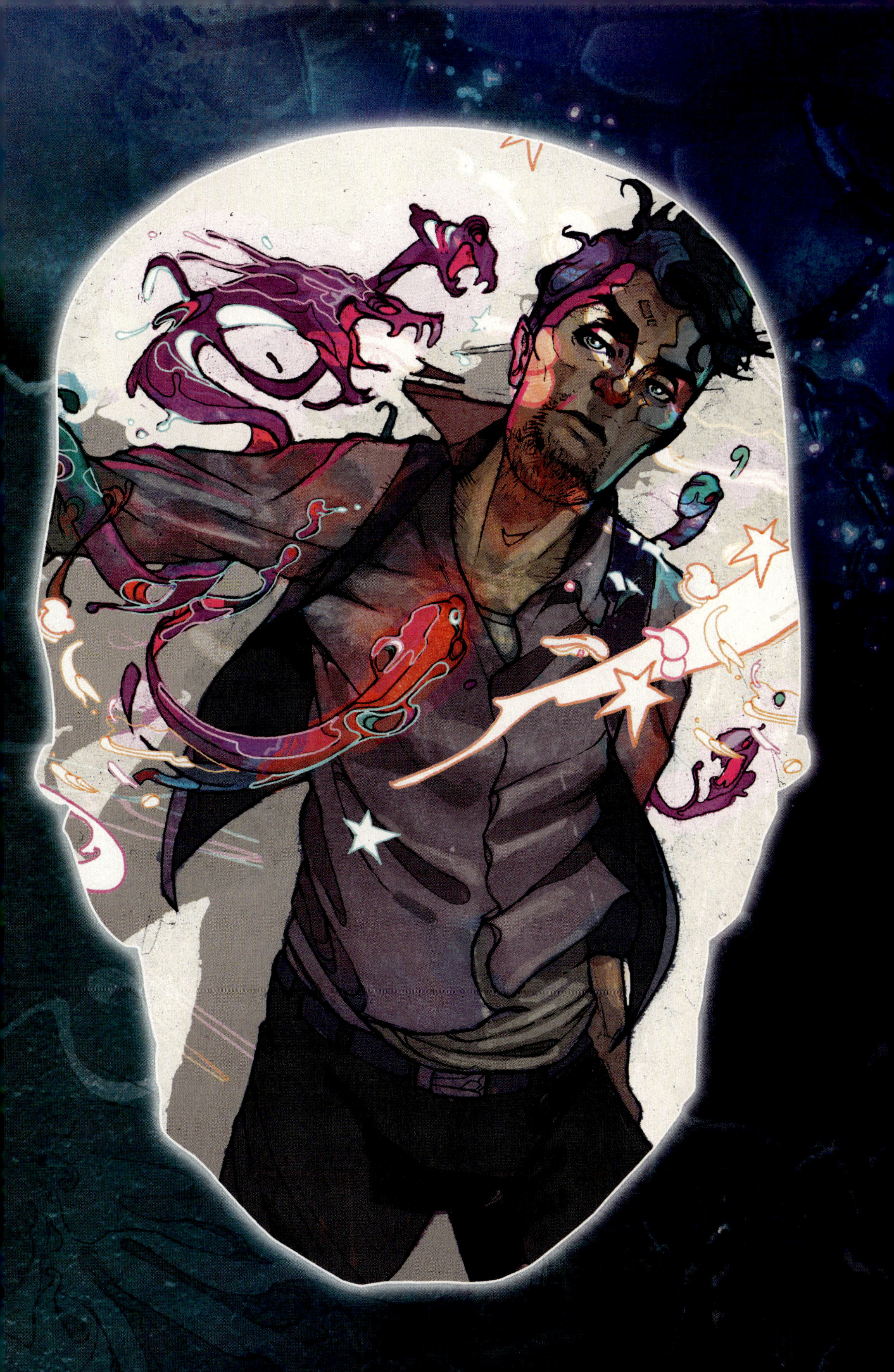

ISSUE 2

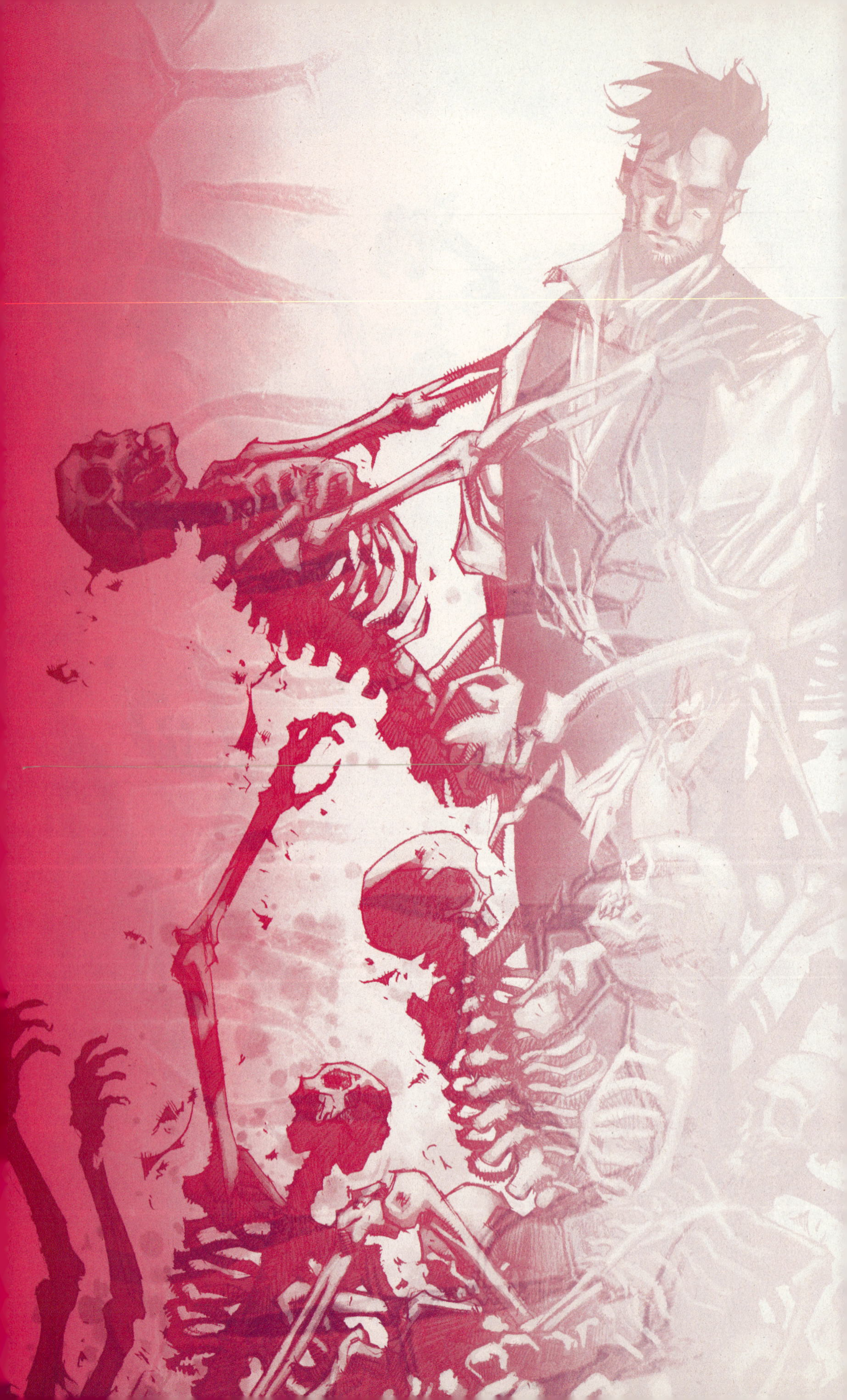

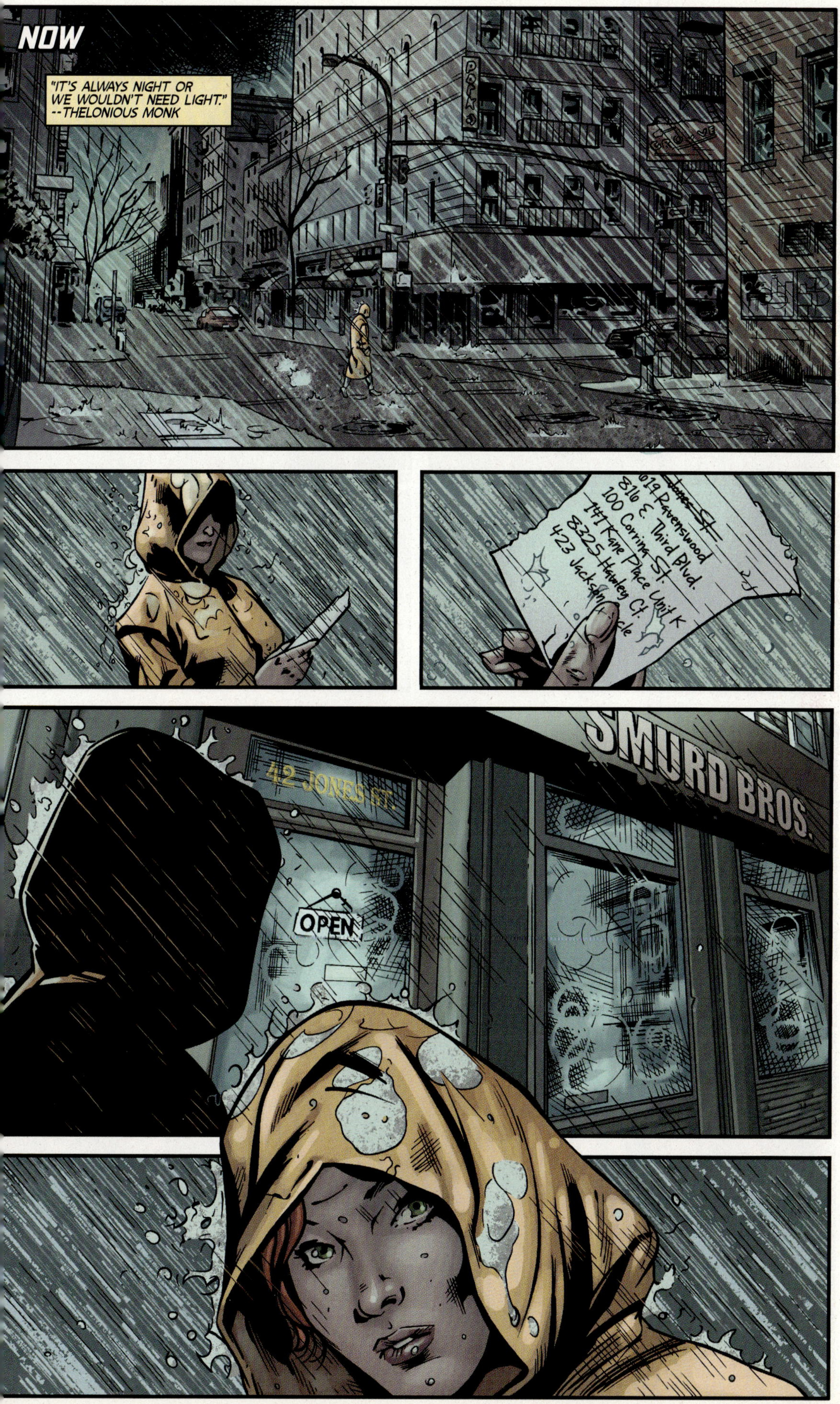
NOW
"IT'S ALWAYS NIGHT OR WE WOULDN'T NEED LIGHT." --THELONIOUS MONK
Jones St.
619 Ravenswood
816 E. Third Blvd.
100 Corring St.
141 Kane Place Unit K
8325 Hawley Ct.
423 Jacks
42 JONES ST.
SMURD BROS.
OPEN

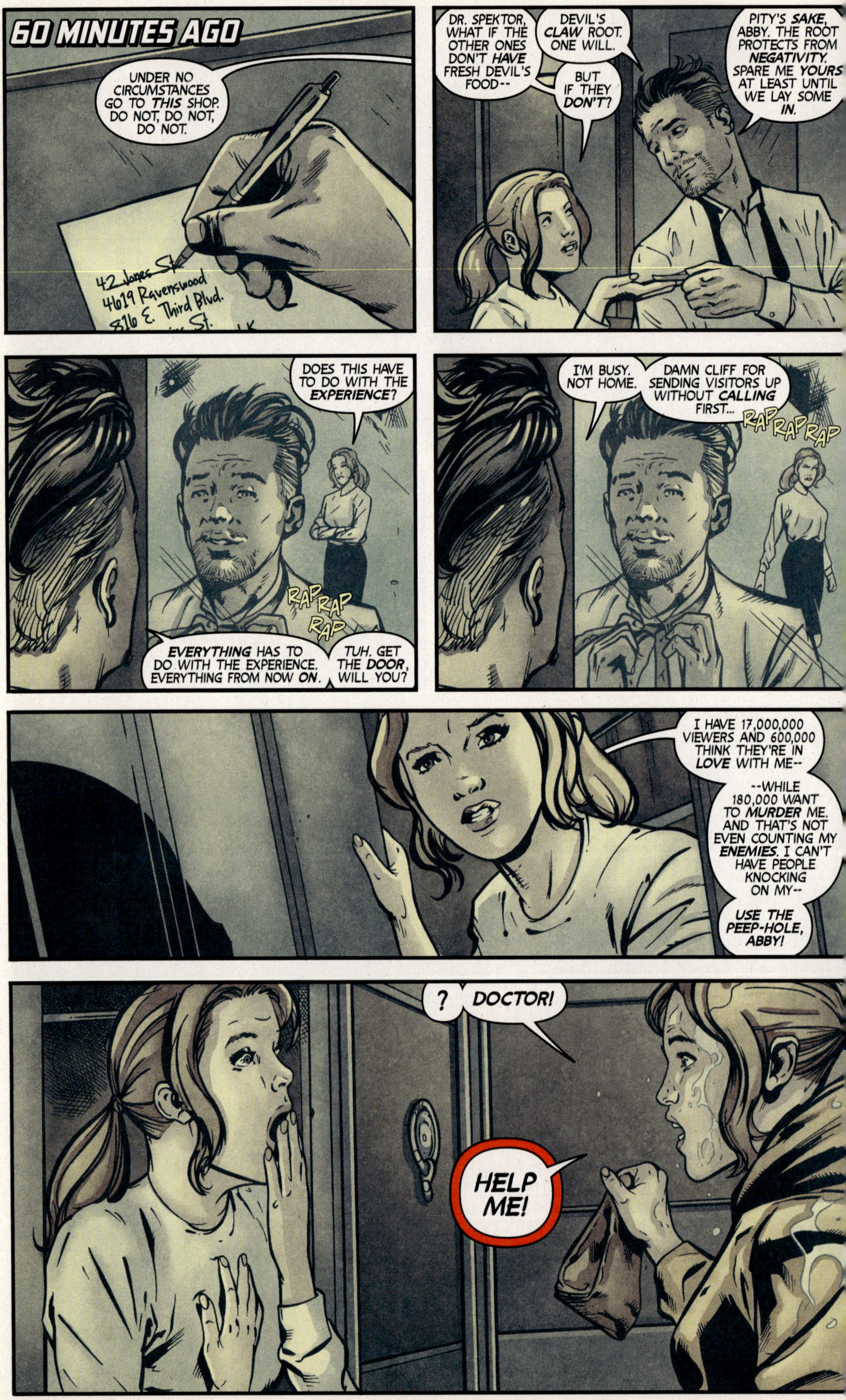

60 MINUTES AGO
UNDER NO CIRCUMSTANCES GO TO THIS SHOP. DO NOT, DO NOT, DO NOT.
42 Jones St.
4619 Ravenswood
816 E. Third Blvd.
DR. SPEKTOR, WHAT IF THE OTHER ONES DON'T HAVE FRESH DEVIL'S FOOD--
DEVIL'S CLAW ROOT. ONE WILL.
BUT IF THEY DON'T?
PITY'S SAKE, ABBY. THE ROOT PROTECTS FROM NEGATIVITY. SPARE ME YOURS AT LEAST UNTIL WE LAY SOME IN.
DOES THIS HAVE TO DO WITH THE EXPERIENCE?
RAP RAP RAP
EVERYTHING HAS TO DO WITH THE EXPERIENCE. EVERYTHING FROM NOW ON.
TUH. GET THE DOOR, WILL YOU?
I'M BUSY. NOT HOME.
DAMN CLIFF FOR SENDING VISITORS UP WITHOUT CALLING FIRST...
RAP RAP RAP
I HAVE 17,000,000 VIEWERS AND 600,000 THINK THEY'RE IN LOVE WITH ME--
--WHILE 180,000 WANT TO MURDER ME. AND THAT'S NOT EVEN COUNTING MY ENEMIES. I CAN'T HAVE PEOPLE KNOCKING ON MY--
USE THE PEEP-HOLE, ABBY!
?
DOCTOR!
HELP ME!

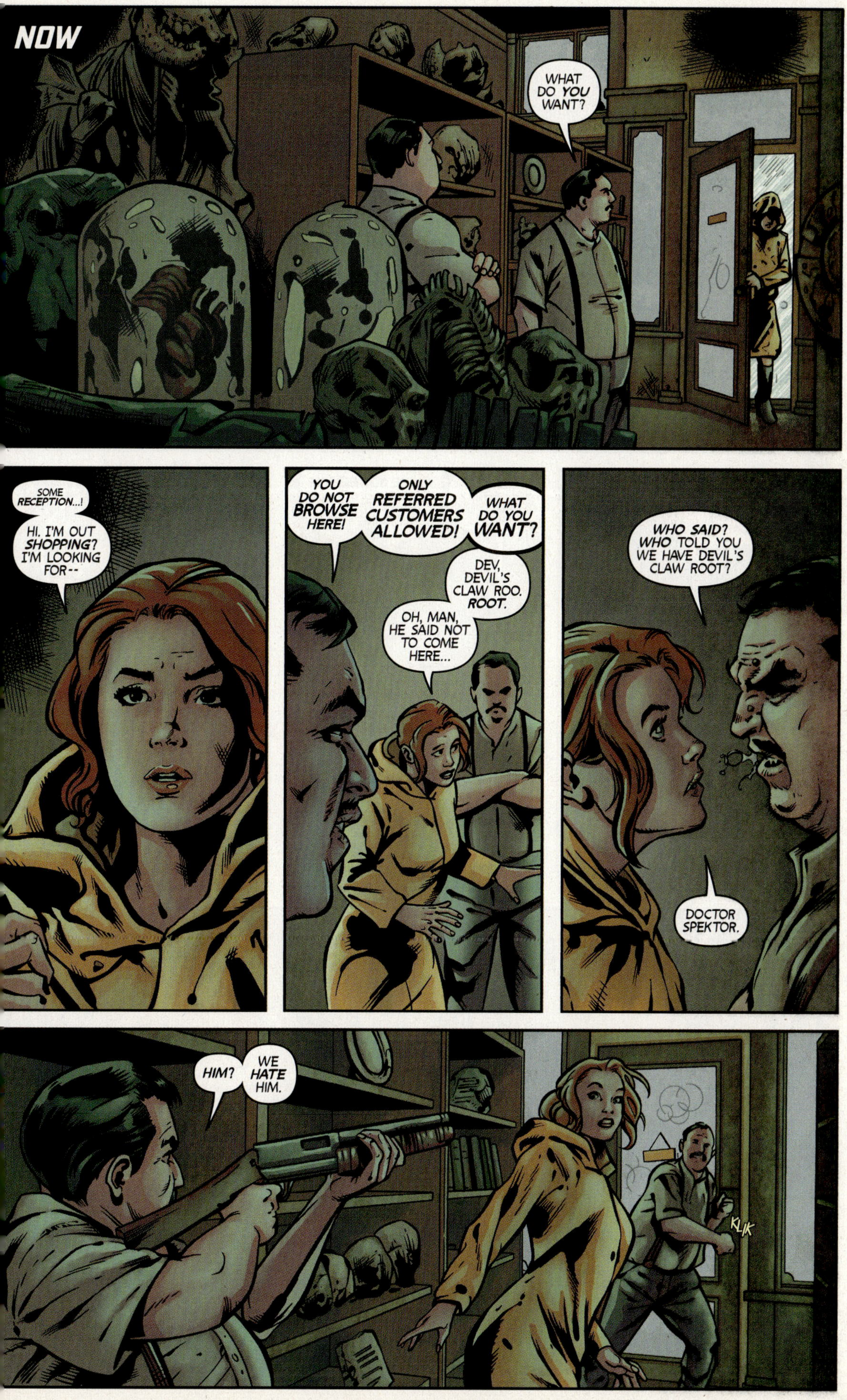
NOW
WHAT DO YOU WANT?
SOME RECEPTION...!
HI. I'M OUT SHOPPING? I'M LOOKING FOR--
YOU DO NOT BROWSE HERE!
ONLY REFERRED CUSTOMERS ALLOWED!
WHAT DO YOU WANT?
DEV, DEVIL'S CLAW ROO. ROOT.
OH, MAN, HE SAID NOT TO COME HERE...
WHO SAID? WHO TOLD YOU WE HAVE DEVIL'S CLAW ROOT?
DOCTOR SPEKTOR.
HIM?
WE HATE HIM.
KLIK

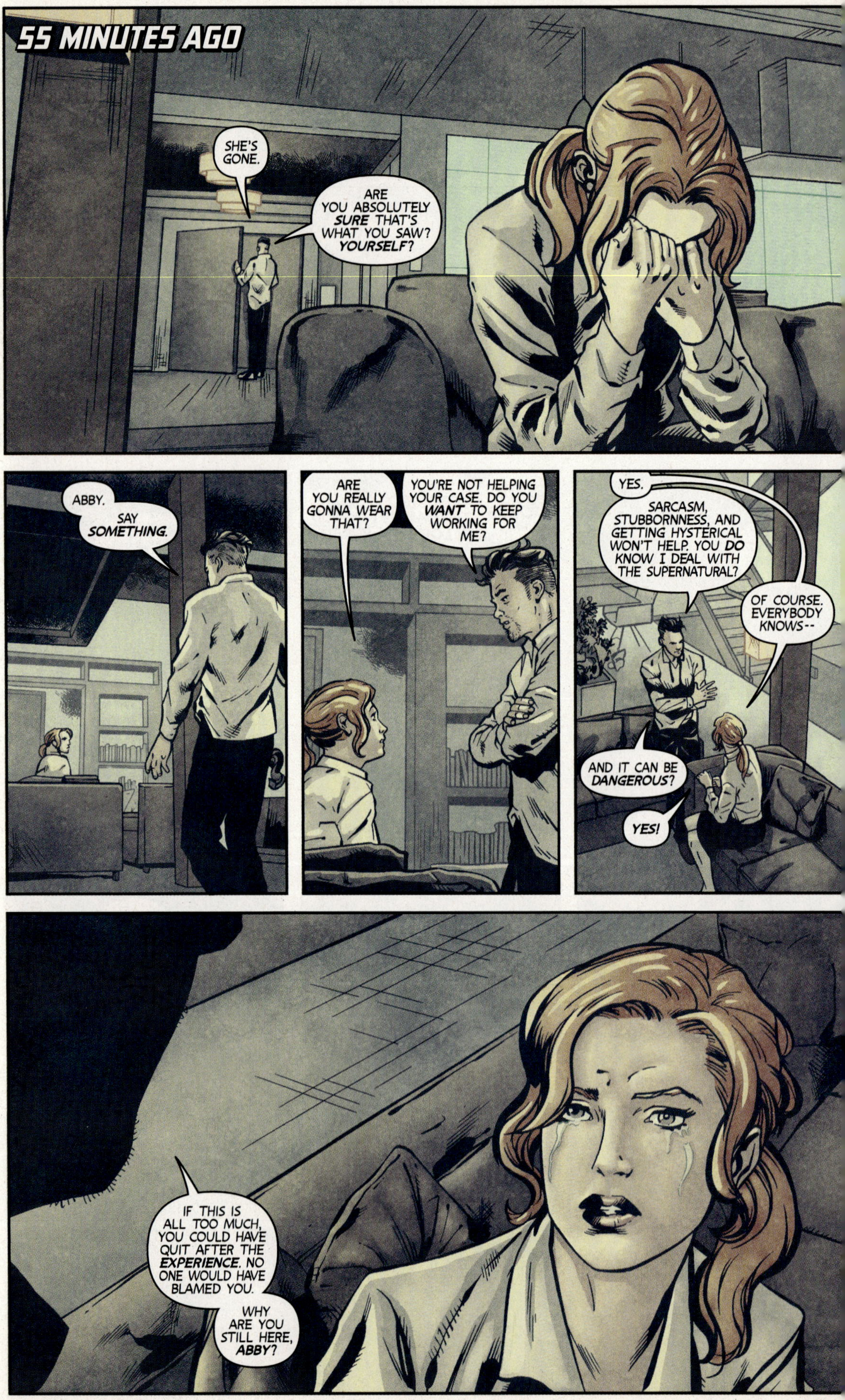
55 MINUTES AGO
SHE'S GONE.
ARE YOU ABSOLUTELY SURE THAT'S WHAT YOU SAW? YOURSELF?
ABBY.
SAY SOMETHING.
ARE YOU REALLY GONNA WEAR THAT?
YOU'RE NOT HELPING YOUR CASE. DO YOU WANT TO KEEP WORKING FOR ME?
YES.
SARCASM, STUBBORNNESS, AND GETTING HYSTERICAL WON'T HELP. YOU DO KNOW I DEAL WITH THE SUPERNATURAL?
OF COURSE. EVERYBODY KNOWS--
AND IT CAN BE DANGEROUS?
YES!
IF THIS IS ALL TOO MUCH, YOU COULD HAVE QUIT AFTER THE EXPERIENCE. NO ONE WOULD HAVE BLAMED YOU.
WHY ARE YOU STILL HERE, ABBY?

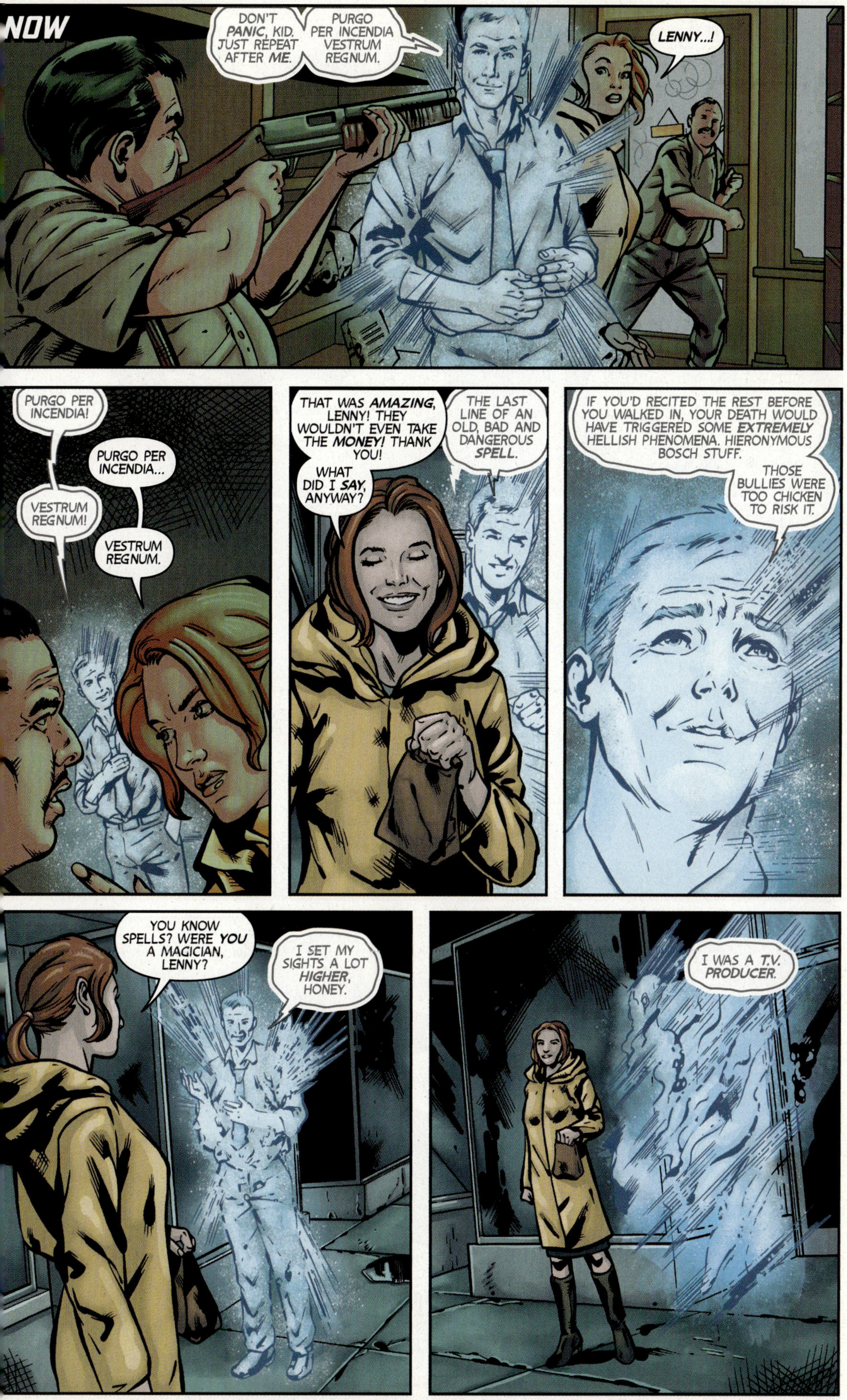
NOW
DON'T PANIC, KID. JUST REPEAT AFTER ME.
PURGO PER INCENDIA VESTRUM REGNUM.
LENNY...!
PURGO PER INCENDIA!
PURGO PER INCENDIA...
VESTRUM REGNUM!
VESTRUM REGNUM.
THAT WAS AMAZING, LENNY! THEY WOULDN'T EVEN TAKE THE MONEY! THANK YOU!
WHAT DID I SAY, ANYWAY?
THE LAST LINE OF AN OLD, BAD AND DANGEROUS SPELL.
IF YOU'D RECITED THE REST BEFORE YOU WALKED IN, YOUR DEATH WOULD HAVE TRIGGERED SOME EXTREMELY HELLISH PHENOMENA. HIERONYMOUS BOSCH STUFF.
THOSE BULLIES WERE TOO CHICKEN TO RISK IT.
YOU KNOW SPELLS? WERE YOU A MAGICIAN, LENNY?
I SET MY SIGHTS A LOT HIGHER, HONEY.
I WAS A T.V. PRODUCER.

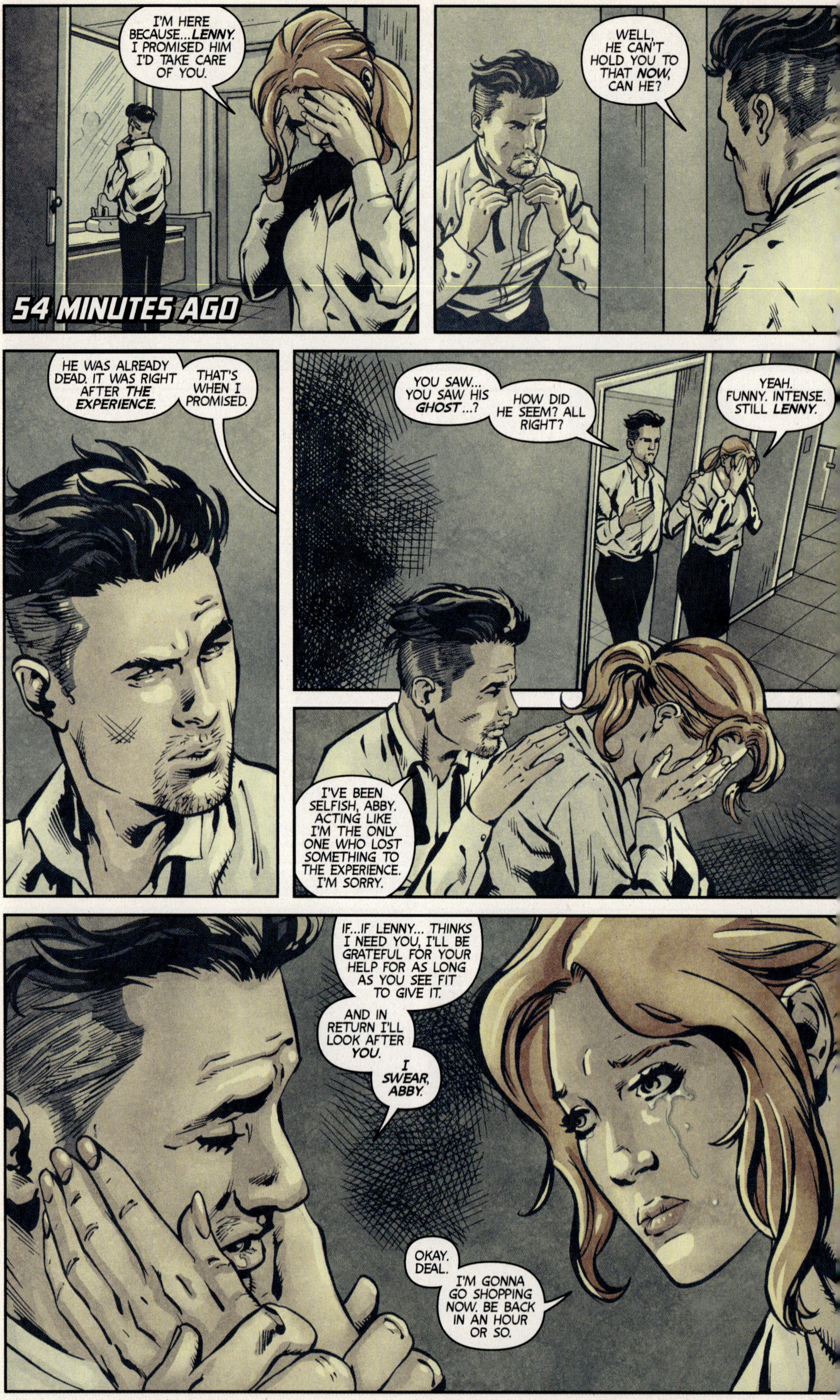
I'M HERE BECAUSE...LENNY. I PROMISED HIM I'D TAKE CARE OF YOU.
54 MINUTES AGO
WELL, HE CAN'T HOLD YOU TO THAT NOW, CAN HE?
HE WAS ALREADY DEAD. IT WAS RIGHT AFTER THE EXPERIENCE.
THAT'S WHEN I PROMISED.
YOU SAW... YOU SAW HIS GHOST...?
HOW DID HE SEEM? ALL RIGHT?
YEAH. FUNNY. INTENSE. STILL LENNY.
I'VE BEEN SELFISH, ABBY. ACTING LIKE I'M THE ONLY ONE WHO LOST SOMETHING TO THE EXPERIENCE. I'M SORRY.
IF...IF LENNY... THINKS I NEED YOU, I'LL BE GRATEFUL FOR YOUR HELP FOR AS LONG AS YOU SEE FIT TO GIVE IT.
AND IN RETURN I'LL LOOK AFTER YOU.
I SWEAR, ABBY.
OKAY. DEAL.
I'M GONNA GO SHOPPING NOW. BE BACK IN AN HOUR OR SO.

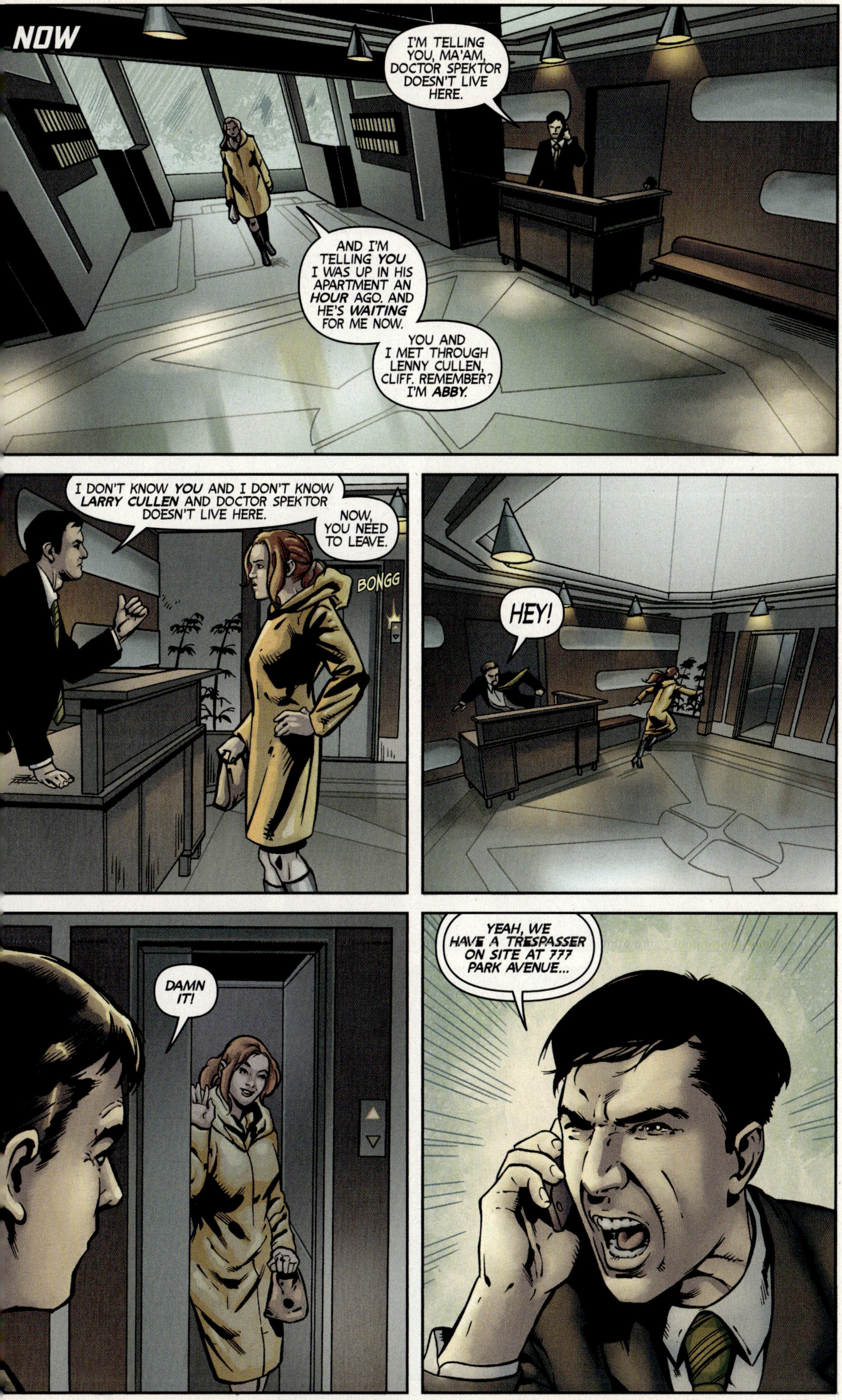
NOW
I'M TELLING YOU, MA'AM, DOCTOR SPEKTOR DOESN'T LIVE HERE.
AND I'M TELLING YOU I WAS UP IN HIS APARTMENT AN HOUR AGO. AND HE'S WAITING FOR ME NOW.
YOU AND I MET THROUGH LENNY CULLEN, CLIFF. REMEMBER? I'M ABBY.
I DON'T KNOW YOU AND I DON'T KNOW LARRY CULLEN AND DOCTOR SPEKTOR DOESN'T LIVE HERE.
NOW, YOU NEED TO LEAVE.
BONGG
HEY!
DAMN IT!
YEAH, WE HAVE A TRESPASSER ON SITE AT 777 PARK AVENUE...

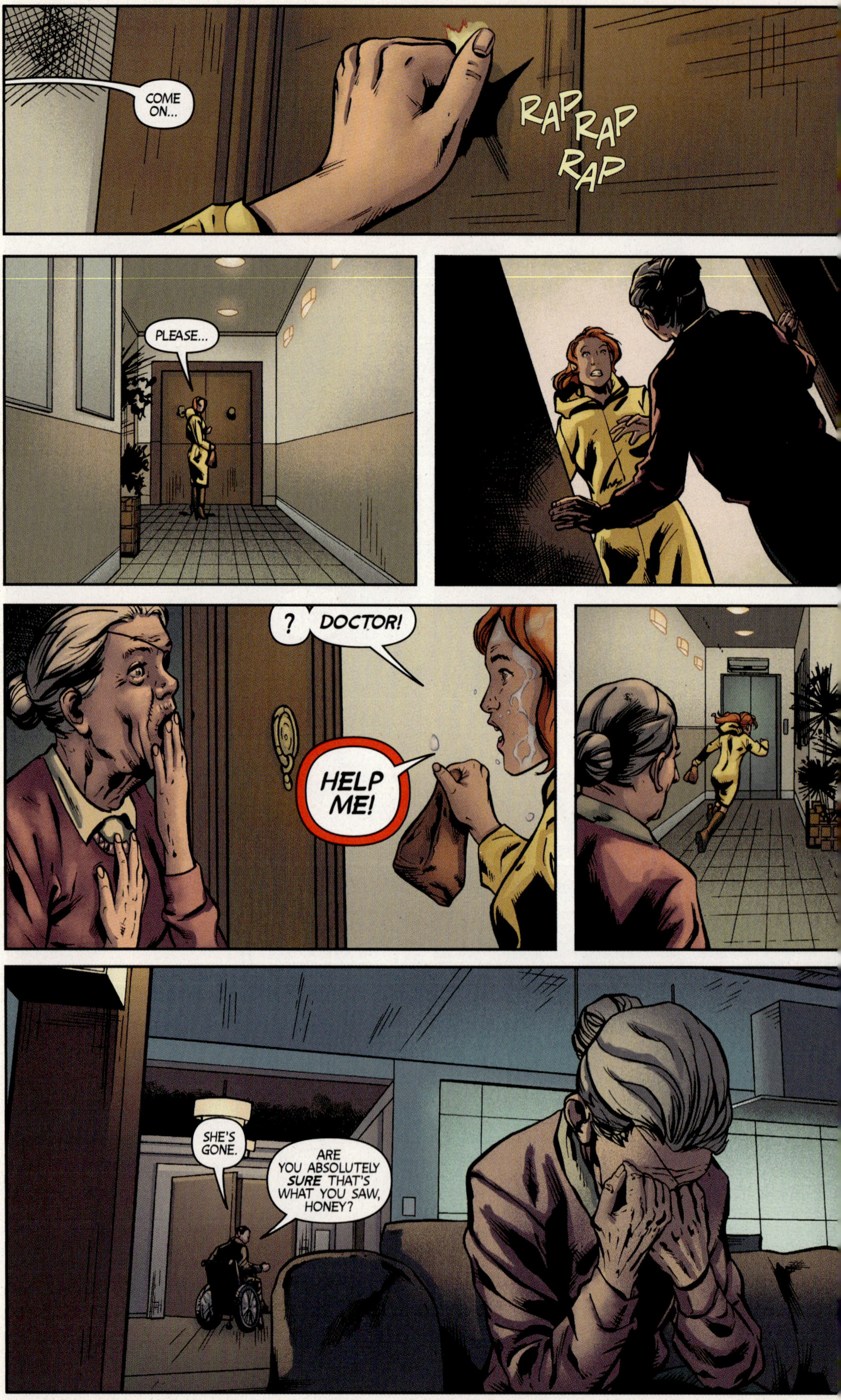
COME ON...
RAP RAP RAP
PLEASE...
?
DOCTOR!
HELP ME!
SHE'S GONE.
ARE YOU ABSOLUTELY SURE THAT'S WHAT YOU SAW, HONEY?

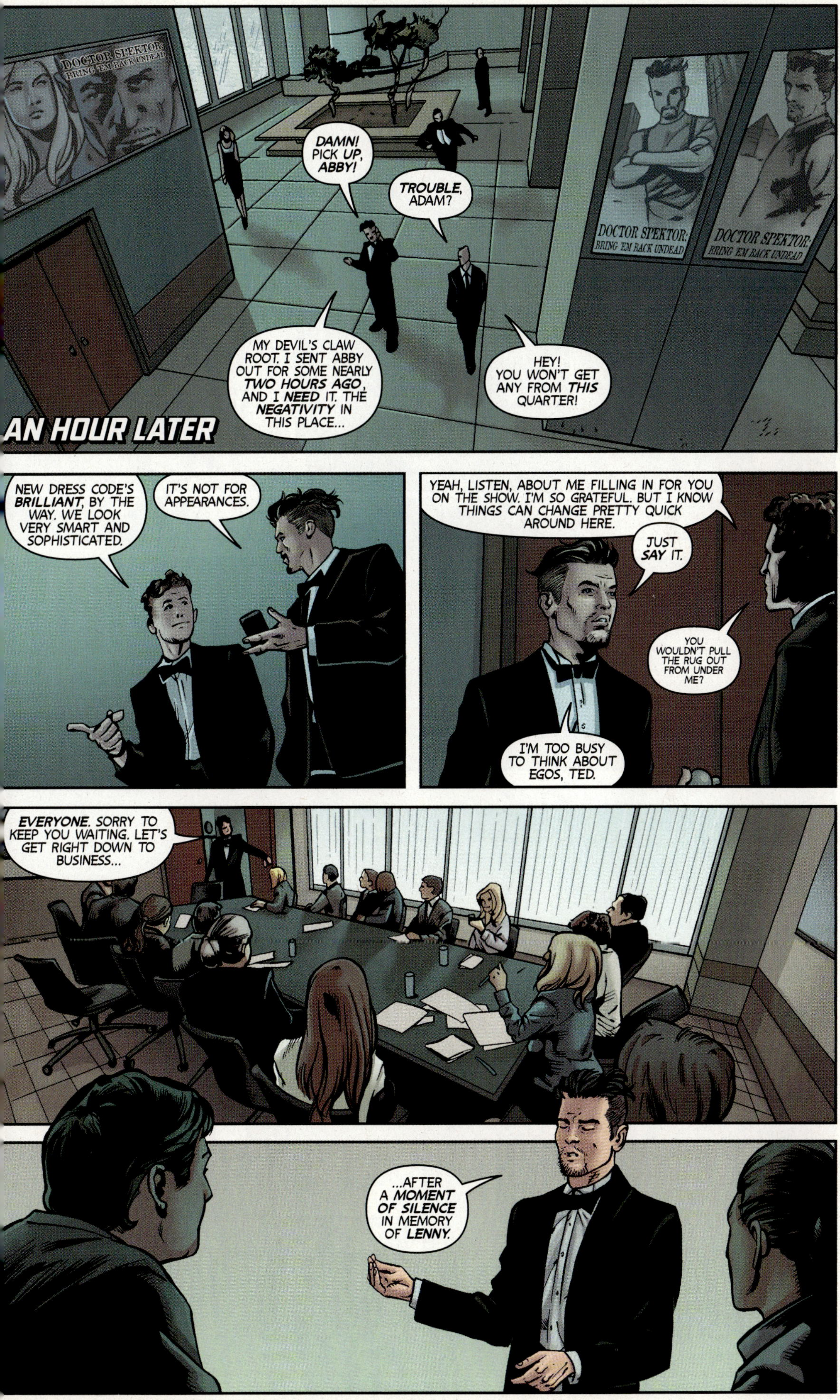
DOCTOR SPEKTOR: BRING 'EM BACK UNDEAD
DAMN! PICK UP, ABBY!
TROUBLE, ADAM?
DOCTOR SPEKTOR: BRING 'EM BACK UNDEAD
DOCTOR SPEKTOR: BRING 'EM BACK UNDEAD
MY DEVIL'S CLAW ROOT. I SENT ABBY OUT FOR SOME NEARLY TWO HOURS AGO, AND I NEED IT. THE NEGATIVITY IN THIS PLACE...
HEY! YOU WON'T GET ANY FROM THIS QUARTER!
AN HOUR LATER
NEW DRESS CODE'S BRILLIANT, BY THE WAY. WE LOOK VERY SMART AND SOPHISTICATED.
IT'S NOT FOR APPEARANCES.
YEAH, LISTEN, ABOUT ME FILLING IN FOR YOU ON THE SHOW. I'M SO GRATEFUL. BUT I KNOW THINGS CAN CHANGE PRETTY QUICK AROUND HERE.
JUST SAY IT.
YOU WOULDN'T PULL THE RUG OUT FROM UNDER ME?
I'M TOO BUSY TO THINK ABOUT EGOS, TED.
EVERYONE. SORRY TO KEEP YOU WAITING. LET'S GET RIGHT DOWN TO BUSINESS...
...AFTER A MOMENT OF SILENCE IN MEMORY OF LENNY.

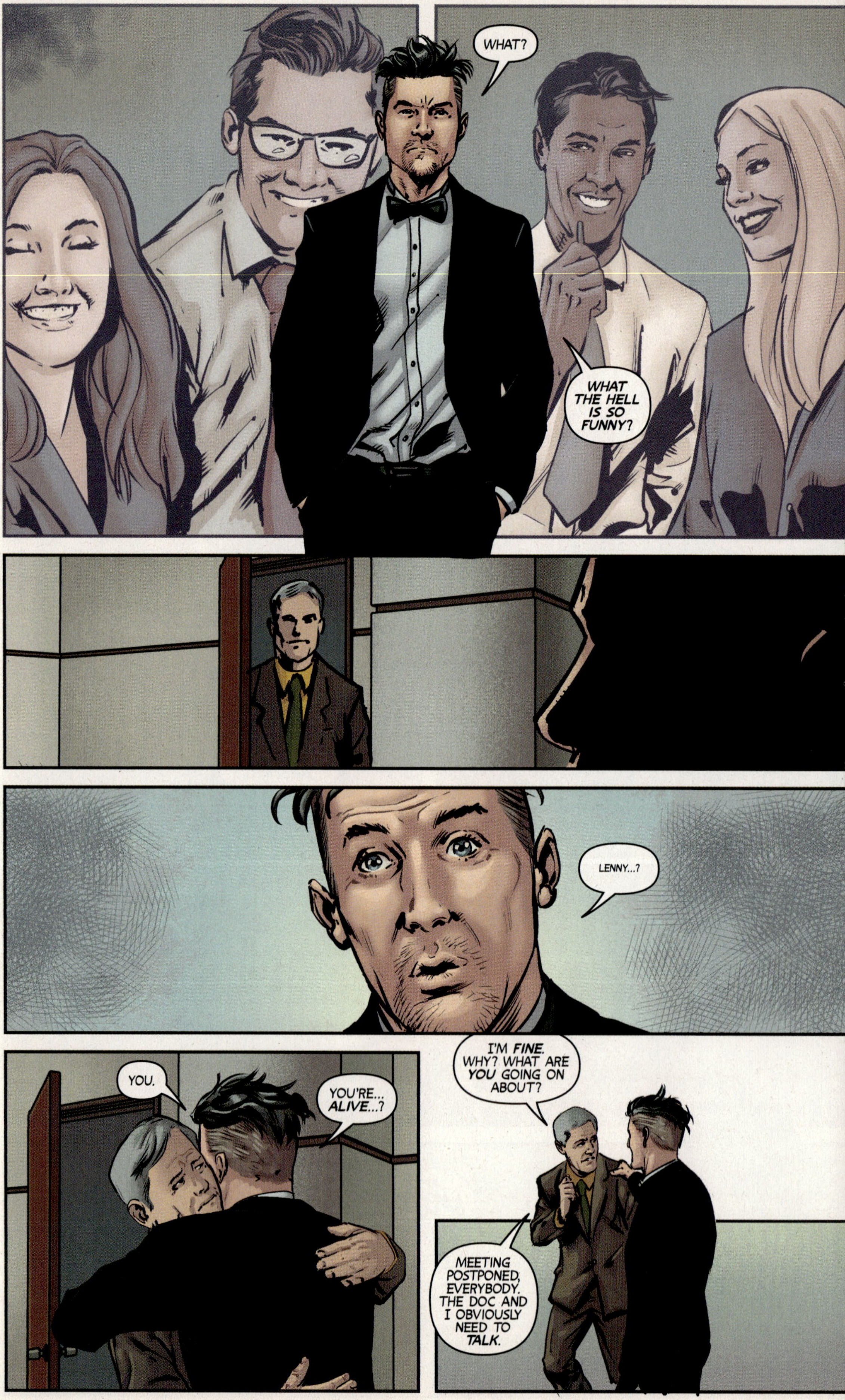
WHAT?
WHAT THE HELL IS SO FUNNY?
LENNY...?
YOU.
YOU'RE... ALIVE...?
I'M FINE. WHY? WHAT ARE YOU GOING ON ABOUT?
MEETING POSTPONED, EVERYBODY. THE DOC AND I OBVIOUSLY NEED TO TALK.

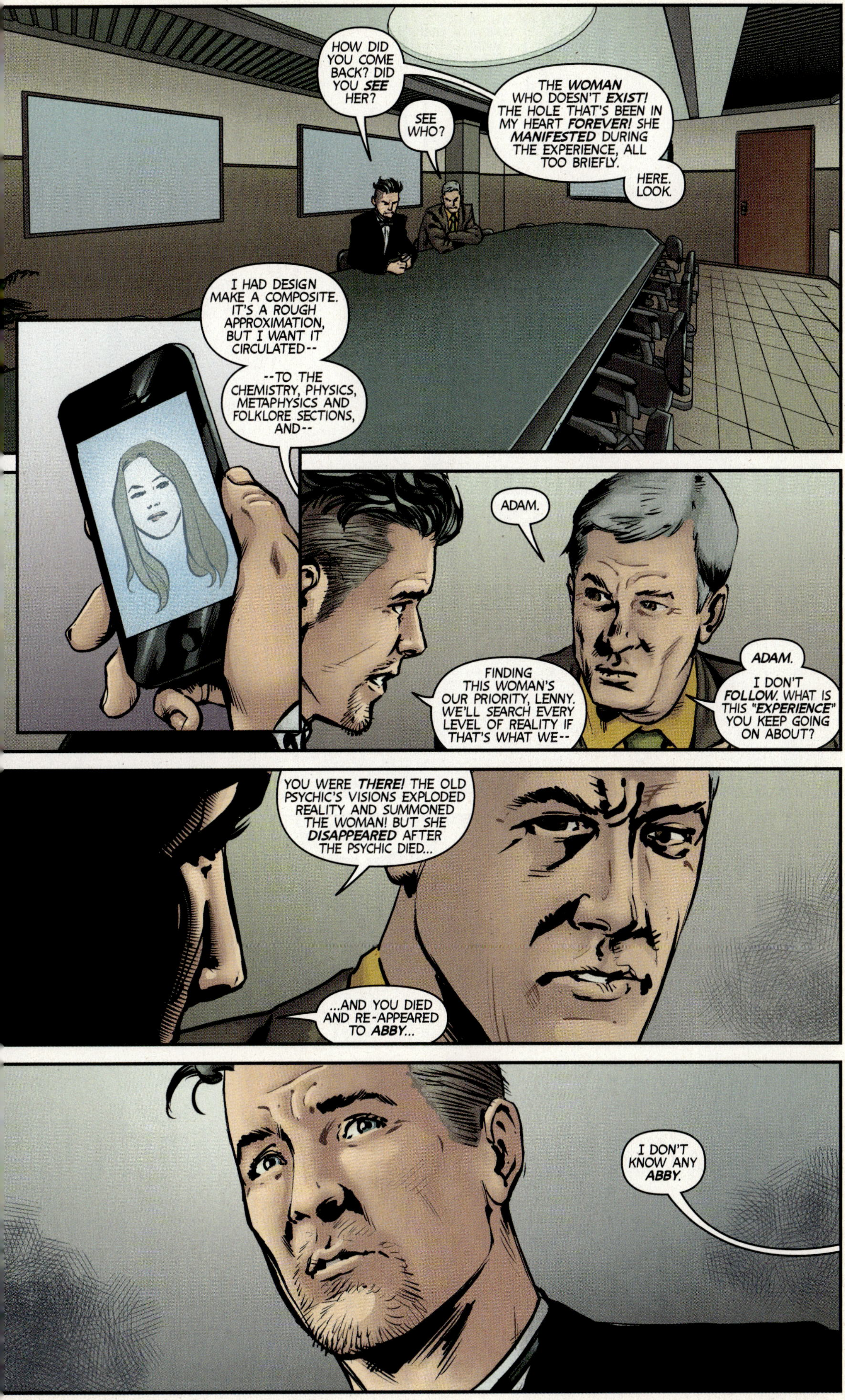
HOW DID YOU COME BACK? DID YOU SEE HER?
SEE WHO?
THE WOMAN WHO DOESN'T EXIST! THE HOLE THAT'S BEEN IN MY HEART FOREVER! SHE MANIFESTED DURING THE EXPERIENCE, ALL TOO BRIEFLY.
HERE. LOOK.
I HAD DESIGN MAKE A COMPOSITE. IT'S A ROUGH APPROXIMATION, BUT I WANT IT CIRCULATED--
--TO THE CHEMISTRY, PHYSICS, METAPHYSICS AND FOLKLORE SECTIONS, AND--
ADAM.
FINDING THIS WOMAN'S OUR PRIORITY, LENNY. WE'LL SEARCH EVERY LEVEL OF REALITY IF THAT'S WHAT WE--
ADAM.
I DON'T FOLLOW. WHAT IS THIS "EXPERIENCE" YOU KEEP GOING ON ABOUT?
YOU WERE THERE! THE OLD PSYCHIC'S VISIONS EXPLODED REALITY AND SUMMONED THE WOMAN! BUT SHE DISAPPEARED AFTER THE PSYCHIC DIED...
...AND YOU DIED AND RE-APPEARED TO ABBY...
I DON'T KNOW ANY ABBY.

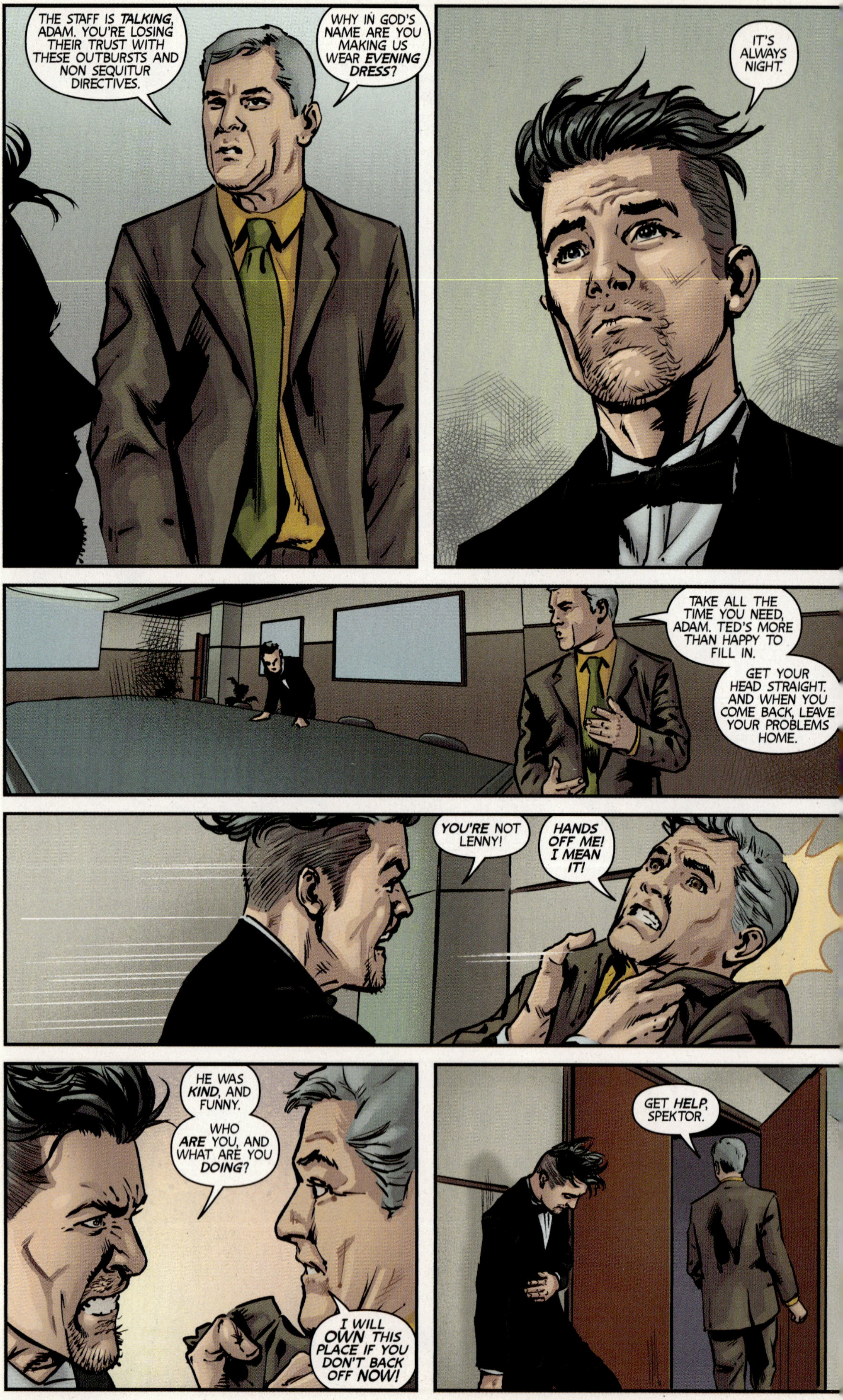
THE STAFF IS **TALKING**, ADAM. YOU'RE LOSING THEIR TRUST WITH THESE OUTBURSTS AND NON SEQUITUR DIRECTIVES.
WHY IN GOD'S NAME ARE YOU MAKING US WEAR **EVENING DRESS**?
IT'S ALWAYS NIGHT.
TAKE ALL THE TIME YOU NEED, ADAM. TED'S MORE THAN HAPPY TO FILL IN.
GET YOUR HEAD STRAIGHT. AND WHEN YOU COME BACK, LEAVE YOUR PROBLEMS HOME.
YOU'RE NOT LENNY!
HANDS OFF ME! I MEAN IT!
HE WAS **KIND**, AND FUNNY.
WHO **ARE** YOU, AND WHAT ARE YOU **DOING**?
I WILL OWN THIS PLACE IF YOU DON'T BACK OFF NOW!
GET **HELP**, SPEKTOR.

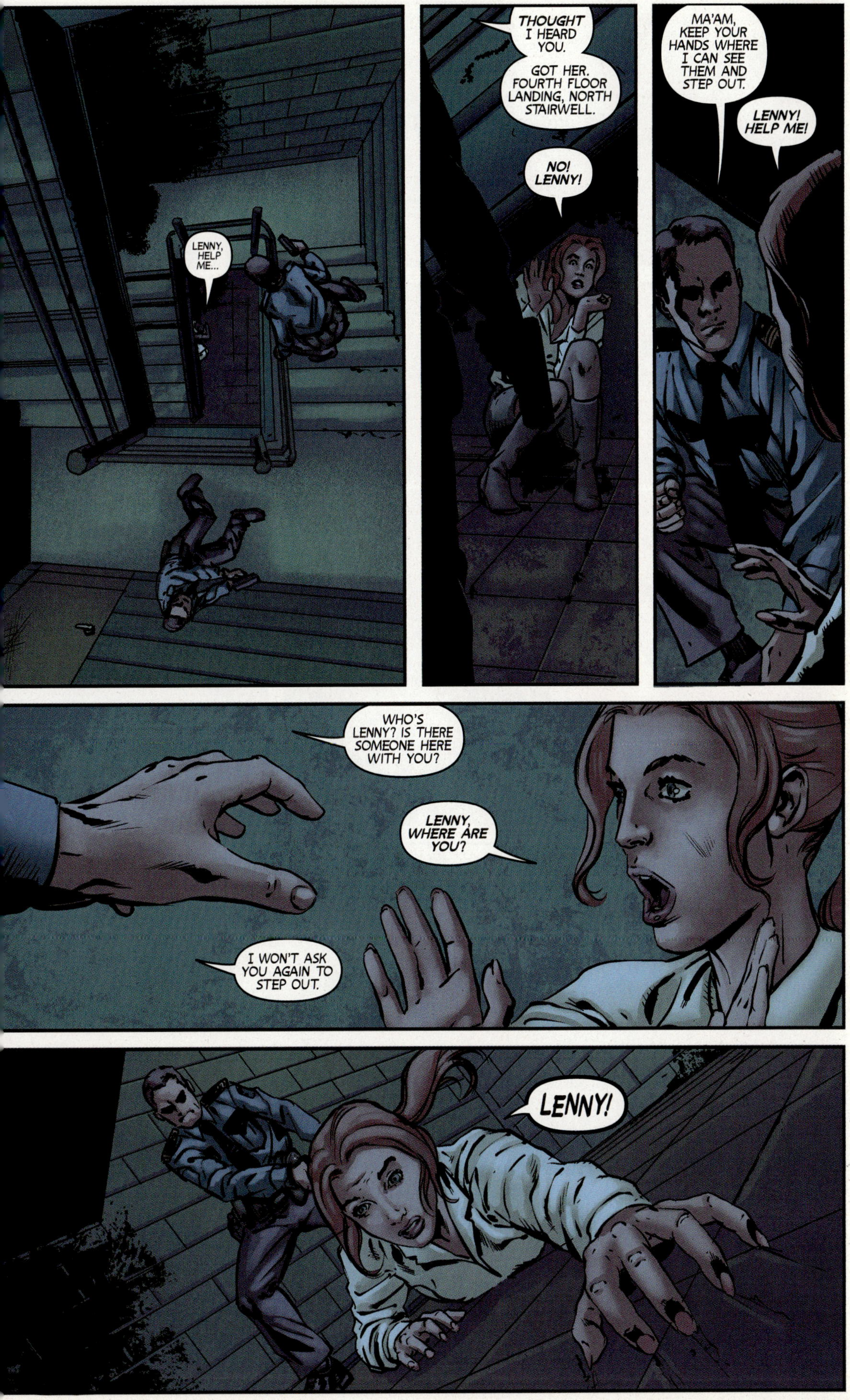
LENNY, HELP ME...
THOUGHT I HEARD YOU.
GOT HER. FOURTH FLOOR LANDING, NORTH STAIRWELL.
NO! LENNY!
MA'AM, KEEP YOUR HANDS WHERE I CAN SEE THEM AND STEP OUT.
LENNY! HELP ME!
WHO'S LENNY? IS THERE SOMEONE HERE WITH YOU?
LENNY, WHERE ARE YOU?
I WON'T ASK YOU AGAIN TO STEP OUT.
LENNY!

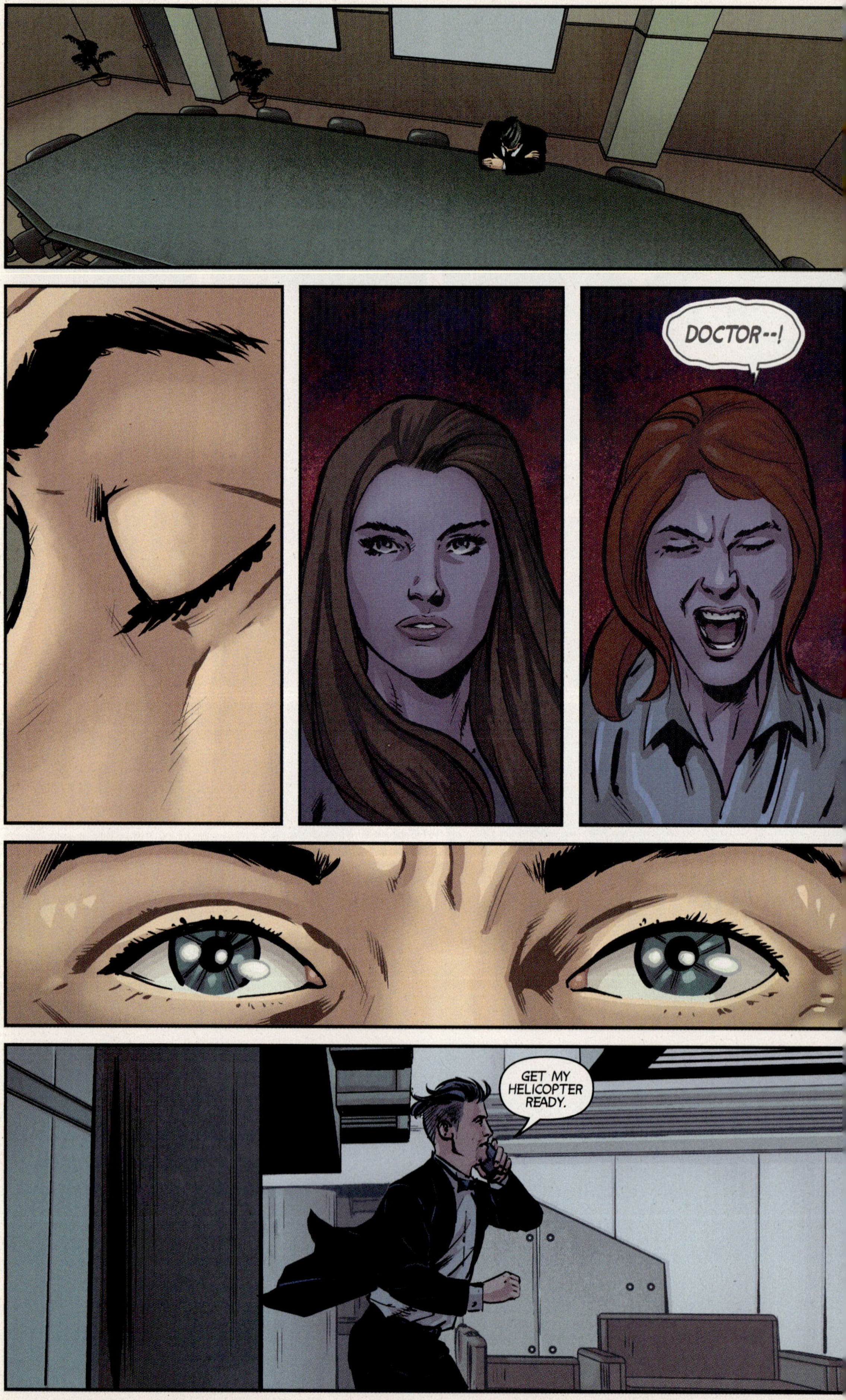
DOCTOR--!
GET MY HELICOPTER READY.

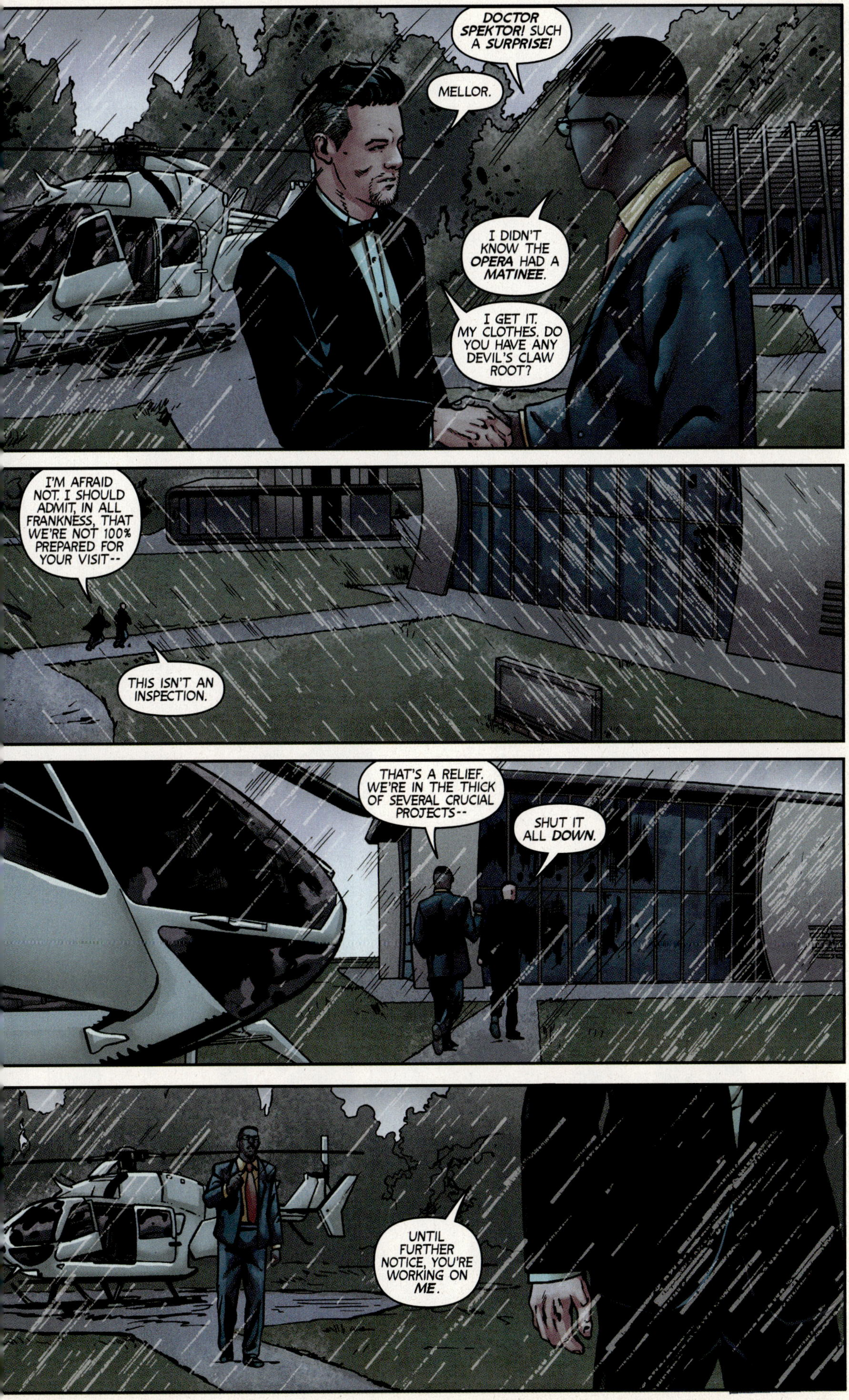
DOCTOR SPEKTOR! SUCH A SURPRISE!
MELLOR.
I DIDN'T KNOW THE OPERA HAD A MATINEE.
I GET IT. MY CLOTHES. DO YOU HAVE ANY DEVIL'S CLAW ROOT?
I'M AFRAID NOT. I SHOULD ADMIT, IN ALL FRANKNESS, THAT WE'RE NOT 100% PREPARED FOR YOUR VISIT--
THIS ISN'T AN INSPECTION.
THAT'S A RELIEF. WE'RE IN THE THICK OF SEVERAL CRUCIAL PROJECTS--
SHUT IT ALL DOWN.
UNTIL FURTHER NOTICE, YOU'RE WORKING ON ME.

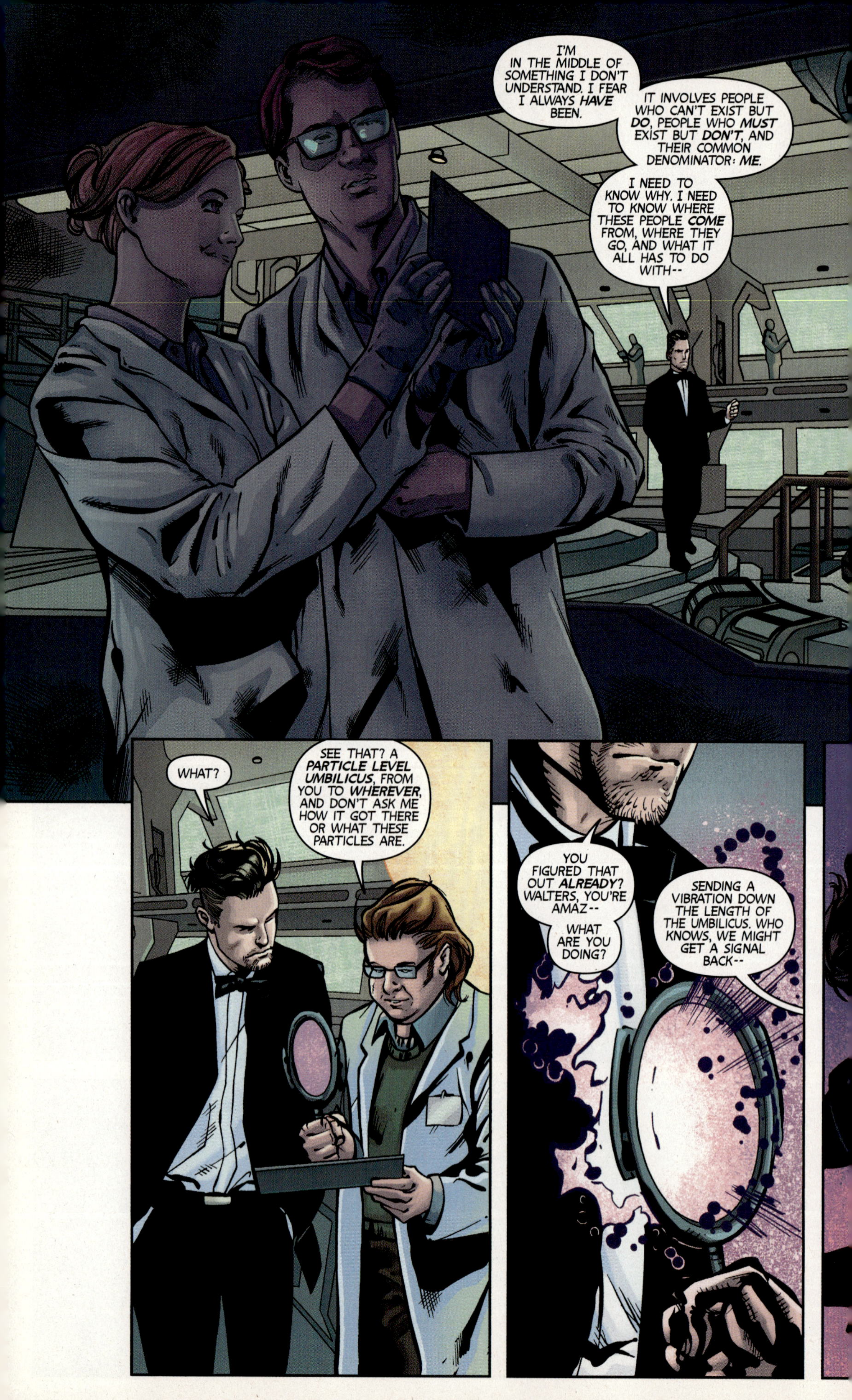
I'M IN THE MIDDLE OF SOMETHING I DON'T UNDERSTAND. I FEAR I ALWAYS HAVE BEEN.
IT INVOLVES PEOPLE WHO CAN'T EXIST BUT DO, PEOPLE WHO MUST EXIST BUT DON'T, AND THEIR COMMON DENOMINATOR: ME.
I NEED TO KNOW WHY. I NEED TO KNOW WHERE THESE PEOPLE COME FROM, WHERE THEY GO, AND WHAT IT ALL HAS TO DO WITH--
WHAT?
SEE THAT? A PARTICLE LEVEL UMBILICUS, FROM YOU TO WHEREVER, AND DON'T ASK ME HOW IT GOT THERE OR WHAT THESE PARTICLES ARE.
YOU FIGURED THAT OUT ALREADY? WALTERS, YOU'RE AMAZ--
WHAT ARE YOU DOING?
SENDING A VIBRATION DOWN THE LENGTH OF THE UMBILICUS. WHO KNOWS, WE MIGHT GET A SIGNAL BACK--

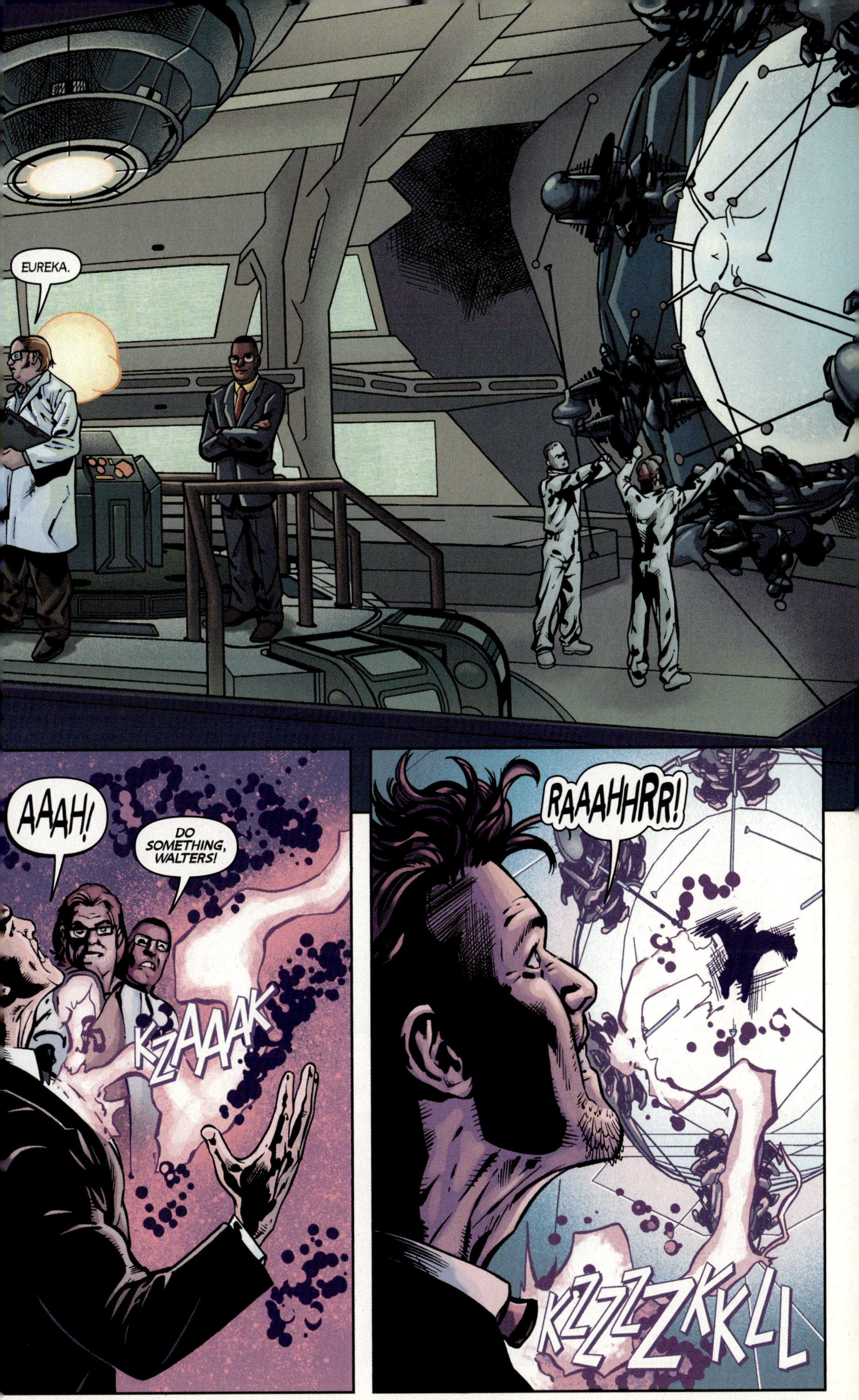
EUREKA.
AAAH!
DO SOMETHING, WALTERS!
KZAAAK
RAAAHHRR!
KZZZZKKLL

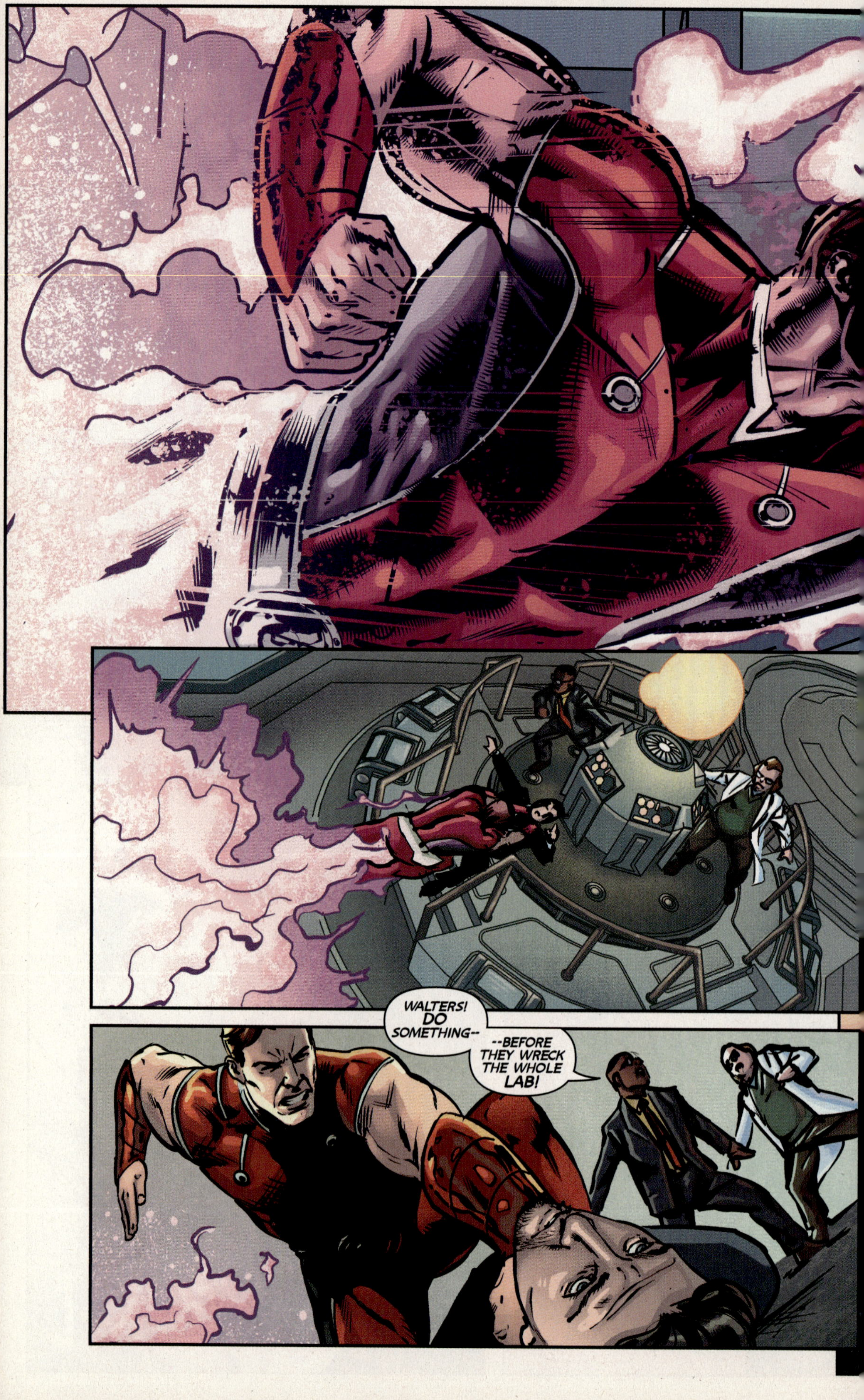
WALTERS! DO SOMETHING--
--BEFORE THEY WRECK THE WHOLE LAB!

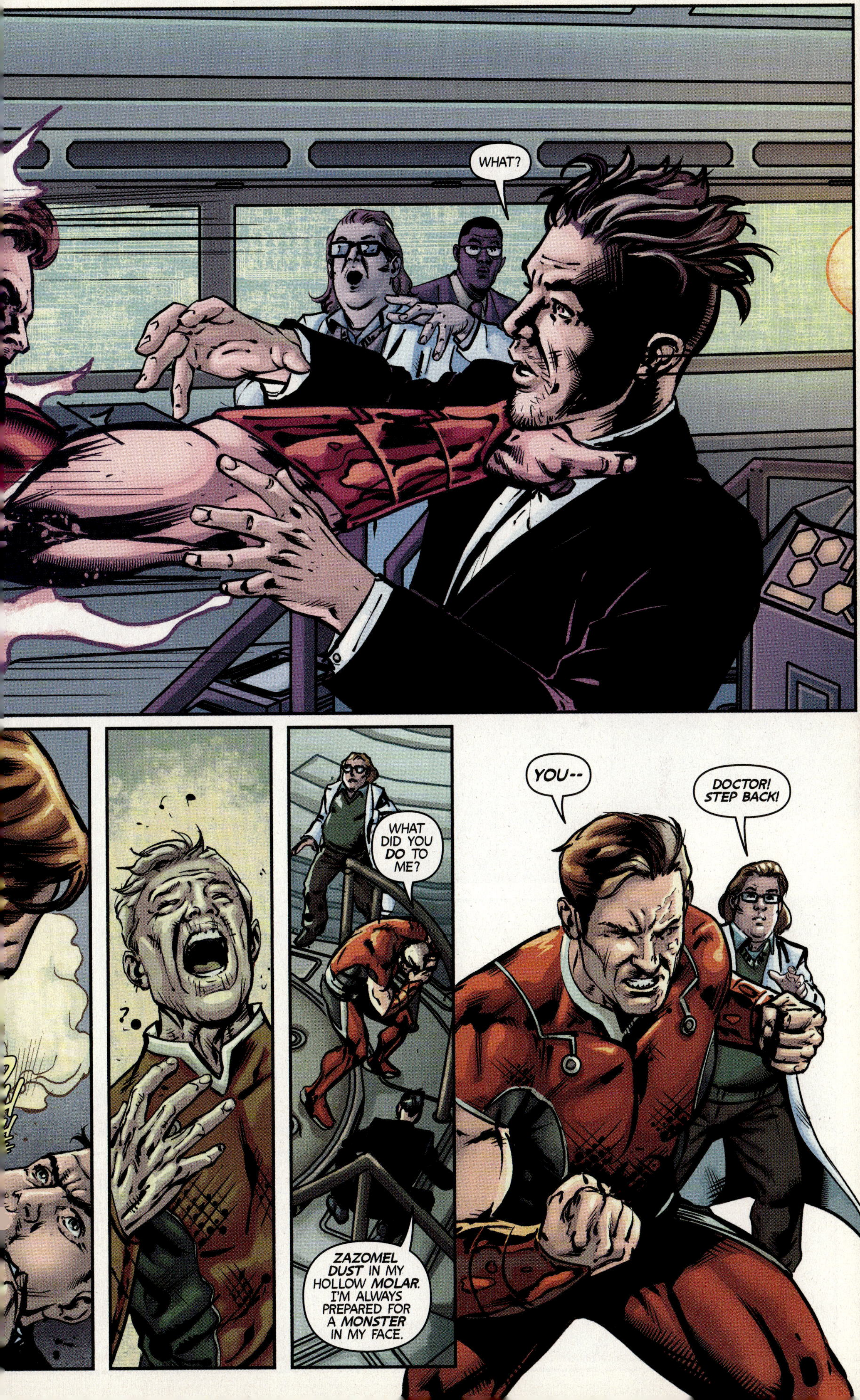
WHAT?
WHAT DID YOU DO TO ME?
ZAZOMEL DUST IN MY HOLLOW MOLAR. I'M ALWAYS PREPARED FOR A MONSTER IN MY FACE.
YOU--
DOCTOR! STEP BACK!

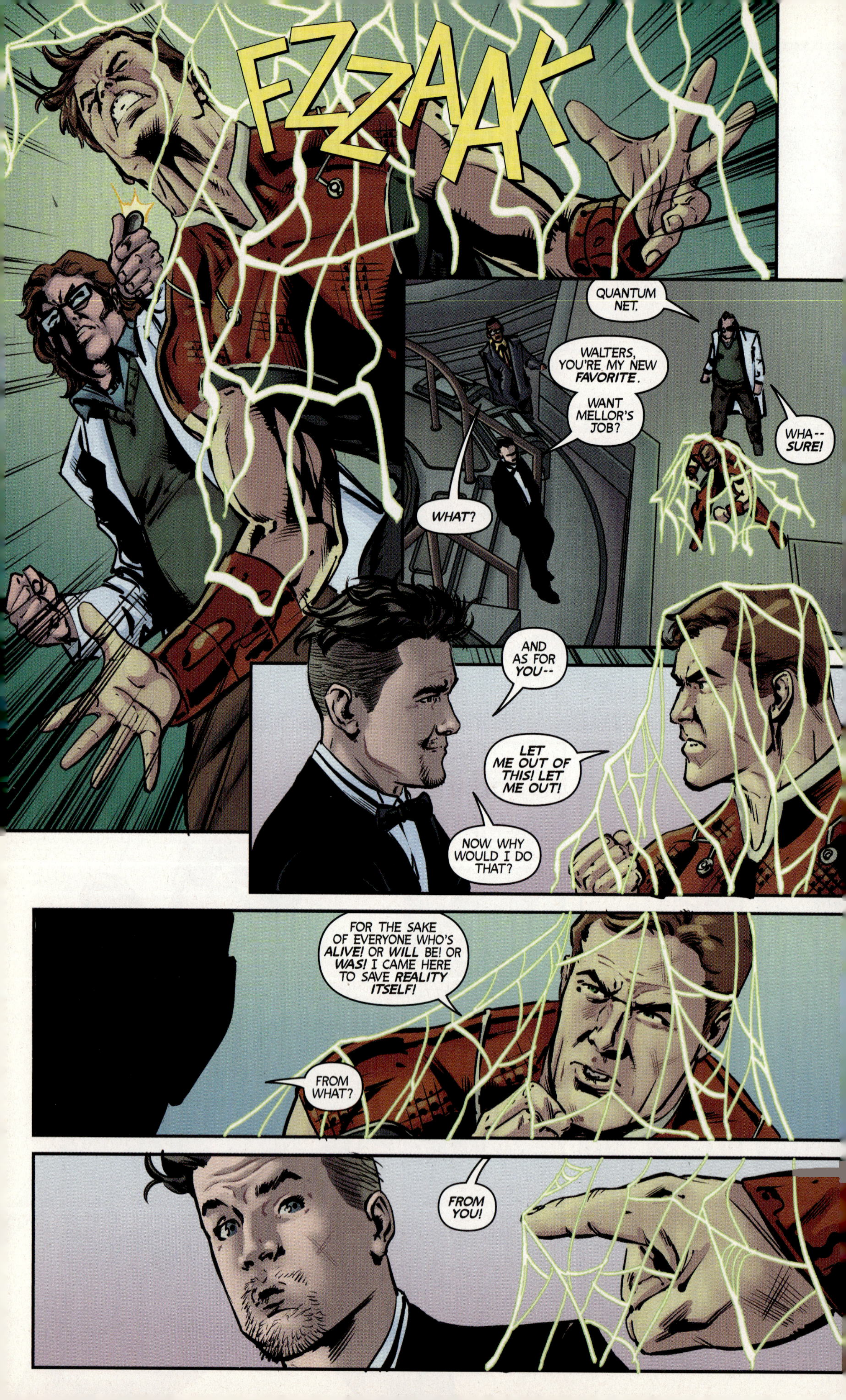
FZZAAK
QUANTUM NET.
WALTERS, YOU'RE MY NEW FAVORITE.
WANT MELLOR'S JOB?
WHAT?
WHA-- SURE!
AND AS FOR YOU--
LET ME OUT OF THIS! LET ME OUT!
NOW WHY WOULD I DO THAT?
FOR THE SAKE OF EVERYONE WHO'S ALIVE! OR WILL BE! OR WAS! I CAME HERE TO SAVE REALITY ITSELF!
FROM WHAT?
FROM YOU!

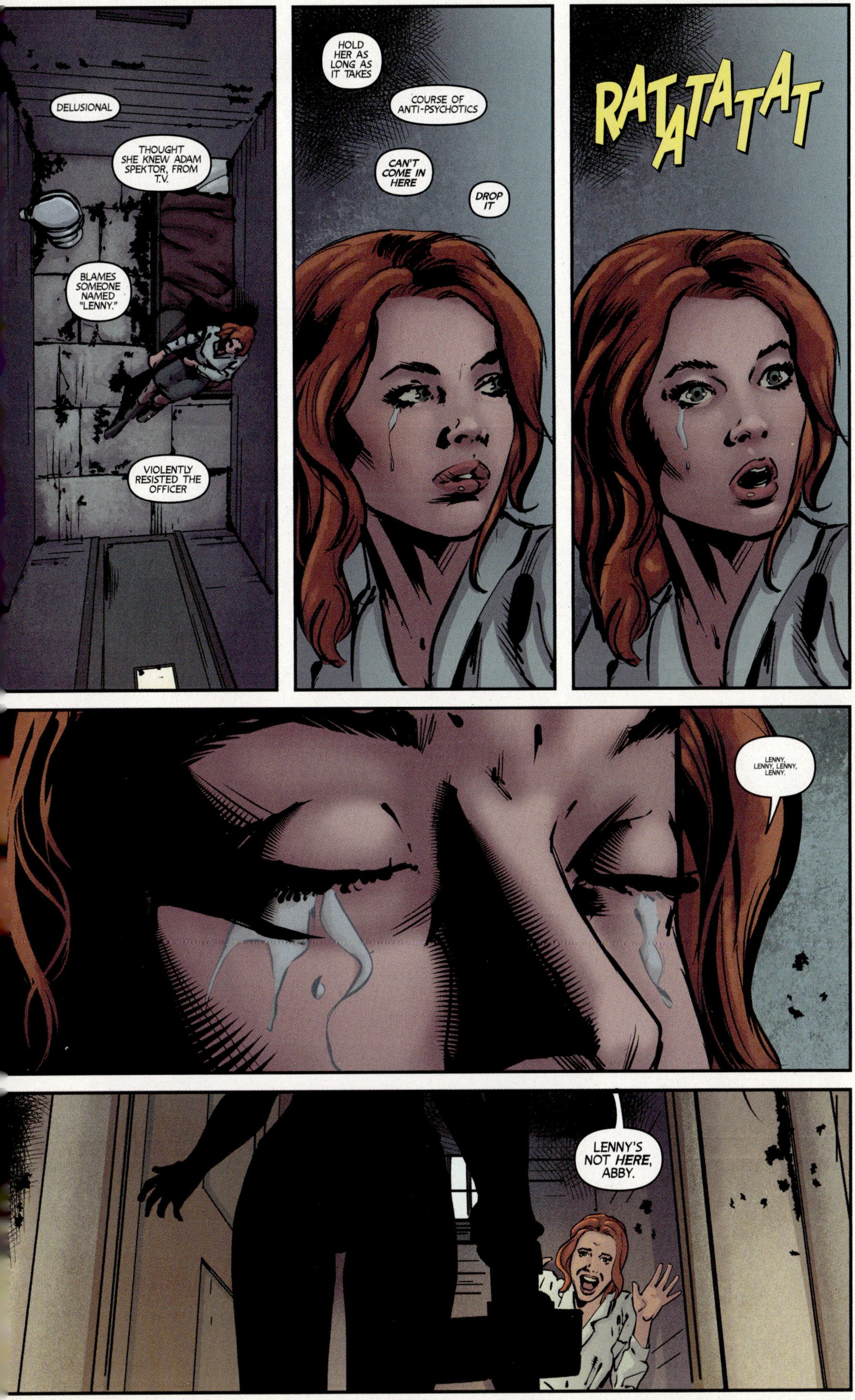

DELUSIONAL
THOUGHT SHE KNEW ADAM SPEKTOR, FROM T.V.
BLAMES SOMEONE NAMED "LENNY."
VIOLENTLY RESISTED THE OFFICER
HOLD HER AS LONG AS IT TAKES
COURSE OF ANTI-PSYCHOTICS
CAN'T COME IN HERE
DROP IT
RATATATATAT
LENNY, LENNY, LENNY, LENNY.
LENNY'S NOT *HERE*, ABBY.

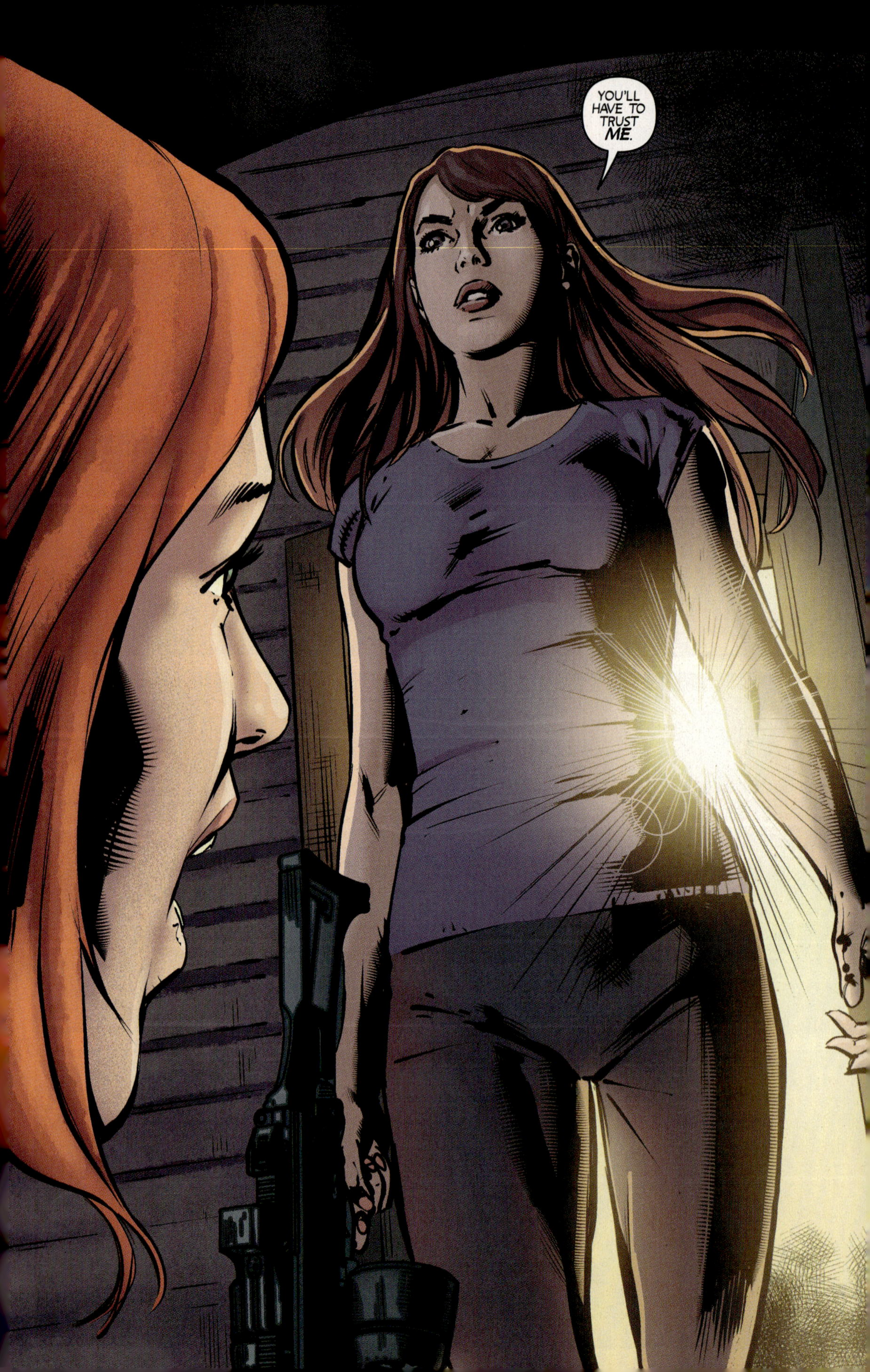
YOU'LL HAVE TO TRUST ME.

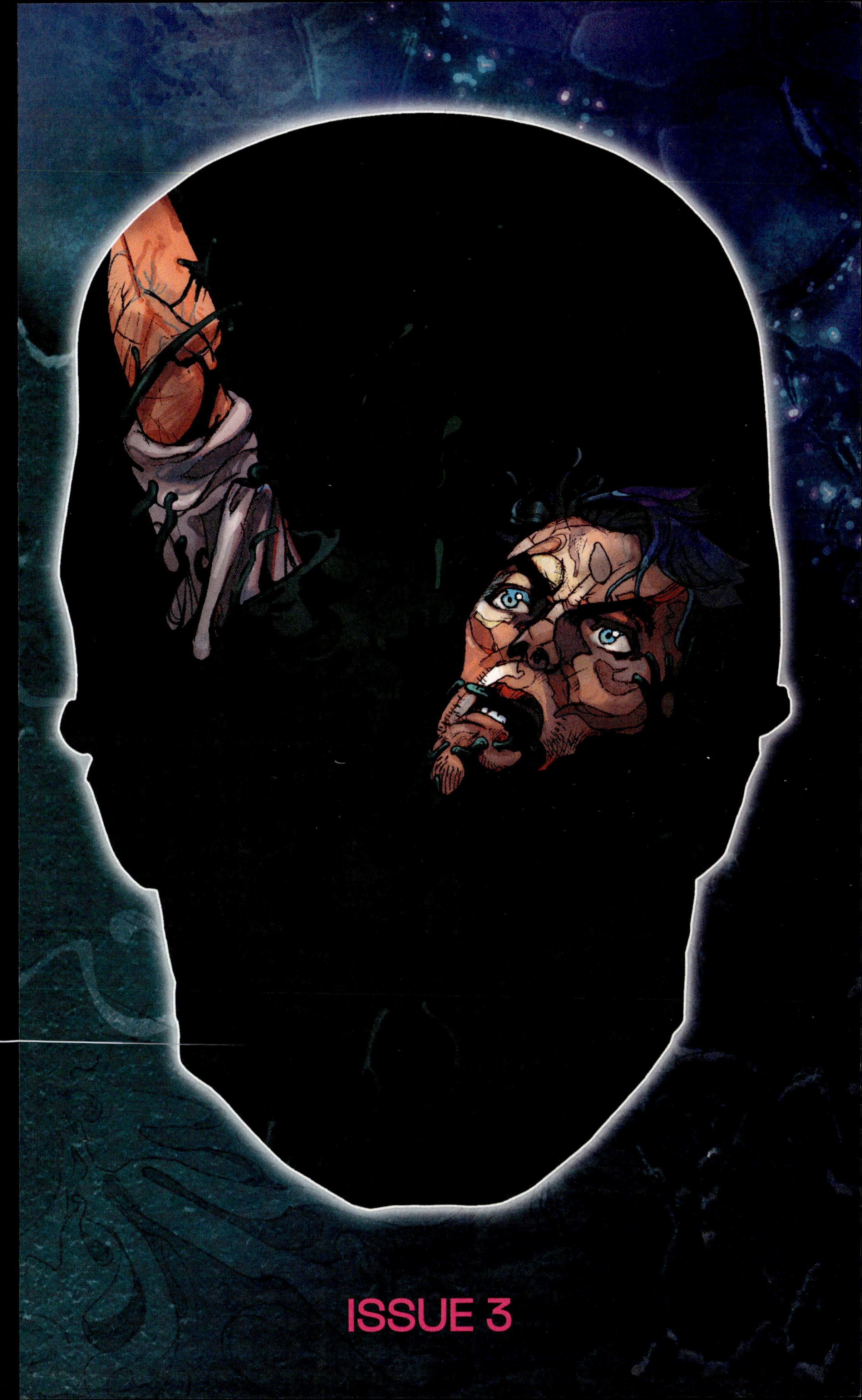
ISSUE 3

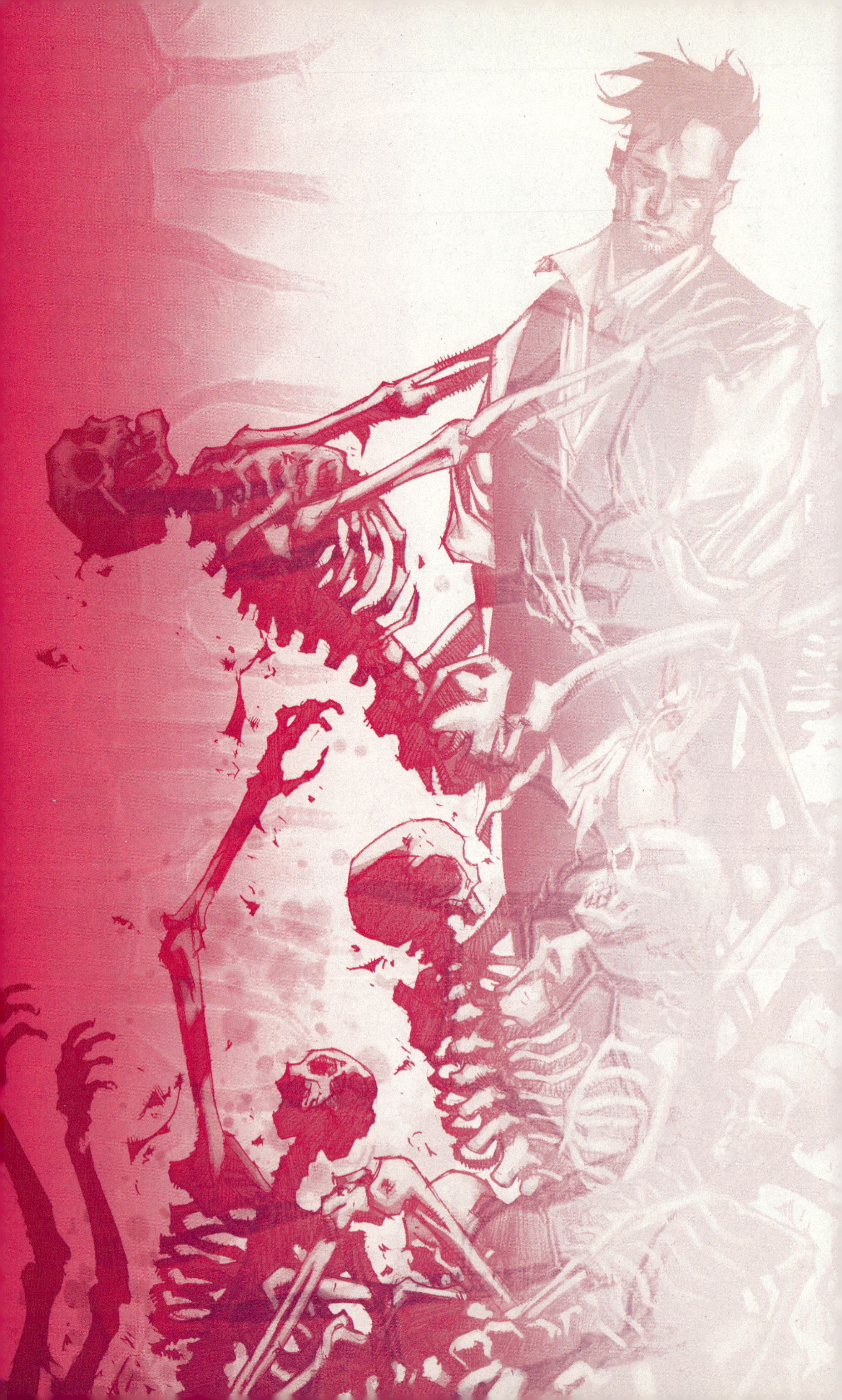

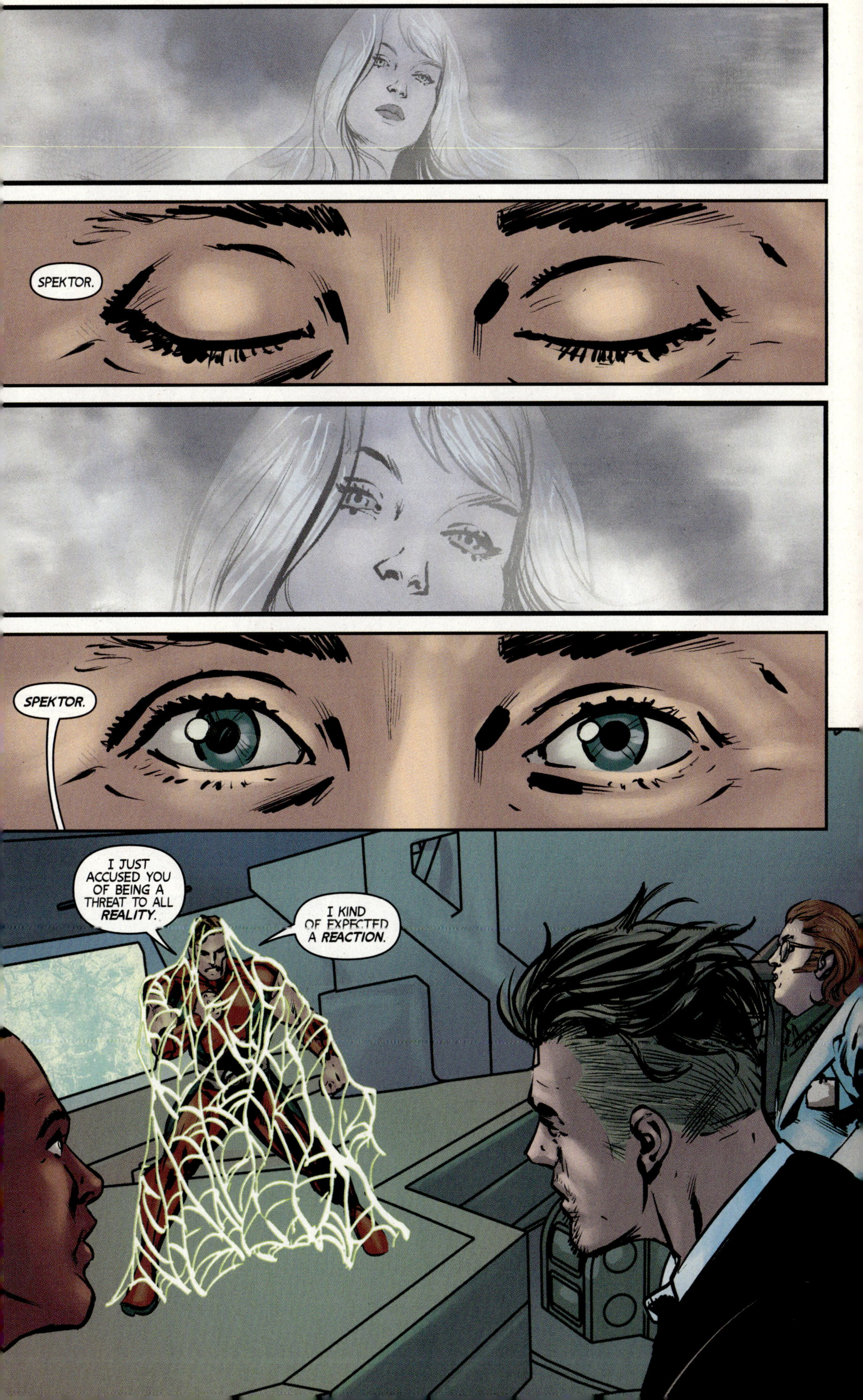
SPEKTOR.
SPEKTOR.
I JUST ACCUSED YOU OF BEING A THREAT TO ALL REALITY.
I KIND OF EXPECTED A REACTION.

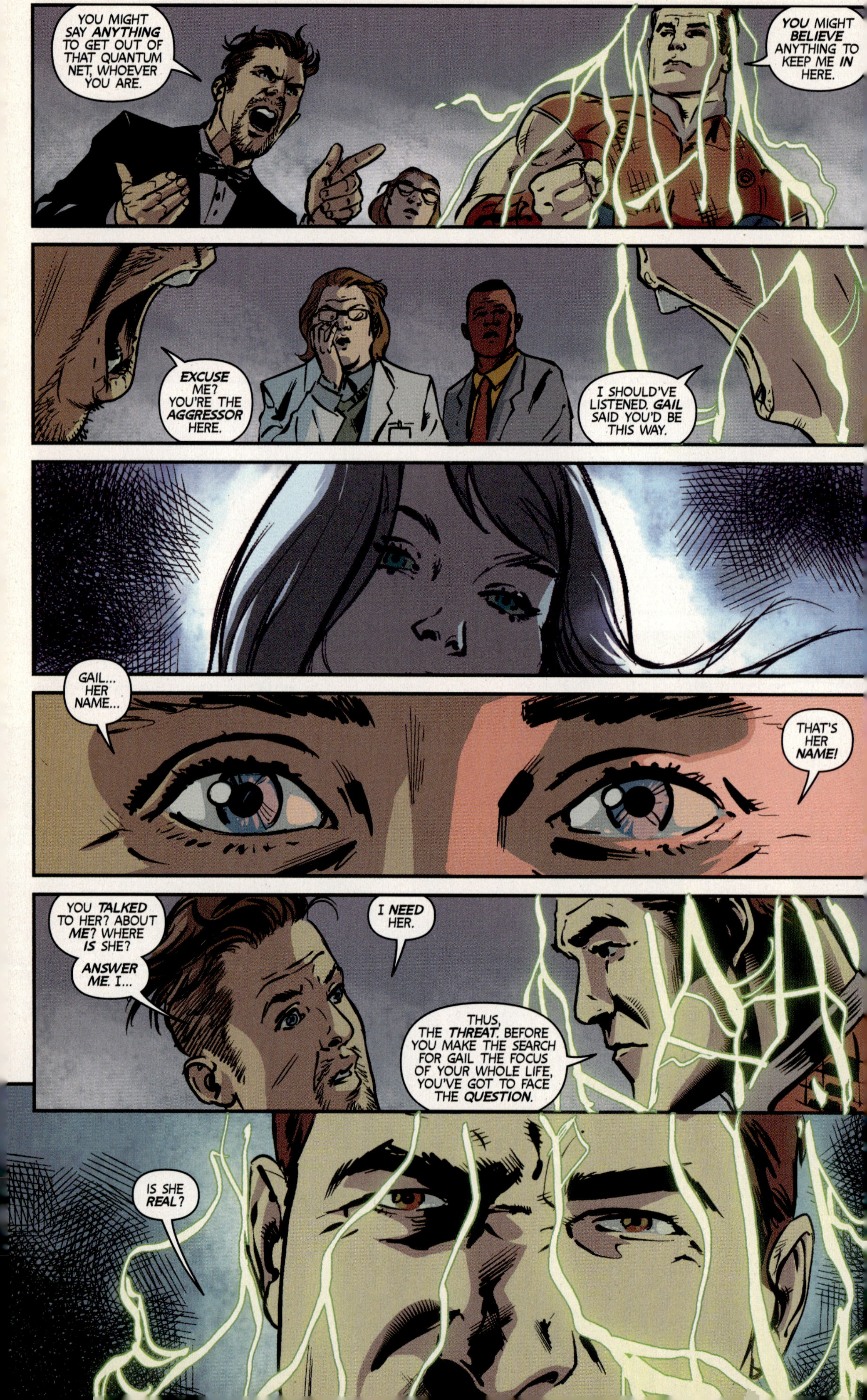
YOU MIGHT SAY ANYTHING TO GET OUT OF THAT QUANTUM NET, WHOEVER YOU ARE.
YOU MIGHT BELIEVE ANYTHING TO KEEP ME IN HERE.
EXCUSE ME? YOU'RE THE AGGRESSOR HERE.
I SHOULD'VE LISTENED. GAIL SAID YOU'D BE THIS WAY.
GAIL... HER NAME...
THAT'S HER NAME!
YOU TALKED TO HER? ABOUT ME? WHERE IS SHE?
ANSWER ME. I...
I NEED HER.
THUS, THE THREAT. BEFORE YOU MAKE THE SEARCH FOR GAIL THE FOCUS OF YOUR WHOLE LIFE, YOU'VE GOT TO FACE THE QUESTION.
IS SHE REAL?

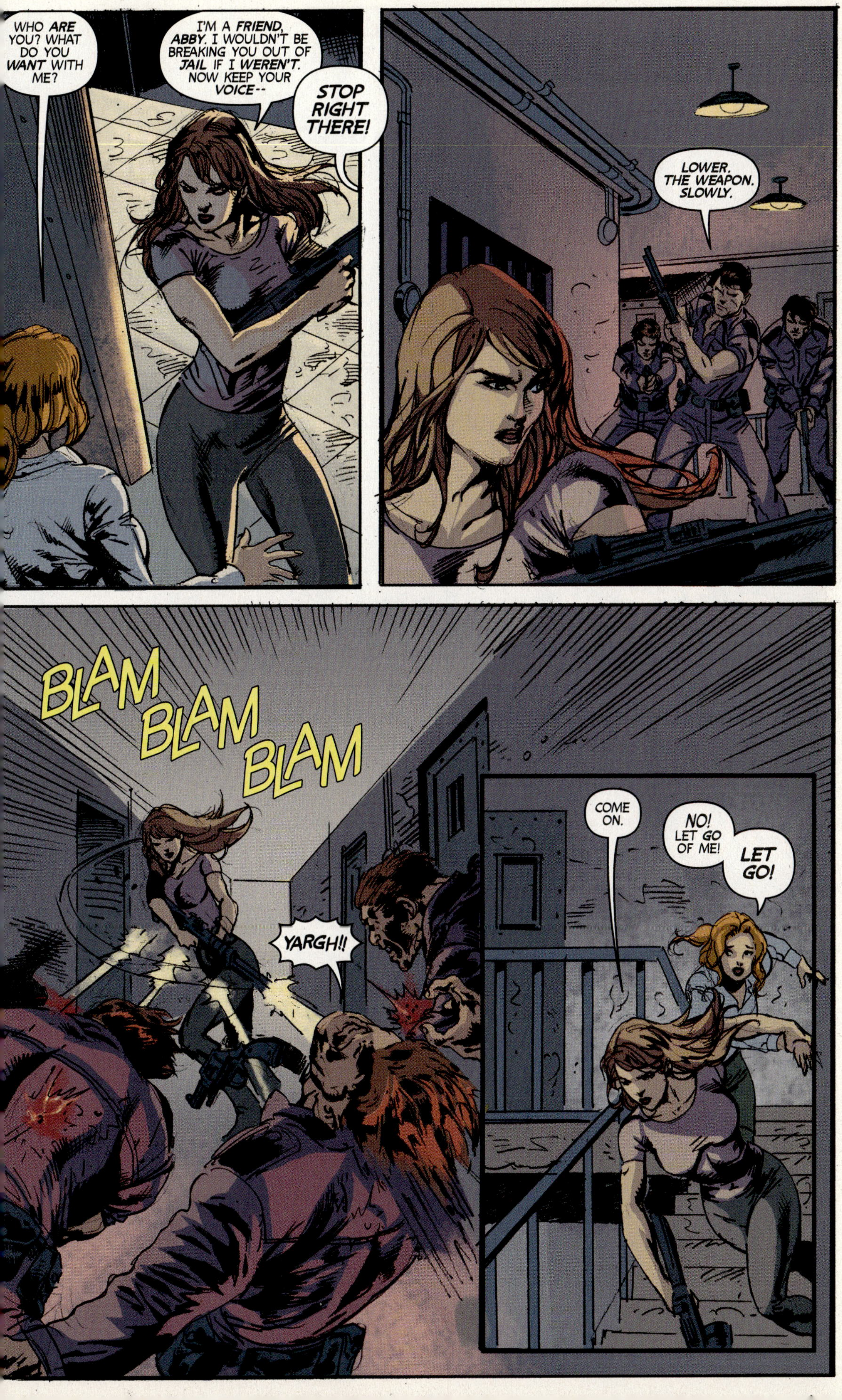
WHO ARE YOU? WHAT DO YOU WANT WITH ME?
I'M A FRIEND, ABBY. I WOULDN'T BE BREAKING YOU OUT OF JAIL IF I WEREN'T. NOW KEEP YOUR VOICE--
STOP RIGHT THERE!
LOWER. THE WEAPON. SLOWLY.
BLAM
BLAM
BLAM
YARGH!!
COME ON.
NO! LET GO OF ME!
LET GO!

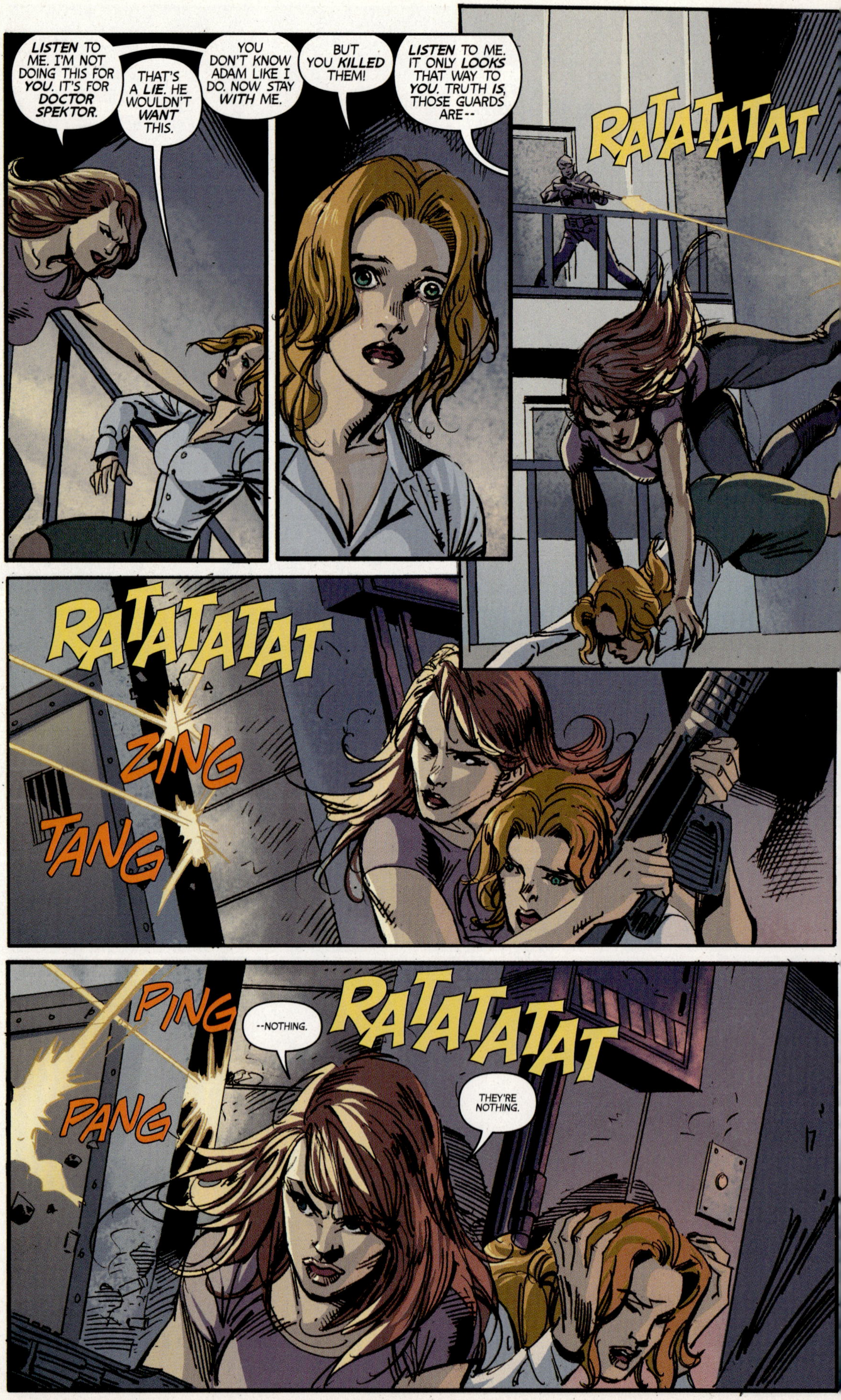
LISTEN TO ME. I'M NOT DOING THIS FOR YOU. IT'S FOR DOCTOR SPEKTOR.
THAT'S A LIE. HE WOULDN'T WANT THIS.
YOU DON'T KNOW ADAM LIKE I DO. NOW STAY WITH ME.
BUT YOU KILLED THEM!
LISTEN TO ME. IT ONLY LOOKS THAT WAY TO YOU. TRUTH IS, THOSE GUARDS ARE--
RATATATAT
RATATATAT
ZING
TANG
PING
PANG
--NOTHING.
RATATATAT
THEY'RE NOTHING.

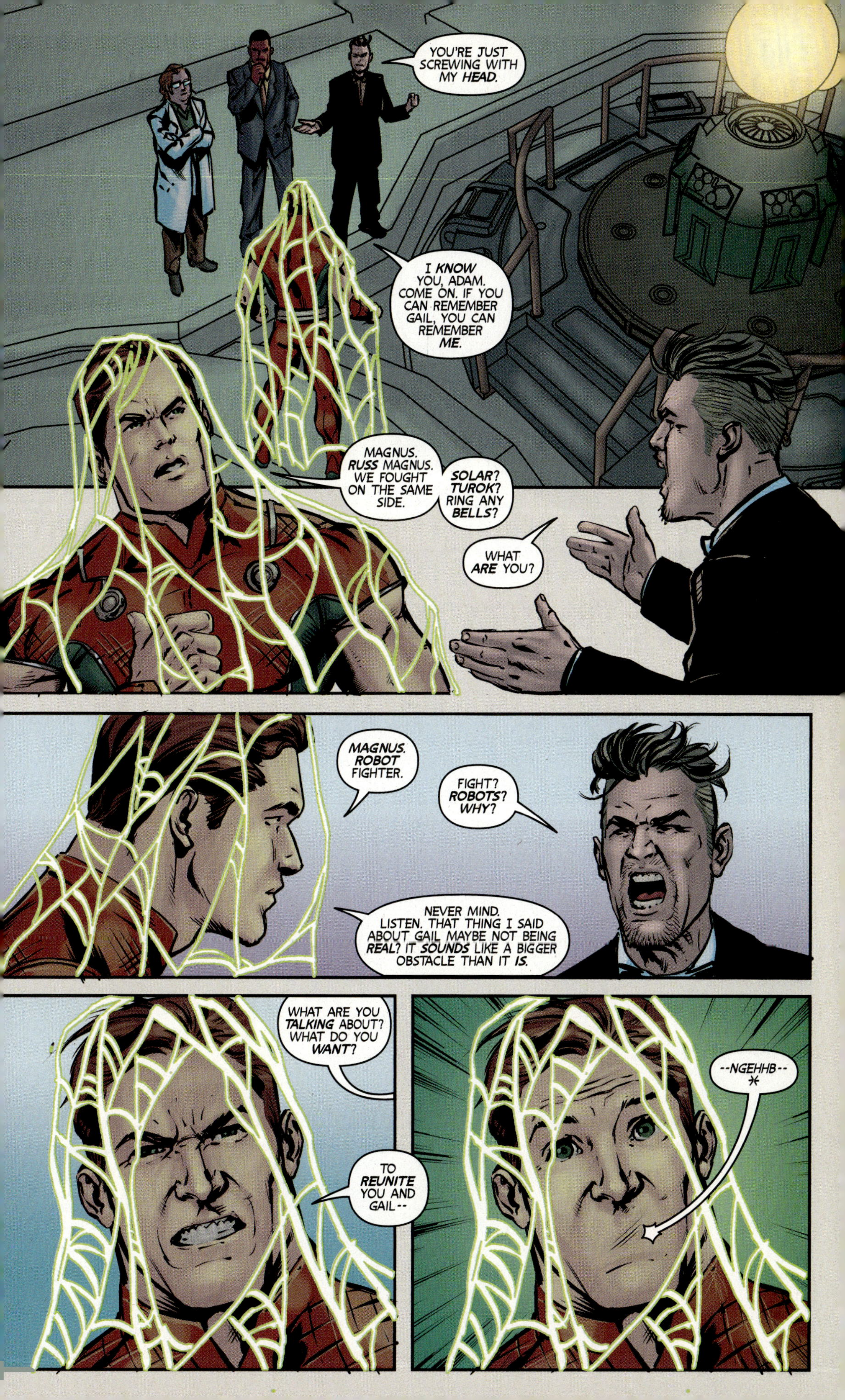
YOU'RE JUST SCREWING WITH MY HEAD.
I KNOW YOU, ADAM. COME ON. IF YOU CAN REMEMBER GAIL, YOU CAN REMEMBER ME.
MAGNUS. RUSS MAGNUS. WE FOUGHT ON THE SAME SIDE.
SOLAR? TUROK? RING ANY BELLS?
WHAT ARE YOU?
MAGNUS. ROBOT FIGHTER.
FIGHT? ROBOTS? WHY?
NEVER MIND. LISTEN. THAT THING I SAID ABOUT GAIL MAYBE NOT BEING REAL? IT SOUNDS LIKE A BIGGER OBSTACLE THAN IT IS.
WHAT ARE YOU TALKING ABOUT? WHAT DO YOU WANT?
TO REUNITE YOU AND GAIL--
--NGEHHB--
*

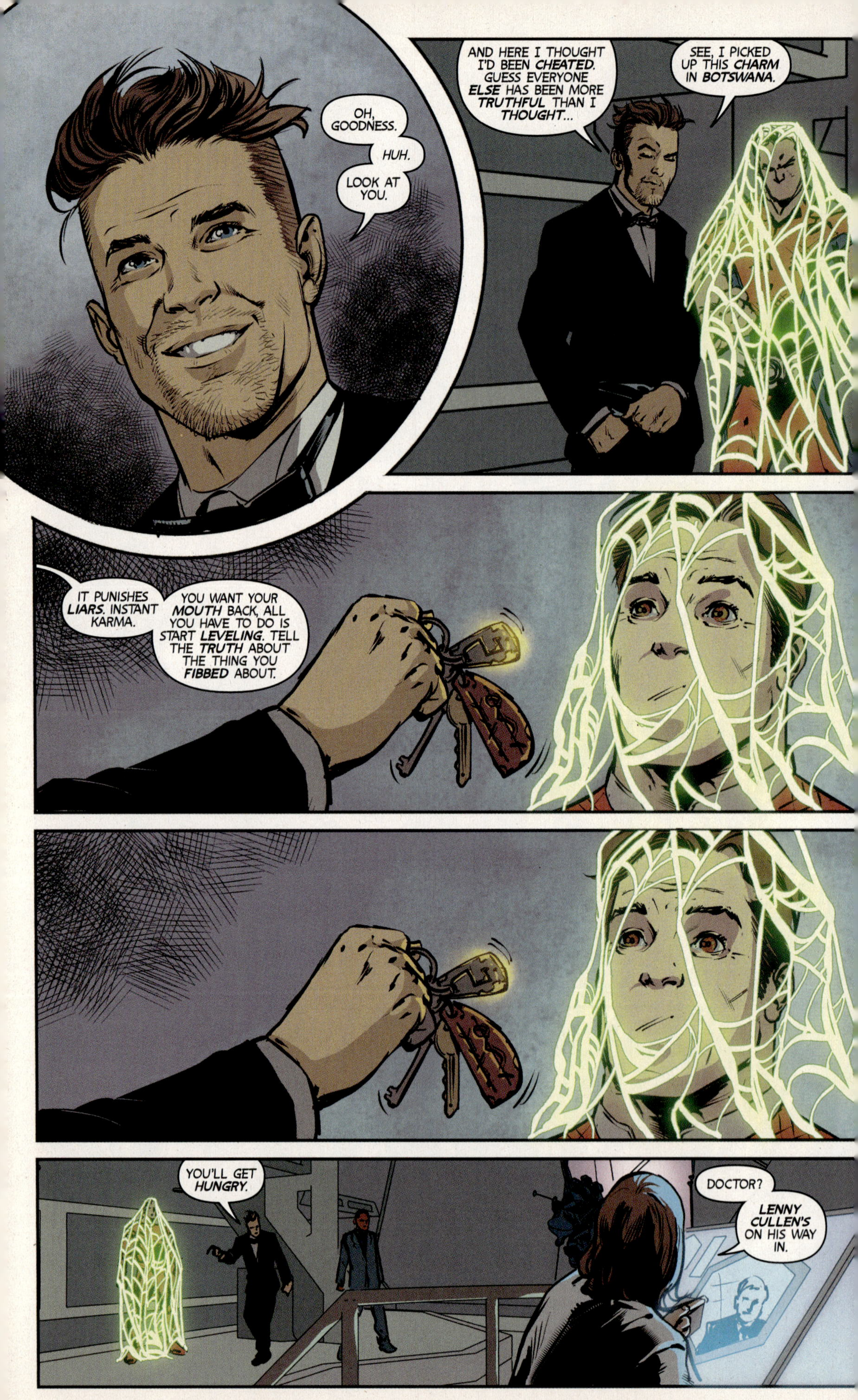

OH, GOODNESS.
HUH.
LOOK AT YOU.
AND HERE I THOUGHT I'D BEEN *CHEATED*. GUESS EVERYONE *ELSE* HAS BEEN MORE *TRUTHFUL* THAN I *THOUGHT*...
SEE, I PICKED UP THIS *CHARM* IN *BOTSWANA*.
IT PUNISHES *LIARS*. INSTANT KARMA.
YOU WANT YOUR *MOUTH* BACK, ALL YOU HAVE TO DO IS START *LEVELING*. TELL THE *TRUTH* ABOUT THE THING YOU *FIBBED* ABOUT.
YOU'LL GET *HUNGRY*.
DOCTOR?
LENNY CULLEN'S ON HIS WAY IN.

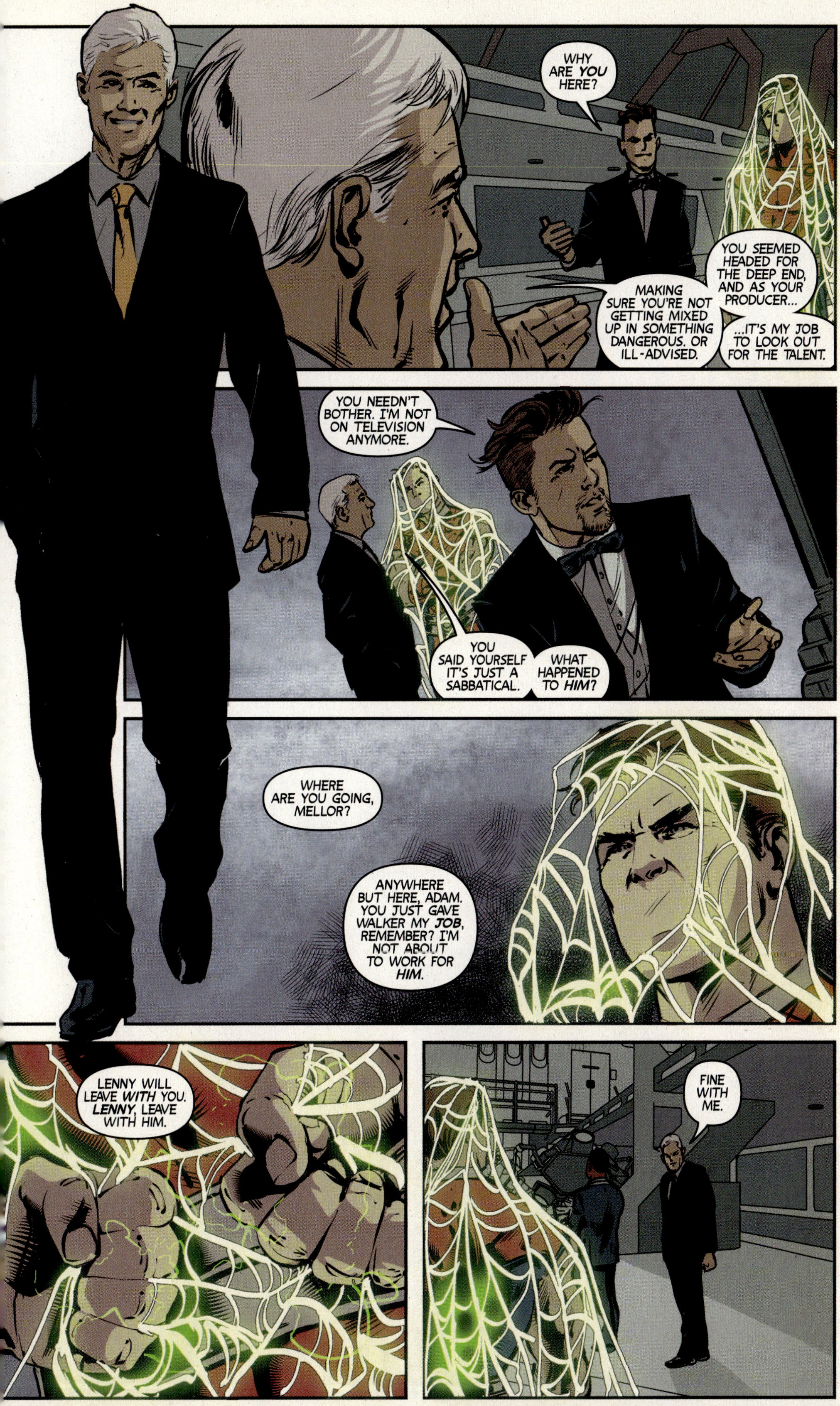
WHY ARE YOU HERE?
MAKING SURE YOU'RE NOT GETTING MIXED UP IN SOMETHING DANGEROUS. OR ILL-ADVISED.
YOU SEEMED HEADED FOR THE DEEP END, AND AS YOUR PRODUCER...
...IT'S MY JOB TO LOOK OUT FOR THE TALENT.
YOU NEEDN'T BOTHER. I'M NOT ON TELEVISION ANYMORE.
YOU SAID YOURSELF IT'S JUST A SABBATICAL.
WHAT HAPPENED TO HIM?
WHERE ARE YOU GOING, MELLOR?
ANYWHERE BUT HERE, ADAM. YOU JUST GAVE WALKER MY JOB, REMEMBER? I'M NOT ABOUT TO WORK FOR HIM.
LENNY WILL LEAVE WITH YOU. LENNY, LEAVE WITH HIM.
FINE WITH ME.

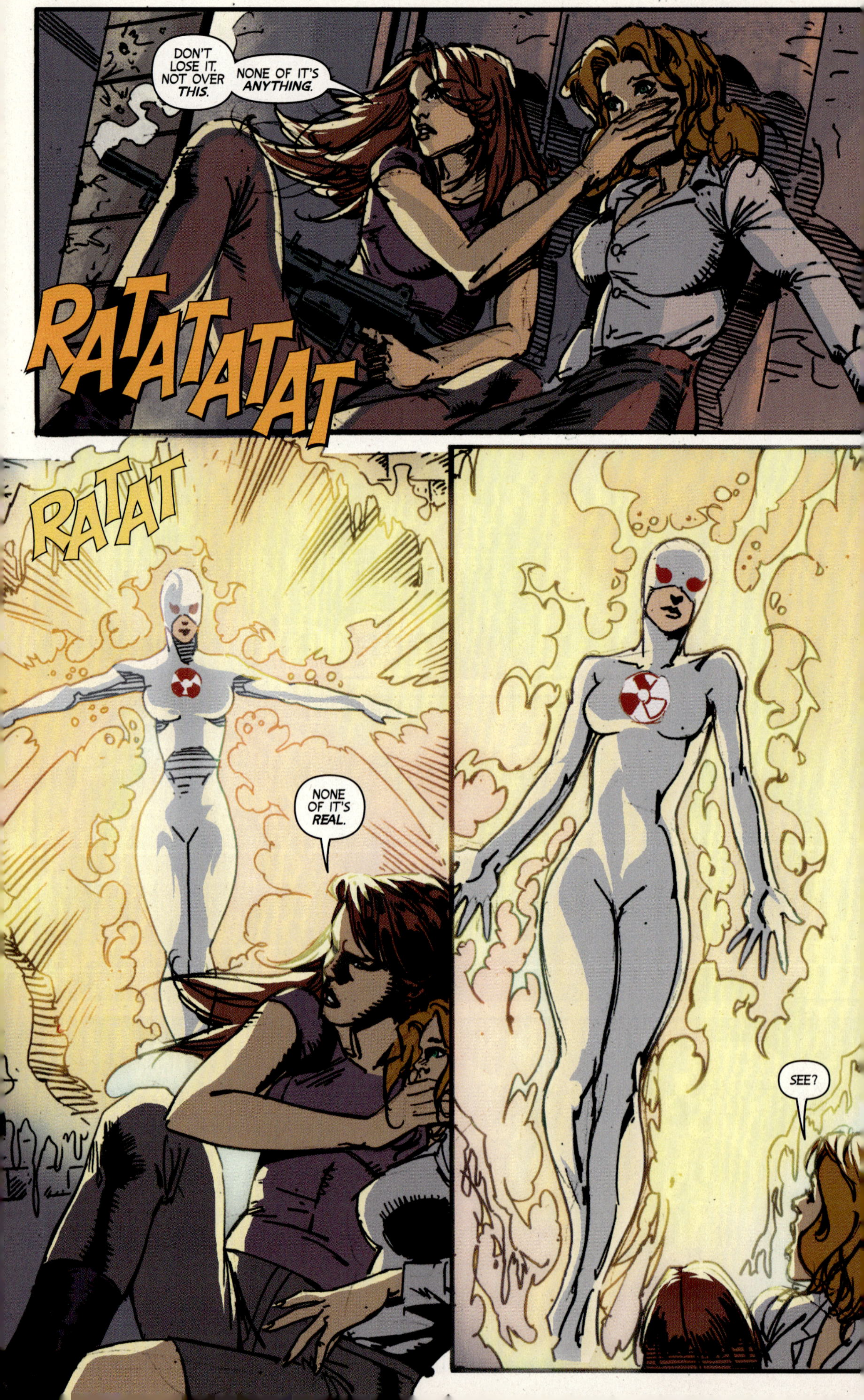
DON'T LOSE IT. NOT OVER *THIS*.
NONE OF IT'S *ANYTHING*.
RATATATAT
RATAT
NONE OF IT'S *REAL*.
SEE?

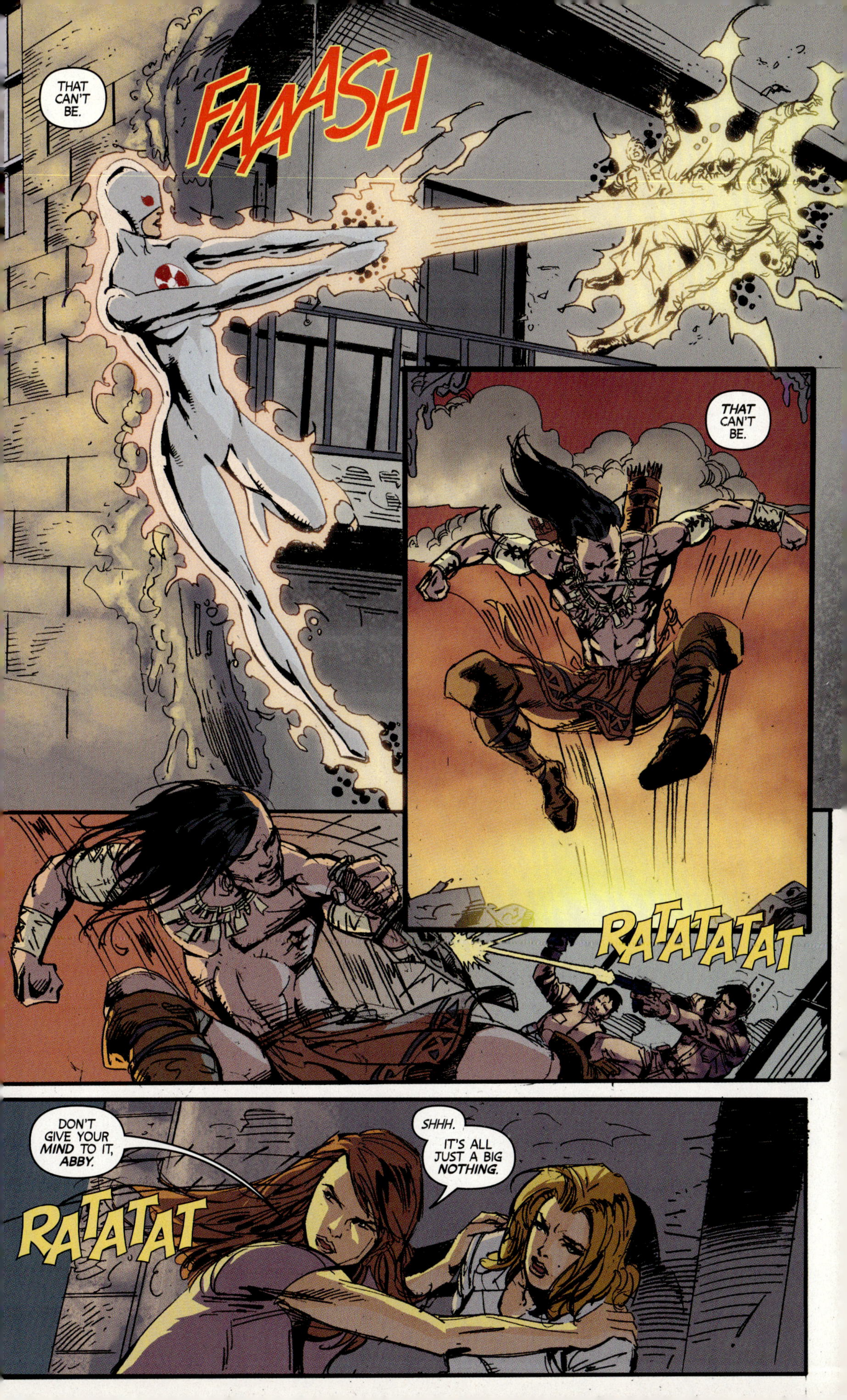
THAT CAN'T BE.
FAAASH
THAT CAN'T BE.
RATATATAT
DON'T GIVE YOUR MIND TO IT, ABBY.
RATATAT
SHHH.
IT'S ALL JUST A BIG NOTHING.

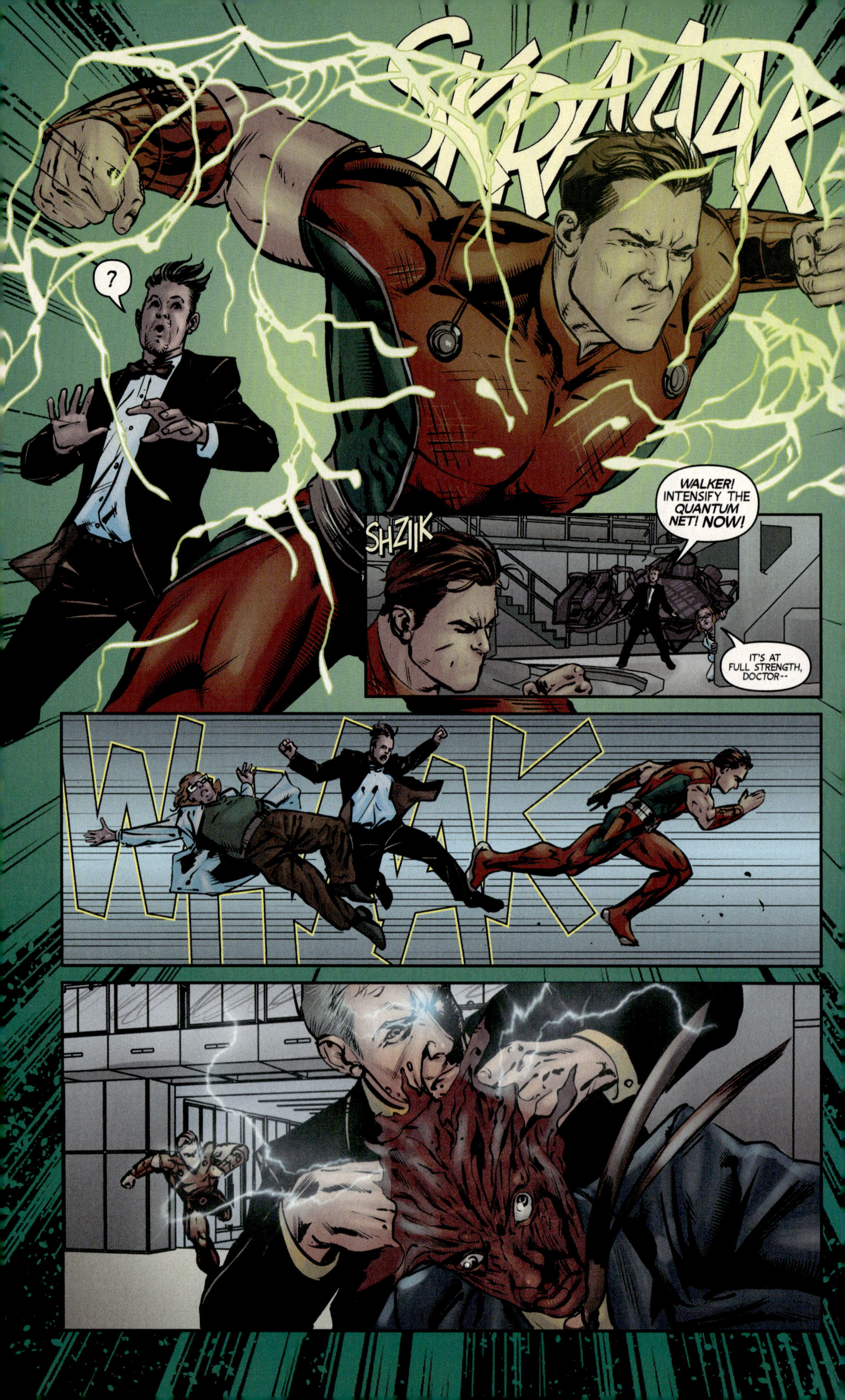
SKRAAAK
?
SHZIIK
WALKER! INTENSIFY THE QUANTUM NET! NOW!
IT'S AT FULL STRENGTH, DOCTOR--
WHAAK

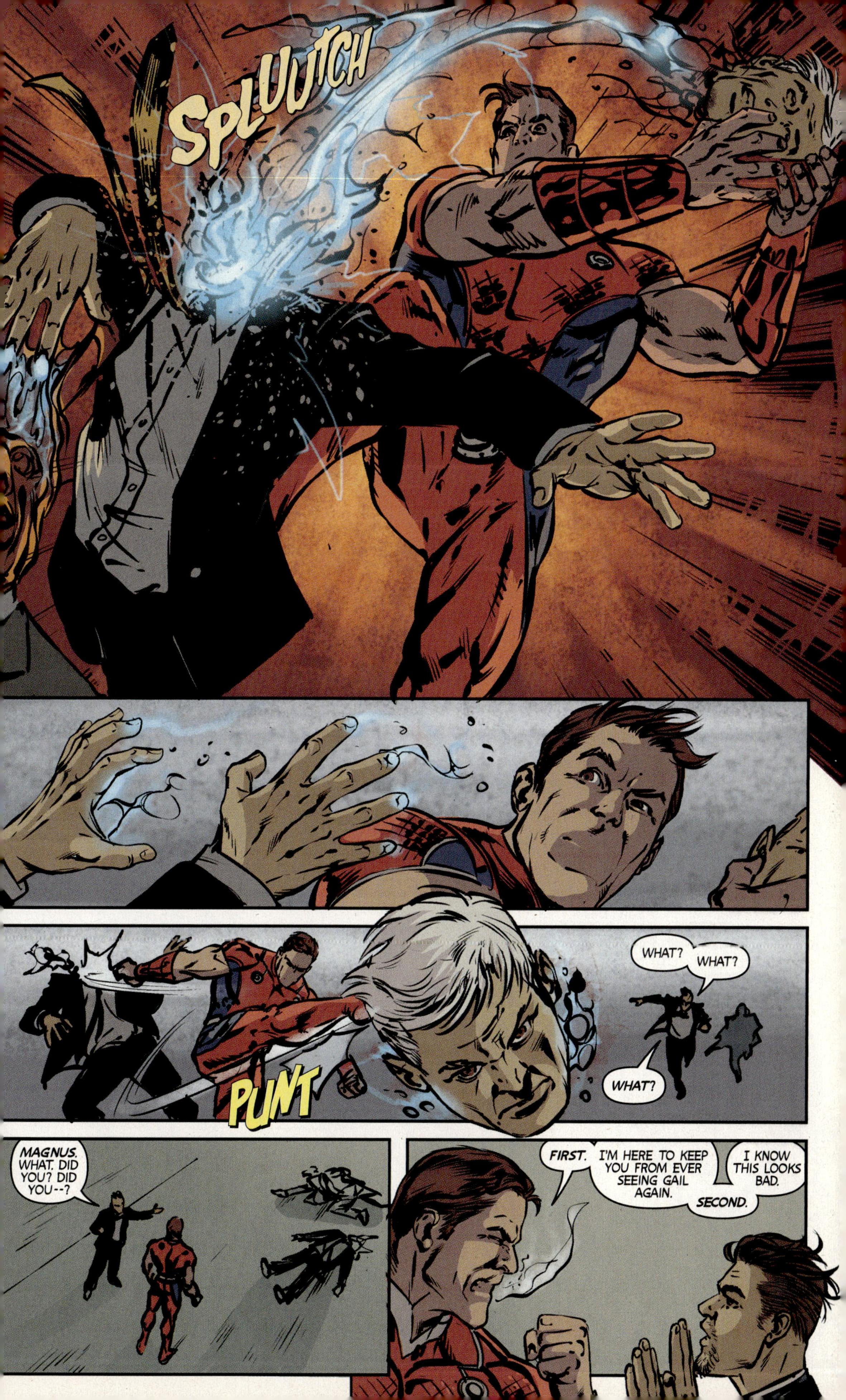
SPLUUTCH
WHAT? WHAT?
WHAT?
PUNT
MAGNUS. WHAT. DID YOU? DID YOU--?
FIRST. I'M HERE TO KEEP YOU FROM EVER SEEING GAIL AGAIN.
SECOND.
I KNOW THIS LOOKS BAD.

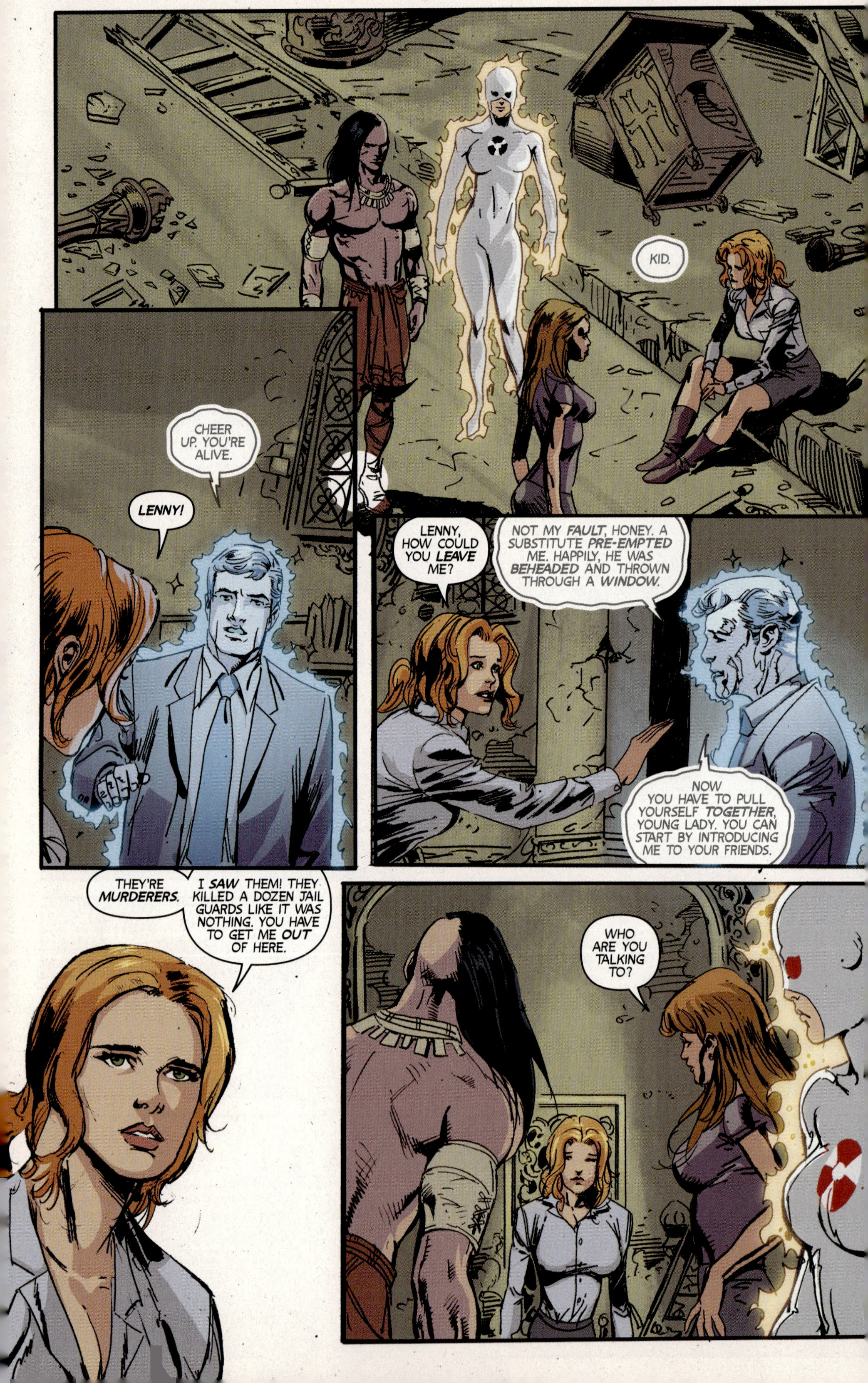
KID.
CHEER UP. YOU'RE ALIVE.
LENNY!
LENNY, HOW COULD YOU LEAVE ME?
NOT MY FAULT, HONEY. A SUBSTITUTE PRE-EMPTED ME. HAPPILY, HE WAS BEHEADED AND THROWN THROUGH A WINDOW.
NOW YOU HAVE TO PULL YOURSELF TOGETHER, YOUNG LADY. YOU CAN START BY INTRODUCING ME TO YOUR FRIENDS.
THEY'RE MURDERERS.
I SAW THEM! THEY KILLED A DOZEN JAIL GUARDS LIKE IT WAS NOTHING. YOU HAVE TO GET ME OUT OF HERE.
WHO ARE YOU TALKING TO?

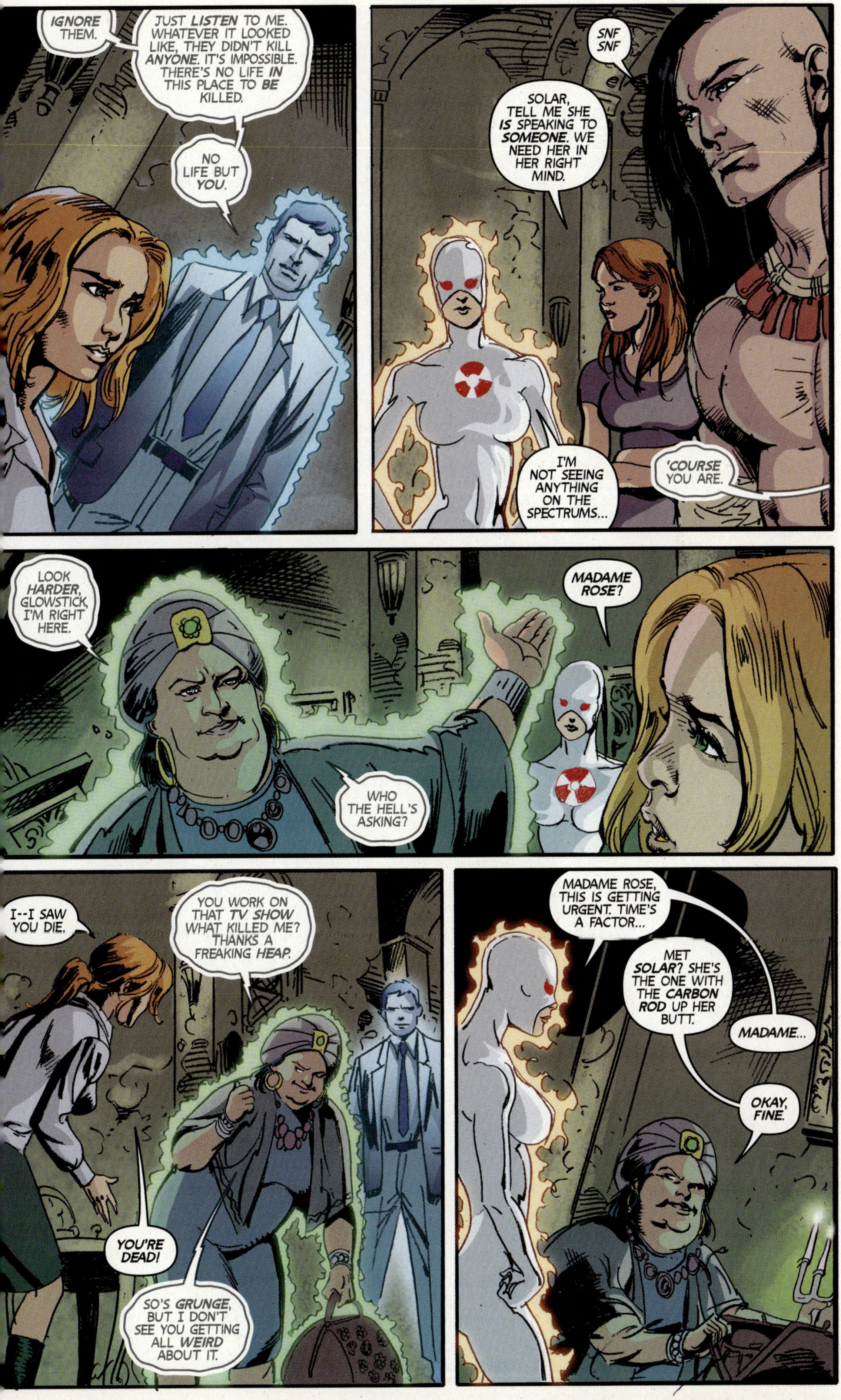
IGNORE THEM.
JUST LISTEN TO ME. WHATEVER IT LOOKED LIKE, THEY DIDN'T KILL ANYONE. IT'S IMPOSSIBLE. THERE'S NO LIFE IN THIS PLACE TO BE KILLED.
NO LIFE BUT YOU.
SNF SNF
SOLAR, TELL ME SHE IS SPEAKING TO SOMEONE. WE NEED HER IN HER RIGHT MIND.
I'M NOT SEEING ANYTHING ON THE SPECTRUMS...
'COURSE YOU ARE.
LOOK HARDER, GLOWSTICK, I'M RIGHT HERE.
MADAME ROSE?
WHO THE HELL'S ASKING?
I--I SAW YOU DIE.
YOU WORK ON THAT TV SHOW WHAT KILLED ME? THANKS A FREAKING HEAP.
YOU'RE DEAD!
SO'S GRUNGE, BUT I DON'T SEE YOU GETTING ALL WEIRD ABOUT IT.
MADAME ROSE, THIS IS GETTING URGENT. TIME'S A FACTOR...
MET SOLAR? SHE'S THE ONE WITH THE CARBON ROD UP HER BUTT.
MADAME...
OKAY, FINE.

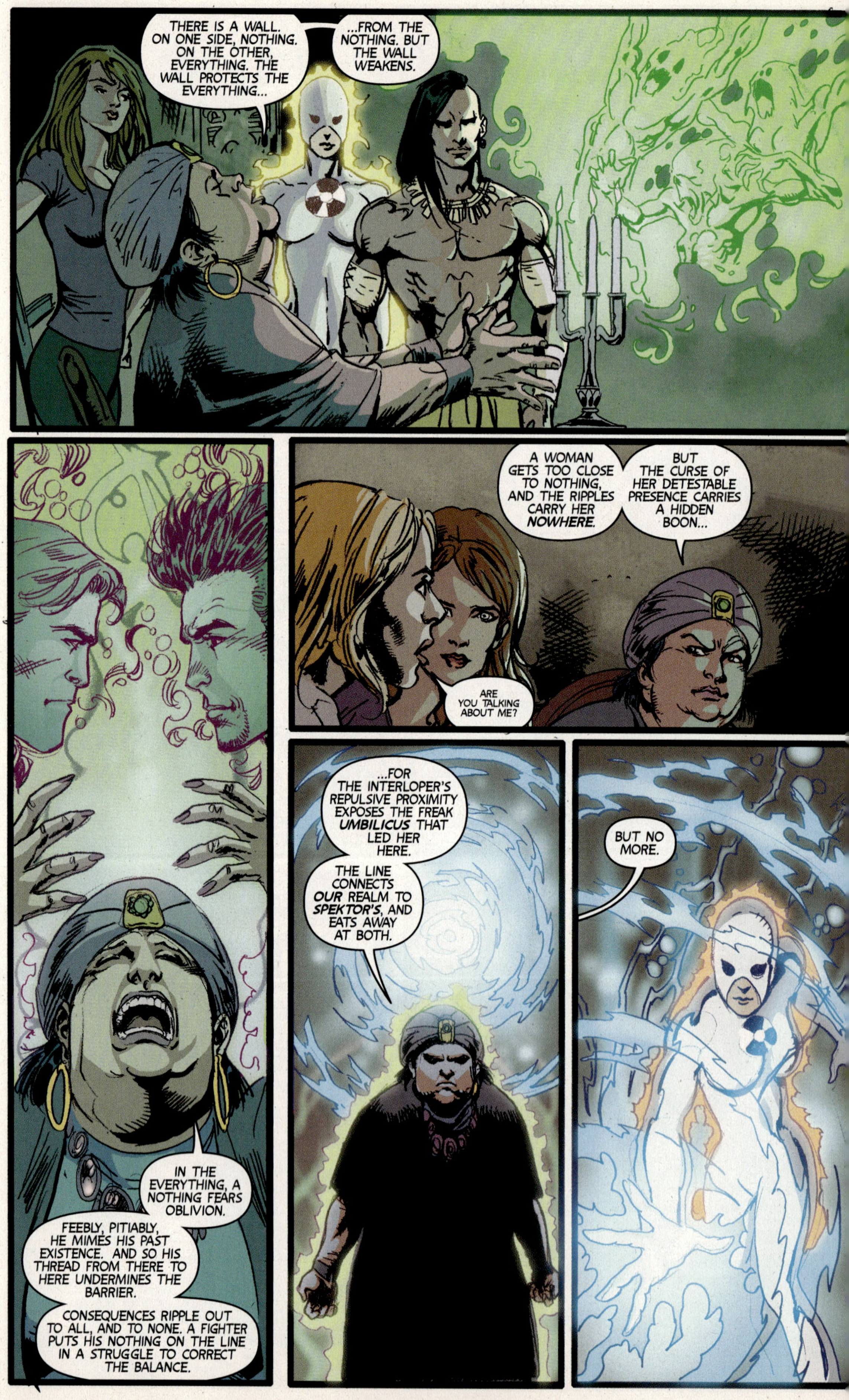

THERE IS A WALL. ON ONE SIDE, NOTHING. ON THE OTHER, EVERYTHING. THE WALL PROTECTS THE EVERYTHING...
...FROM THE NOTHING. BUT THE WALL WEAKENS.
IN THE EVERYTHING, A NOTHING FEARS OBLIVION.
FEEBLY, PITIABLY, HE MIMES HIS PAST EXISTENCE. AND SO HIS THREAD FROM THERE TO HERE UNDERMINES THE BARRIER.
CONSEQUENCES RIPPLE OUT TO ALL, AND TO NONE. A FIGHTER PUTS HIS NOTHING ON THE LINE IN A STRUGGLE TO CORRECT THE BALANCE.
A WOMAN GETS TOO CLOSE TO NOTHING, AND THE RIPPLES CARRY HER *NOWHERE*.
BUT THE CURSE OF HER DETESTABLE PRESENCE CARRIES A HIDDEN BOON...
ARE YOU TALKING ABOUT ME?
...FOR THE INTERLOPER'S REPULSIVE PROXIMITY EXPOSES THE FREAK *UMBILICUS* THAT LED HER HERE.
THE LINE CONNECTS *OUR* REALM TO *SPEKTOR'S*, AND EATS AWAY AT BOTH.
BUT NO MORE.

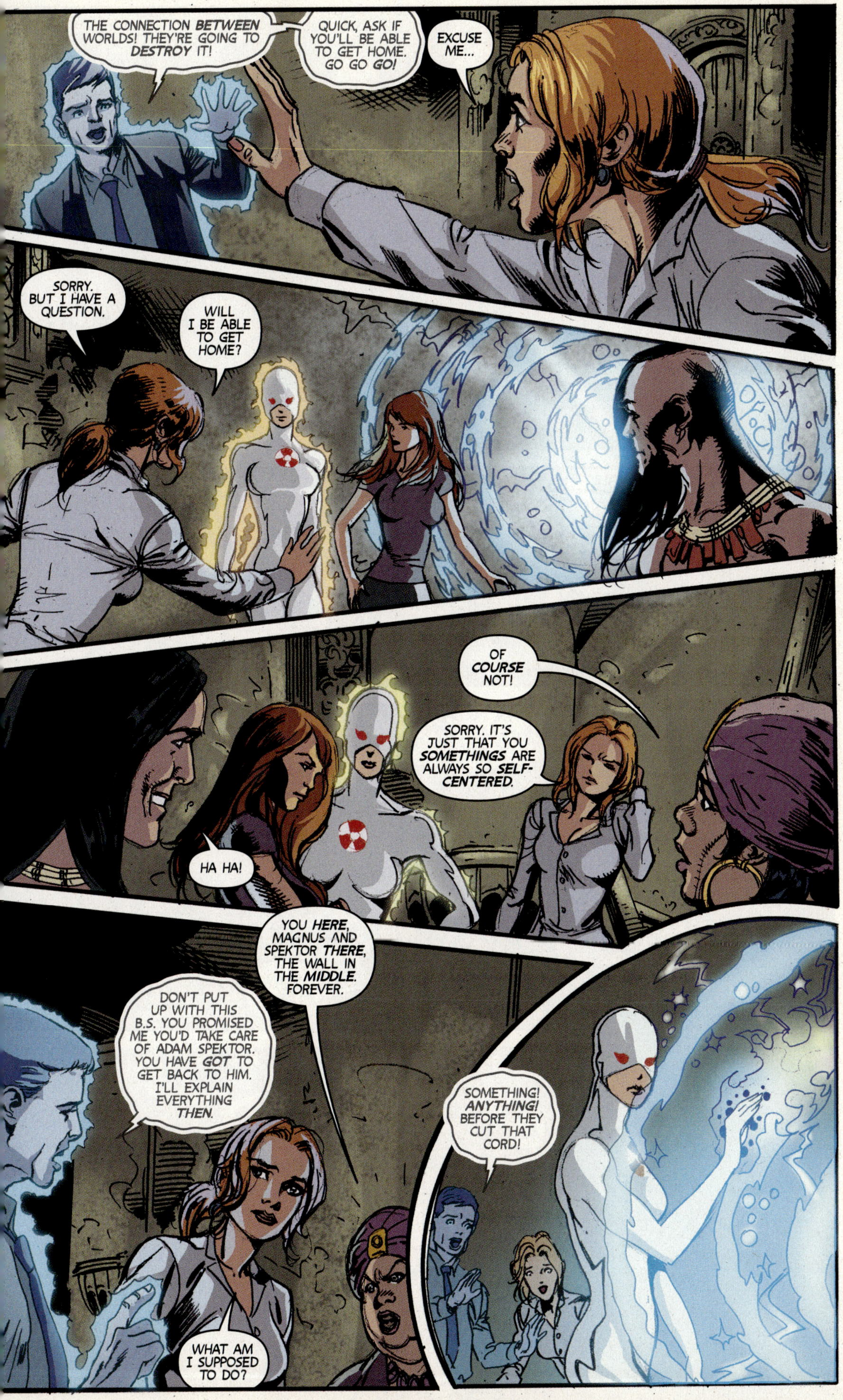
THE CONNECTION BETWEEN WORLDS! THEY'RE GOING TO DESTROY IT!
QUICK, ASK IF YOU'LL BE ABLE TO GET HOME. GO GO GO!
EXCUSE ME...
SORRY. BUT I HAVE A QUESTION.
WILL I BE ABLE TO GET HOME?
OF COURSE NOT!
SORRY. IT'S JUST THAT YOU SOMETHINGS ARE ALWAYS SO SELF-CENTERED.
HA HA!
YOU HERE, MAGNUS AND SPEKTOR THERE, THE WALL IN THE MIDDLE. FOREVER.
DON'T PUT UP WITH THIS B.S. YOU PROMISED ME YOU'D TAKE CARE OF ADAM SPEKTOR. YOU HAVE GOT TO GET BACK TO HIM. I'LL EXPLAIN EVERYTHING THEN.
SOMETHING! ANYTHING! BEFORE THEY CUT THAT CORD!
WHAT AM I SUPPOSED TO DO?

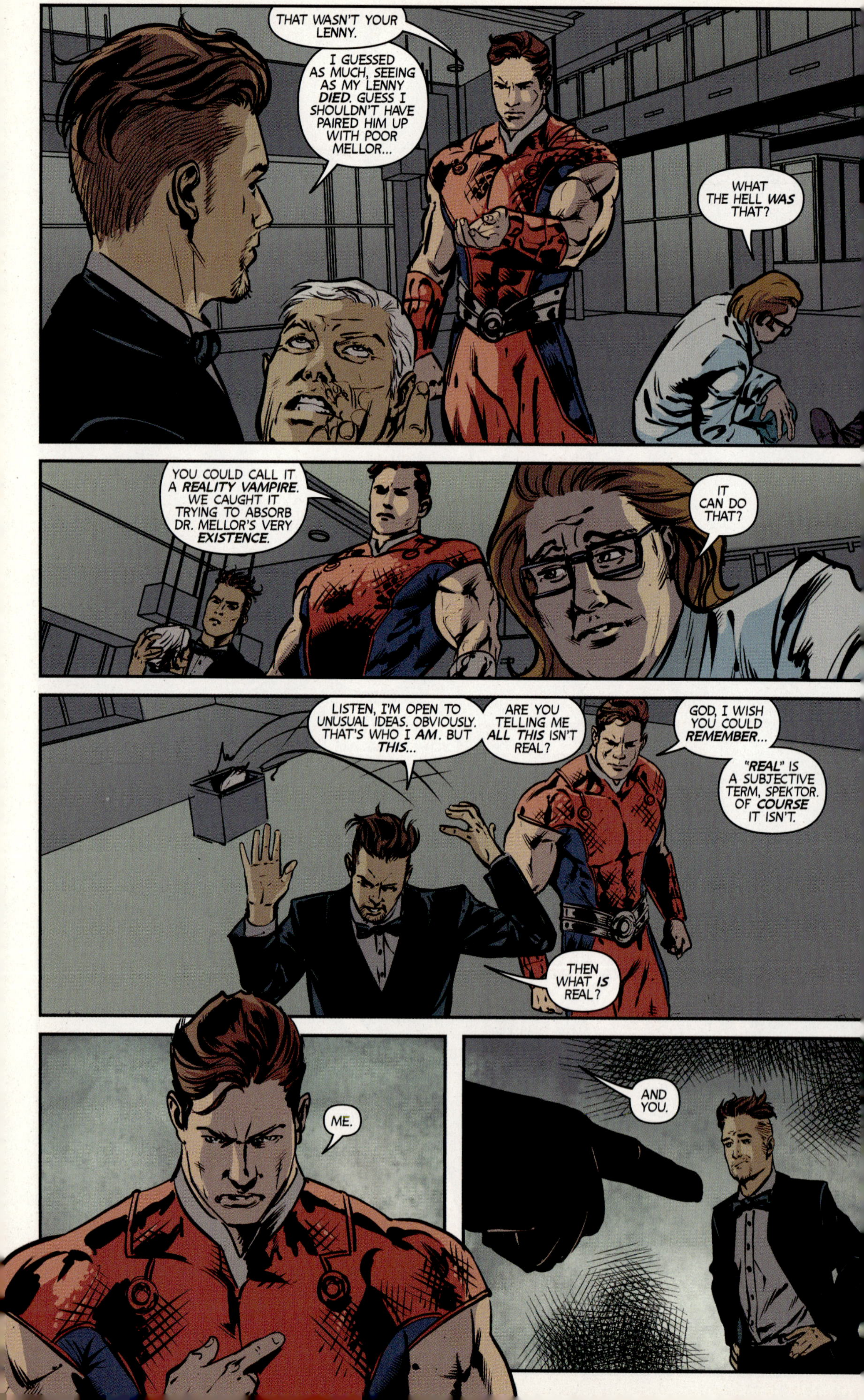
THAT WASN'T YOUR LENNY.
I GUESSED AS MUCH, SEEING AS MY LENNY DIED. GUESS I SHOULDN'T HAVE PAIRED HIM UP WITH POOR MELLOR...
WHAT THE HELL WAS THAT?
YOU COULD CALL IT A REALITY VAMPIRE. WE CAUGHT IT TRYING TO ABSORB DR. MELLOR'S VERY EXISTENCE.
IT CAN DO THAT?
LISTEN, I'M OPEN TO UNUSUAL IDEAS. OBVIOUSLY. THAT'S WHO I AM. BUT THIS...
ARE YOU TELLING ME ALL THIS ISN'T REAL?
GOD, I WISH YOU COULD REMEMBER...
"REAL" IS A SUBJECTIVE TERM, SPEKTOR. OF COURSE IT ISN'T.
THEN WHAT IS REAL?
ME.
AND YOU.

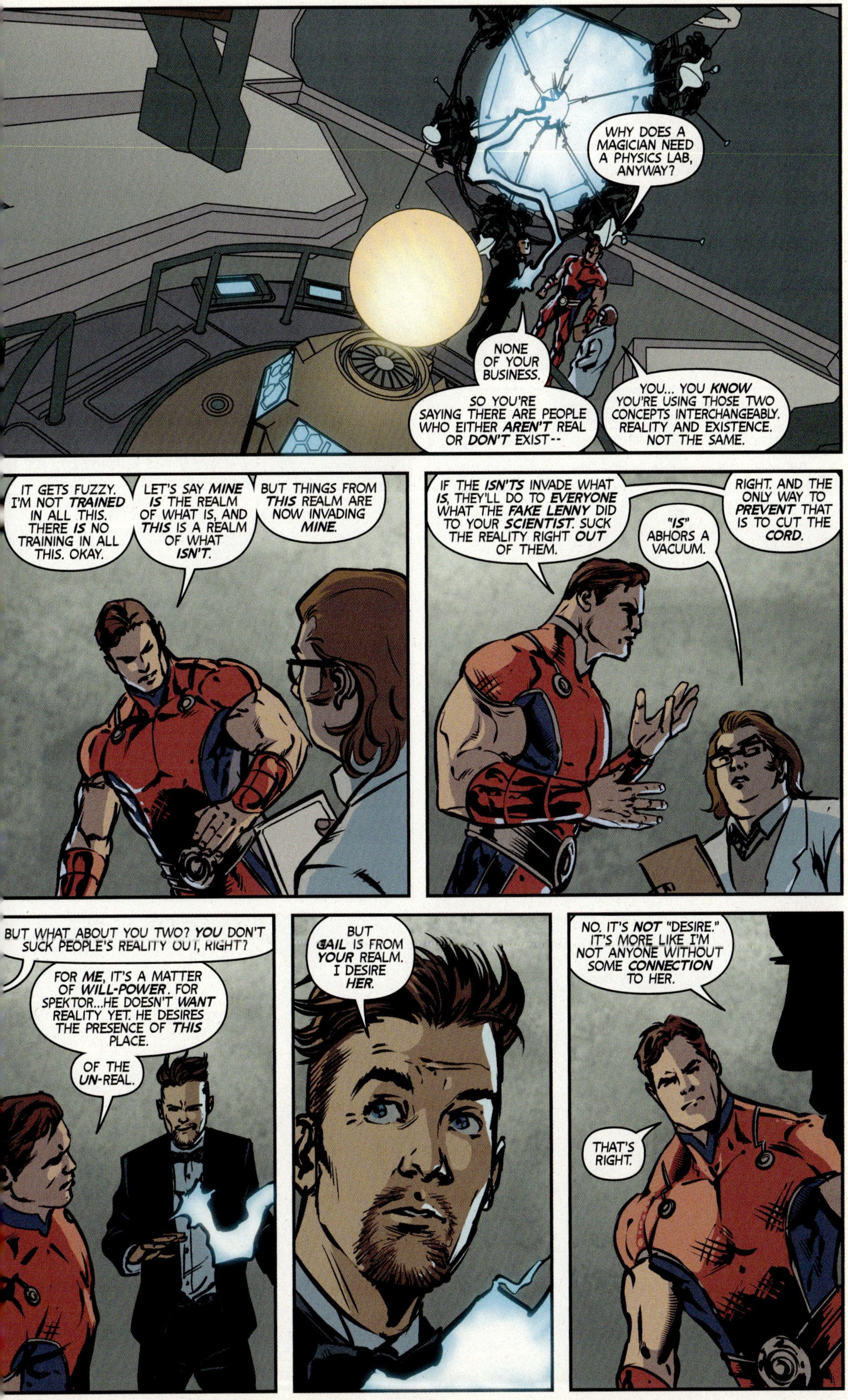
WHY DOES A MAGICIAN NEED A PHYSICS LAB, ANYWAY?
NONE OF YOUR BUSINESS.
SO YOU'RE SAYING THERE ARE PEOPLE WHO EITHER **AREN'T** REAL OR **DON'T** EXIST--
YOU... YOU **KNOW** YOU'RE USING THOSE TWO CONCEPTS INTERCHANGEABLY. REALITY AND EXISTENCE. NOT THE SAME.
IT GETS FUZZY. I'M NOT **TRAINED** IN ALL THIS. THERE **IS** NO TRAINING IN ALL THIS. OKAY.
LET'S SAY **MINE IS** THE REALM OF WHAT IS, AND **THIS** IS A REALM OF WHAT **ISN'T**.
BUT THINGS FROM **THIS** REALM ARE NOW INVADING **MINE**.
IF THE **ISN'TS** INVADE WHAT **IS**, THEY'LL DO TO **EVERYONE** WHAT THE **FAKE LENNY** DID TO YOUR **SCIENTIST**. SUCK THE REALITY RIGHT **OUT** OF THEM.
"**IS**" ABHORS A VACUUM.
RIGHT. AND THE ONLY WAY TO **PREVENT** THAT IS TO CUT THE **CORD**.
BUT WHAT ABOUT YOU TWO? **YOU** DON'T SUCK PEOPLE'S REALITY OUT, RIGHT?
FOR **ME**, IT'S A MATTER OF **WILL-POWER**. FOR SPEKTOR...HE DOESN'T **WANT** REALITY YET. HE DESIRES THE PRESENCE OF **THIS** PLACE.
OF THE **UN**-REAL.
BUT **GAIL** IS FROM **YOUR** REALM. I DESIRE **HER**.
NO. IT'S **NOT** "DESIRE." IT'S MORE LIKE I'M NOT ANYONE WITHOUT SOME **CONNECTION** TO HER.
THAT'S RIGHT.

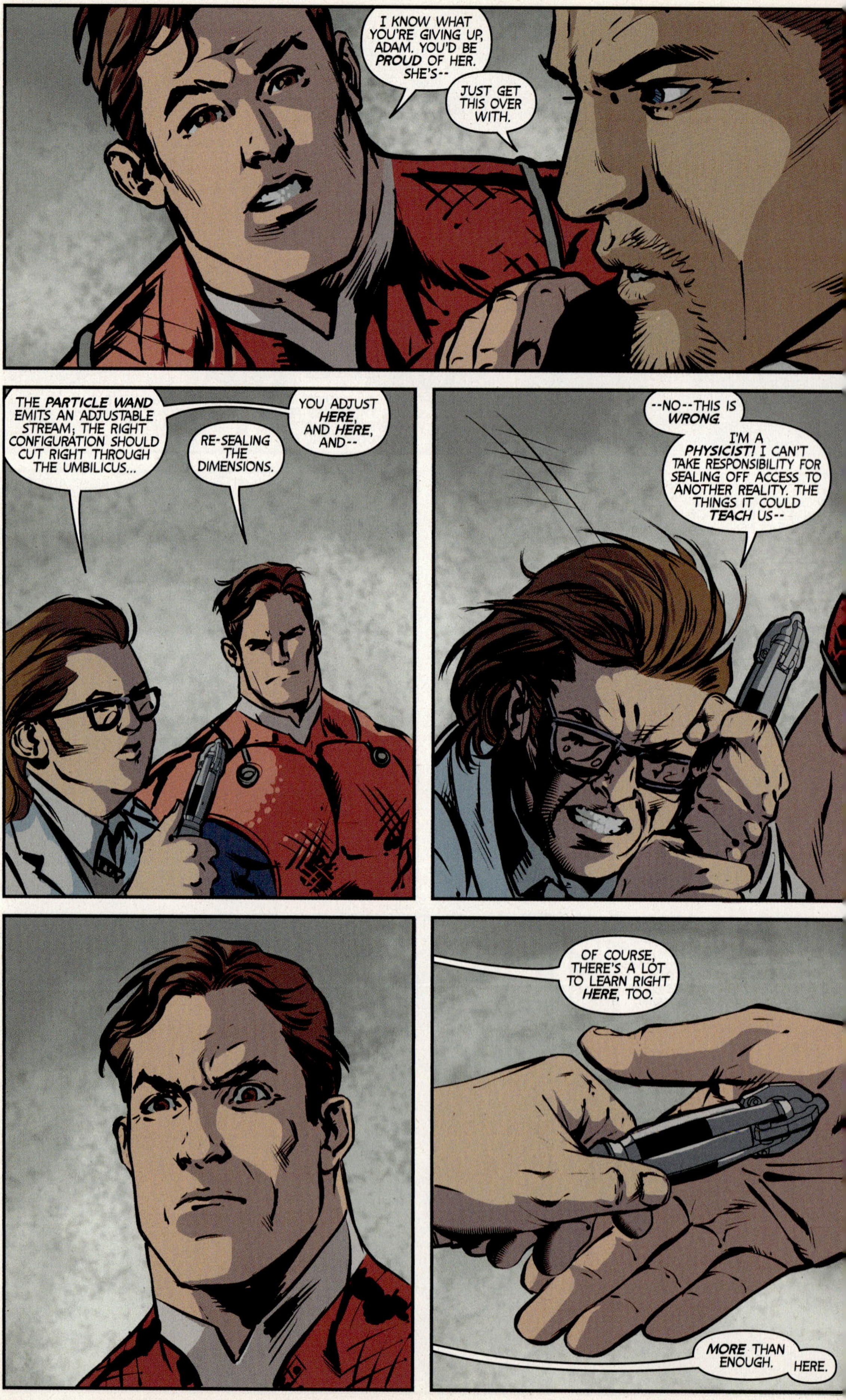
I KNOW WHAT YOU'RE GIVING UP, ADAM. YOU'D BE PROUD OF HER. SHE'S--
JUST GET THIS OVER WITH.
THE PARTICLE WAND EMITS AN ADJUSTABLE STREAM; THE RIGHT CONFIGURATION SHOULD CUT RIGHT THROUGH THE UMBILICUS...
RE-SEALING THE DIMENSIONS.
YOU ADJUST HERE, AND HERE, AND--
--NO--THIS IS WRONG.
I'M A PHYSICIST! I CAN'T TAKE RESPONSIBILITY FOR SEALING OFF ACCESS TO ANOTHER REALITY. THE THINGS IT COULD TEACH US--
OF COURSE, THERE'S A LOT TO LEARN RIGHT HERE, TOO.
MORE THAN ENOUGH.
HERE.

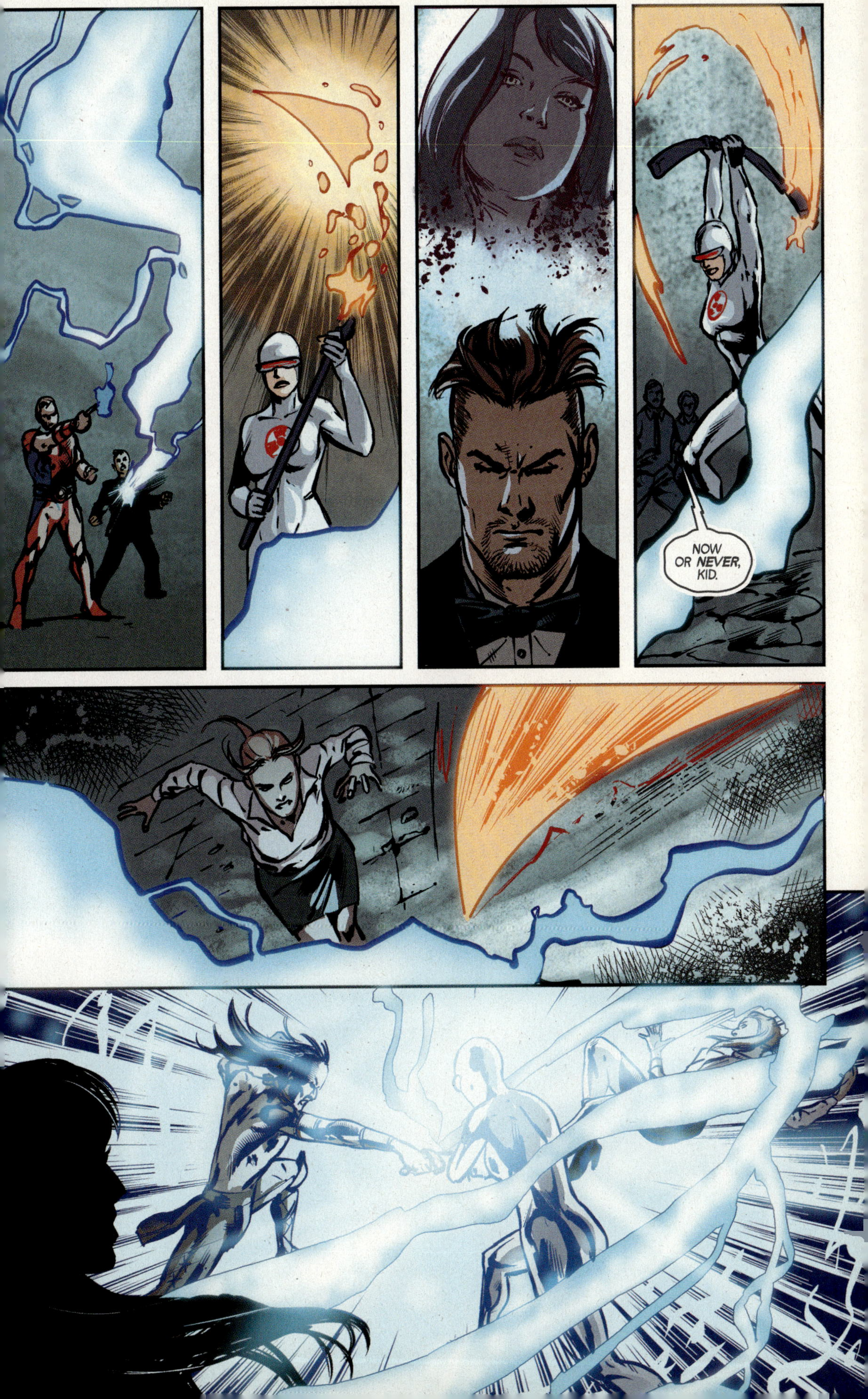
NOW OR NEVER, KID.

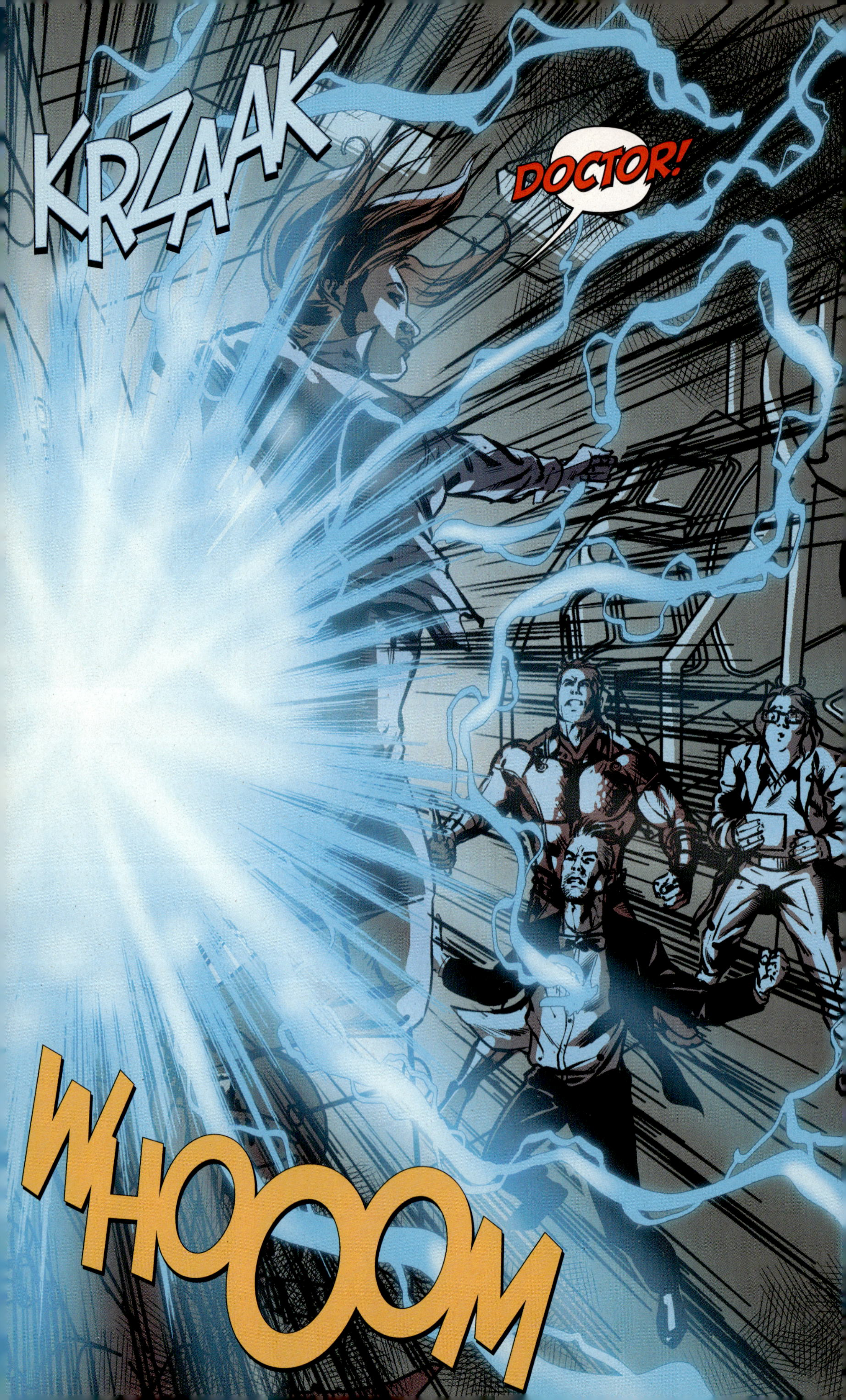
KRZAAK
DOCTOR!
WHOOOM

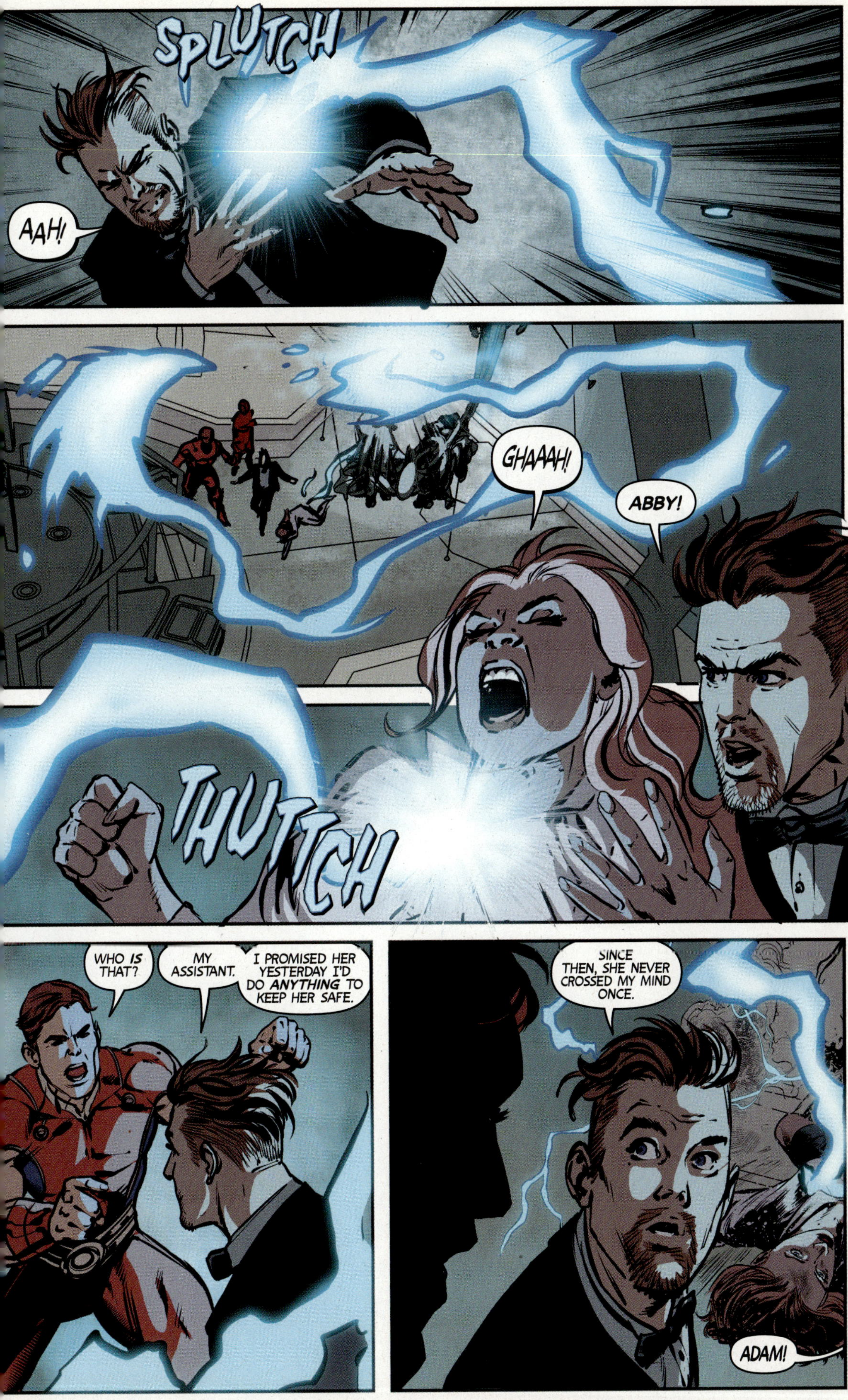
SPLUTCH
AAH!
GHAAAH!
ABBY!
THUTTCH
WHO IS THAT?
MY ASSISTANT.
I PROMISED HER YESTERDAY I'D DO ANYTHING TO KEEP HER SAFE.
SINCE THEN, SHE NEVER CROSSED MY MIND ONCE.
ADAM!

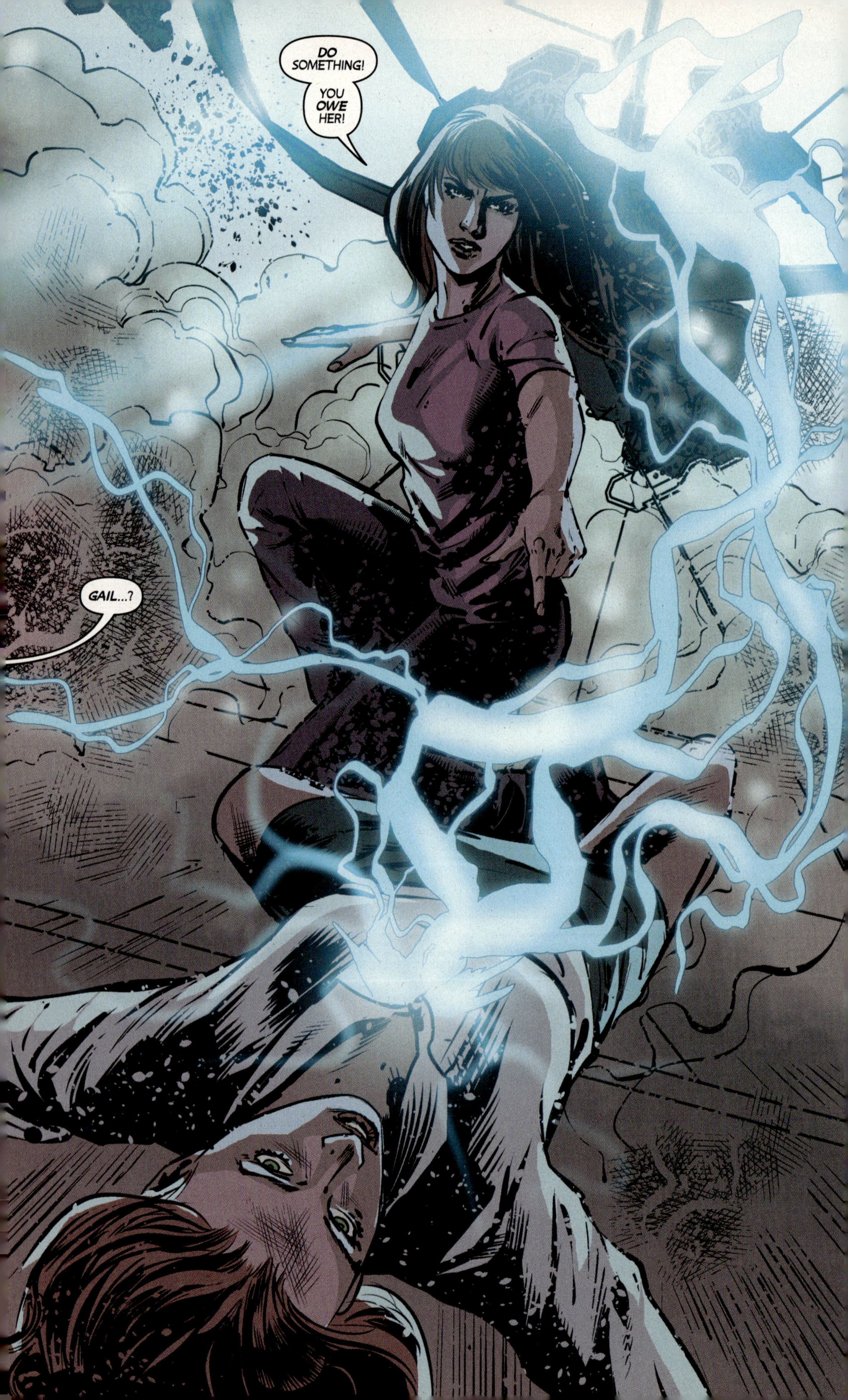
DO SOMETHING!
YOU OWE HER!
GAIL...?

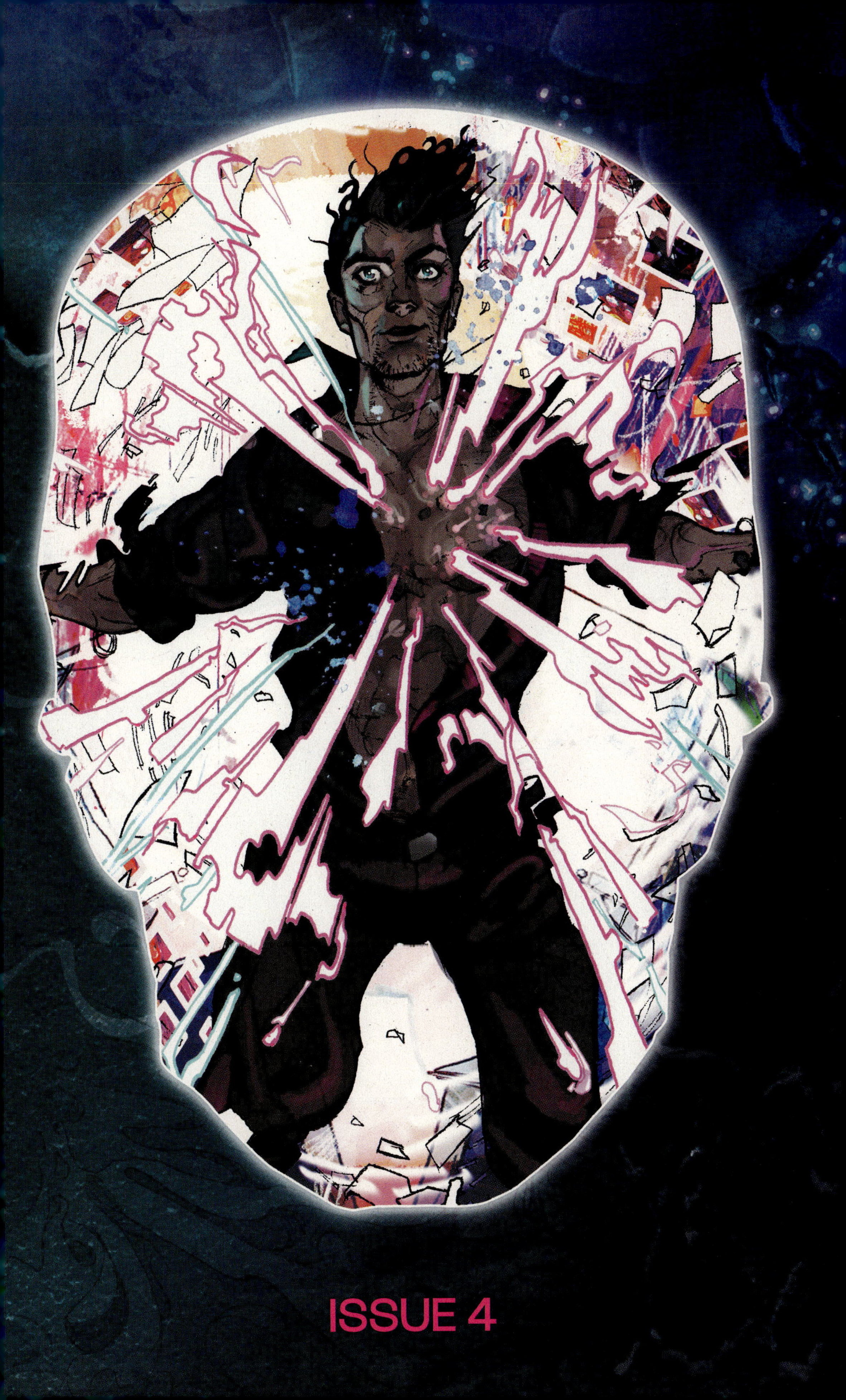
ISSUE 4

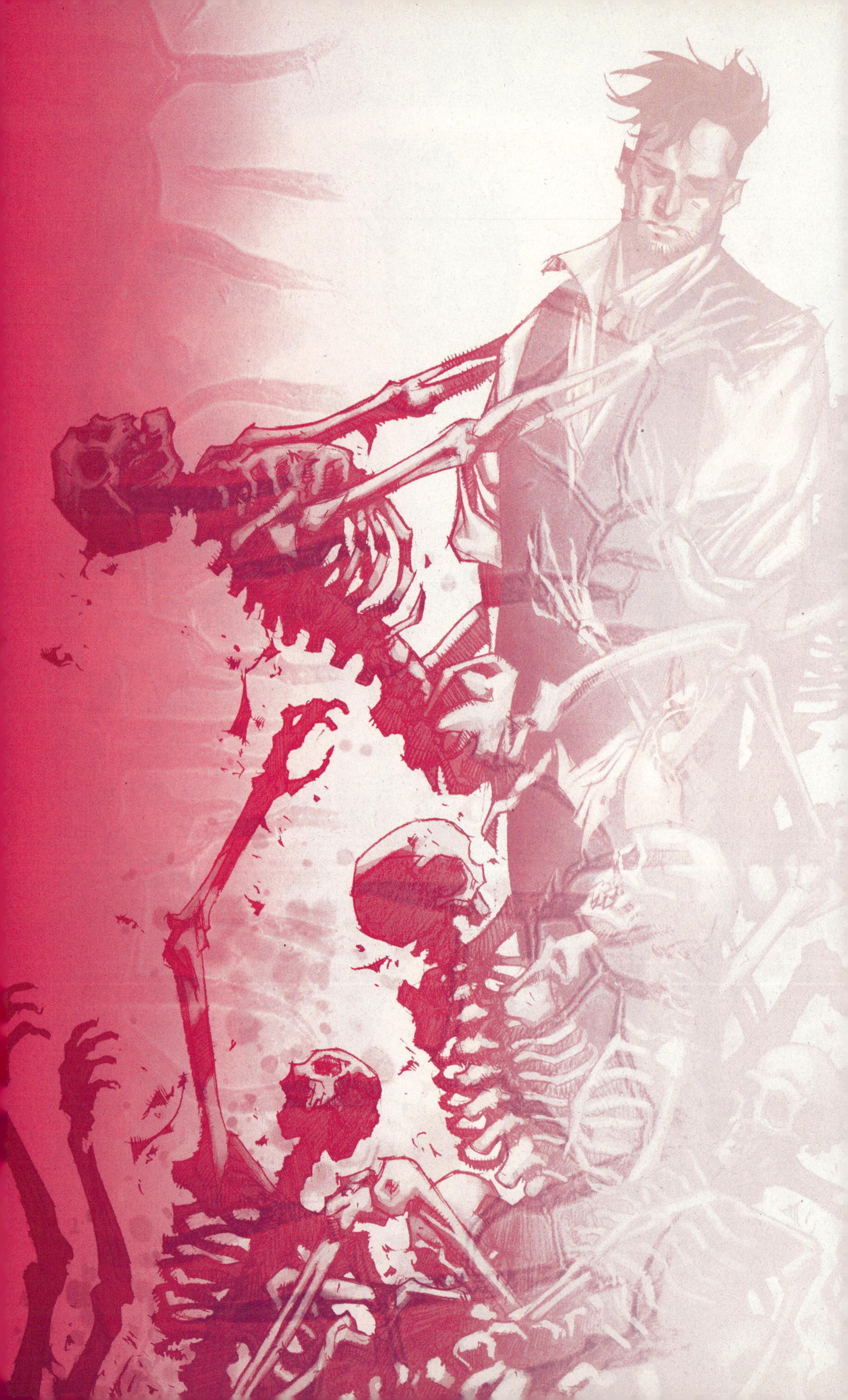

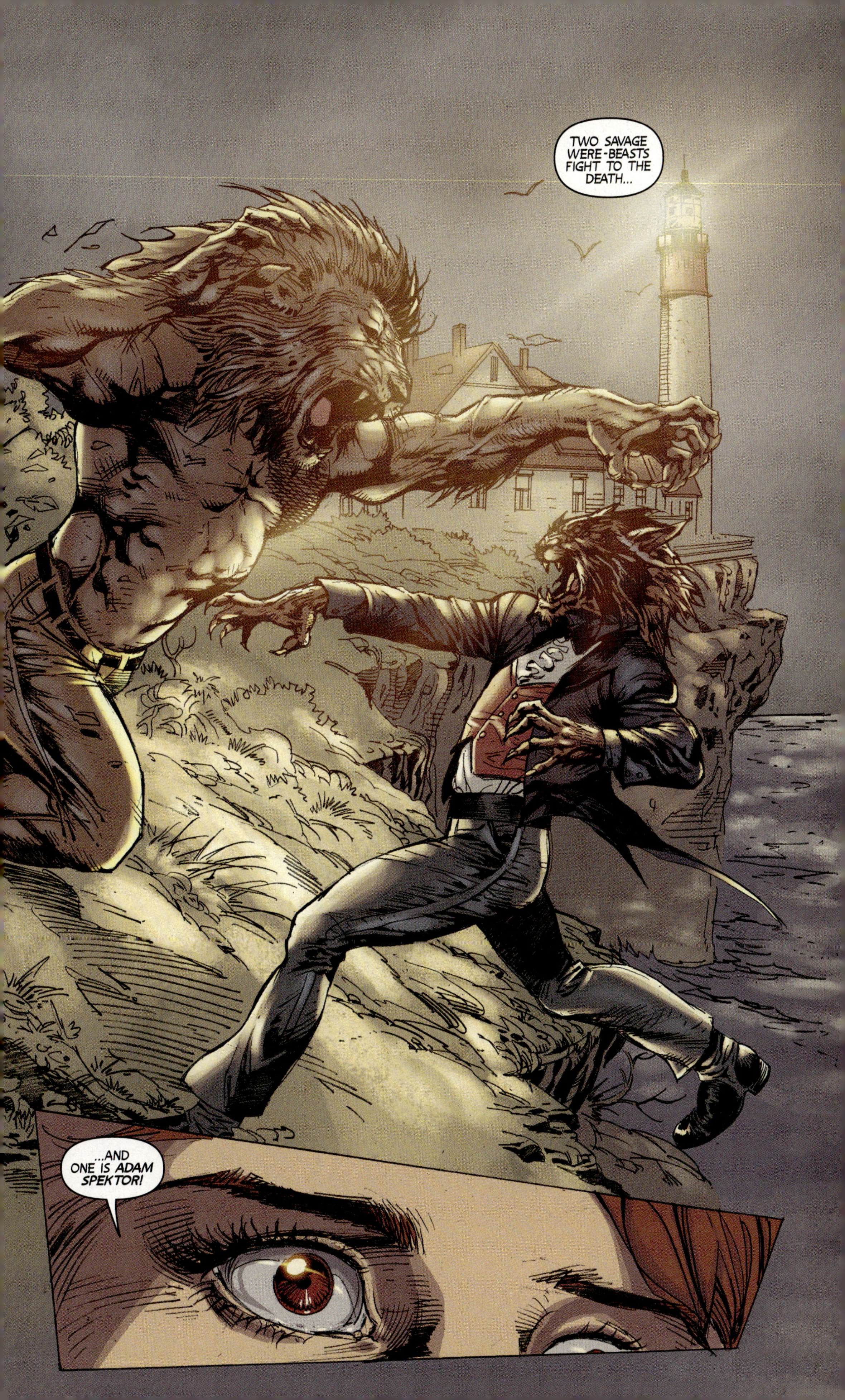
TWO SAVAGE WERE-BEASTS FIGHT TO THE DEATH...
...AND ONE IS *ADAM SPEKTOR!*

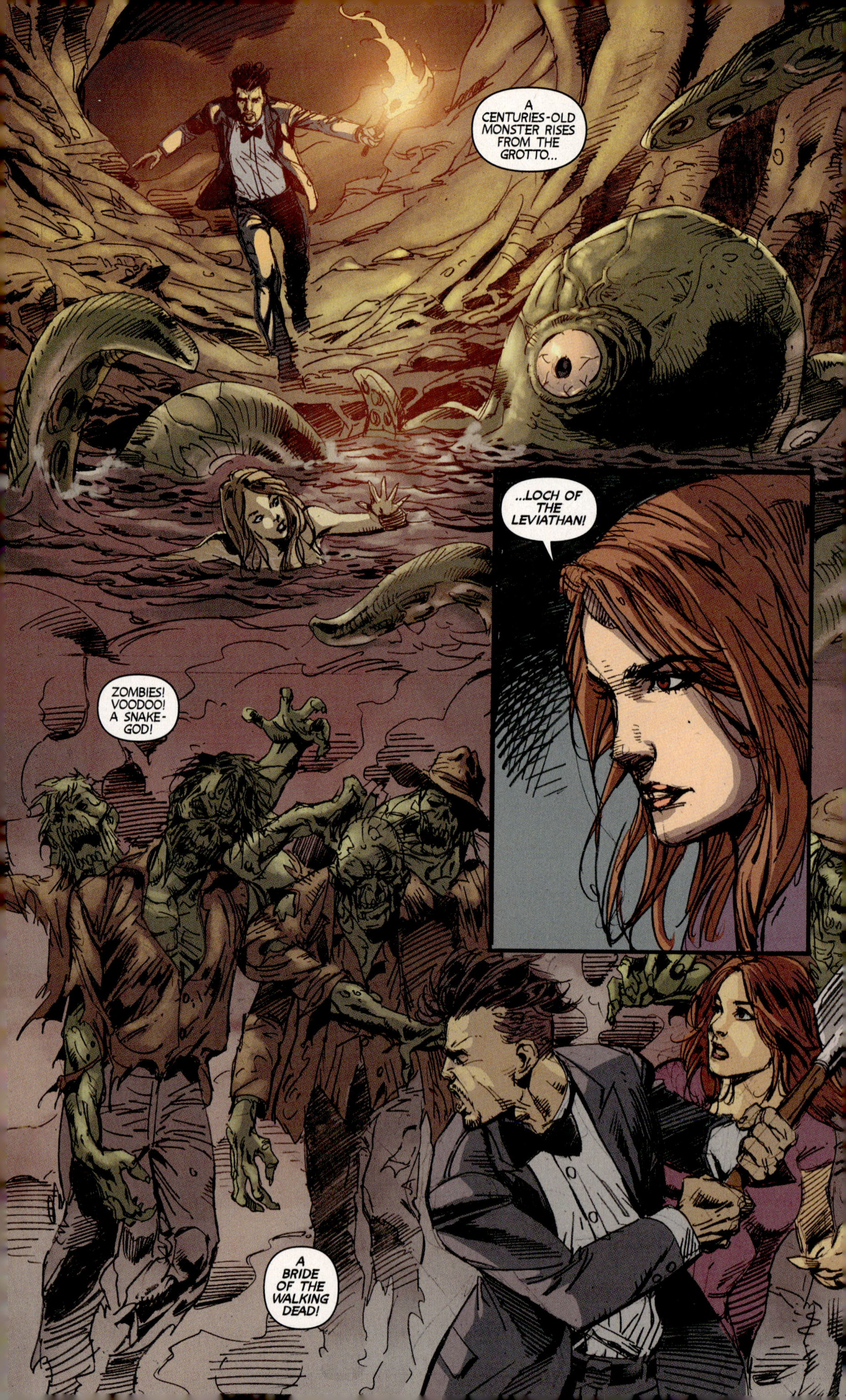
A CENTURIES-OLD MONSTER RISES FROM THE GROTTO...
...LOCH OF THE LEVIATHAN!
ZOMBIES! VOODOO! A SNAKE-GOD!
A BRIDE OF THE WALKING DEAD!

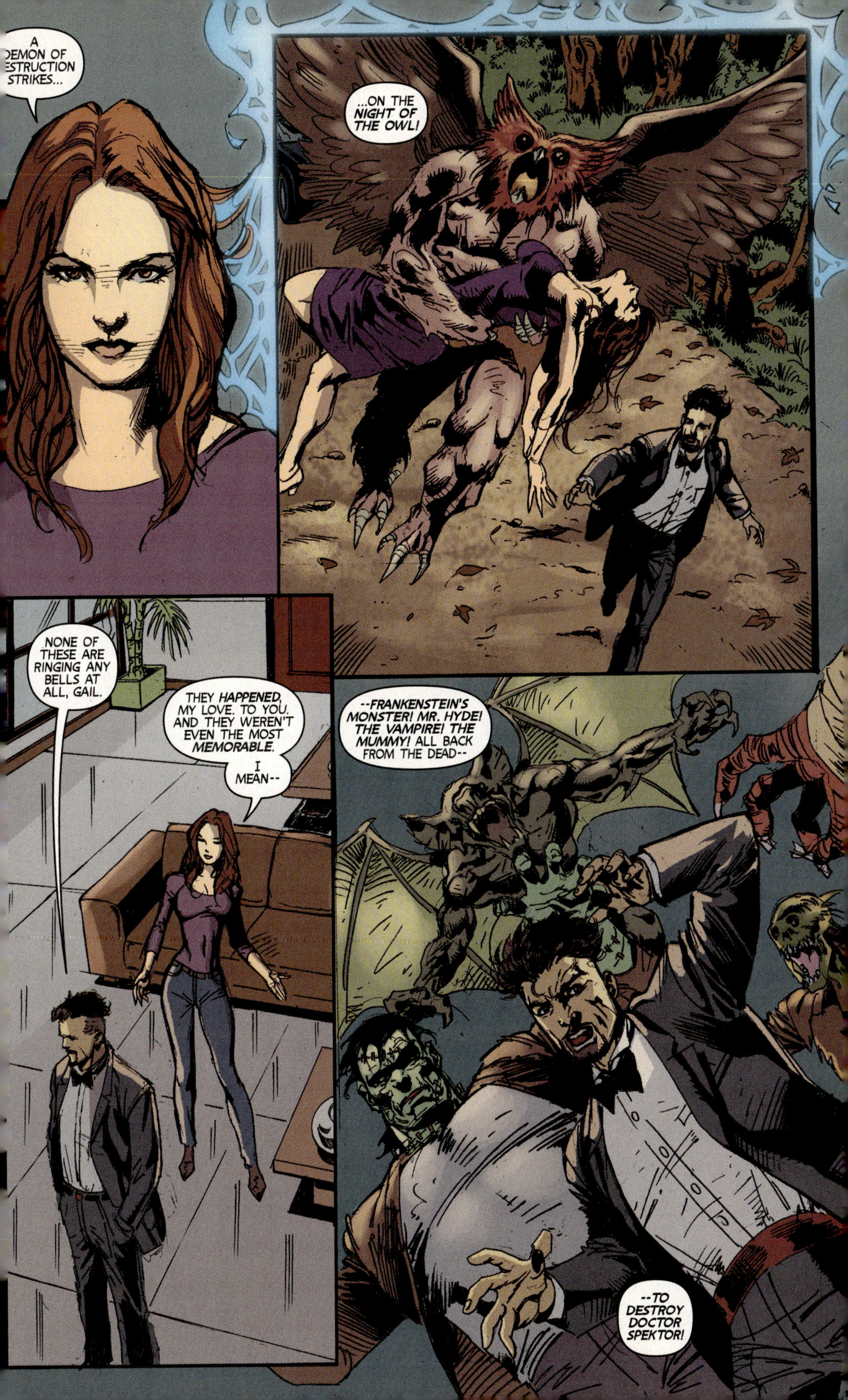
A DEMON OF DESTRUCTION STRIKES...
...ON THE NIGHT OF THE OWL!
NONE OF THESE ARE RINGING ANY BELLS AT ALL, GAIL.
THEY HAPPENED, MY LOVE. TO YOU. AND THEY WEREN'T EVEN THE MOST MEMORABLE.
I MEAN--
--FRANKENSTEIN'S MONSTER! MR. HYDE! THE VAMPIRE! THE MUMMY! ALL BACK FROM THE DEAD--
--TO DESTROY DOCTOR SPEKTOR!

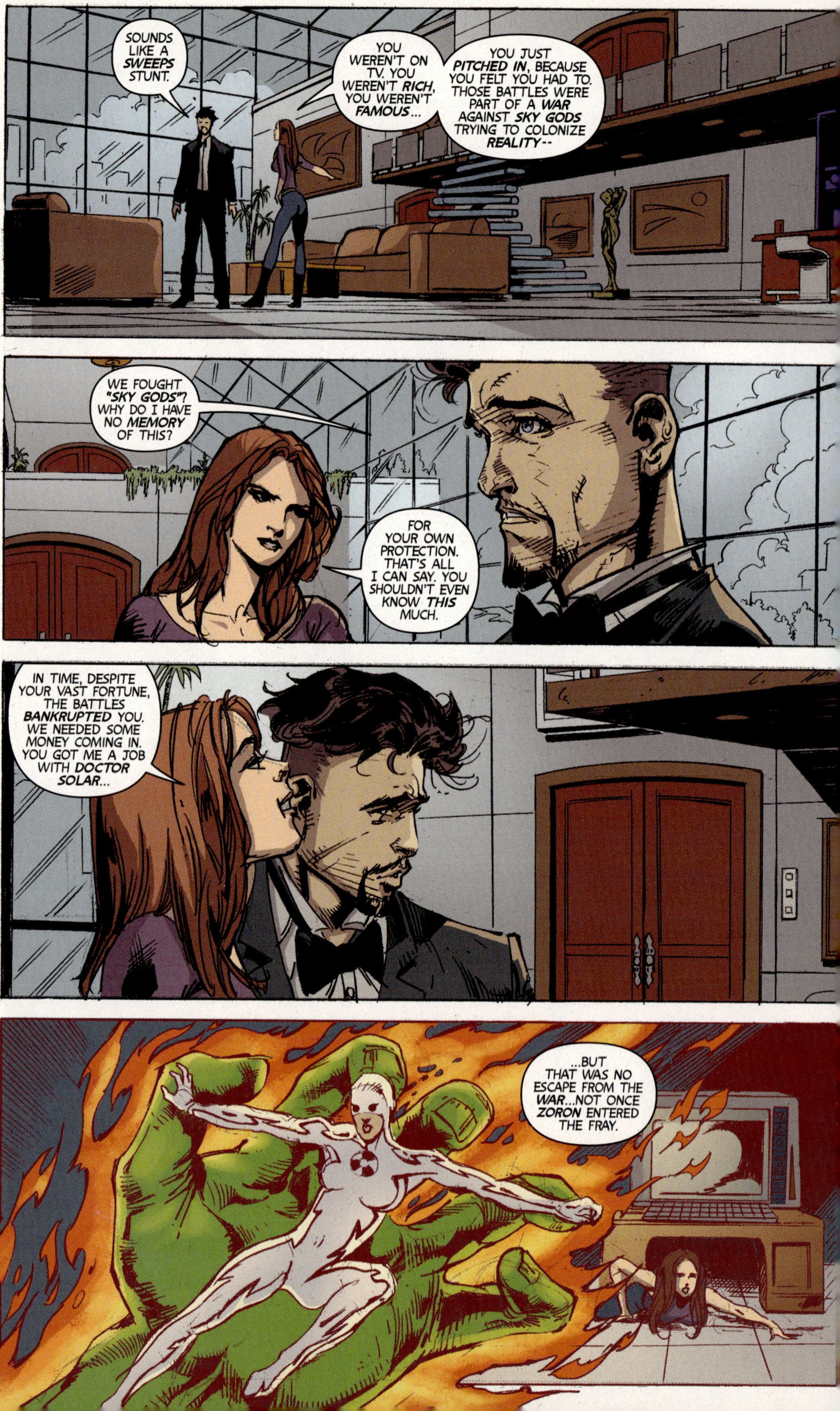
SOUNDS LIKE A SWEEPS STUNT.
YOU WEREN'T ON TV, YOU WEREN'T RICH, YOU WEREN'T FAMOUS...
YOU JUST PITCHED IN, BECAUSE YOU FELT YOU HAD TO. THOSE BATTLES WERE PART OF A WAR AGAINST SKY GODS TRYING TO COLONIZE REALITY--
WE FOUGHT "SKY GODS"? WHY DO I HAVE NO MEMORY OF THIS?
FOR YOUR OWN PROTECTION. THAT'S ALL I CAN SAY. YOU SHOULDN'T EVEN KNOW THIS MUCH.
IN TIME, DESPITE YOUR VAST FORTUNE, THE BATTLES BANKRUPTED YOU. WE NEEDED SOME MONEY COMING IN. YOU GOT ME A JOB WITH DOCTOR SOLAR...
...BUT THAT WAS NO ESCAPE FROM THE WAR...NOT ONCE ZORON ENTERED THE FRAY.

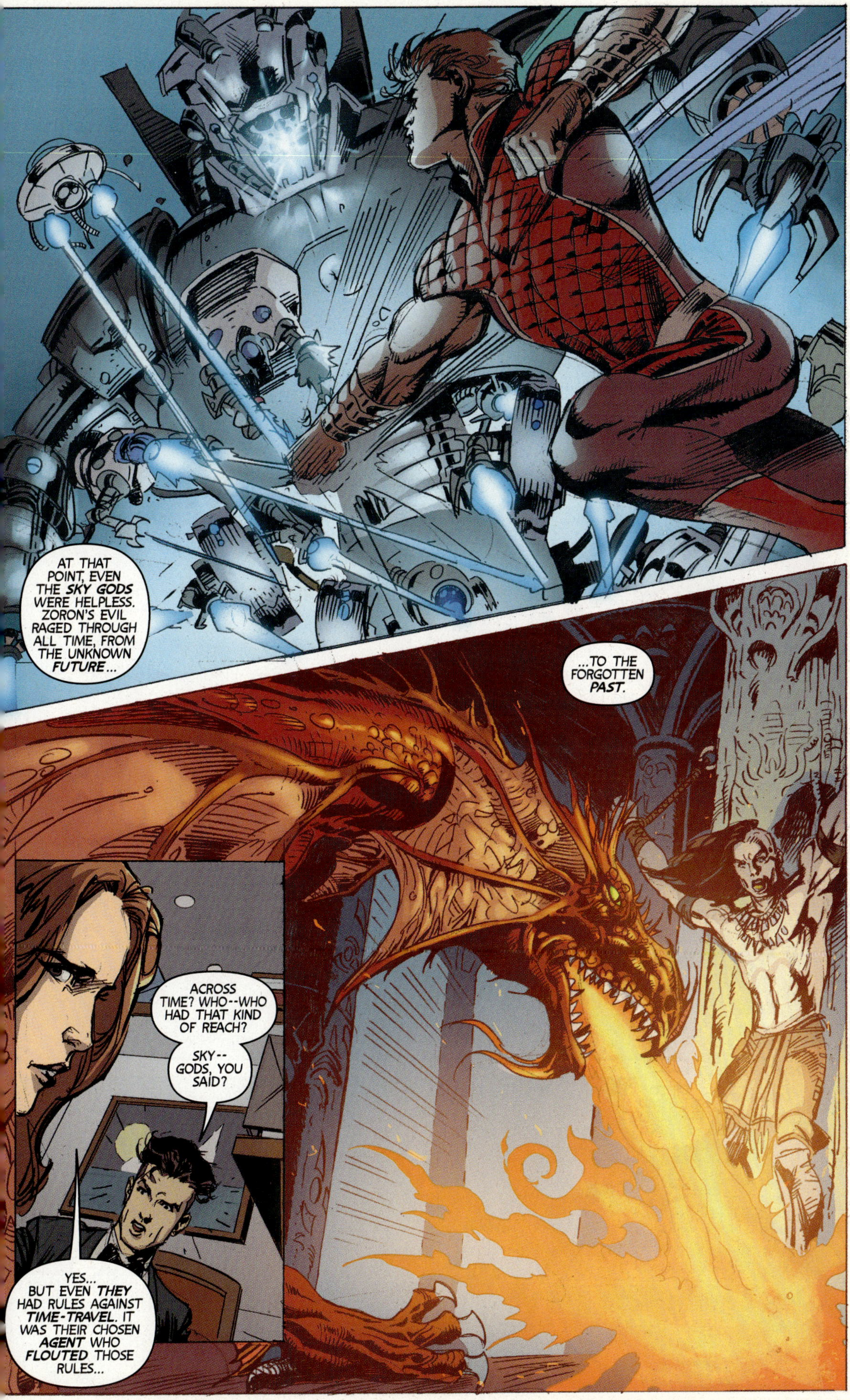
AT THAT POINT, EVEN THE SKY GODS WERE HELPLESS. ZORON'S EVIL RAGED THROUGH ALL TIME, FROM THE UNKNOWN FUTURE...
...TO THE FORGOTTEN PAST.
ACROSS TIME? WHO--WHO HAD THAT KIND OF REACH?
SKY-- GODS, YOU SAID?
YES... BUT EVEN THEY HAD RULES AGAINST TIME-TRAVEL. IT WAS THEIR CHOSEN AGENT WHO FLOUTED THOSE RULES...

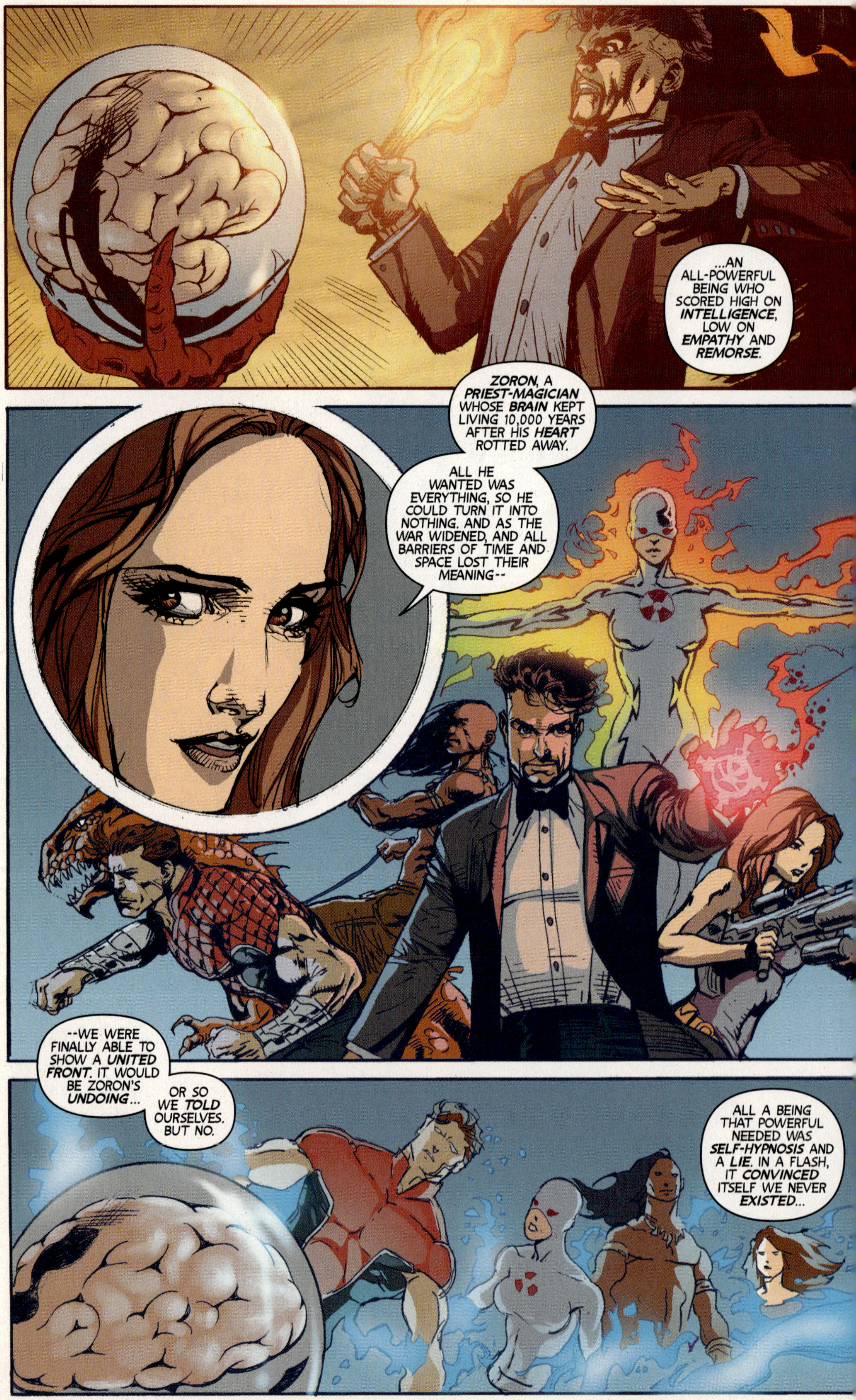
...AN ALL-POWERFUL BEING WHO SCORED HIGH ON INTELLIGENCE, LOW ON EMPATHY AND REMORSE.
ZORON, A PRIEST-MAGICIAN WHOSE BRAIN KEPT LIVING 10,000 YEARS AFTER HIS HEART ROTTED AWAY.
ALL HE WANTED WAS EVERYTHING, SO HE COULD TURN IT INTO NOTHING. AND AS THE WAR WIDENED, AND ALL BARRIERS OF TIME AND SPACE LOST THEIR MEANING--
--WE WERE FINALLY ABLE TO SHOW A UNITED FRONT. IT WOULD BE ZORON'S UNDOING...
OR SO WE TOLD OURSELVES. BUT NO.
ALL A BEING THAT POWERFUL NEEDED WAS SELF-HYPNOSIS AND A LIE. IN A FLASH, IT CONVINCED ITSELF WE NEVER EXISTED...

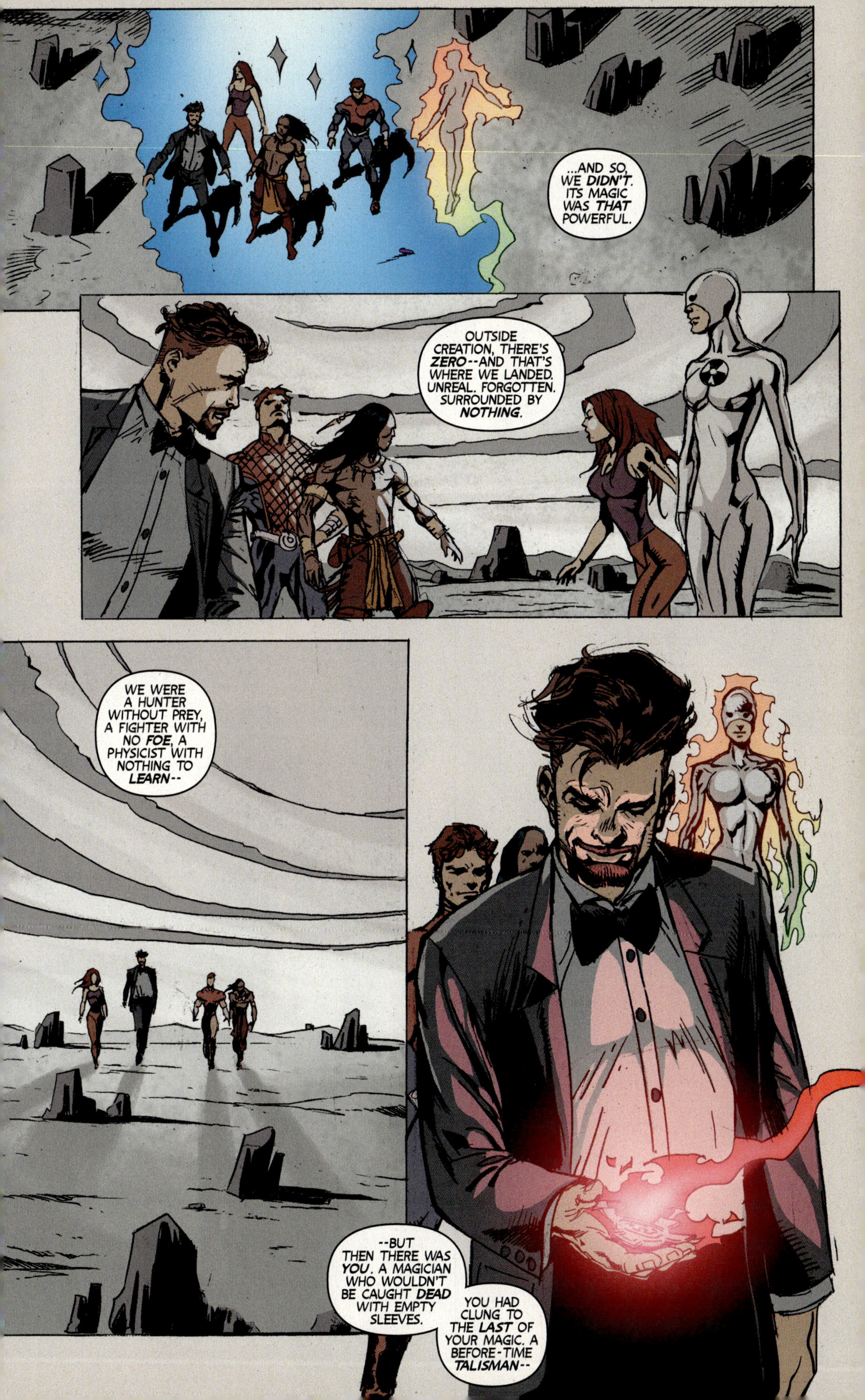
...AND SO, WE DIDN'T. ITS MAGIC WAS THAT POWERFUL.
OUTSIDE CREATION, THERE'S ZERO--AND THAT'S WHERE WE LANDED. UNREAL. FORGOTTEN. SURROUNDED BY NOTHING.
WE WERE A HUNTER WITHOUT PREY, A FIGHTER WITH NO FOE, A PHYSICIST WITH NOTHING TO LEARN--
--BUT THEN THERE WAS YOU. A MAGICIAN WHO WOULDN'T BE CAUGHT DEAD WITH EMPTY SLEEVES.
YOU HAD CLUNG TO THE LAST OF YOUR MAGIC. A BEFORE-TIME TALISMAN--

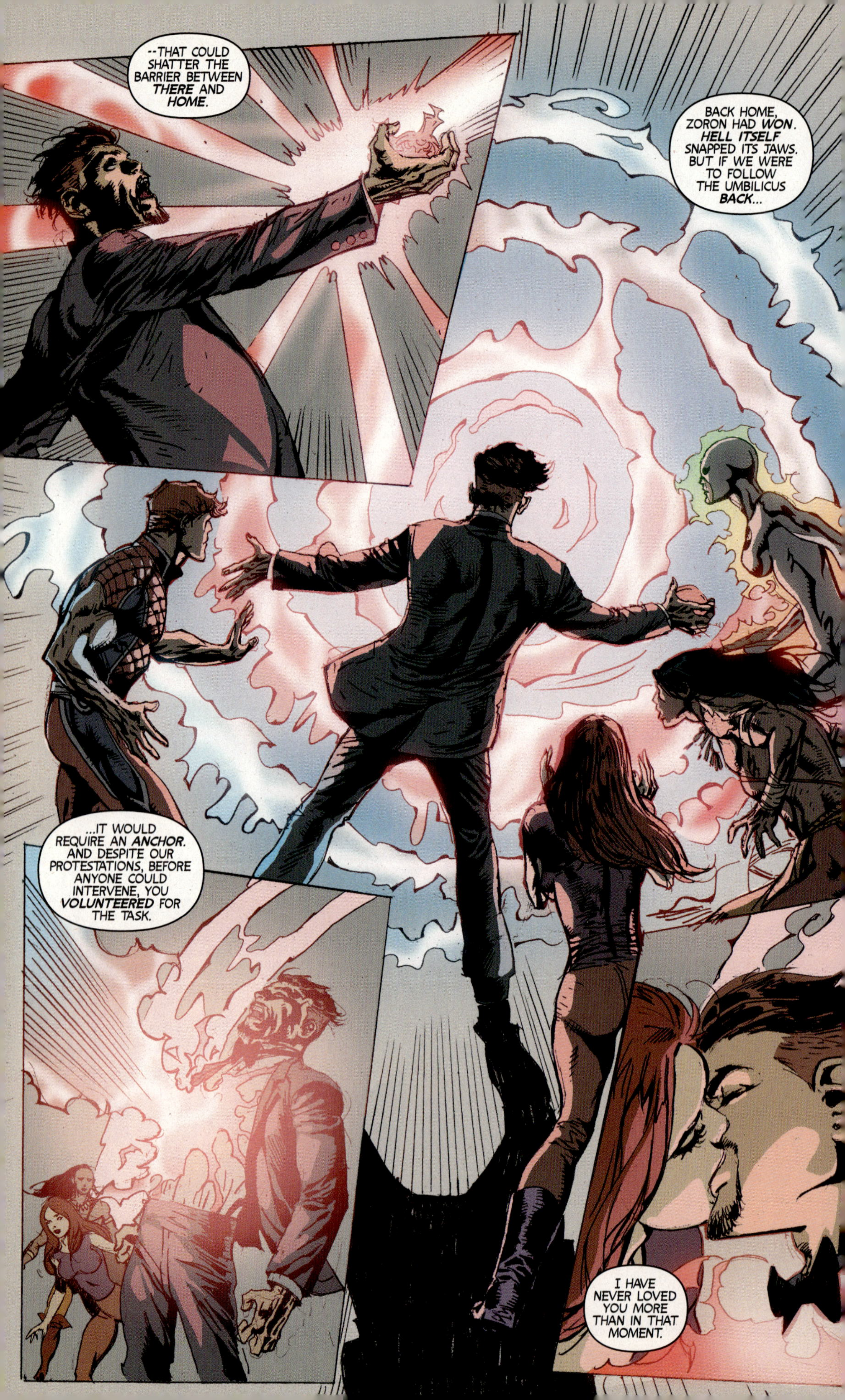
--THAT COULD SHATTER THE BARRIER BETWEEN THERE AND HOME.
BACK HOME, ZORON HAD WON. HELL ITSELF SNAPPED ITS JAWS, BUT IF WE WERE TO FOLLOW THE UMBILICUS BACK...
...IT WOULD REQUIRE AN ANCHOR. AND DESPITE OUR PROTESTATIONS, BEFORE ANYONE COULD INTERVENE, YOU VOLUNTEERED FOR THE TASK.
I HAVE NEVER LOVED YOU MORE THAN IN THAT MOMENT.

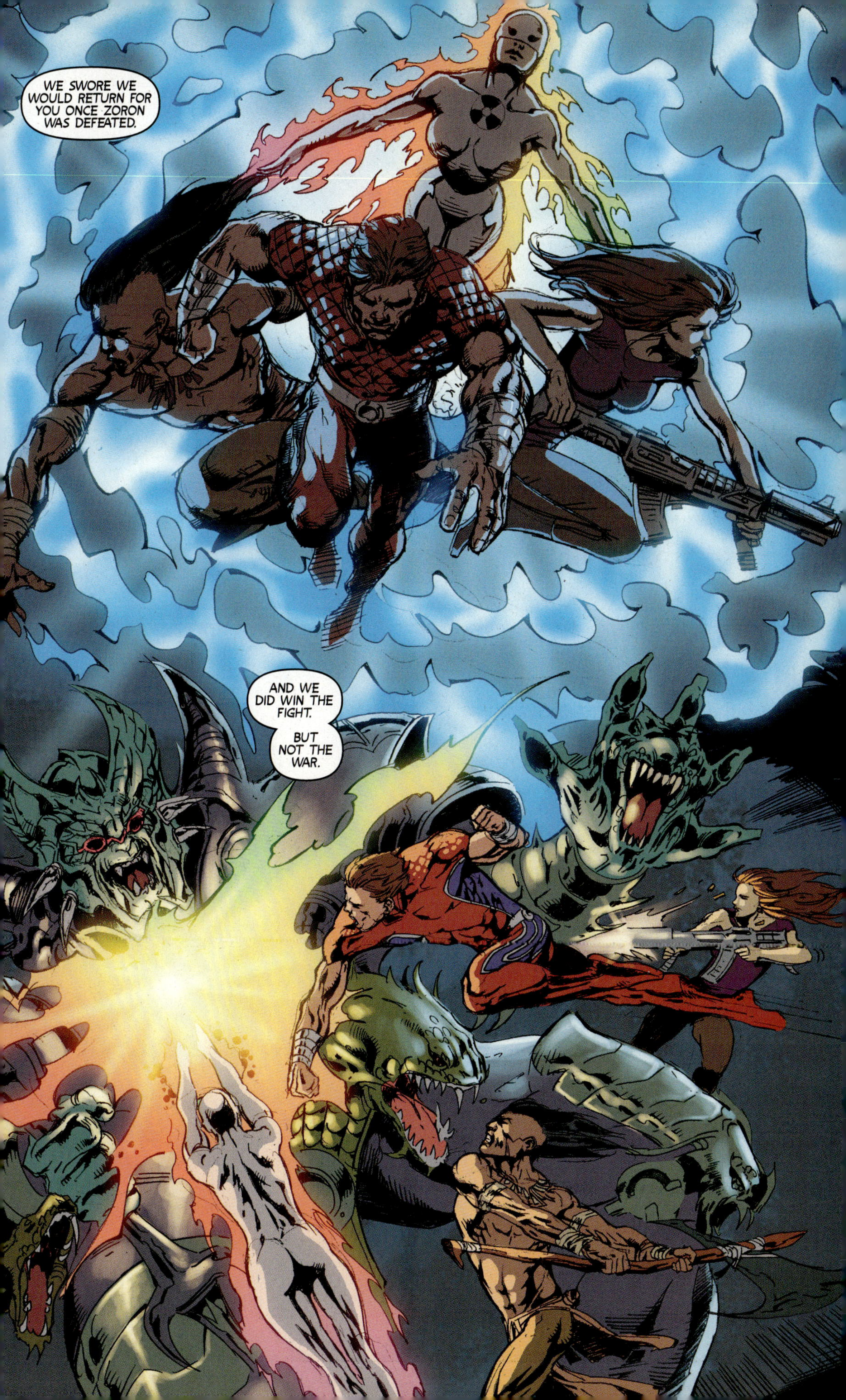
WE SWORE WE WOULD RETURN FOR YOU ONCE ZORON WAS DEFEATED.
AND WE DID WIN THE FIGHT.
BUT NOT THE WAR.

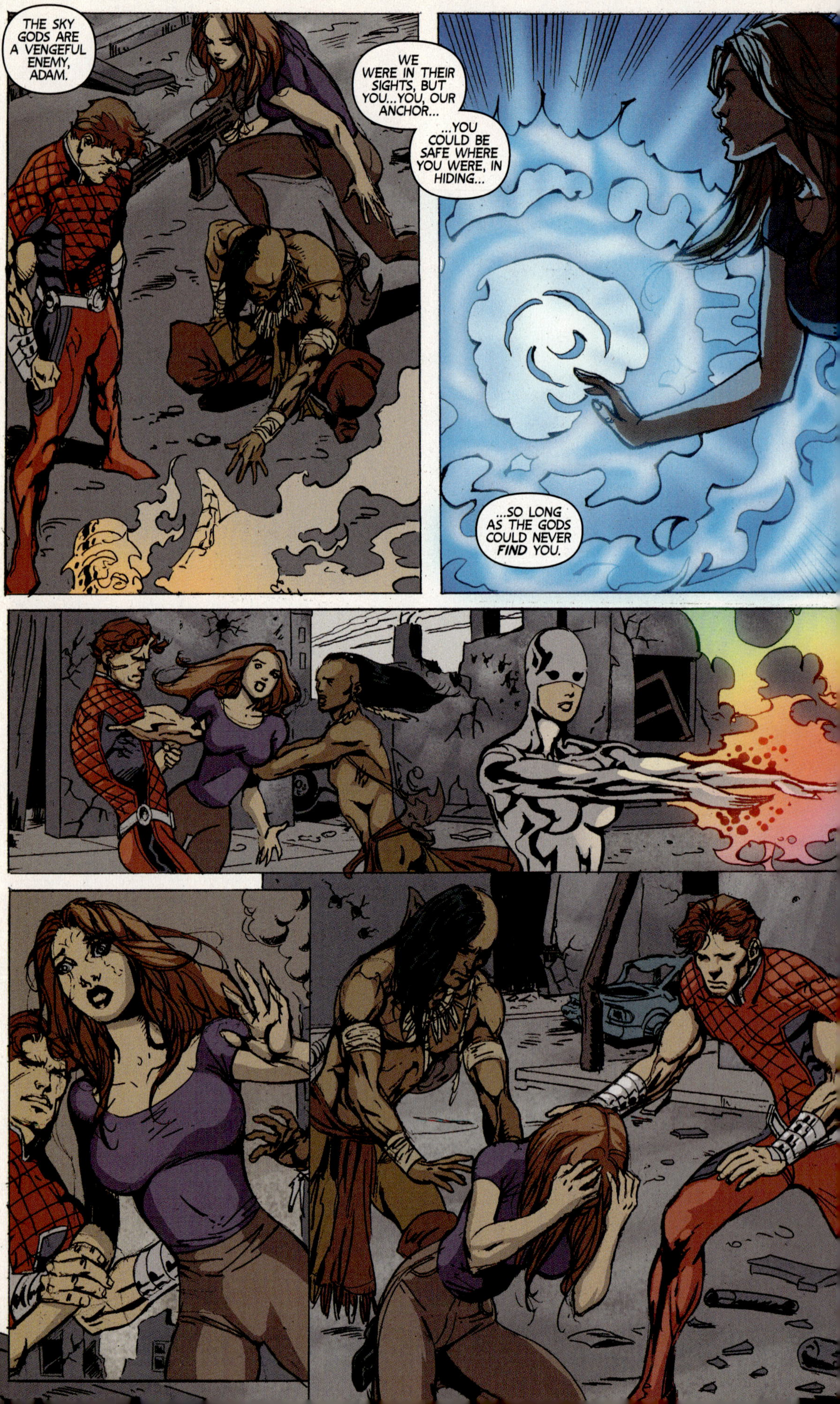
THE SKY GODS ARE A VENGEFUL ENEMY, ADAM.
WE WERE IN THEIR SIGHTS, BUT YOU...YOU, OUR ANCHOR...
...YOU COULD BE SAFE WHERE YOU WERE, IN HIDING...
...SO LONG AS THE GODS COULD NEVER FIND YOU.

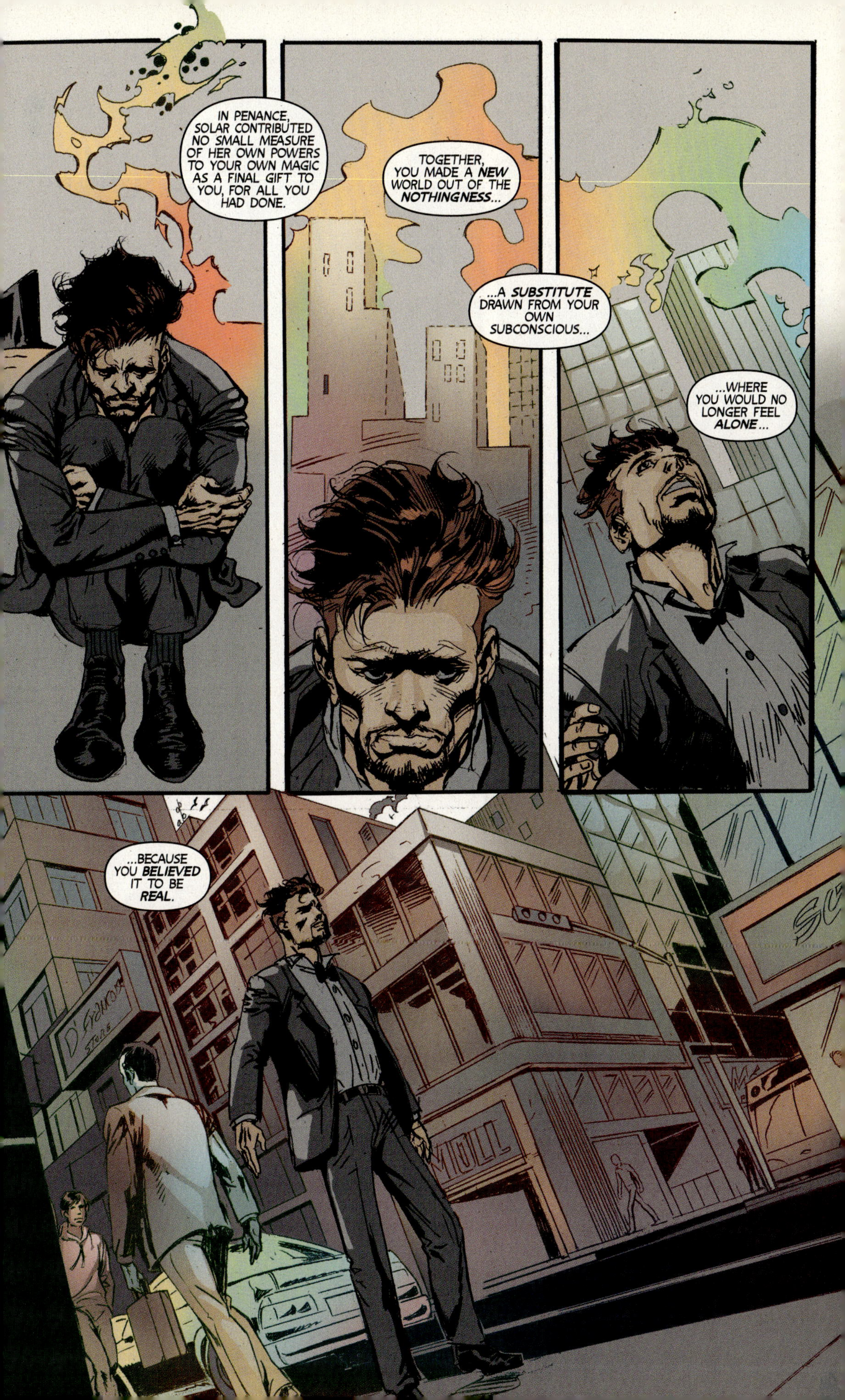
IN PENANCE, SOLAR CONTRIBUTED NO SMALL MEASURE OF HER OWN POWERS TO YOUR OWN MAGIC AS A FINAL GIFT TO YOU, FOR ALL YOU HAD DONE.
TOGETHER, YOU MADE A *NEW* WORLD OUT OF THE *NOTHINGNESS*...
...A *SUBSTITUTE* DRAWN FROM YOUR OWN SUBCONSCIOUS...
...WHERE YOU WOULD NO LONGER FEEL *ALONE*...
...BECAUSE YOU *BELIEVED* IT TO BE *REAL*.

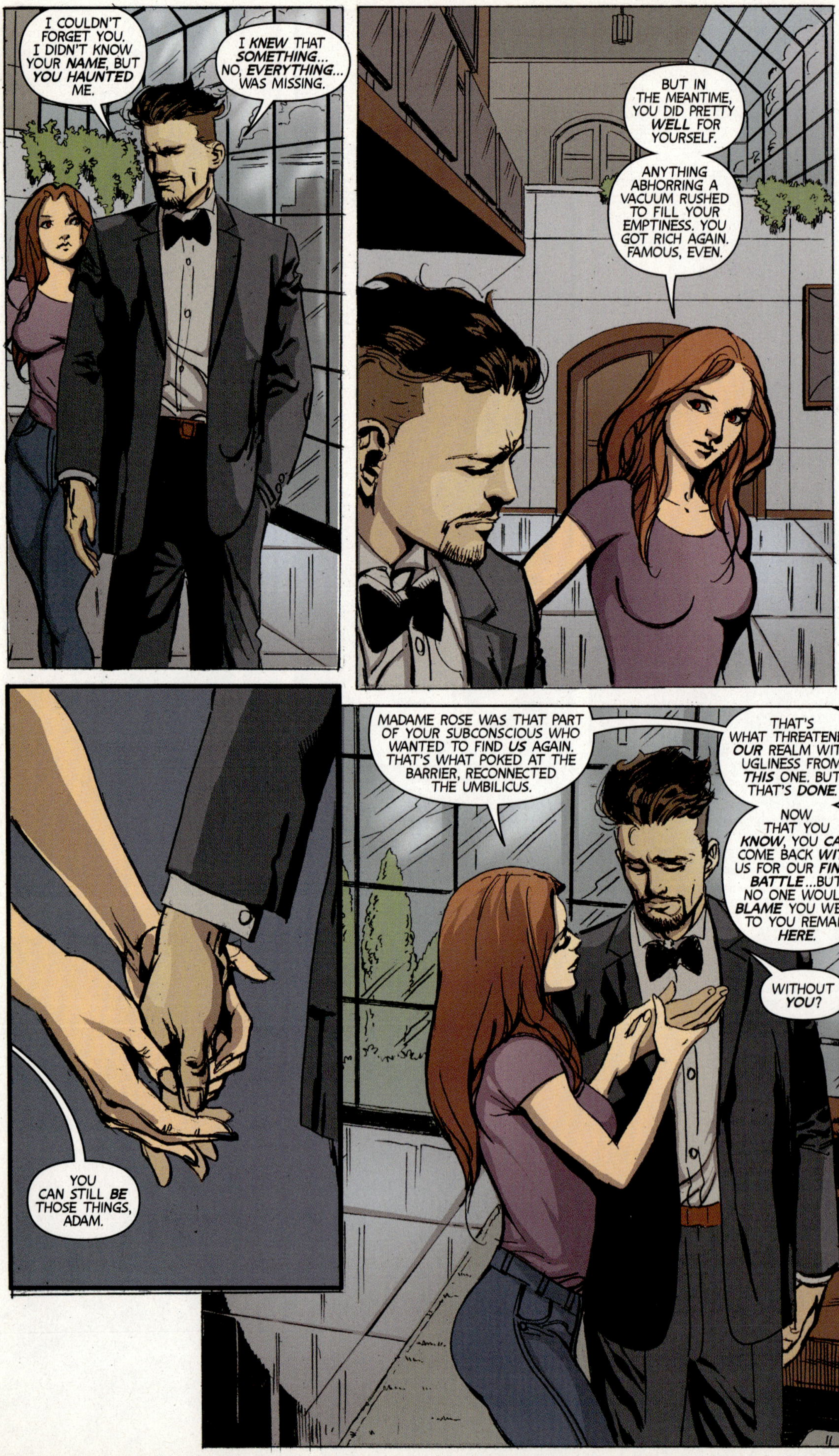
I COULDN'T FORGET YOU. I DIDN'T KNOW YOUR NAME, BUT YOU HAUNTED ME.
I KNEW THAT SOMETHING... NO, EVERYTHING... WAS MISSING.
BUT IN THE MEANTIME, YOU DID PRETTY WELL FOR YOURSELF.
ANYTHING ABHORRING A VACUUM RUSHED TO FILL YOUR EMPTINESS. YOU GOT RICH AGAIN. FAMOUS, EVEN.
YOU CAN STILL BE THOSE THINGS, ADAM.
MADAME ROSE WAS THAT PART OF YOUR SUBCONSCIOUS WHO WANTED TO FIND US AGAIN. THAT'S WHAT POKED AT THE BARRIER, RECONNECTED THE UMBILICUS.
THAT'S WHAT THREATENED OUR REALM WITH UGLINESS FROM THIS ONE. BUT THAT'S DONE.
NOW THAT YOU KNOW, YOU CAN COME BACK WITH US FOR OUR FINAL BATTLE...BUT NO ONE WOULD BLAME YOU WERE TO YOU REMAIN HERE.
WITHOUT YOU?

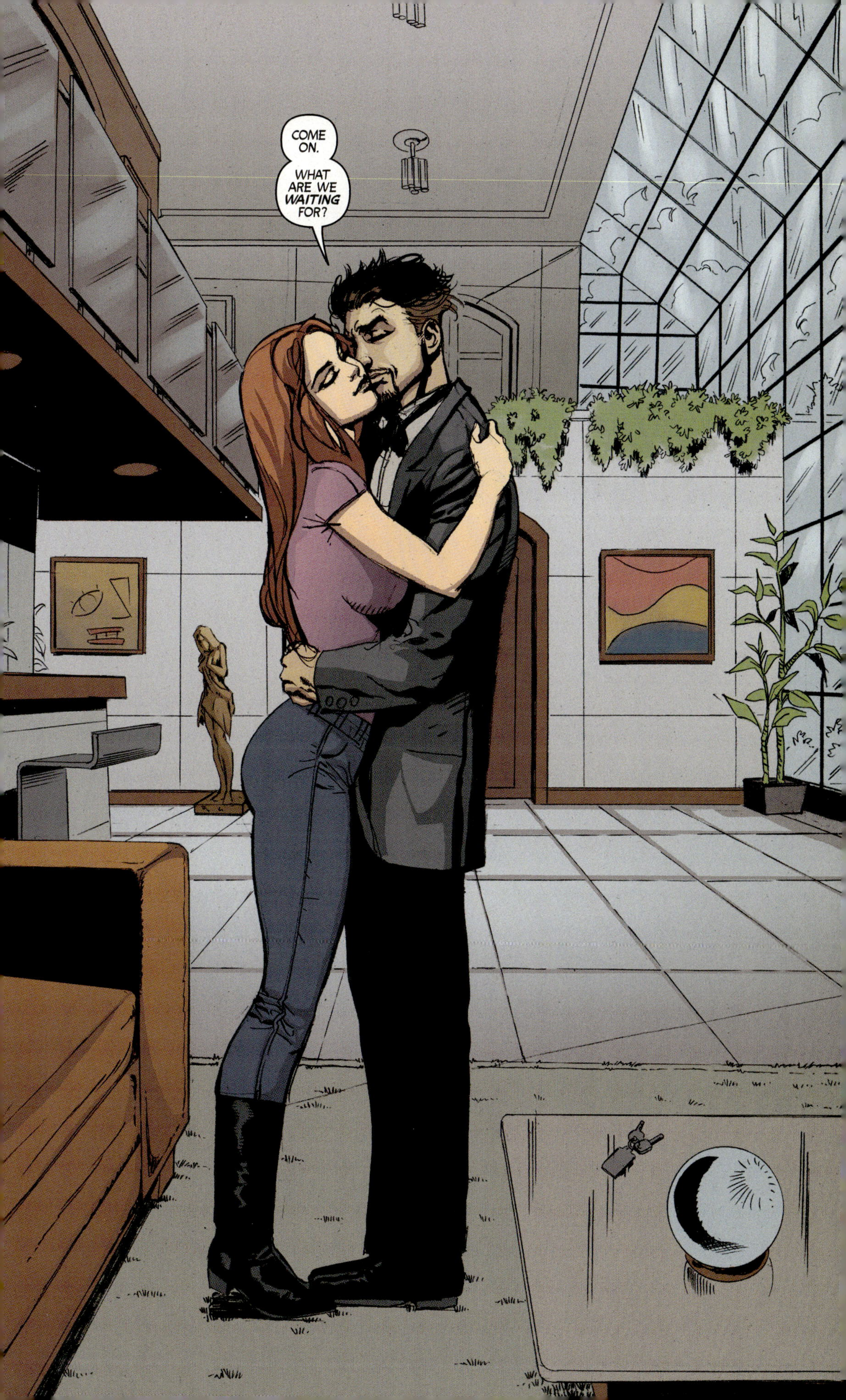
COME ON.
WHAT ARE WE *WAITING* FOR?

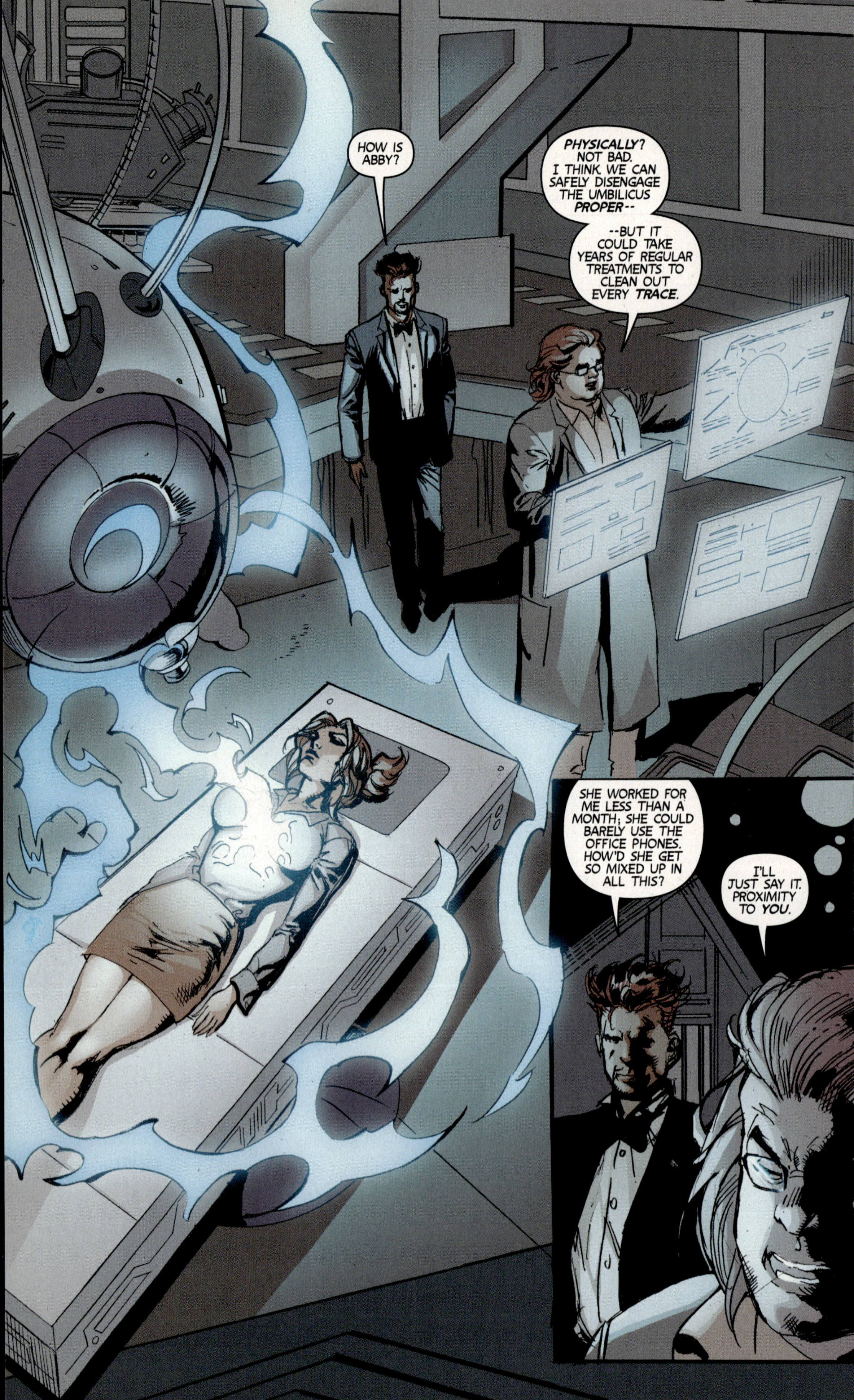
HOW IS ABBY?
PHYSICALLY? NOT BAD. I THINK WE CAN SAFELY DISENGAGE THE UMBILICUS *PROPER*--
--BUT IT COULD TAKE YEARS OF REGULAR TREATMENTS TO CLEAN OUT EVERY *TRACE*.
SHE WORKED FOR ME LESS THAN A MONTH; SHE COULD BARELY USE THE OFFICE PHONES. HOW'D SHE GET SO MIXED UP IN ALL THIS?
I'LL JUST SAY IT. PROXIMITY TO *YOU*.

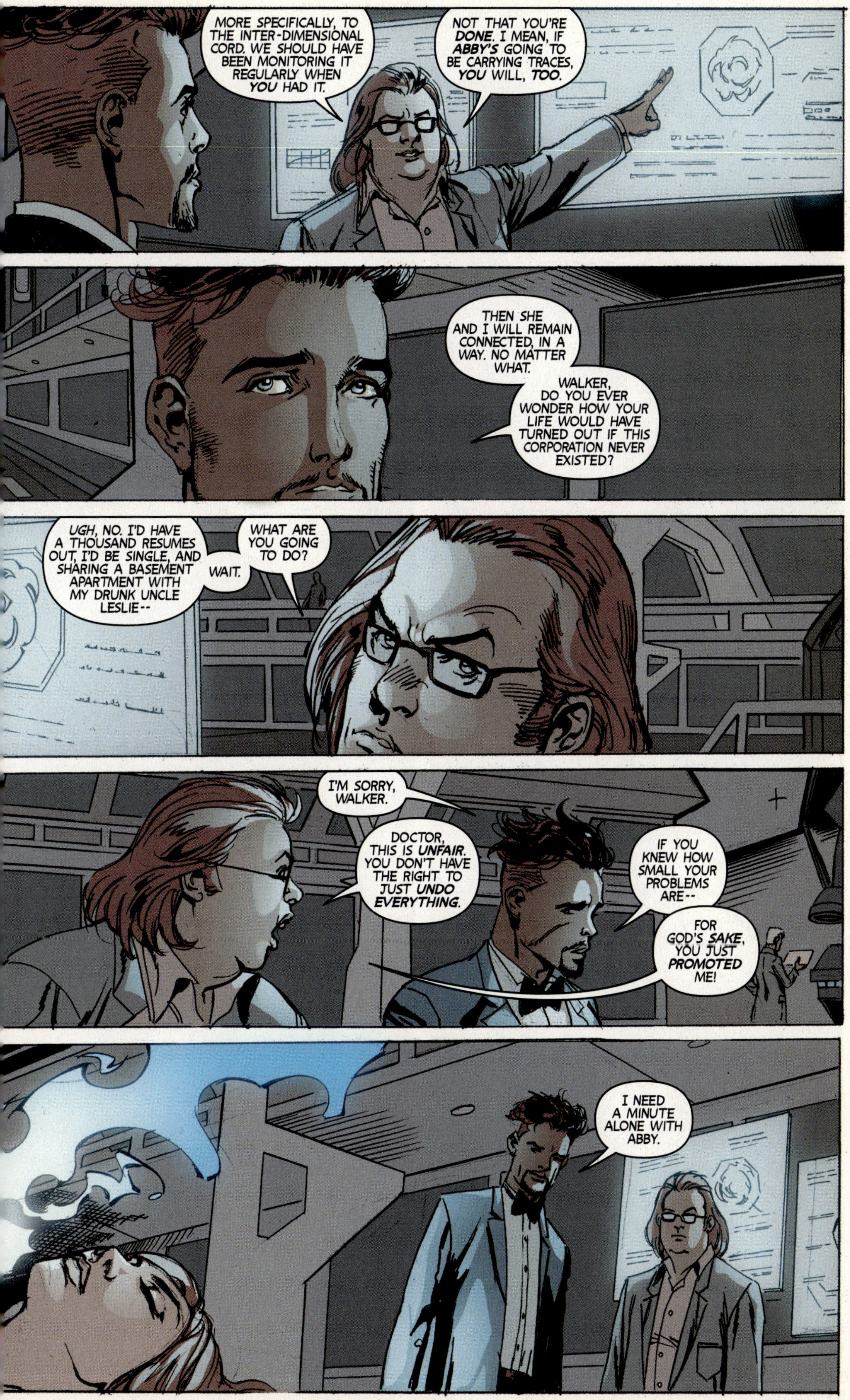
MORE SPECIFICALLY, TO THE INTER-DIMENSIONAL CORD. WE SHOULD HAVE BEEN MONITORING IT REGULARLY WHEN YOU HAD IT.
NOT THAT YOU'RE DONE. I MEAN, IF ABBY'S GOING TO BE CARRYING TRACES, YOU WILL, TOO.
THEN SHE AND I WILL REMAIN CONNECTED, IN A WAY. NO MATTER WHAT.
WALKER, DO YOU EVER WONDER HOW YOUR LIFE WOULD HAVE TURNED OUT IF THIS CORPORATION NEVER EXISTED?
UGH, NO. I'D HAVE A THOUSAND RESUMES OUT, I'D BE SINGLE, AND SHARING A BASEMENT APARTMENT WITH MY DRUNK UNCLE LESLIE--
WAIT.
WHAT ARE YOU GOING TO DO?
I'M SORRY, WALKER.
DOCTOR, THIS IS UNFAIR. YOU DON'T HAVE THE RIGHT TO JUST UNDO EVERYTHING.
IF YOU KNEW HOW SMALL YOUR PROBLEMS ARE--
FOR GOD'S SAKE, YOU JUST PROMOTED ME!
I NEED A MINUTE ALONE WITH ABBY.

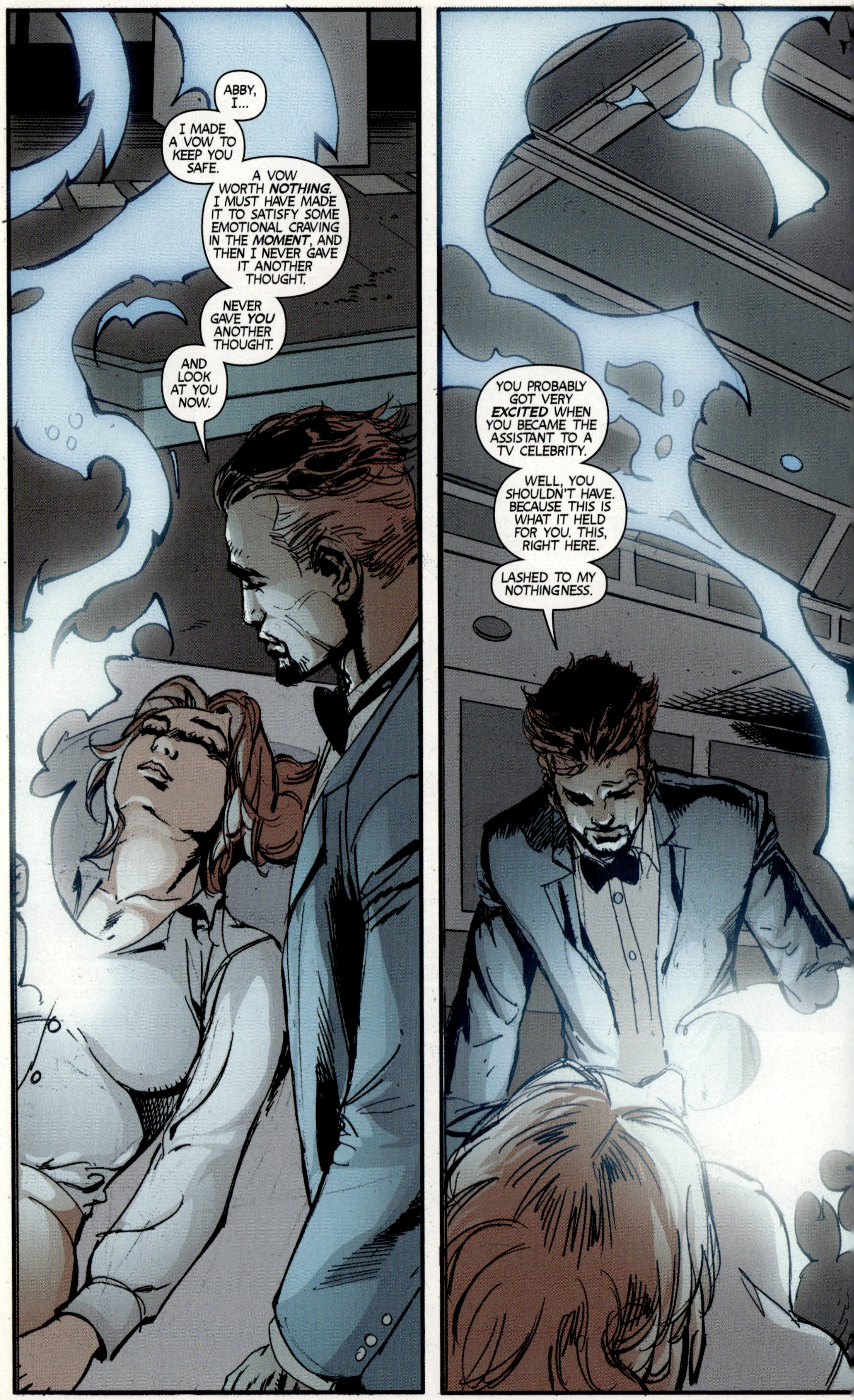
ABBY, I...
I MADE A VOW TO KEEP YOU SAFE.
A VOW WORTH NOTHING. I MUST HAVE MADE IT TO SATISFY SOME EMOTIONAL CRAVING IN THE MOMENT, AND THEN I NEVER GAVE IT ANOTHER THOUGHT.
NEVER GAVE YOU ANOTHER THOUGHT.
AND LOOK AT YOU NOW.
YOU PROBABLY GOT VERY EXCITED WHEN YOU BECAME THE ASSISTANT TO A TV CELEBRITY.
WELL, YOU SHOULDN'T HAVE. BECAUSE THIS IS WHAT IT HELD FOR YOU. THIS, RIGHT HERE.
LASHED TO MY NOTHINGNESS.

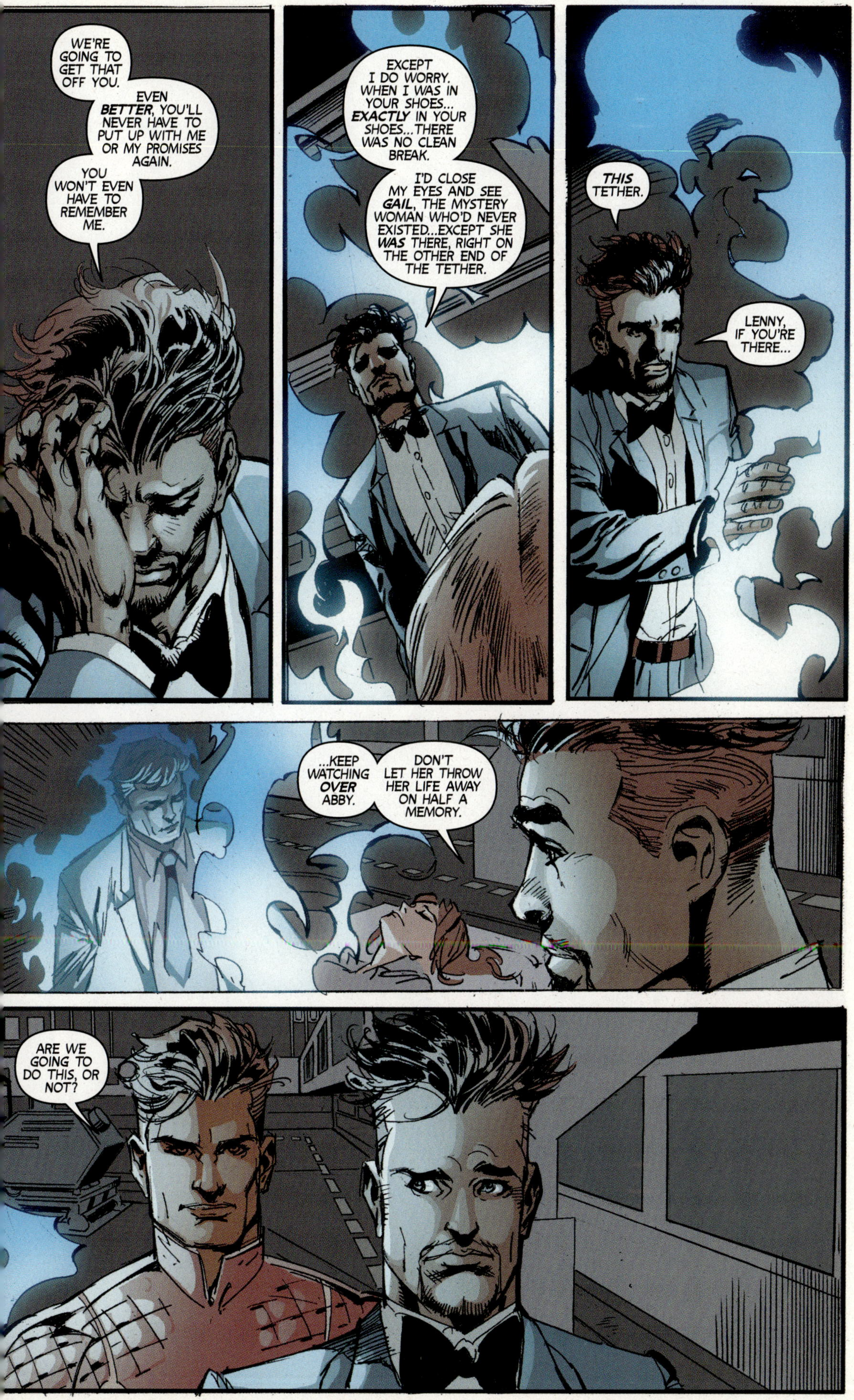

WE'RE GOING TO GET THAT OFF YOU.
EVEN BETTER, YOU'LL NEVER HAVE TO PUT UP WITH ME OR MY PROMISES AGAIN.
YOU WON'T EVEN HAVE TO REMEMBER ME.
EXCEPT I DO WORRY. WHEN I WAS IN YOUR SHOES... EXACTLY IN YOUR SHOES...THERE WAS NO CLEAN BREAK.
I'D CLOSE MY EYES AND SEE GAIL, THE MYSTERY WOMAN WHO'D NEVER EXISTED...EXCEPT SHE WAS THERE, RIGHT ON THE OTHER END OF THE TETHER.
THIS TETHER.
LENNY, IF YOU'RE THERE...
...KEEP WATCHING OVER ABBY.
DON'T LET HER THROW HER LIFE AWAY ON HALF A MEMORY.
ARE WE GOING TO DO THIS, OR NOT?

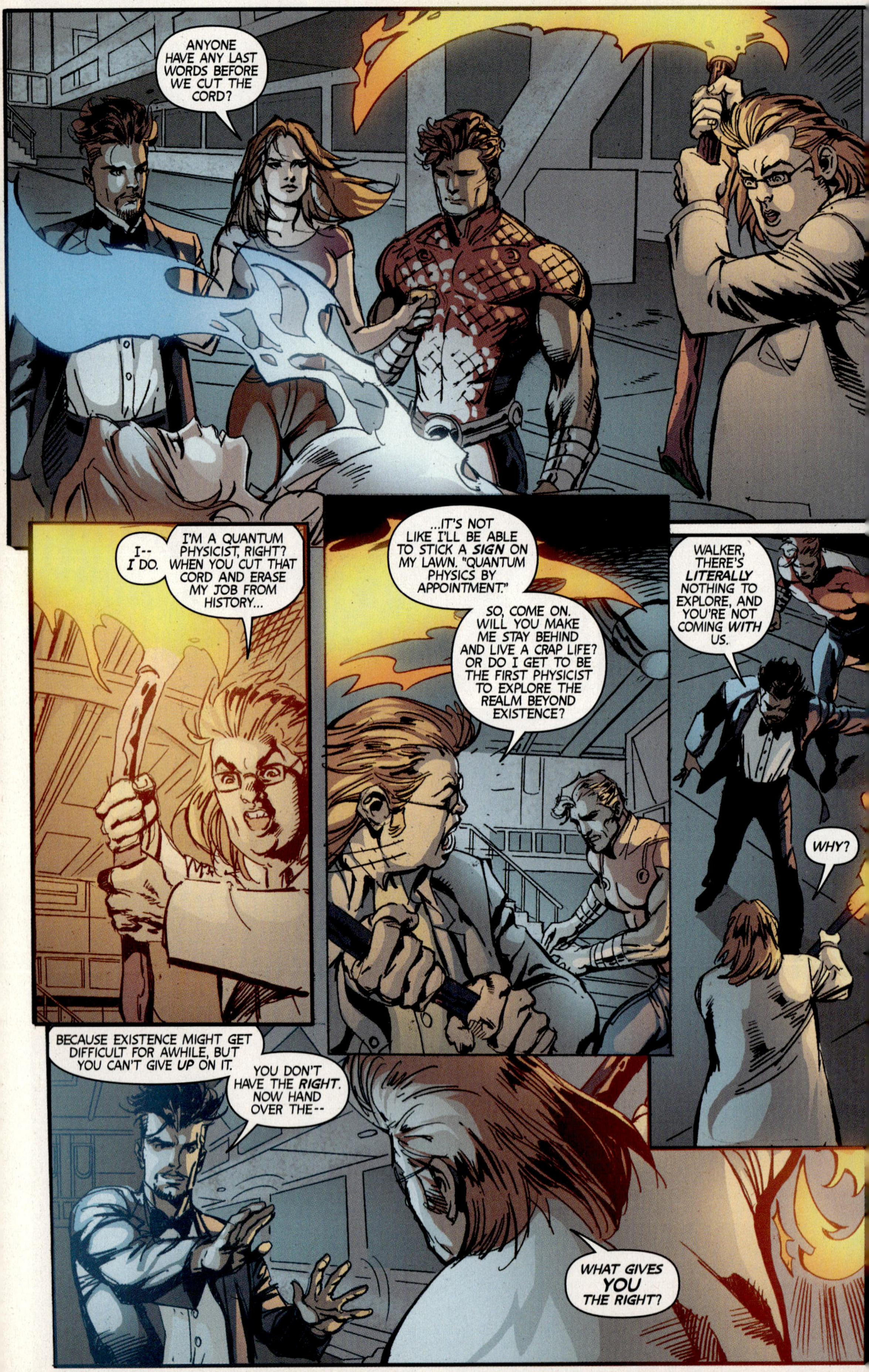
ANYONE HAVE ANY LAST WORDS BEFORE WE CUT THE CORD?
I-- I DO.
I'M A QUANTUM PHYSICIST, RIGHT? WHEN YOU CUT THAT CORD AND ERASE MY JOB FROM HISTORY...
...IT'S NOT LIKE I'LL BE ABLE TO STICK A SIGN ON MY LAWN. "QUANTUM PHYSICS BY APPOINTMENT."
SO, COME ON. WILL YOU MAKE ME STAY BEHIND AND LIVE A CRAP LIFE? OR DO I GET TO BE THE FIRST PHYSICIST TO EXPLORE THE REALM BEYOND EXISTENCE?
WALKER, THERE'S LITERALLY NOTHING TO EXPLORE, AND YOU'RE NOT COMING WITH US.
WHY?
BECAUSE EXISTENCE MIGHT GET DIFFICULT FOR AWHILE, BUT YOU CAN'T GIVE UP ON IT.
YOU DON'T HAVE THE RIGHT. NOW HAND OVER THE--
WHAT GIVES YOU THE RIGHT?

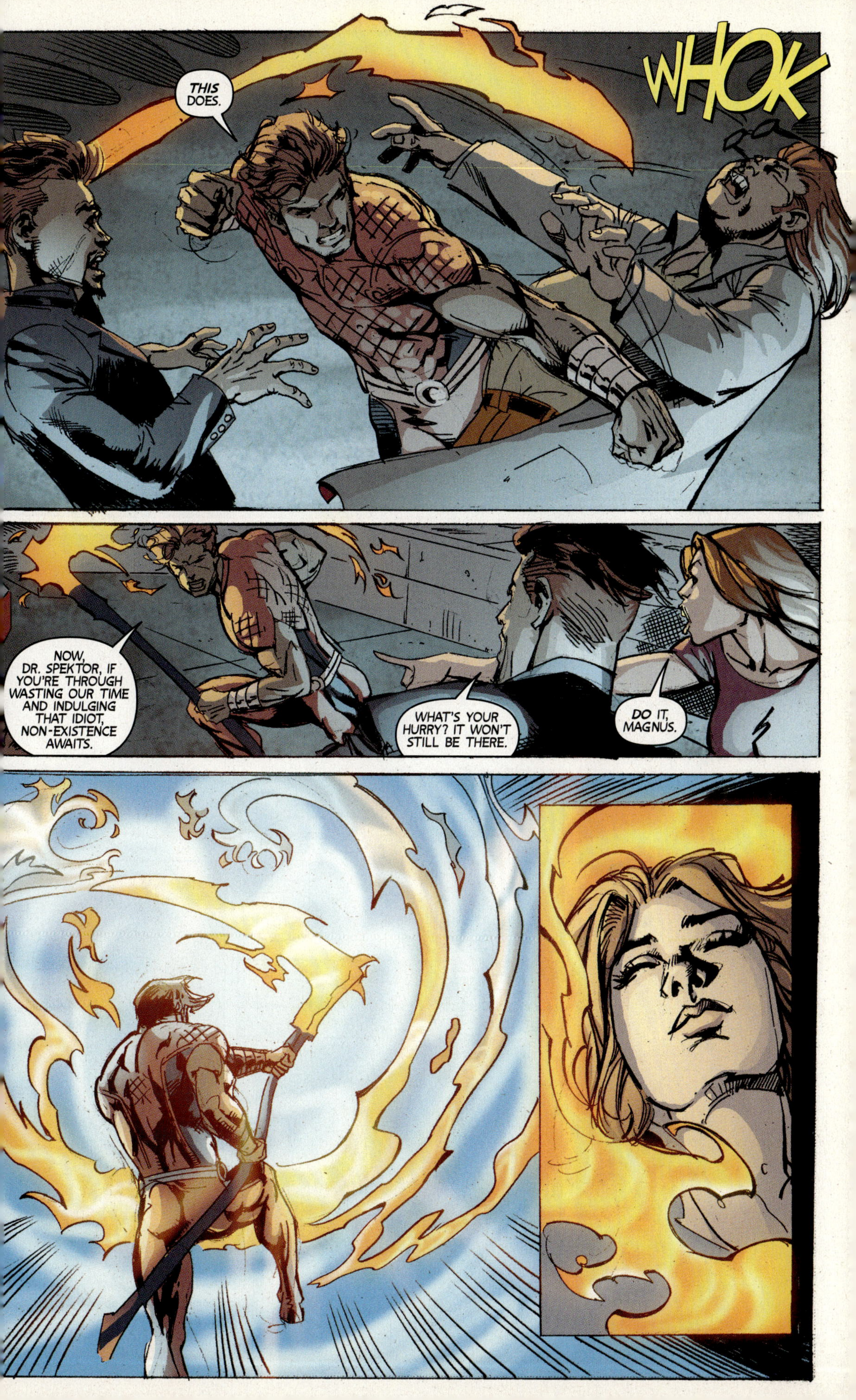
THIS DOES.
WHOK
NOW, DR. SPEKTOR, IF YOU'RE THROUGH WASTING OUR TIME AND INDULGING THAT IDIOT, NON-EXISTENCE AWAITS.
WHAT'S YOUR HURRY? IT WON'T STILL BE THERE.
DO IT, MAGNUS.

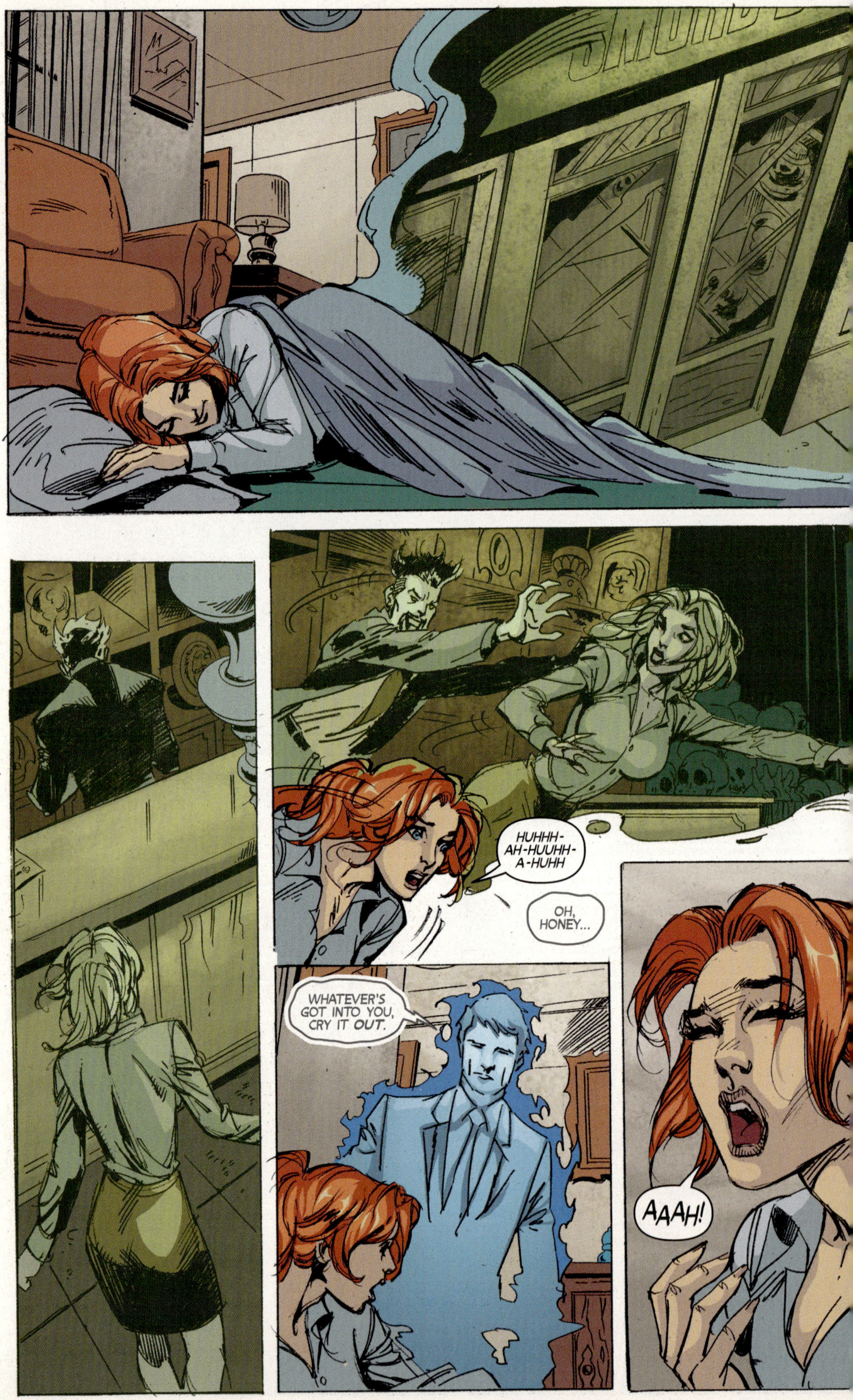

HUHHH-AH-HUUHH-A-HUHH
OH, HONEY...
WHATEVER'S GOT INTO YOU, CRY IT OUT.
AAAH!

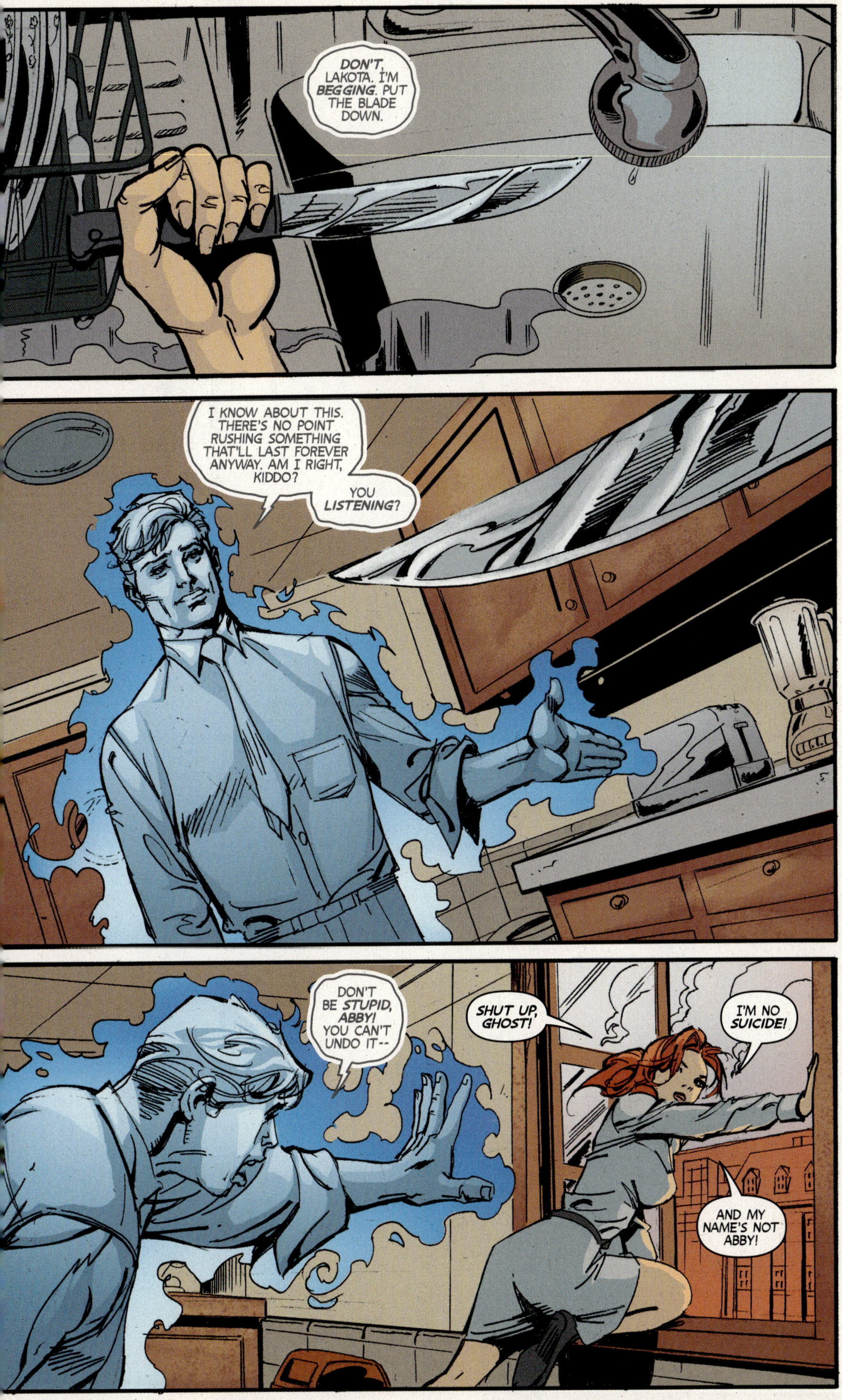
DON'T, LAKOTA. I'M BEGGING. PUT THE BLADE DOWN.
I KNOW ABOUT THIS. THERE'S NO POINT RUSHING SOMETHING THAT'LL LAST FOREVER ANYWAY. AM I RIGHT, KIDDO?
YOU LISTENING?
DON'T BE STUPID, ABBY! YOU CAN'T UNDO IT--
SHUT UP, GHOST!
I'M NO SUICIDE!
AND MY NAME'S NOT ABBY!

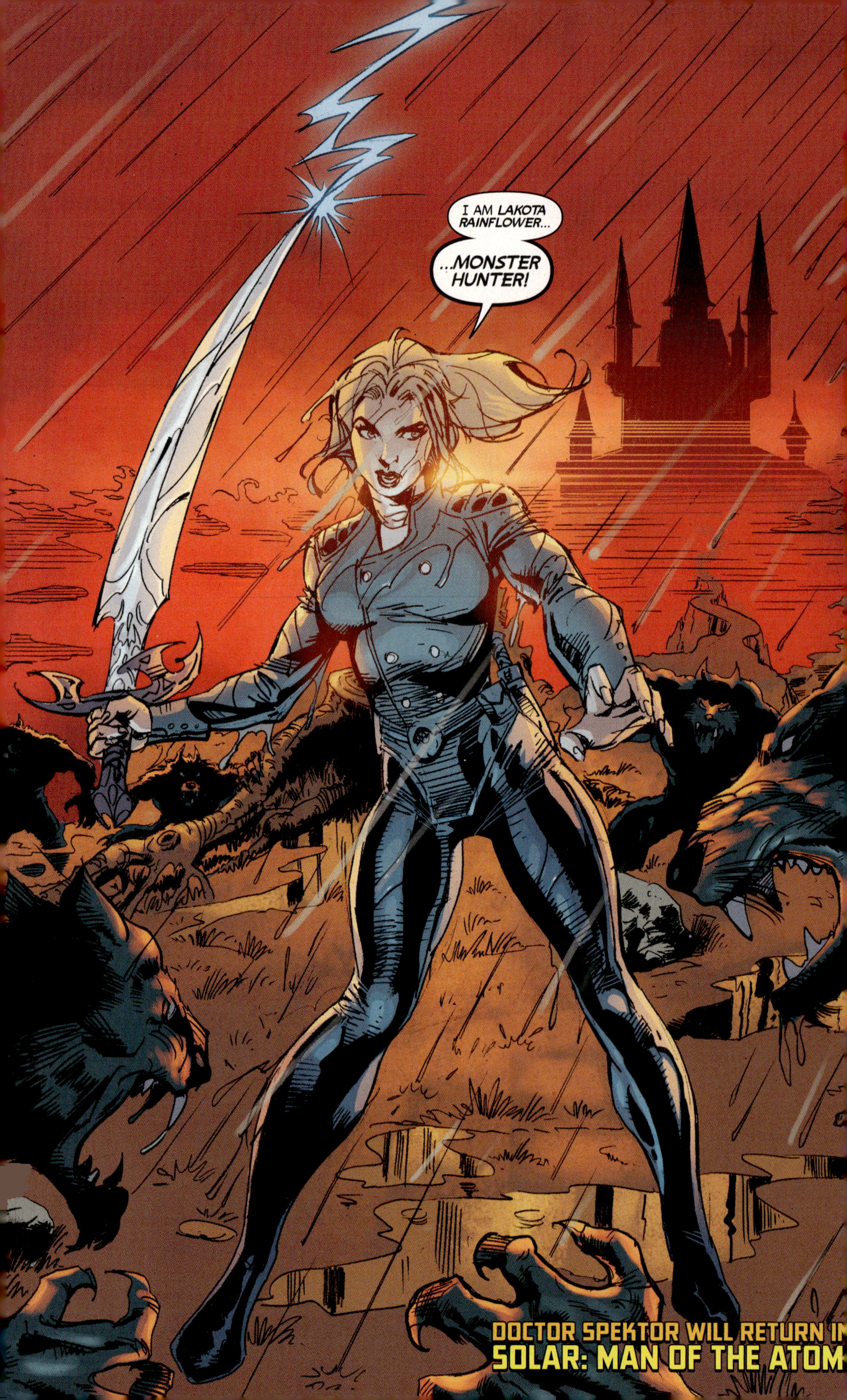
I AM LAKOTA RAINFLOWER...
...MONSTER HUNTER!
DOCTOR SPEKTOR WILL RETURN IN
SOLAR: MAN OF THE ATOM

BONUS MATERIAL

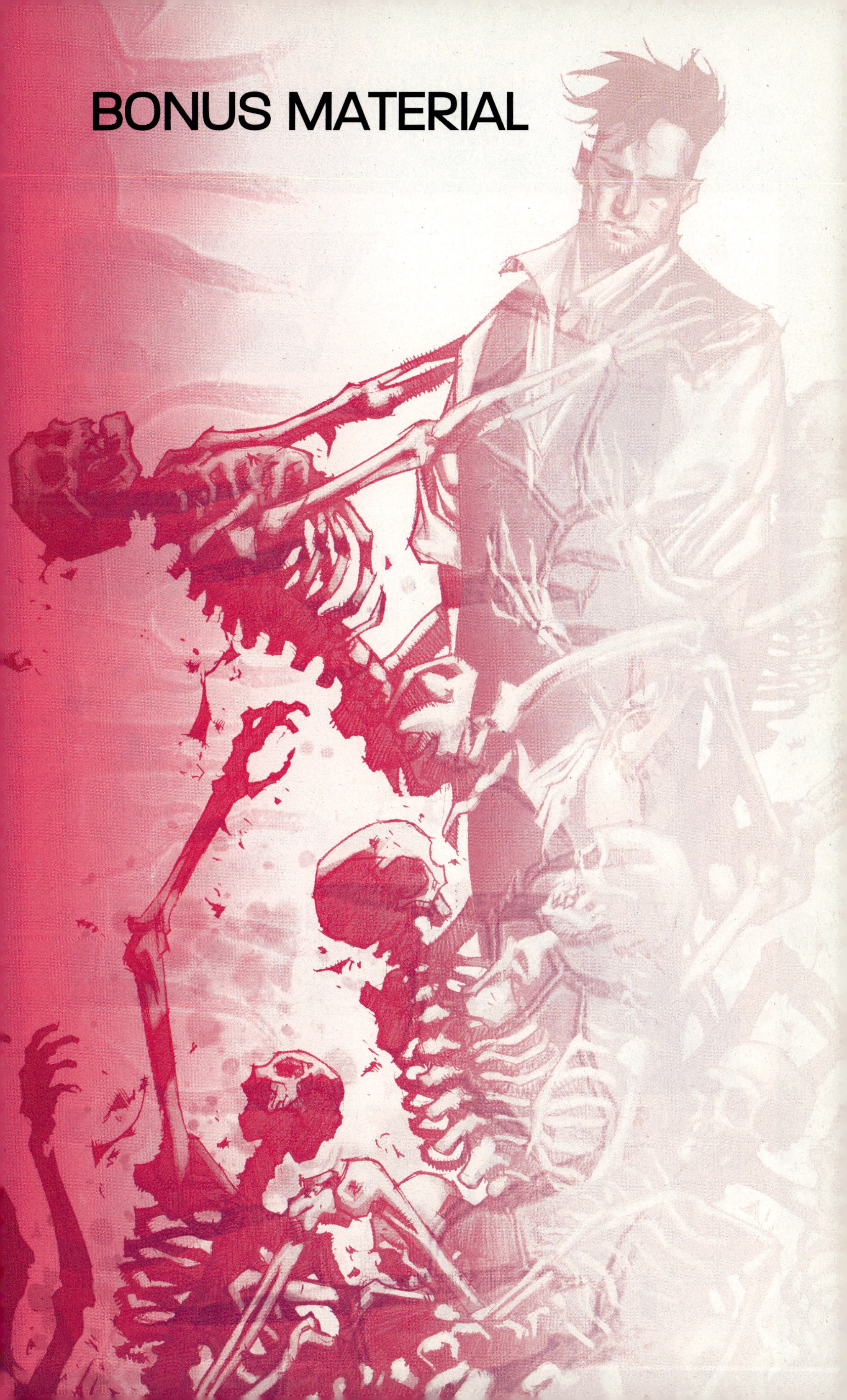

THE OCCULT FILES OF DOCTOR SPEKTOR #1

WRITTEN BY MARK WAID
EDITED BY NATE COSBY

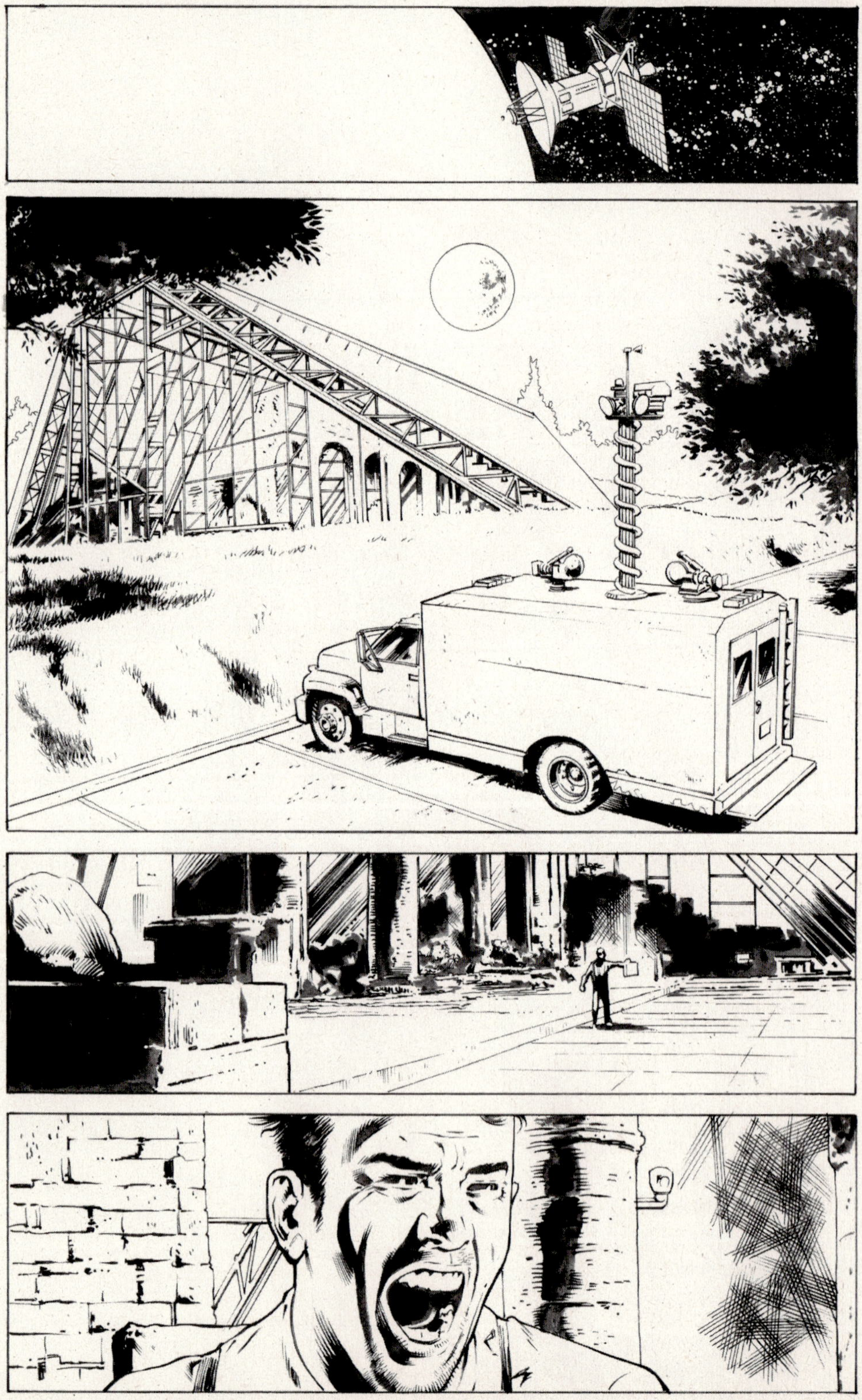

PAGE ONE

PANEL ONE: EARTH ORBIT. A BROADCAST SATELLITE MARKED WITH SPEKTOR'S CORPORATE LOGO.

TAILLESS/elec: Three...

BIG PANEL TWO: EXTERIOR, A CLEAR NIGHT. NORWAY'S HAMAR RUINS (http://bit.ly/13sm3Ez), A MODERN GLASS-AND-STEEL-FRAME STRUCTURE WRAPPED AROUND THE SURVIVING WALLS OF A 13TH CENTURY CATHEDRAL. THE INTERIOR IS LIT FAINTLY BY SECURITY LIGHTS.

    A SATELLITE BROADCAST VAN MARKED WITH SPEKTOR'S LOGO IS PARKED NEARBY.

TAILLESS/elec: ...two...

PANEL THREE: INSIDE THE GLASS STRUCTURE, A MYSTERIOUS FIGURE (DOCTOR SPEKTOR) HOLDS A CARRYING CASE. WE DON'T NEED TO SEE HIM TOO PROMINENTLY OR TOO CLEARLY.

TAILLESS/elec: ...ONE...

PANEL FOUR: INSIDE. SPEKTOR, YELLING DRAMATICALLY INTO A HEADSET MIC, POSED FOR ACTION. A SMALL BUT CONSPICUOUS VIDEO CAMERA IS MOUNTED ON THE WALL BEHIND HIM; HE HAS PLANTED SUCH CAMERAS THROUGHOUT THE FACILITY.

TAILLESS/elec: You're ON, Doctor.

SPEKTOR: I'm at the ruins of Norway's 13th Century HAMAR CATHEDRAL. My global pursuit of an ANCIENT EVIL ends HERE, with ITS death...or MINE.

SPEKTOR: RACKENHAM! VAMPIRE! SHOW YOURSELF!

PAGE TWO

PANEL ONE: INSIDE THE BROADCAST TRUCK. THREE PEOPLE:

    ENGINEER GRETA WISE, GEEK-WITH-GLASSES, WORKS THE CONTROL PANEL.

    PRODUCER LENNY CULLEN, FIFTYISH, EXPERIENCED, HARD-BITTEN AND SARCASTIC. THINK ED ASNER OR RIP TORN. HE LOOKS OVER GRETA'S SHOULDER AND GIVES AN ORDER.

    GRETA AND LENNY ARE WEARING HEADSETS.

ON-AIR PERSONALITY TED MOREHOUSE--AN ENERGETIC RYAN SEACREST CROSSED WITH A DEPRESSIVE HANK KINGSLEY--CHECKS HIS REFLECTION IN A MIRROR. (NOTE: IN THE PROPOSAL, TED WAS CALLED NESTOR GABEL, AN EVOCATIVE NAME THAT COULDN'T BE MORE WRONG FOR HIM.)

MONITORS SHOW THE CATHEDRAL RUIN INTERIOR, AND MAYBE A SHADOWY SUGGESTION OF SPEKTOR.

TAILLESS/elec: Ashamed to be seen, are you? I would be too, if I subsisted on the blood of the YOUNG and HELPLESS!

LENNY: That's our cue to raid the fridge. Give me Meghan, then Dara

PANEL TWO: TV SCREEN. SPEKTOR SHARES THE SCREEN WITH A GRAPHIC: A SNAPSHOT OF A SMILING TEN-YEAR OLD GIRL.

SPEKTOR/
ELECTRONIC: Like MEGHAN THOMS, abducted two days short of her ELEVENTH BIRTHDAY, then found drained of blood and viciously UNDEAD. She had to be NULLIFIED.

SPEKTOR/
ELECTRONIC: A parent's worst nightmare made impossibly WORSE.

PANEL THREE: TV SCREEN. SAME, EXCEPT A NEW GRAPHIC: A WEDDING RECEPTION SNAPSHOT OF A VERY HAPPY YOUNG BRIDE AND GROOM.

SPEKTOR/
ELECTRONIC: And DARA GULASKI, mother of an infant son, living the happiest time of her life, until...

SPEKTOR/
ELECTRONIC: ...until...

PANEL FOUR: BROADCAST TRUCK. ONSCREEN: SPEKTOR BURIES HIS FACE IN HIS HANDS. LENNY SNARLS AT THE IMAGE. TED GLANCES AWAY FROM HIS MIRROR TO ADMIRE SPEKTOR.

TAILLESS/elec: FORGIVE me. It's when I remember the VICTIMS that I KNOW destiny has set me on my truest path.

LENNY: What IS this, "The Bachelor"? Next he'll be blithering about "the journey."

TED: No, it's GOOD. It's IMPORTANT to show emotion!

PANEL FIVE: BACK IN THE CATHEDRAL. SPEKTOR, REACTING BRAVELY TO

AN EVIL PRESENCE.

SPEKTOR: I feel the cold gust of Rackenham's PRESENCE. It circles me, watching, waiting for its moment to strike.

SPEKTOR: It knows I am ARMED.

 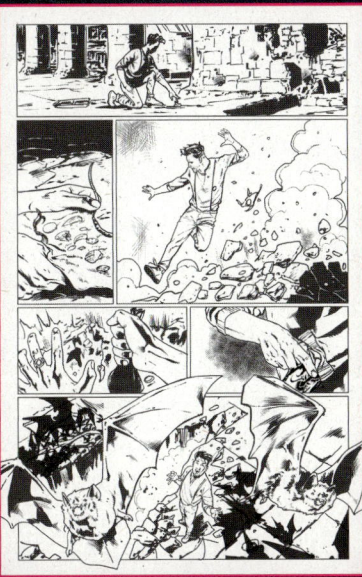 

PAGE THREE

PANEL ONE: SPEKTOR PULLS A SQUARE OF BLACK FABRIC FROM HIS CASE, WHICH WE CAN NOW SEE IS A TATTERED ANTIQUE VALISE.

SPEKTOR: Perhaps, like many viewers, the creature is familiar with THE ARCANE ARSENAL--

SPEKTOR: --my talisman collection valuated by Christie's at more than $100,000,000.

PANEL TWO: SPEKTOR UNFOLDS THE FABRIC ON THE FLOOR, REVEALING NEAT ROWS OF ATTACHED RELICS, LIKE A JEWELER'S DISPLAY. THERE ARE CARVINGS; A PIECE OF BONE; RELIGIOUS OBJECTS; A SMALL, FULL POUCH.

SPEKTOR: I brought with me some of the arsenal's most potent ANTI-VAMPIRE--

PANEL THREE: THE FLOOR OPENS UP! IT'S STARTING TO SWALLOW THE MOUNTED TALISMANS!

SFX: SKRAAK

SMALL PANEL FOUR: CLOSE-UP. SPEKTOR'S HAND SNATCHES THE SMALL POUCH AS THE OTHER TALISMANS FALL. (NOTE: SPEKTOR IS WEARING A SHOWY RING.)

SFX: KRAK

SFX: SKREE

SMALL PANEL FIVE: SPEKTOR SLIPS THE POUCH UP HIS SLEEVE.

SFX: REEE

PANEL SIX: BATS FLY UP THROUGH THE CREVICE, OVERWHELMING SPEKTOR.

SFX: SKREEEE

PAGE FOUR

HUGE PANEL ONE: THE BATS DISPERSE INTO VAPOR! THE VAPOR CARESSES RACKENHAM, A CLASSIC CHRISTOPHER LEE/DRACULA-STYLE VAMPIRE, WHO HOVERS MENACINGLY ABOVE THE OFF-BALANCE SPEKTOR!

PANEL TWO: INTERIOR TV TRUCK. ONSCREEN: THE SAME SHOT AS LAST PANEL, BUT THE VAMPIRE IS MISSING. TED SQUINTS DISAPPROVINGLY AT THE SCREEN. LENNY SCOWLS AND YELLS INTO HER HEADSET.

TED: Jesus! Can't you get a SHOT of it?

LENNY: How long have you worked here, Ted? Bloodsuckers don't PHOTOGRAPH, genius!

LENNY: DOC! MAKE-UP!

PANEL THREE: TIGHT ON SPEKTOR THUMBING OPEN HIS RING--

PANEL FOUR: --AND HE SHOOTS A BLAST OF WHITE PIGMENT FROM HIS RING, SOAKING THE VAMPIRE'S FACE AND CHEST.

SFX: TSSS-SS-SS

RACKENHAM: AAAH!

COPY OF PANEL 2
COPY OF PANEL 2

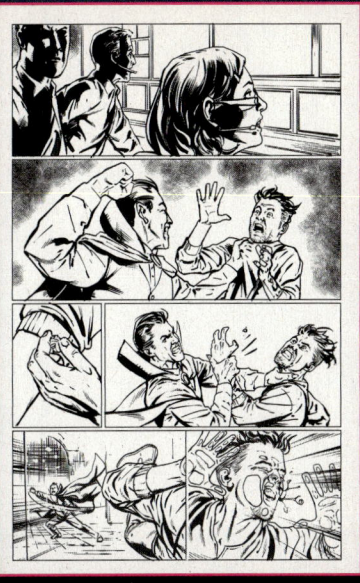

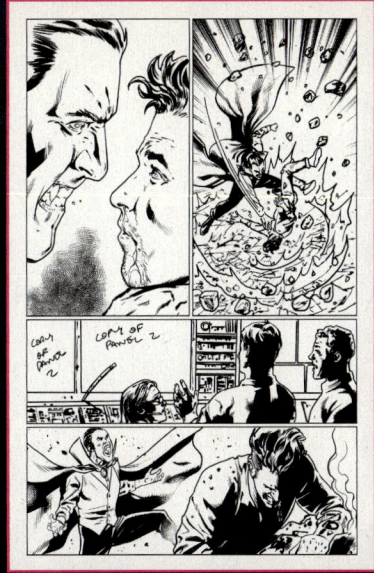

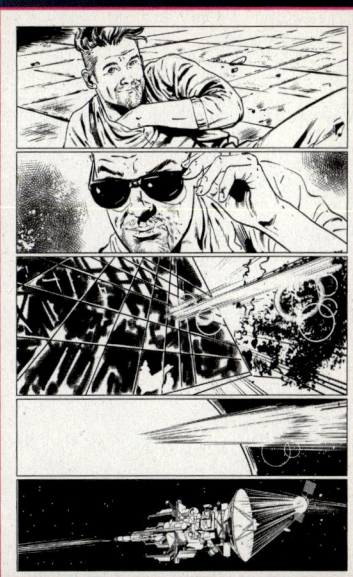

PAGE FIVE

PANEL ONE: TV TRUCK. LENNY, TED. TED FROWNS AT THE SCREEN, EMBARRASSED. ONSCREEN: THE ANGRY VAMPIRE--RATHER, THE PART OF HIM THAT'S SPLATTERED WITH PIGMENT--IS NOW VISIBLE.

TED/small: I knew that.

LENNY: Doc, MOVE!

PANEL TWO: FURIOUS RACKENHAM SNATCHES SPEKTOR AND ARCS TOWARD THE GLASS CEILING.

RACKHAM: THIS IS OVER! I KILL YOU NOW!

SMALL PANEL THREE: EXTREME CLOSE-UP. SPEKTOR FURTIVELY PULLS THE POUCH FROM HIS SLEEVE.

PANEL FOUR: SNARLING RACKENHAM SNAPS SPEKTOR'S WRIST. THE POUCH FALLS.

SFX: SKAKK

SPEKTOR: AAH!

PANEL FIVE: ANGRY RACKENHAM THROWS SPEKTOR AGAINST THE GLASS WALL!

SFX: KSSSHH

PAGE SIX

PANEL ONE: THE SNEERING VAMPIRE YANKS RAG-DOLL SPEKTOR BACK TOWARDS HIM BY THE THROAT.

RACKENHAM: TELL ME WHAT YOU HAD UP YOUR SLEEVE! TELL ME!

RACKENHAM: GARLIC?

SPEKTOR/weak: J=KOFF= Jade.

RACKENHAM: OH, OF COURSE! WHY GO CHEAP?

PANEL TWO: RACKENHAM FLINGS SPEKTOR TO THE GROUND.

RACKENHAM: The RICH MAN'S undead-repellent MUST be superior to the PEASANTS'!

PANEL THREE: TV TRUCK. LENNY, TED AND GRETA STARE AT THEIR SCREENS IN SHOCK! ONSCREEN: ANGRY RACKENHAM PICKS SPEKTOR UP AGAIN!

TAILLESS/ELEC: You're an arrogant FOOL, Spektor! I represent OLDER powers!

TAILLESS/elec: The power of SHADOWS!

TAILLESS/elec: The power of the GRAVE!

TAILLESS/elec: All YOU have are the toys your FORTUNE can buy!

PANEL FOUR, BIG: THE VAMPIRE LOOMS OVER SEEMINGLY DEFEATED SPEKTOR.

RACKENHAM: You cannot WIN by throwing MONEY at ME!

PAGE SEVEN

PANEL ONE: ANGLE FAVORING THE SHADOWY SPEKTOR, WHO SMILES WEAKLY AS A YELLOW LIGHT ILLUMINATES HIS JAW. HE'S PULLING SOMETHING FROM HIS BREAST POCKET.

SPEKTOR: Yeah?

PANEL TWO: GRINNING, SPEKTOR POPS ON A PAIR OF SUNGLASSES.

PANEL THREE: RACKENHAM LOOKS UP WARILY THROUGH THE GLASS TO SEE WHAT LOOKS LIKE A BRIGHT COMET ROCKETING DIRECTLY

TOWARDS HIM!

PANEL FOUR: WE BACKTRACK, FOLLOWING THE RAY OF LIGHT TO THE STRATOSPHERE--

PANEL FIVE: --AND TWO SPEKTOR-LOGO SATELLITES. ONE HAS A MIRROR-APPENDAGE THAT PASSES THE BEAM FROM THE OFF-PANEL SUN TO THE SECOND SATELLITE; THE SECOND SATELLITE REFLECTS THE BEAM DOWN TO EARTH.

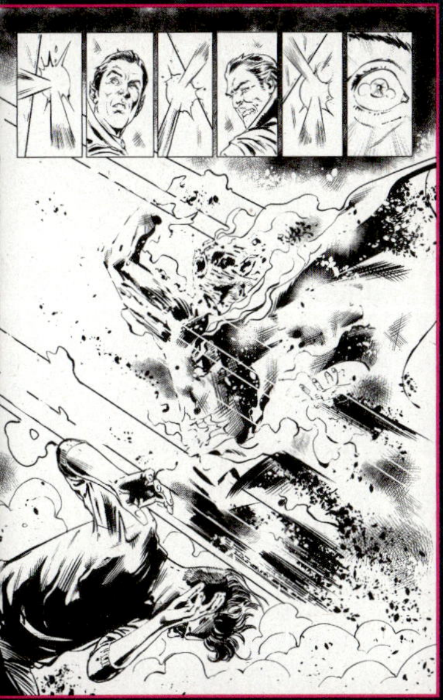

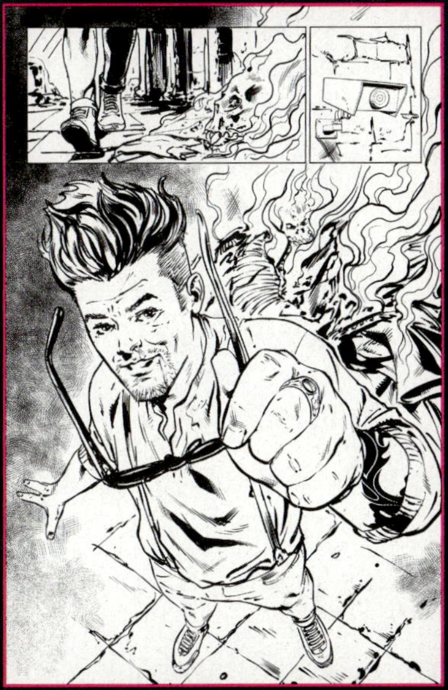

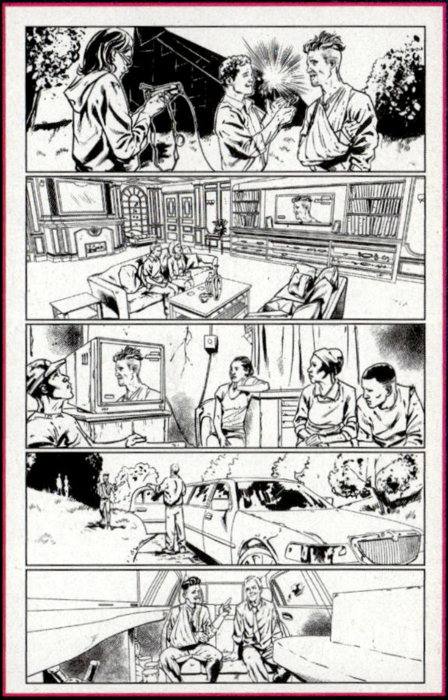

PAGE TEN

PANEL ONE: SOON AFTER. THE BANGED-UP DOC'S BROKEN WRIST HAS BEEN BANDAGED, AS HAVE SEVERAL CUTS. TED CHEERFULLY INTERVIEWS HIM ON CAMERA OUTSIDE THE RUIN. GRETA OPERATES A CAMERA WITH A BIG MICROPHONE ATTACHED.

TED: Long haul, Doctor Spektor, but you won. How does this victory stack up against past seasons?

SPEKTOR: Wouldn't want to live through "CITY OF WOLVES" or "LUNASAUR" again, Ted. But from now on I'll have to say RACKENHAM was the WORST.

PANEL TWO: THE FAMILY ROOM OF A MANSION. A HAPPY, WELL-OFF OLDER COUPLE WATCHES THIS INTERVIEW ON A MASSIVE TV; THEY LOOK LIKE MODELS FOR A STOCK PHOTOGRAPH IN AN AD FOR SOME PRESCRIPTION DRUG. ONSCREEN: CAMERA TIGHT ON TED AND SPEKTOR.

TED/Elec: Ratings held steady, which means your fans were with you every step of the way. Can you talk about the difference that made?

SPEKTOR/Elec: Huge. When you look a killer in the eyes, and it has the strength of TEN, and it's APPLYING that strength to your BONES...

PANEL THREE: A POOR FAMILY WATCHES THIS INTERVIEW ON A LITTLE TV ONSCREEN: A CLOSE-UP OF THE CHARMING DOCTOR SPEKTOR, POINTING AND LOOKING RIGHT INTO THE CAMERA.

ELECTRONIC: ...You need a deep source to draw from. And mine is knowing that YOU'RE out there pulling for ME.

ELECTRONIC: Seriously. It sounds like I'm sh=BEEP=ing you, but I'm not. Thank you ALL, and have a good night free from fear.

PANEL FOUR: A LITTLE WHILE LATER, BACK AT THE RUIN. SPEKTOR APPROACHES HIS CHAUFFERED STRETCH LIMO. A GRINNING LENNY HOLDS THE DOOR OPEN FOR HIM.

LENNY: How many VAMPIRES do we have to kill before the SATELLITE stunt earns out?

SPEKTOR: We'll get 'em ALL, Lenny. How'd I look?

LENNY: Like the great monster-hunting star you ARE, kid.

LENNY: Oh, just so you know, I sent for a crew to recover those precious TALISMANS you lost--

PANEL FIVE: BACK OF THE LIMO. LENNY AND SPEKTOR SMIRK.

SPEKTOR: Cheap copies. Forget it.

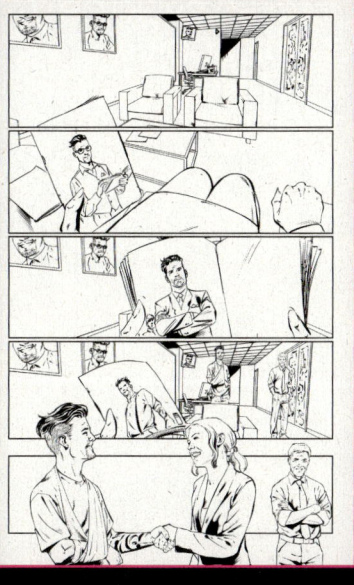

PAGE ELEVEN

PANEL ONE: SUBJECTIVE POV. THROUGH THE EYES OF <u>ABBY DODGE</u>, A WOMAN IN HER EARLY 20s, SITTING IN THE GRAND WAITING ROOM OF THE SPEKTOR EXECUTIVE SUITE AFTER A JOB INTERVIEW. ACROSS FROM US IS THE HUGE WOODEN DOOR TO SPEKTOR'S OFFICE, AN ANTIQUE RECOVERED FROM A MEDEIVAL CASTLE. NEXT TO THAT IS AN EMPTY DESK.

    A WALL-MOUNTED TV SHOWS AN AD FOR SPEKTOR'S TV SHOW. ONSCREEN, SPEKTOR IS SPEAKING TO THE CAMERA AGAINST A BACKDROP OF FOG. HE SMILES FAKE-SHEEPISHLY AND DISPLAYS HIS BANDAGED WRIST.

    WE--ABBY--ARE LOOKING THROUGH A FEW GLOSSY ANNUAL REPORTS FANNED OUT ON A TABLE. THE FIRST BEARS THE LOGO <u>SPEKTOR COMMUNICATIONS</u>, A PHOTO OF SPEKTOR AND THE HEADLINES:

HEADLINES:
- CABLE/SATELLITE
- STREAMING
- MOTION PICTURES
- PUBLISHING
- SOFTWARE
- MUSIC

TV/Elec: When "DOCTOR SPEKTOR: BRING 'EM BACK UNDEAD" returns in three weeks, I confront a SPIRITUALIST I hope is NOT strong enough to break my wrist.

LINKED: So we'll see you on the 27th for an episode we're calling--

PANEL TWO: ABBY'S SUBJECTIVE POV, LOOKING AT THE ANNUAL REPORT FOR SPEKTOR RESEARCH. ON ITS COVER, BESPECTACLED SPEKTOR LOOKS STUDIOUS POSING WITH A HUGE, OPEN, ANTIQUE BOOK.

    ONSCREEN: THE WORD "TRIAL" IN SMOKY LETTERING IS SUPERIMPOSED OVER SPEKTOR.

HEADLINES:
- PHYSICS
- CHEMISTRY
- METAPHYSICS
- ANTHROPOLOGY
- FOLKLORE
- FUTURISM

TV/Elec/off: "--THE TRIAL OF MADAME ROSE."

PANEL THREE: ABBY'S POV, LOOKING AT A PAGE HEADLINED SPEKTOR CAPITAL. SPEKTOR IN A SUIT AND HARDHAT POSING ON A FACTORY FLOOR WITH SMILING, MULTIRACIAL WORKERS. A REAL MITT ROMNEY SHOT.

HEADLINES:
- RETAIL & DINING
- FINANCIAL SERVICES
- INDUSTRIAL & ENERGY
- TECHNOLOGY & TELECOM

PANEL FOUR: ABBY'S POV; SHE LOOKS UP FROM THE COVER OF DOC, HIS FAN MAGAZINE, TO SEE SPEKTOR AND LENNY STARING AT HER AS THEY EMERGE FROM THE INNER OFFICE. SPEKTOR'S WRIST IS STILL BANDAGED TIL FURTHER NOTICE.

    THE MAGAZINE COVER HAS A BEEFCAKE SHOT OF SPEKTOR, AND THE HEADLINES:

HEADLINES:
- BEST EPISODES
- SCARIEST MONSTERS
- MOST POWERFUL TALISMANS
- WHAT'S NEXT

SPEKTOR: Abby Horne?

PANEL FIVE: OUR FIRST SUBJECTIVE VIEW. ABBY'S ON HER FEET,

THRILLED. SPEKTOR SHAKES HER HAND. LENNY GRINS AT HER.

SPEKTOR: CONGRATULATIONS, Abby. The job is yours.

ABBY: It IS? That's GREAT!

LENNY: How's it FEEL to be the mad doctor's newest HUNCHBACK?

PAGE TWELVE

PANEL ONE: TWO WEEKS LATER. ABBY--DRESSED IN DIFFERENT BUSINESS ATTIRE, NATCH--SITS AT THE FORMERLY VACANT DESK OUTSIDE SPEKTOR'S DOOR. THE SAME COMMERCIAL IS RUNNING ON THE TV SET. BORED ABBY RECITES ALONG WITH IT.

TV/Elec AND
ABBY/
Two tails: When "DOCTOR SPEKTOR: BRING 'EM BACK UNDEAD" returns next week, I confront a SPIRITUALIST I hope is NOT strong enough to break my wrist.

LINKED: So we'll see you on the 27th for an episode we're calling--

PANEL TWO: LENNY APPROACES. SHE MAKES A FACE AT HIM.

TV/Elec: "--THE TRIAL OF MADAME ROSE."

ABBY: She's just some old lady. Why go after HER?

LENNY: The BUDGET episodes make the Rackenhams and Lunasaurs POSSIBLE, kiddo. What's his MOOD?

PANEL THREE: BLAND ABBY, APPALLED LENNY.

ABBY: I don't know. He's not IN yet.

LENNY: He stayed HOME? And you LET him?

PANEL FOUR: LENNY PULLS ABBY BY THE WRIST TO THE EXIT.

ABBY: LET him? I'm not his BOSS.

LENNY: Bigger than THAT. You're his ASSISTANT. I hired you to TAKE CARE of him. When you TAKE CARE of someone, THEY don't call the SHOTS.

PANEL FIVE: CLOSE SHOT. CONFUSED ABBY, RESOLUTE LENNY.

ABBY: Where we going?

LENNY: To SAVE him.

PAGE THIRTEEN

PANEL ONE: EXTERIOR, SUNNY DAY. A MANHATTAN HIGH-RISE TOPPED WITH SOME SPEKTORISH, MAGICAL-MEDIEVAL DETAIL TO SET IT OFF FROM BORING SKYSCRAPERS; NOT DEVIL HORNS. MAYBE BAT WINGS. OR ODDLY SHAPED WINDOWS IN THE PENTHOUSE. ANYWAY...

ELECTRONIC: ...and after destroying his big, bad VAMPIRE, DOCTOR SPEKTOR wants to do what?

PANEL TWO: INTERIOR, SPEKTOR'S PENTHOUSE BEDROOM. THE CURTAINS ARE DRAWN. THE ONLY LIGHT COMES FROM THE TV, TUNED TO A TALK SHOW. SPEKTOR IS IN BED, TURNED AWAY FROM THE SCREEN HIS HEAD BURIED IN PILLOWS.

TV/Elec: Annihilate a little old psychic from Central Florida? From the high perch atop his media and financial empire?

PANEL THREE: CLOSE-UP. SPEKTOR, BETWEEN TWO PILLOWS. HIS EYES ARE SHUT TIGHT.

ELECTRONIC: Is it ME, or is Spektor becoming a BULLY?

ELECTRONIC: I disagree, Bill--

PANEL FOUR: AN ETHEREAL SHOT OF WHAT SPEKTOR SEES WITH HIS EYES CLOSED: BLACKNESS, AND THE FACE OF A WOMAN, OR SMEARED, OR BLURRED, OR SHADOWED OR TURNED AWAY FROM US--HOWEVER YOU ACCOMPLISH IT, HE CAN'T QUITE SEE HER.

ELECTRONIC: --after all Spektor's done, I think we can give him the benefit of the doubt on this. Besides--

PANEL FIVE: SAME AS PANEL THREE. SPEKTOR OPENS HIS EYES. HE'S SHEDDING TEARS.

ELECTRONIC: --I look forward to his snarky PUT-DOWNS.

PAGE FOURTEEN

PANEL ONE: INTERIOR, THE GLOOMY FRONT HALL OF SPEKTOR'S APARTMENT. THE DOOR OPENS IN; IT'S LENNY, FOLLOWED BY A NERVOUS ABBY.

THE WALLS OF THE CREEPILY-LIT HALL ARE DECORATED WITH MOUNTED MONSTER HEADS, LIKE HUNTING TROPHIES. A WEREWOLF, A VAMPIRE, A MUMMY, A LIZARD-MAN, WHATEVER.

ABBY/small: I STILL don't know what we're SAVING him from.

LENNY: Himself. And it's MY fault, kid. Not yours.

PANEL TWO: AS THEY CREEP ALONG THE DARK HALLWAY, ABBY LOOKS SIDELONG AT THE MONSTER MASKS. SHE'S GETTING A SERIOUS CASE OF THE CREEPS.

LENNY: I should have known after the RACKENHAM finale set the all-time goddamn RATINGS record, of all the stinking luck.

ABBY: Should have known WHAT?

PANEL THREE: CLOSE-UP OF LENNY. GENTLE CONCERN ON HIS FACE. HE LOVES SPEKTOR LIKE A SON.

LENNY: He SEEMS okay, kid, but there's something MISSING. Something he NEEDS. Whether he's IMAGINING that or not, he can still FEEL it.

LENNY: His SHRINK thinks he's just chasing down monsters 'til he finds one bad enough to kill the one that's EATING him.

PANEL FOUR: THEY PAUSE AT THE CLOSED DOOR OF SPEKTOR'S BEDROOM.

ABBY: I still don't get it. A MONSTER'S eating him?

LENNY: He's eating HIMSELF. See, every time America's sweetheart has one of his BIG SUCCESSES--

PANEL FIVE: LENNY GENTLY PUSHES THE DOOR OPEN. IN THE GLOOM, HE SEES THE CHAOS OF BEDDING THAT IS SPEKTOR.

LENNY/Small: --he IMPLODES.

LENNY: GOOD MORNING, DARLING! Time to greet the NEW DAY!

SPEKTOR: Nnhh.

PANEL SIX: NERVOUS ABBY'S POV. SPEKTOR SITS UP, BURYING HIS FACE IN HIS HANDS. LENNY PULLS A CURTAIN OPEN, LETTING IN BRIGHT SUNLIGHT.

SPEKTOR: They hate me.

LENNY: You wish. THAT, you could FACE.

SPEKTOR: I need her.

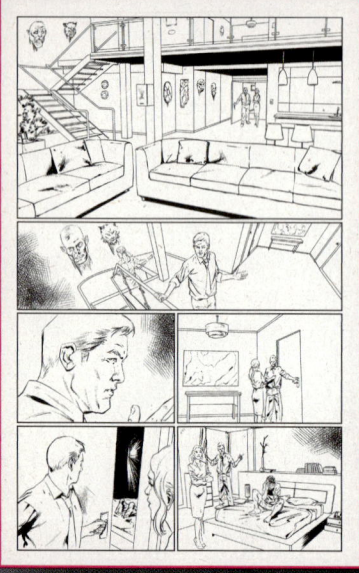  

PAGE FIFTEEN

PANEL ONE: IN FOREGROUND, SPEKTOR FURTIVELY PULLS A TALISMAN FROM UNDER HIS PILLOW. CONCERNED LENNY PLEADS WITH SPEKTOR; ABBY STANDS A LITTLE BEHIND LENNY, NOT KNOWING WHAT TO MAKE OF SPEKTOR.

LENNY: Oh, God.

LENNY: Adam, we've been THROUGH this. She's not REAL, buddy--

PANEL TWO: EXTERIOR, SIDEWALK. LENNY IS IN THE SAME POSE AS LAST PANEL; ABBY CRIES OUT IN ALARM. THEY'VE BEEN TELEPORTED.

ABBY: AAH!

LENNY: Oh, goddamn it!

ABBY: WHAT'S HAPPENING?

PANEL THREE: LENNY FEELS STUPID. ABBY IS VERY UPSET.

LENNY: TELEPORT talisman. He gave us the BUM'S RUSH, kid.

ABBY: What's going ON? Why's he such a BASKET CASE?

PANEL FOUR: THEY WALK. ABBY'S STILL WOUND UP. HE SCOLDS HER.

LENNY: Don't CALL him that. It's your PRIVILEGE to assist a great
                     man at his most VULNERABLE.

LENNY: He falls apart after a big success--like clockwork--because he
                     needs to SHARE it with someone.

ABBY: Like a THERAPIST?

LENNY: Someone in PARTICULAR.

PANEL FIVE: LENNY STOPS AND FACES ABBY. THE STORY HE'S TELLING IS SERIOUS.

LENNY: Only she doesn't EXIST. He says he almost SEES her when
                     he closes his eyes--but not QUITE.

LENNY: He has no actual MEMORY of this person. Just a FEELING.

LENNY: Just a HURT.

PANEL SIX: SPEKTOR'S DARKENED ROOM. HE'S ONCE AGAIN BURROWED INTO THE BEDDING. THE VAGUE FACE OF THE WOMAN IS SUPERIMPOSED OVER THE SCENE.

PAGE SIXTEEN

PANEL ONE: INTERIOR, TV STUDIO, SPEKTOR'S TALK SHOW. HE AND MADAME ROSE SIT AT A TABLE IN FRONT OF A SPEKTOR-LOGO BACKDROP. ROSE IS A CLASSIC, STEREOTYPE-EMBRACING SPIRITUALIST OF THE MARIA OUSPENSKAYA SCHOOL; ORDINARILY, SHE'D BE IN A CIRCUS TENT USING A CRYSTAL BALL TO FORETELL LISA SIMPSON'S FUTURE. A MAKEUP ARTIST GIVES HER A FINAL DAB.

       A SMILING LENNY, WEARING A HEADSET AND HOLDING AN iPAD, GIVES SPEKTOR A DOSE OF PRE-SHOW ENCOURAGEMENT. SPEKTOR GREETS HIM SHEEPISHLY.

       ABBY WATCHES A MONITOR; IF WE SEE THE SCREEN, AND WE DON'T HAVE TO, IT'S A LIVE SHOT OF SPEKTOR AND MADAME ROSE.

LENNY: Hello, gorgeous! Don't YOU look like a million bucks!

SPEKTOR: Thanks. Work makes all the difference. Hey, I'm really
                     SORRY about the telepor--

LENNY: PAST HISTORY, kid! And on a related note, I'm loving the new Audi, thanks!

PANEL TWO: REVERSE ANGLE. LENNY BACKS AWAY. SPEKTOR GAZES AT ABBY, WHO'S IGNORING HIM. THE FLOOR DIRECTOR GIVES SPEKTOR THE COUNTDOWN 'TIL AIR.

SPEKTOR: Good. I guess Abby likes hers, too. We haven't heard from her lawyer, right?

LENNY: Very funny. Now clear your mind of everything but the leg I want you to break.

DIRECTOR: Three...two...one...

PANEL THREE: SPEKTOR SPEAKS TO THE CAMERA, EXUDING CHARM.

SPEKTOR: Tonight: we're live with MADAME ROSE, a spiritualist. That's someone who talks to DEAD PEOPLE, like DR. DOOLITTLE talks to ALPACAS.

SPEKTOR: Over the last thirty years, she's built a nice career scamming the bereaved. After tonight, she'll need to hire a spiritualist to TALK to that career.

PANEL FOUR: SPEKTOR SPEAKS MOCKINGLY TO MADAME ROSE. SHE SCOWLS.

SPEKTOR: Now, Madame, you accepted quite a handsome payment to be with us tonight, knowing that I intend to destroy your reputation on live TV.

SPEKTOR: Is money THAT irresistible?

PANEL FIVE: ANGLE FAVORING MADAME ROSE. SHE'S NOT SEEING THE HUMOR.

MADAME: No, no, no. My VISIONS are irresistible.

SPEKTOR: I'll be the judge of that. Lay some ON me.

PAGE SEVENTEEN

THREE SMALL PANELS, FOLLOWED BY A TWO-THIRDS SPLASH.

PANEL ONE: MADAME ROSE COVERS HER EYES WITH A VEIL AND ASSUMES A POSE OF GREAT CONCENTRATION. SPEKTOR GRINS AT THE CAMERA.

MADAME: The departed, they live in a place beyond time. Past, future, alternate presents--all the same to them.
MADAME: These revelations are their gift to me. To the world THROUGH me.

SPEKTOR: Are we getting to some actual visions soon? Because so far, all I'm hearing is your eHarmony profile.

PANEL TWO: ANGLE FAVORING THE SMIRKING SPEKTOR. MADAME ROSE APPEARS TO BE IN DEEP CONCENTRATION, OR A TRANCE.

MADAME/weakly: A boy warrior guts a fallen spinosaurus...

SPEKTOR: As one would. IF the earth were 4,000 years old.
MADAME/weakly: A rebel fighter plunges his fist into an oppressor's torso...pulls out sizzling wires...

PANEL THREE: CLOSER STILL ON THE SMIRKING SPEKTOR. REALLY PLEASED WITH HIMSELF.

SPEKTOR: You have a violent imagination.

MADAME/Off/
Weak: The sun cremates a living man...and replaces his body...with itself...

SPEKTOR: Now THAT just sounds--

TWO-THIRDS SPLASH: PULL BACK. SPEKTOR IS GAPING, STUNNED TO SEE THE STOIC MADAME ROSE'S VISIONS MANIFEST IN THE STUDIO.

A FUTURISTIC MACHINE--PERHAPS THE CENTRAL UNIT OF AN ENERGY-RESEARCH LAB--CONTAINS A BURST OF ENERGY VISIBLE THROUGH CLEAR SHIELDING.

SOLAR (ERICA SELESKI, IN COSTUME), TUROK AND MAGNUS SOUNDLESSLY SHOUT A DESPERATE WARNING AT SPEKTOR.

THE SHADOW OF A PTERODACTYL FALLS FROM ABOVE.

A VILLAINOUS ROBOT FROM THE MAGNUS SERIES--ITS CHEST OPEN, TUBES FLAILING, LUBRICANT SPLASHING--STRUGGLES TO ITS FEET. RAZORS PROTRUDE FROM ITS FINGERS.

SPEKTOR'S TV CREW BEHAVES AS THOUGH EVERYTHING IS NORMAL; ONLY SPEKTOR SEES THE VISION.

PAGE EIGHTEEN

PANEL ONE: THE FATALLY WOUNDED ROBOT LURCHES TOWARD SPEKTOR MADAME ROSE CRIES OUT A WARNING.

SPEKTOR: Okay, STOP it. Can you STOP it? CLEARLY I was WRONG. You have a POWER.

MADAME: YOU see them, TOO! That has never HAPPENED. Your sensitivity is--

MADAME: CAREFUL! DO NOT LET THEM TOUCH--!

PANEL TWO: LENNY'S POV, NO VISIONS VISIBLE. DOCTOR SPEKTOR CRIES OUT IN AGONY, SEEMINGLY REACTING TO NOTHING; A BLOODY SLASH APPEARS UP AND DOWN HIS SLEEVE. LENNY RUSHES TOWARD HIM.

SPEKTOR: AAAH!

LENNY: DOC!

PANEL THREE: THE VISIONS ARE AGAIN VISIBLE TO US. THE ROBOT THAT JUST SLASHED SPEKTOR NOW RUNS LENNY THROUGH WITH A BLADE, KILLING HIM INSTANTLY.

SPEKTOR SEEMS TO BE LOOKING ON IN ALARM, BUT WE'LL LEARN THAT HE'S SEEING SOMETHING EVEN MORE COMPELLING IN THE DISTANCE PAST LENNY.

LENNY: DOC, What--

LENNY: =HKKK--*=

PANEL FOUR: REVERSE ANGLE. SPEKTOR IS FLABBERGASTED TO SEE A YOUNG MAN AND WOMAN, OBLIVIOUS TO THE DISASTROUS SURROUNDINGS AND AT EASE. THE WOMAN IS THE ONE FROM SPEKTOR'S VISIONS-- THE WOMAN WHO DOESN'T EXIST, BUT SHOULD! [TUROK, SOLAR AND MAGNUS ARE GONE.]

LENNY/Off: DOC!

SMALL PANEL FIVE: CLOSE-UP: FLABBERGASTED SPEKTOR, GAZING AT THE OFF-PANEL WOMAN.

SPEKTOR: You.

PAGE NINETEEN

PANEL ONE: THE ROBOT RAISES ITS BLOODY CLAW, MENACING ABBY. ITS OPEN CHEST IS SIZZLING AND SPUTTERING. ABBY CRIES OUT.

ABBY: DON'T!

ABBY/Big: PLEASE!

ABBY/Bigger: DOC!

PANEL TWO: THE ROBOT DROPS DEAD. ABBY STEPS BACK, SHAKEN.

ABBY/Small: Help...

PANEL THREE: SPEKTOR LUNGES AT THE MYSTERY WOMAN, TOUCHING HER! ABBY LOOKS ON IN ALARM!

ABBY: NO!

HUGE PANEL FOUR: REALITY EXPLODES! A HUGE DISCHARGE OF ENERGY! THE ROBOT AND THE ENERGY DEVICE BREAK INTO DISSOLVING FRAGMENTS! SPEKTOR AND THE WOMAN AND ABBY AND LENNY AND THE CREW CRY OUT IN AGONY!

SFX/Big: WHAROOMOORAHW

PAGE TWENTY

PANEL ONE: A SUDDEN CALM AFTER THE STORM! THE APPARITIONS ARE GONE! SPEKTOR STARES, HEARTBROKEN, AT THE EMPTY SPACE WHERE THE WOMAN STOOD!

SPEKTOR: The WOMAN...! Where--where IS she?

SPEKTOR: Madame Rose, TELL me! WHERE DID SHE GO?

OFF: She's not answering, Doctor.

PANEL TWO: TO HIS HORROR, SPEKTOR SEES THAT MADAME ROSE IS DEAD IN HER SEAT! THE FLOOR DIRECTOR KNEELS NEXT TO HER, IS TAKING HER NECK PULSE AND WRIST PULSE, SOLEMNLY.

DIRECTOR: Must have had a heart attack or something. GET ME THAT DEFIB IN THE BREAK ROOM--!

OFF: Doctor--

PANEL THREE: SPEKTOR TURNS TO SEE A CRYING ABBY, CRADLING LENNY'S CORPSE!

ABBY: Look.

ABBY: Lenny.

PANEL FOUR: SPEKTOR CROUCHES, GENTLY BRUSHES THE BACKS OF HIS FINGERTIPS AGAINST LENNY'S CHEEK. SPEKTOR'S HORRIFIED. TEARS STING HIS EYES. ABBY IS SOBBING.

SPEKTOR: No...

PAGE TWENTY-ONE

PANEL ONE: SPEKTOR LOOKS UP TO SEE THE MYSTERY WOMAN AND HER YOUNG MAN, ALL GHOSTLY AND TRANSPARENT, WALKING CALMLY

TO THE EXIT. STILL CRADLING LENNY, ABBY GLOWERS AT HIM.

SPEKTOR: She's LEAVING.

SPEKTOR: I have to go.

ABBY: Doctor, NO!

PANEL TWO: SPEKTOR HEADS TO THE EXIT. ABBY BITTERLY CALLS AFTER HIM.

SPEKTOR: I can't let her get away! You have to understand.

ABBY: He tried to SAVE you!

PANEL THREE: FRAMED BY THE DOOR, SPEKTOR TURNS AND DARKLY APOLOGIZES.

SPEKTOR: I'm sorry.

PANEL FOUR: ABBY CRADLES LENNY AND SOBS WITH ANGER.

ABBY: After all you DID for him. All the things. He--

ABBY/Small: He only cares about himself.

OFF: It doesn't MATTER.

PAGE TWENTY-TWO

PANEL ONE: ABBY LOOKS UP TO SEE--LENNY'S TRANSLUCENT GHOST! HE SPEAKS TO HER GENTLY.

ABBY: What?

LENNY: I said it doesn't MATTER. Go AFTER him.

ABBY: Lenny?

PANEL TWO: CLOSE-UP OF LENNY. KIND AND BEATIFIC AND TRANSLUCENT, LIKE THE GHOST OF OBI-WAN KENOBI.

LENNY: Don't worry about ME, kid. It's too LATE. Look after the DOC.

ABBY/Off: What? NO! After how he treated YOU?

LENNY: He NEEDS you. And it's what I WANT. Honest.

ABBY/Off: But--

PANEL THREE: THE GHOST OF LENNY YELLS AT HER. SHE SCRAMBLES TO HER FEET.

LENNY: FOR GOD'S SAKES, ABBY! DO THE DAMN JOB I HIRED YOU FOR!

PANEL FOUR: ABBY RUNS TO THE EXIT.

ABBY: DOCTOR!

ABBY/Big: WAIT!

BLURB: NEXT: GHOST WORLD

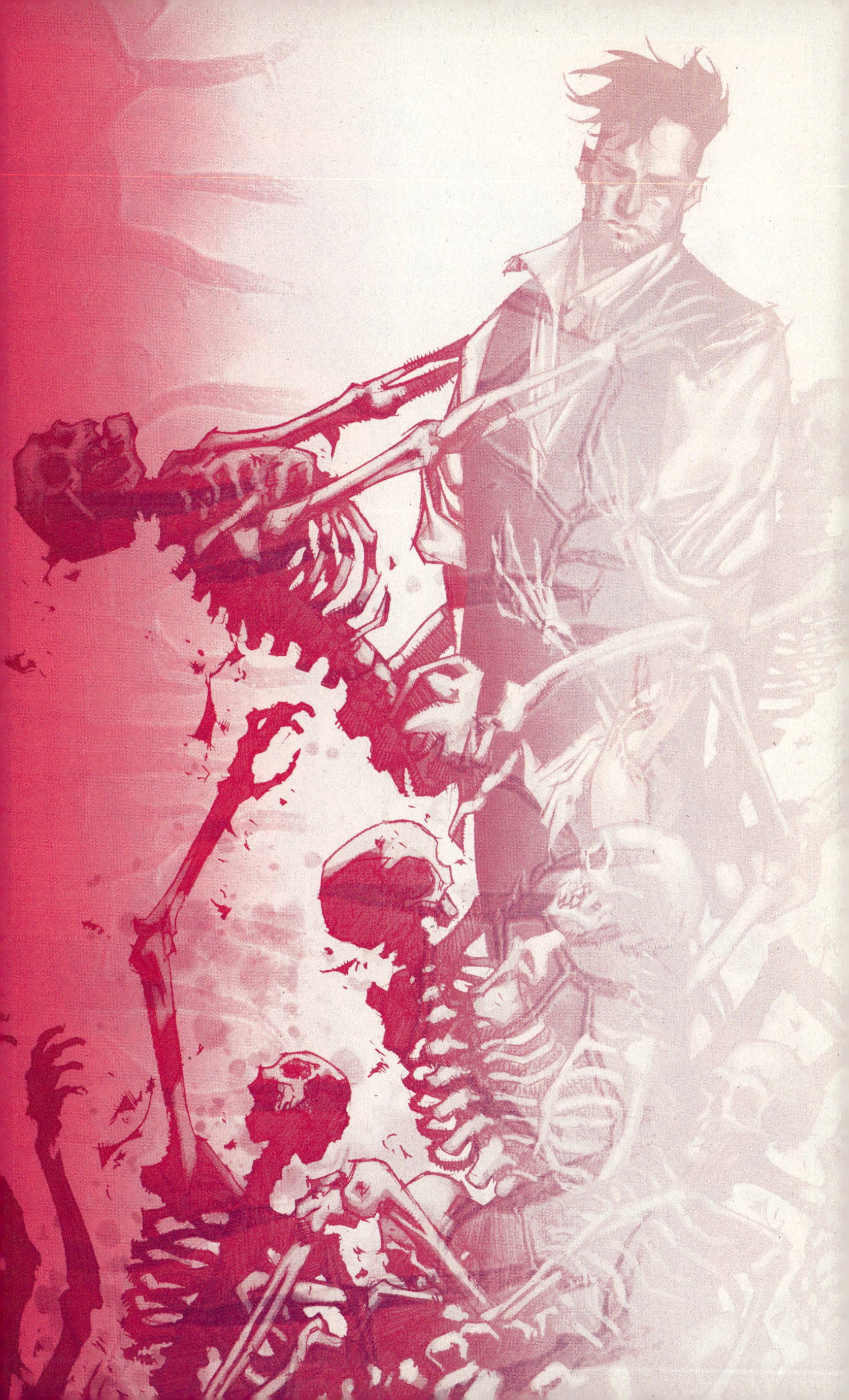

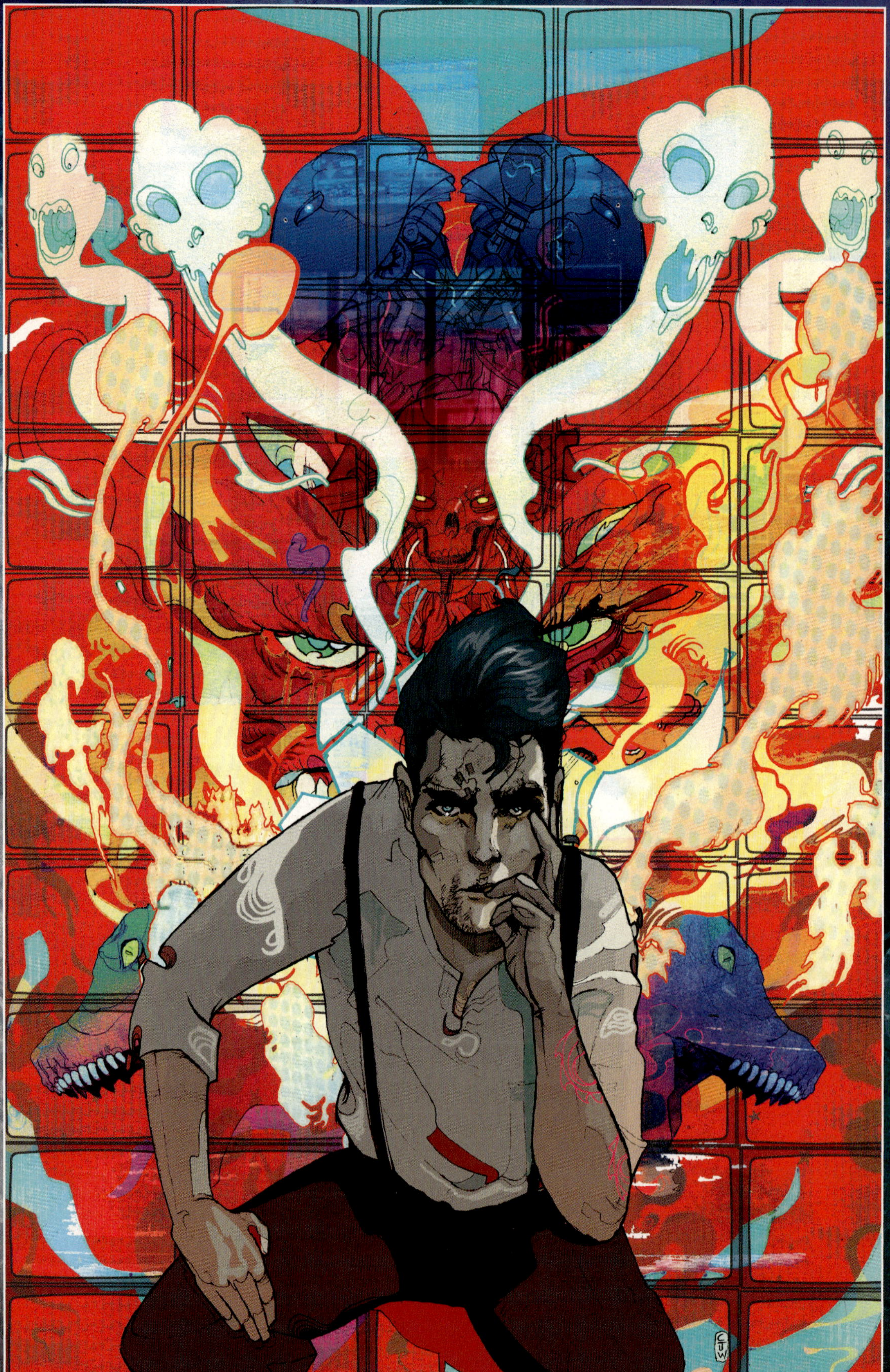

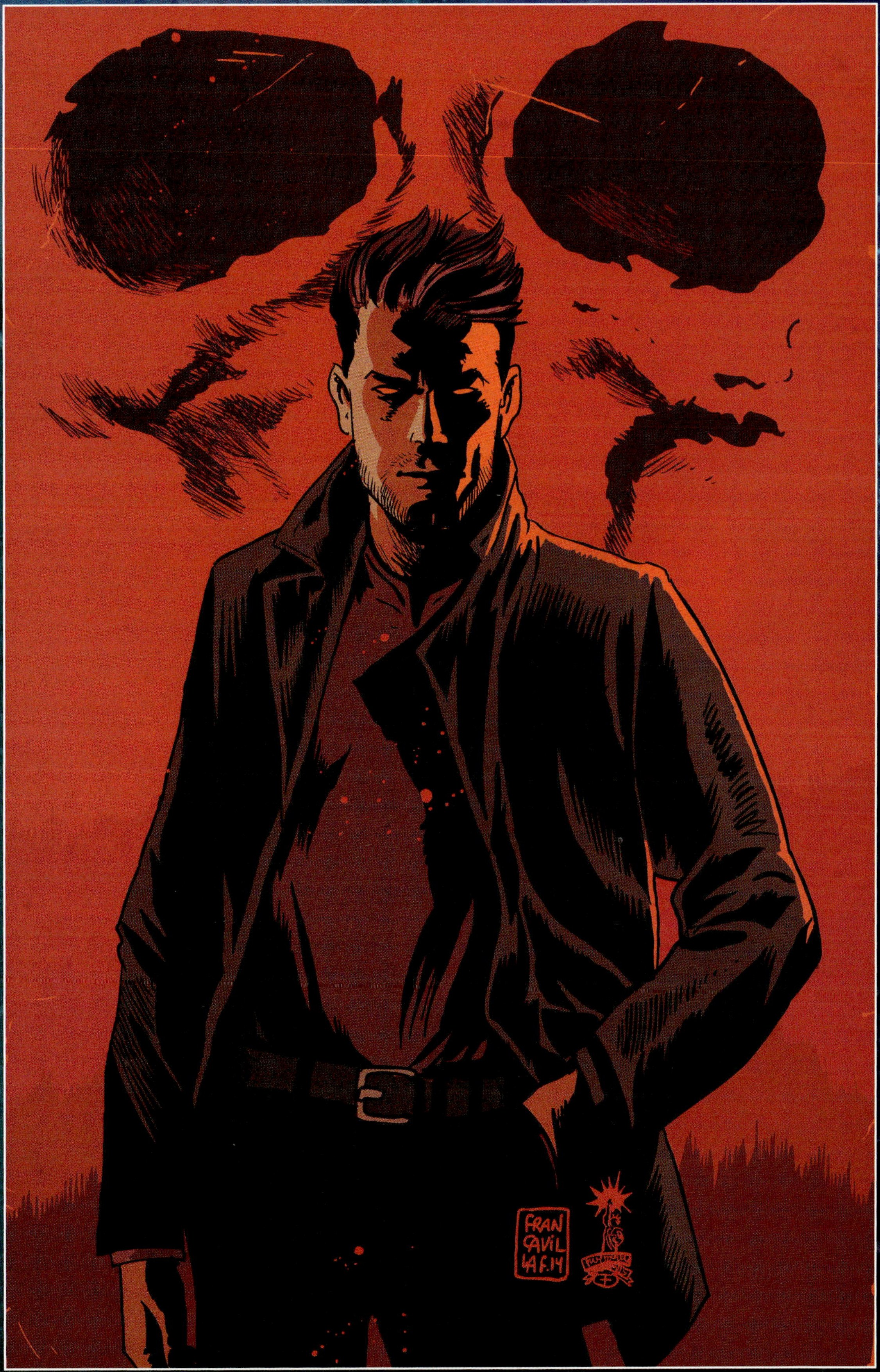
FRAN
CAVIL
LA F.14

issue #1 cover by FRANCESCO FRANCAVILLA

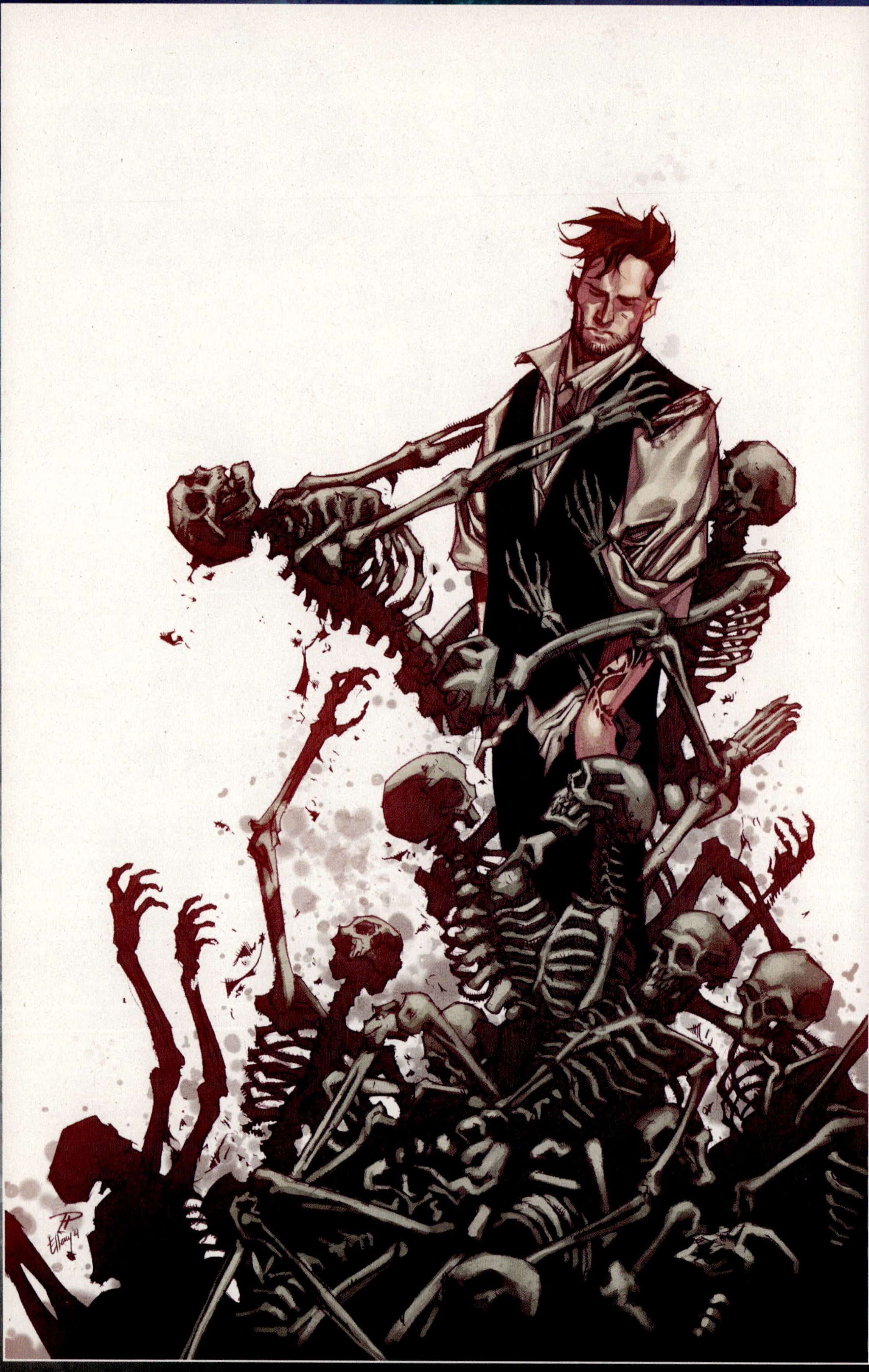

issue #1 cover by PHIL HESTER

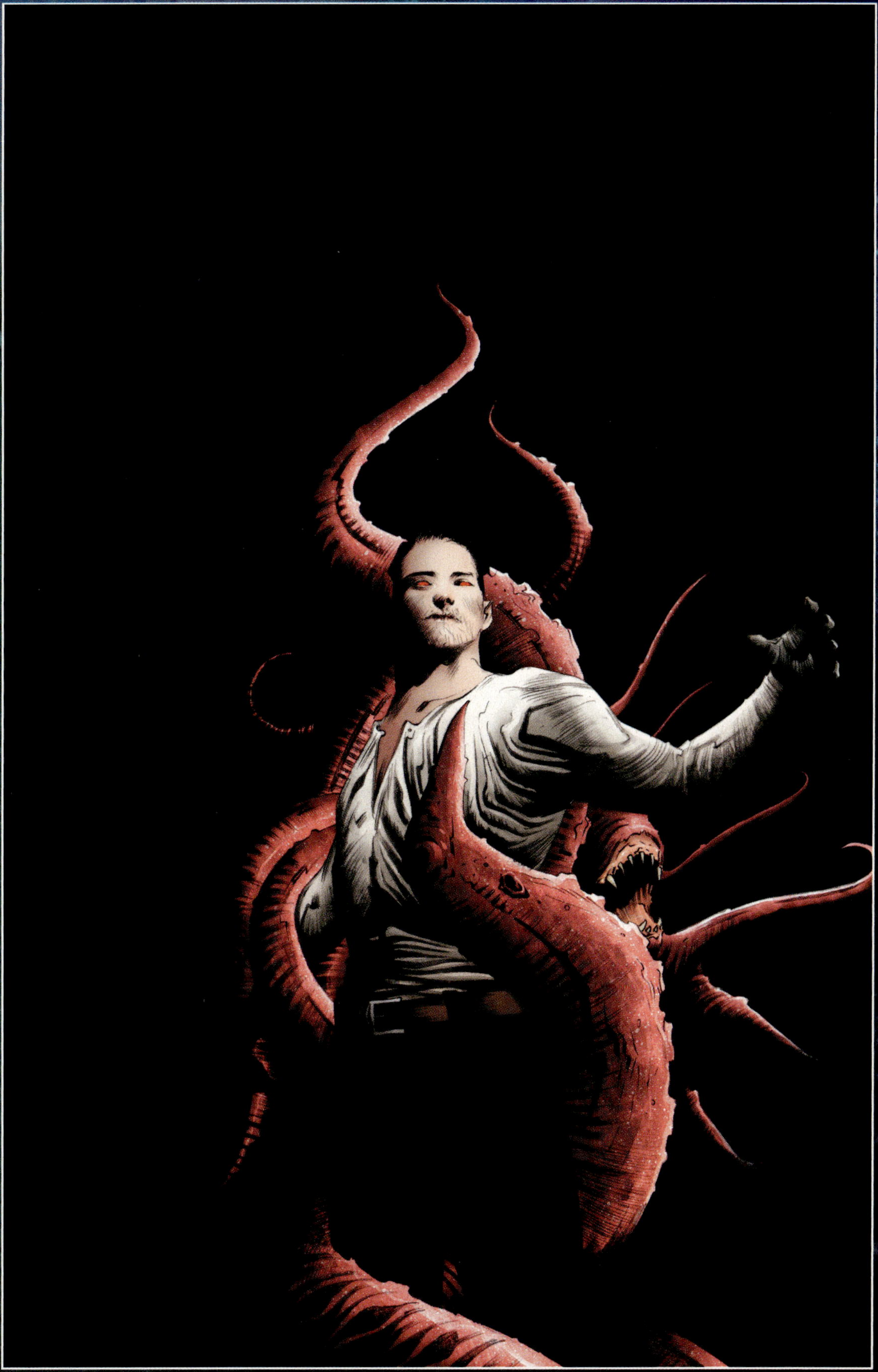

issue #1 cover by JAE LEE
colors by JUNE CHUNG

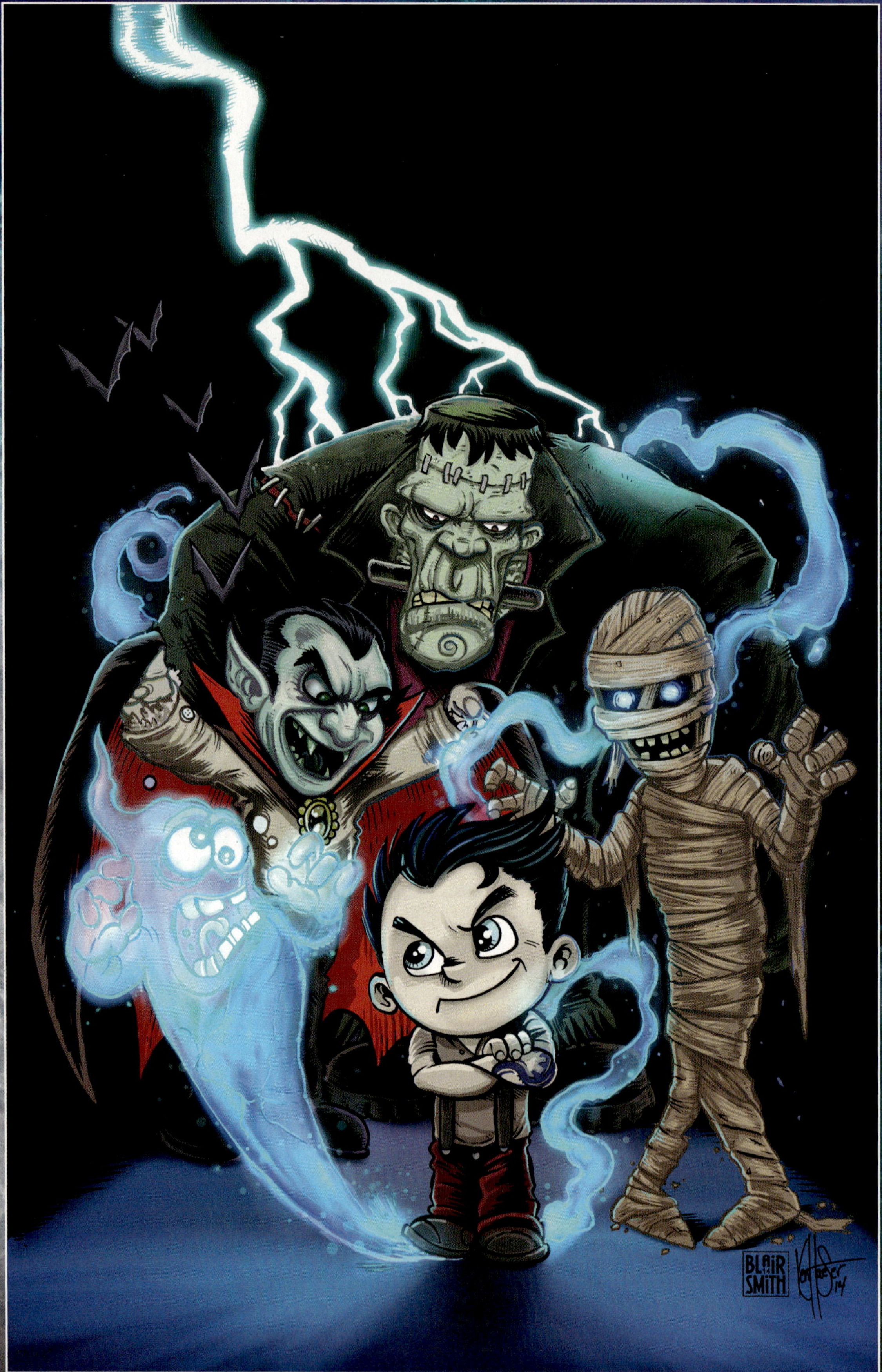
BLAIR SMITH

issue #1 cover by KEN HAESER

colors by BLAIR SMITH

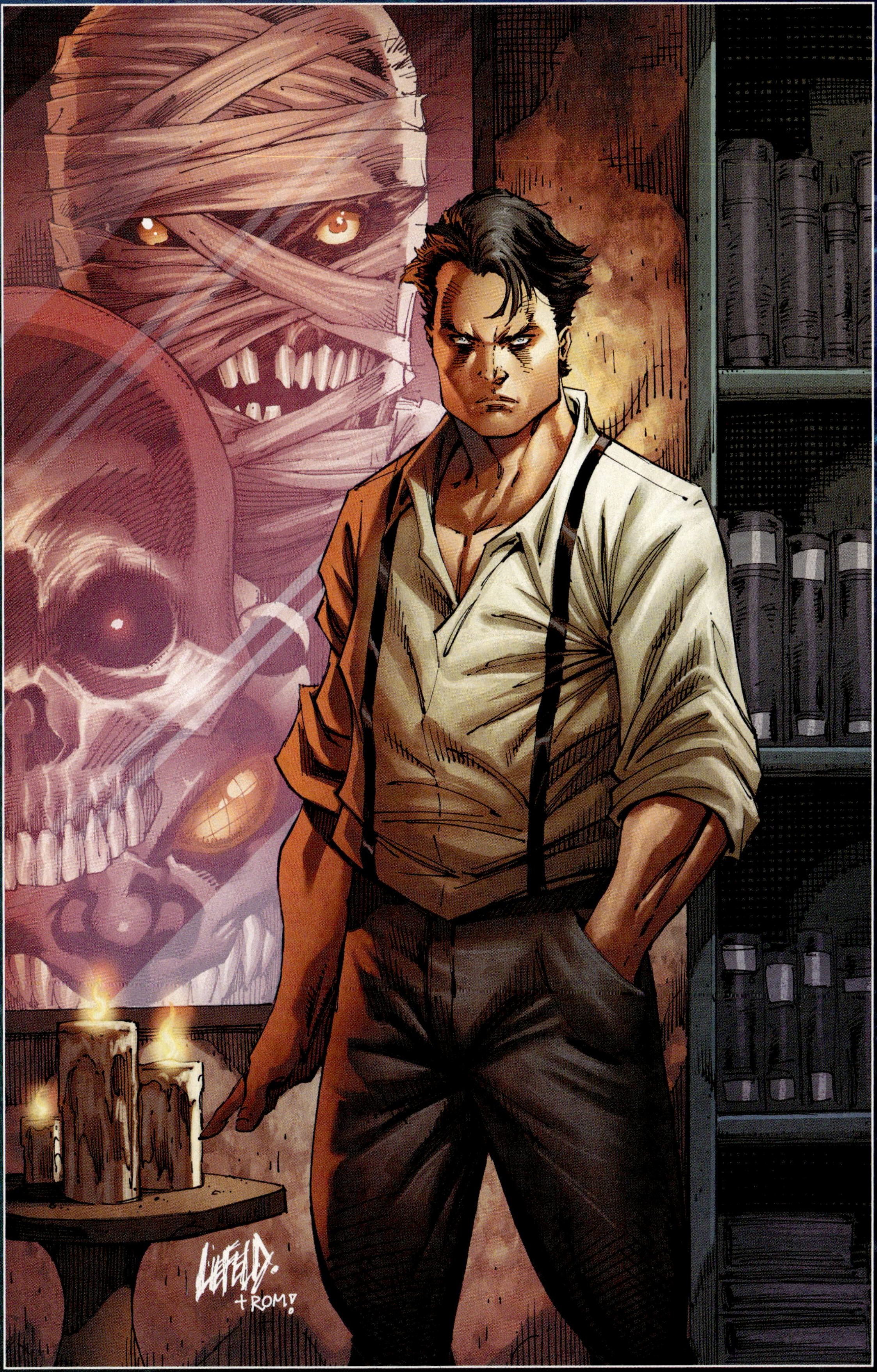

issue #1 cover by ROB LIEFELD
colors by ANDY TROY

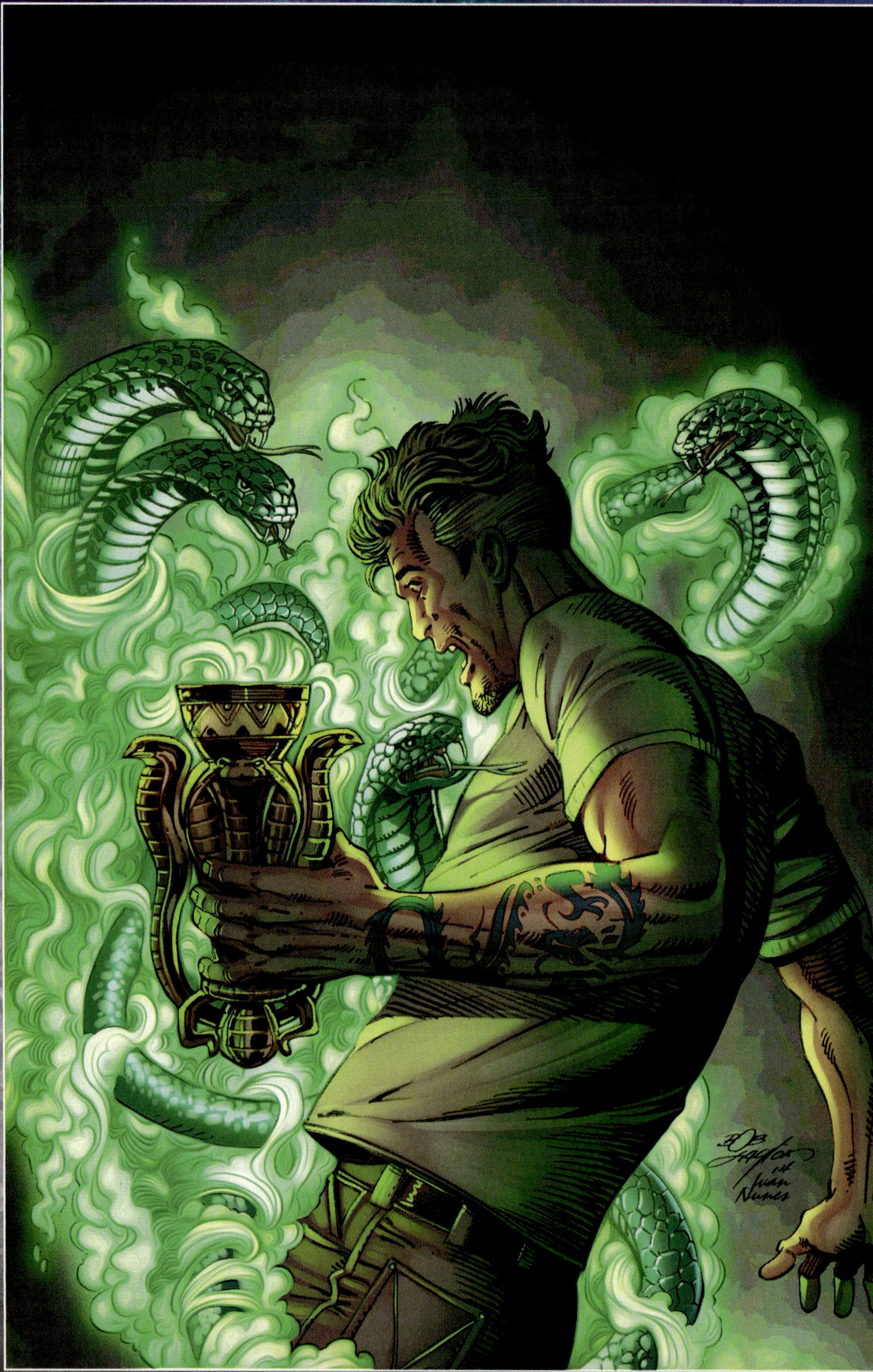
Bob Layton
Ivan Nunes

issue #1 cover by BOB LAYTON
colors by IVAN NUNES

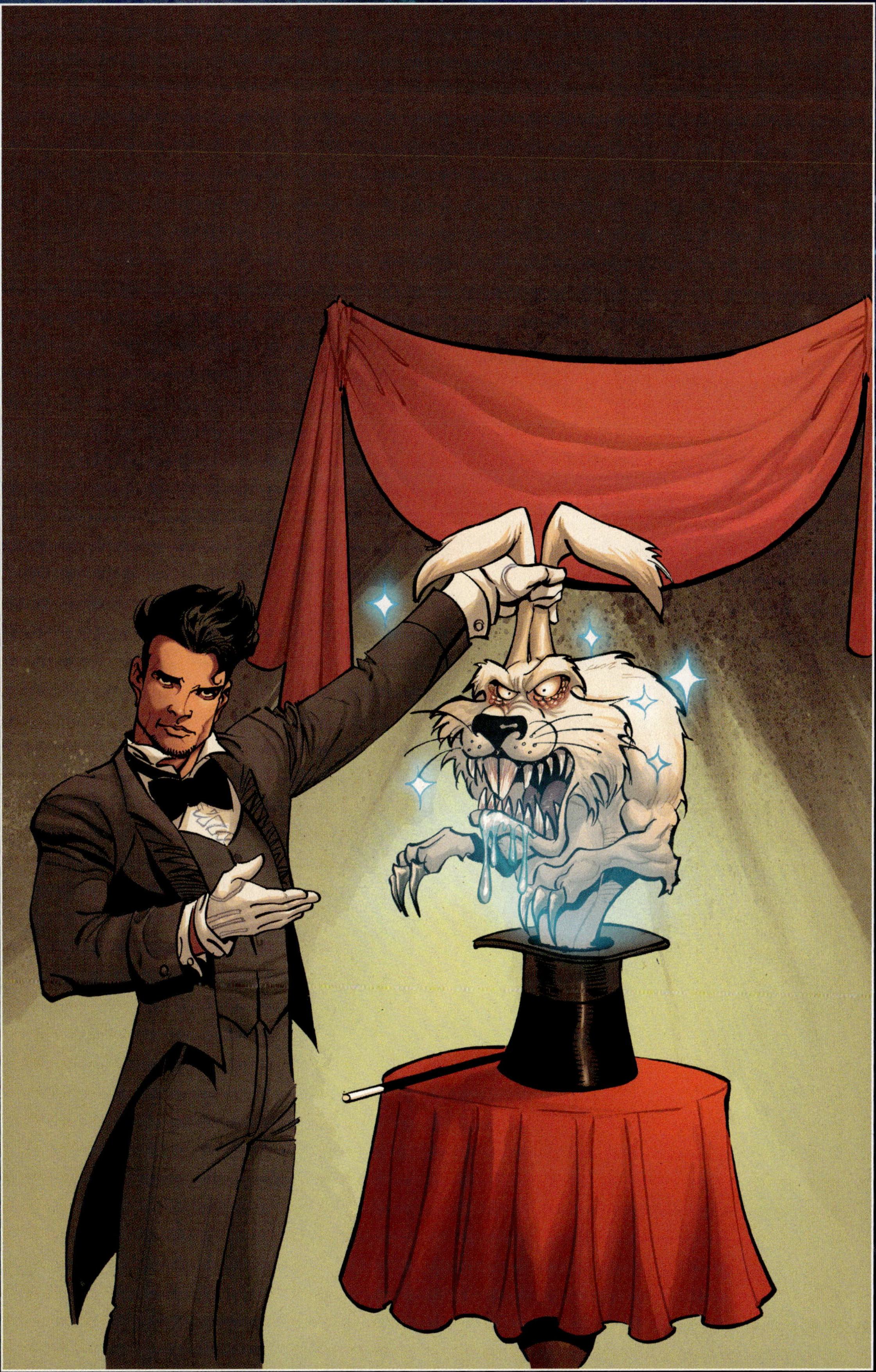

issue #1 "retailer heroic exclusive" cover by ROBERTO CASTRO
colors by ADRIANO LUCAS

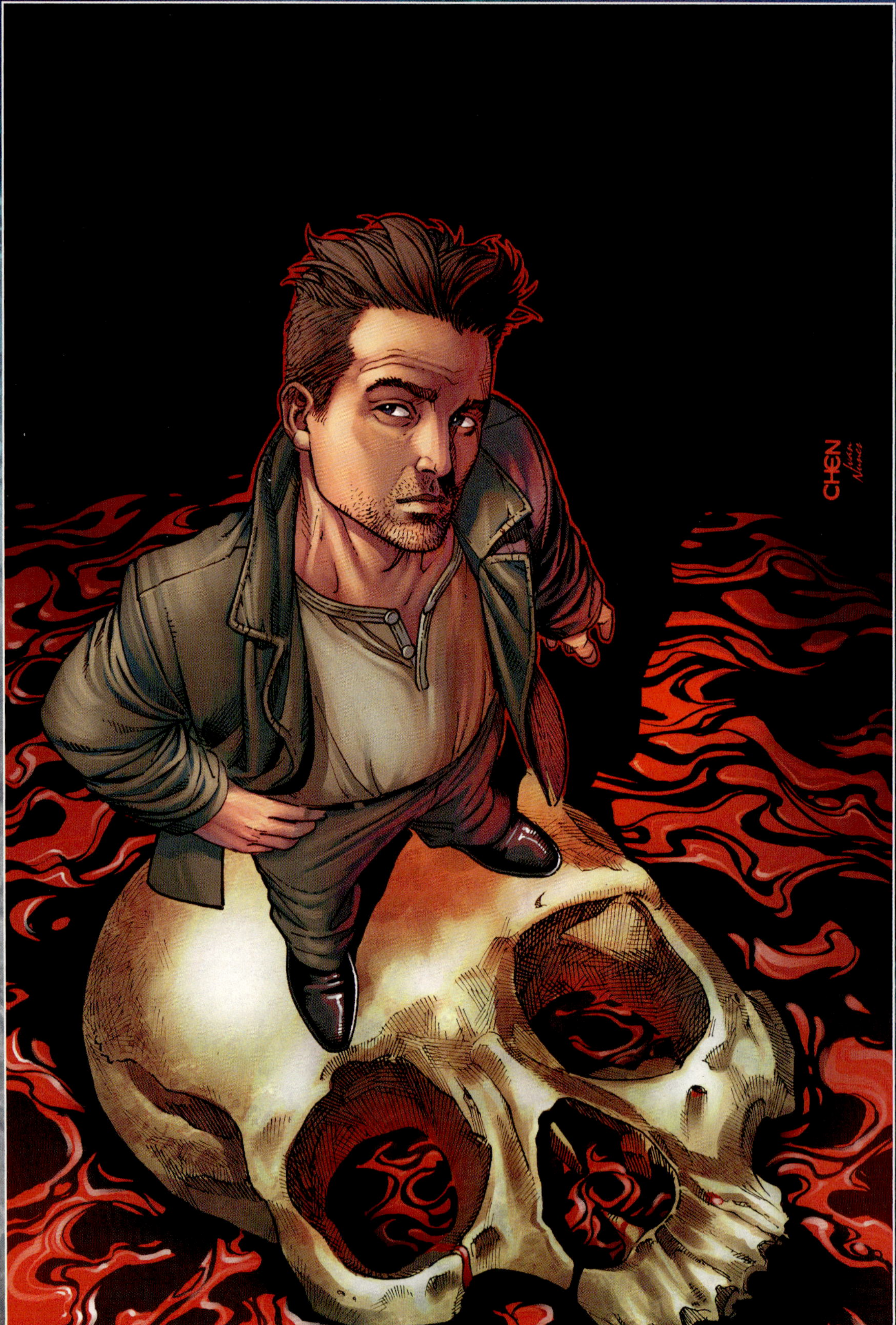
CHEN

issue #1 cards, comics, and collectibles exclusive cover by SEAN CHEN

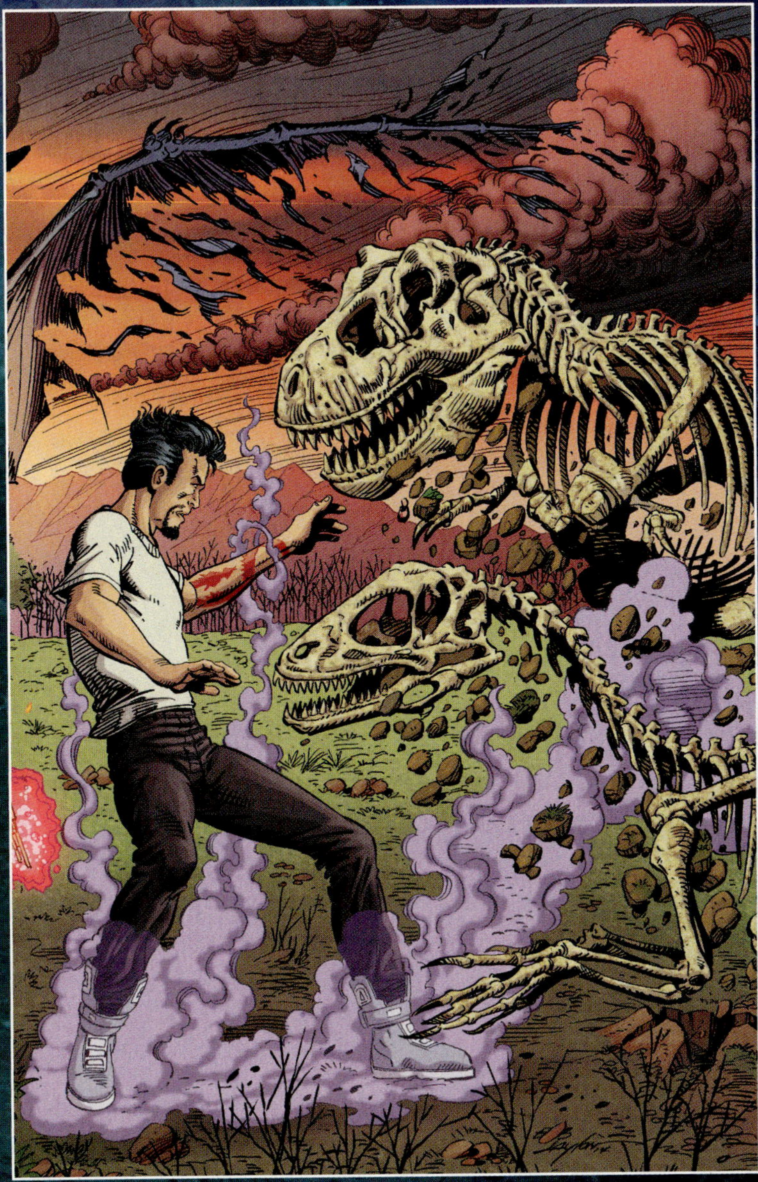

issue #1 sharps comics exclusive cover by BOB LAYTON
colors by MIKE CAVALLARO

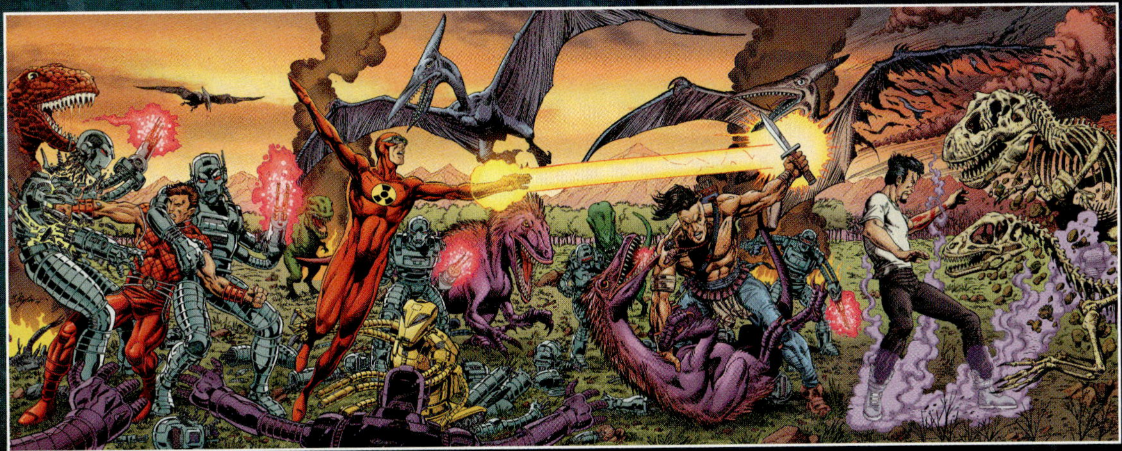

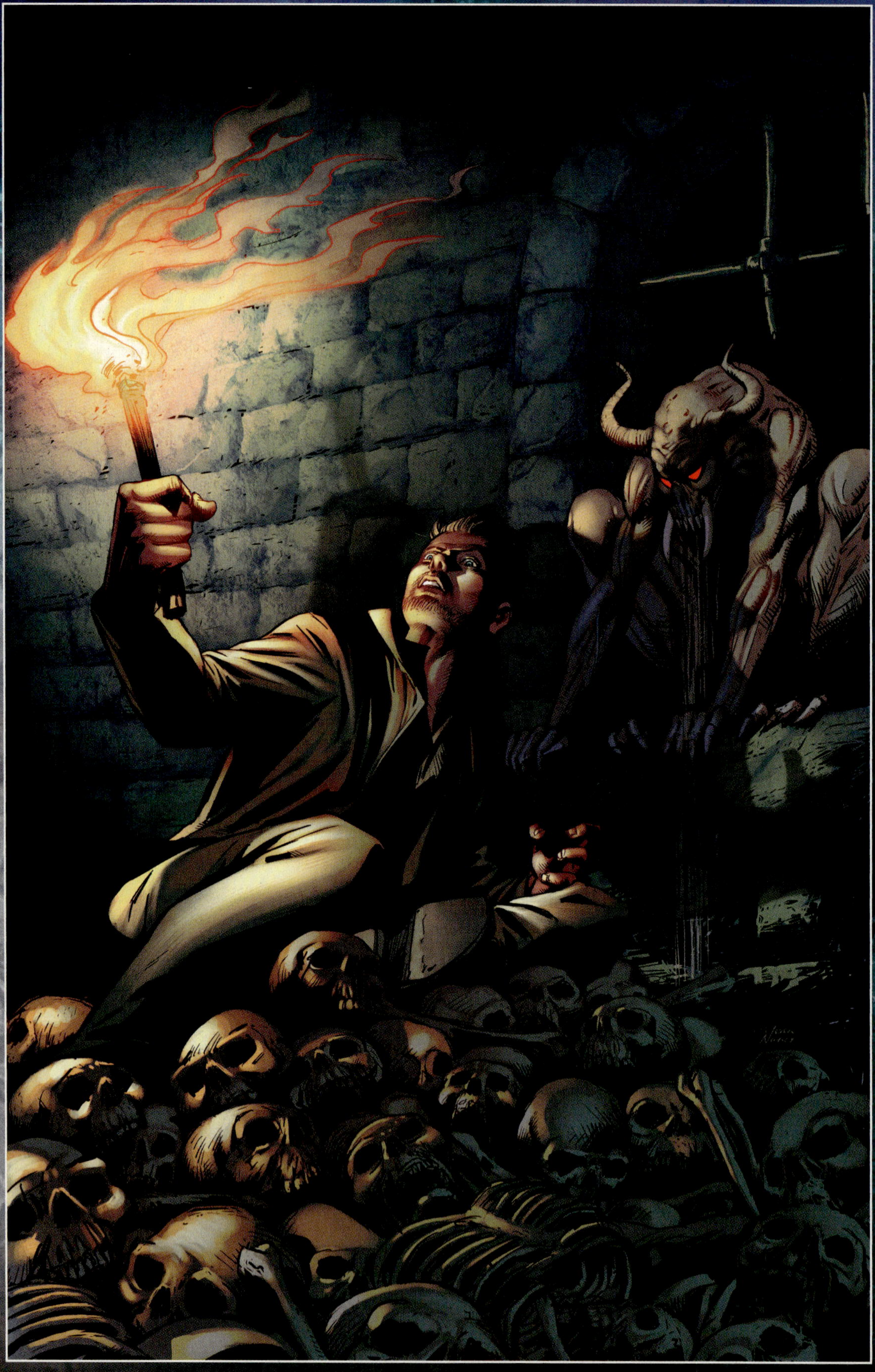

issue #1 second print cover by JOSÉ MALAGA
colors by IVAN NUNES

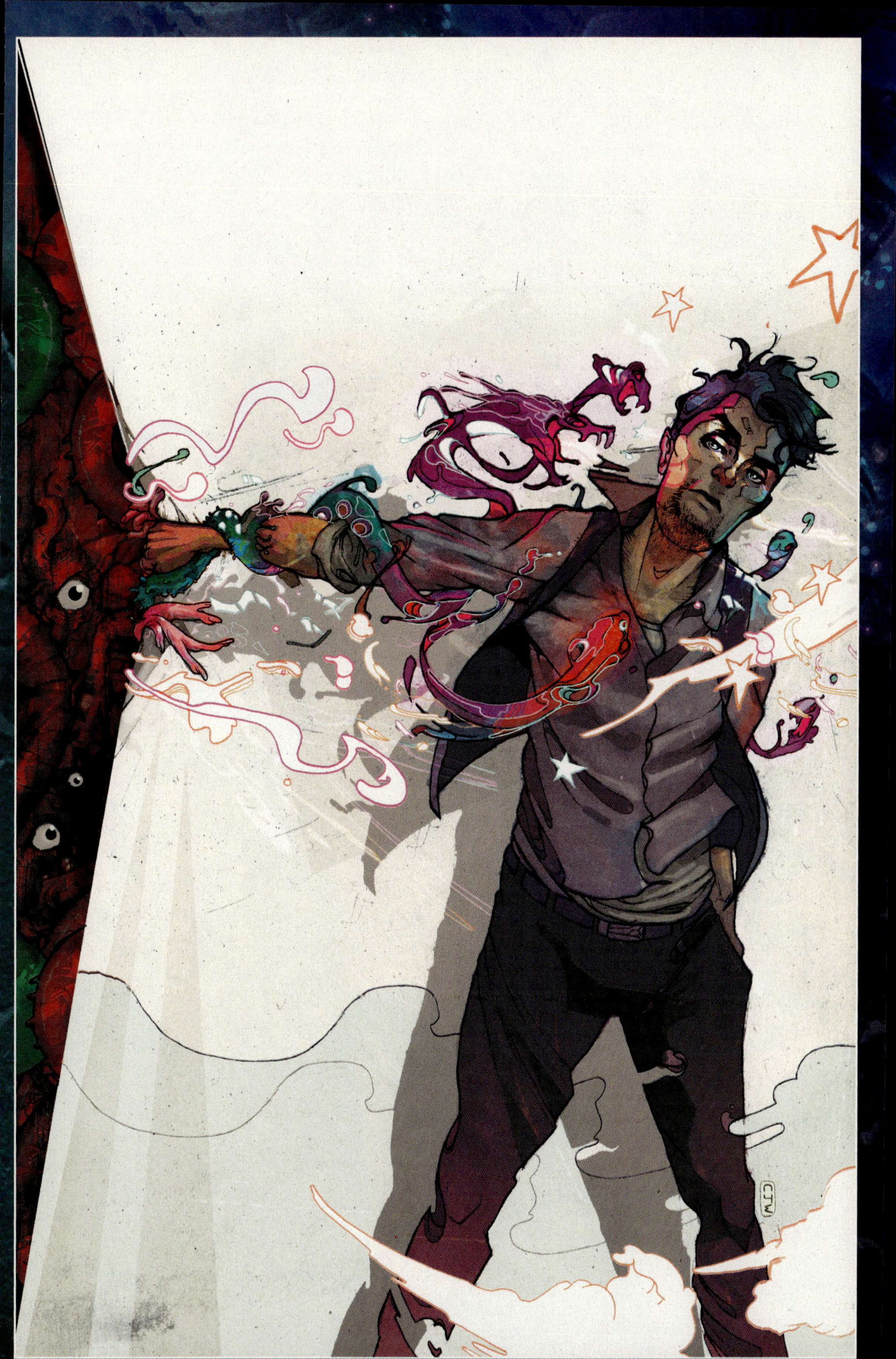
CJW

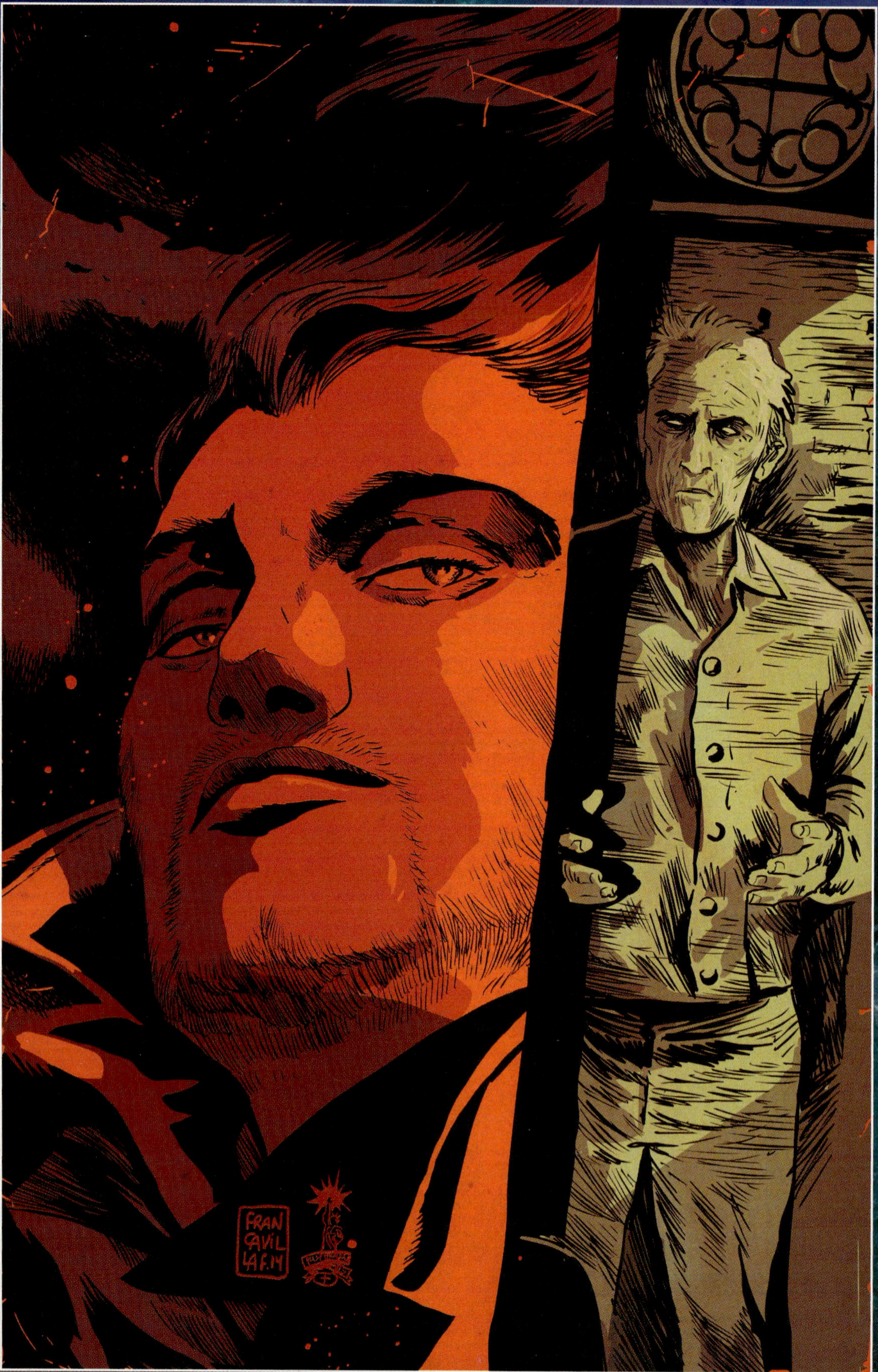
FRAN
CAVIL
LA F.14

issue #2 cover by FRANCESCO FRANCAVILLA

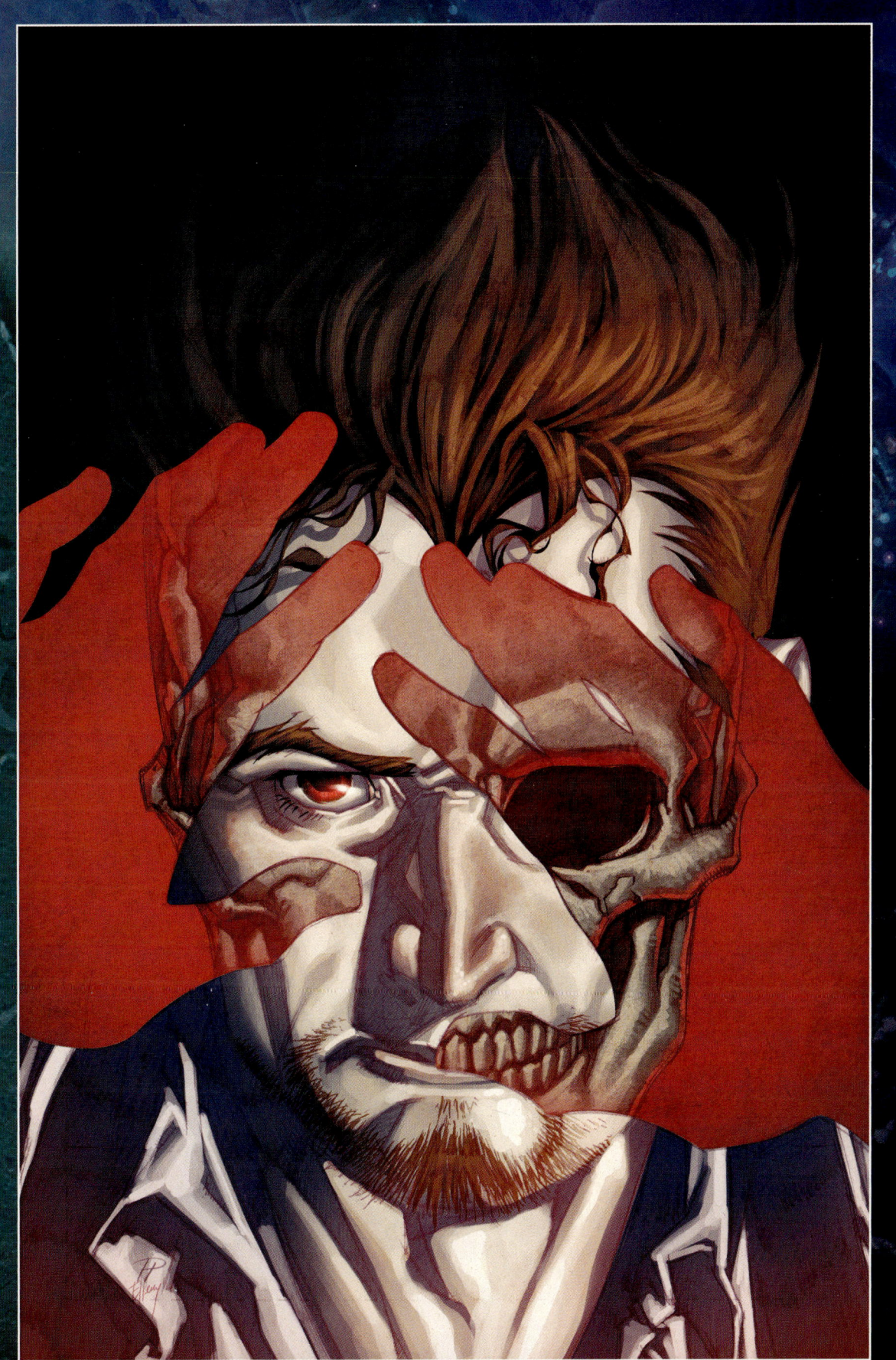

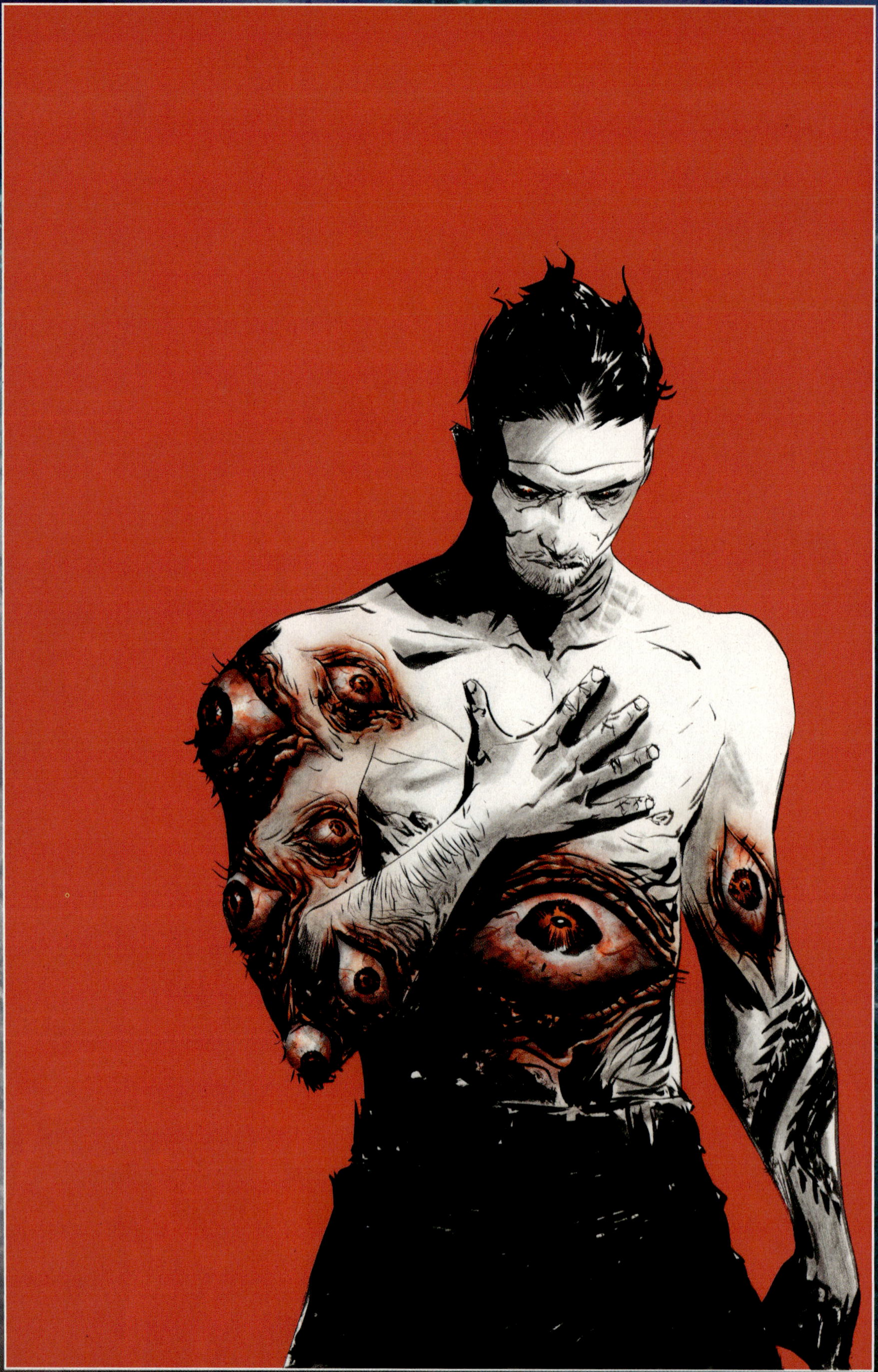

issue #2 cover by JAE LEE
colors by JUNE CHUNG

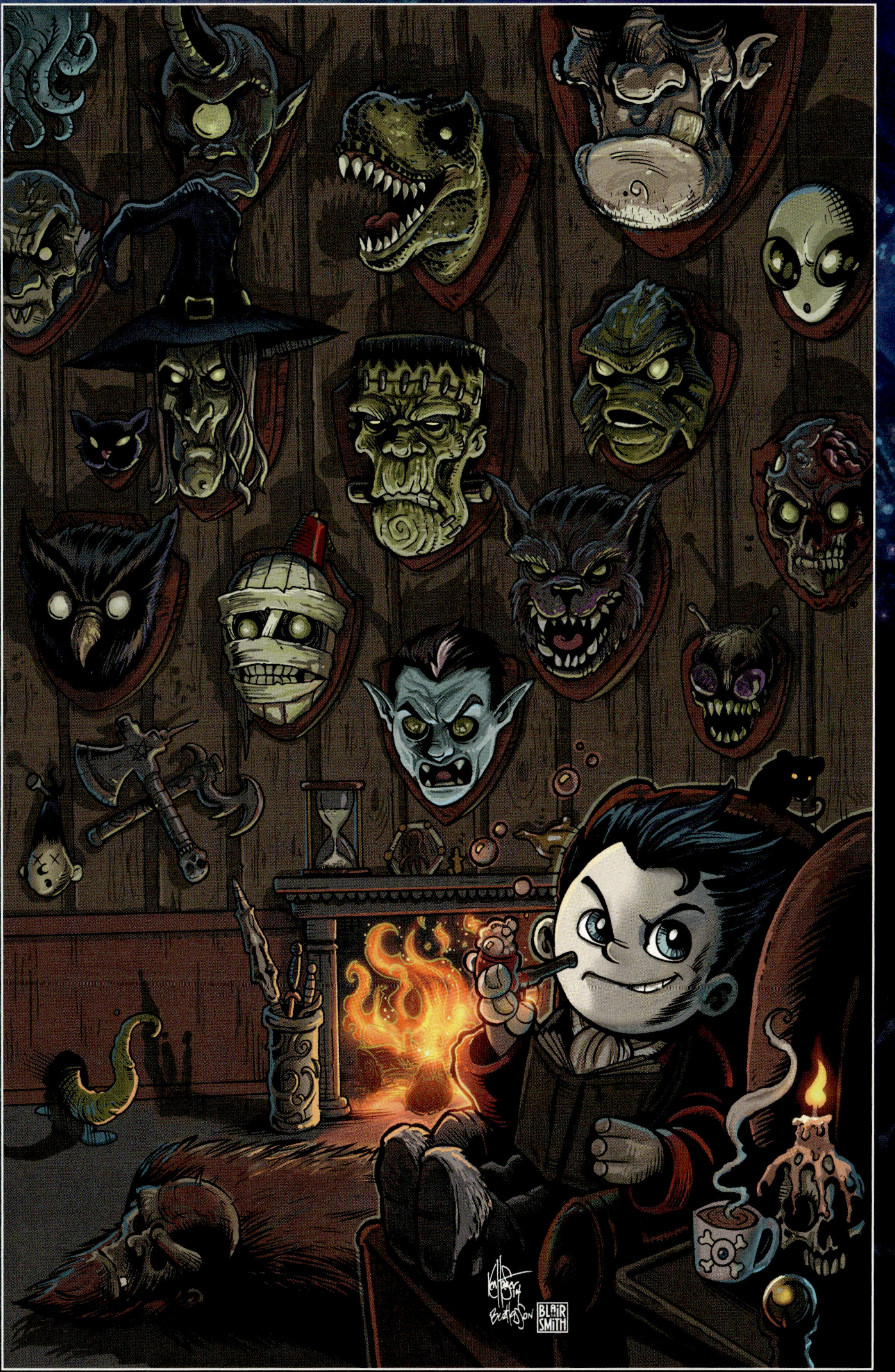
BLAIR SMITH

issue #2 cover by KEN HAESER

colors by BLAIR SMITH

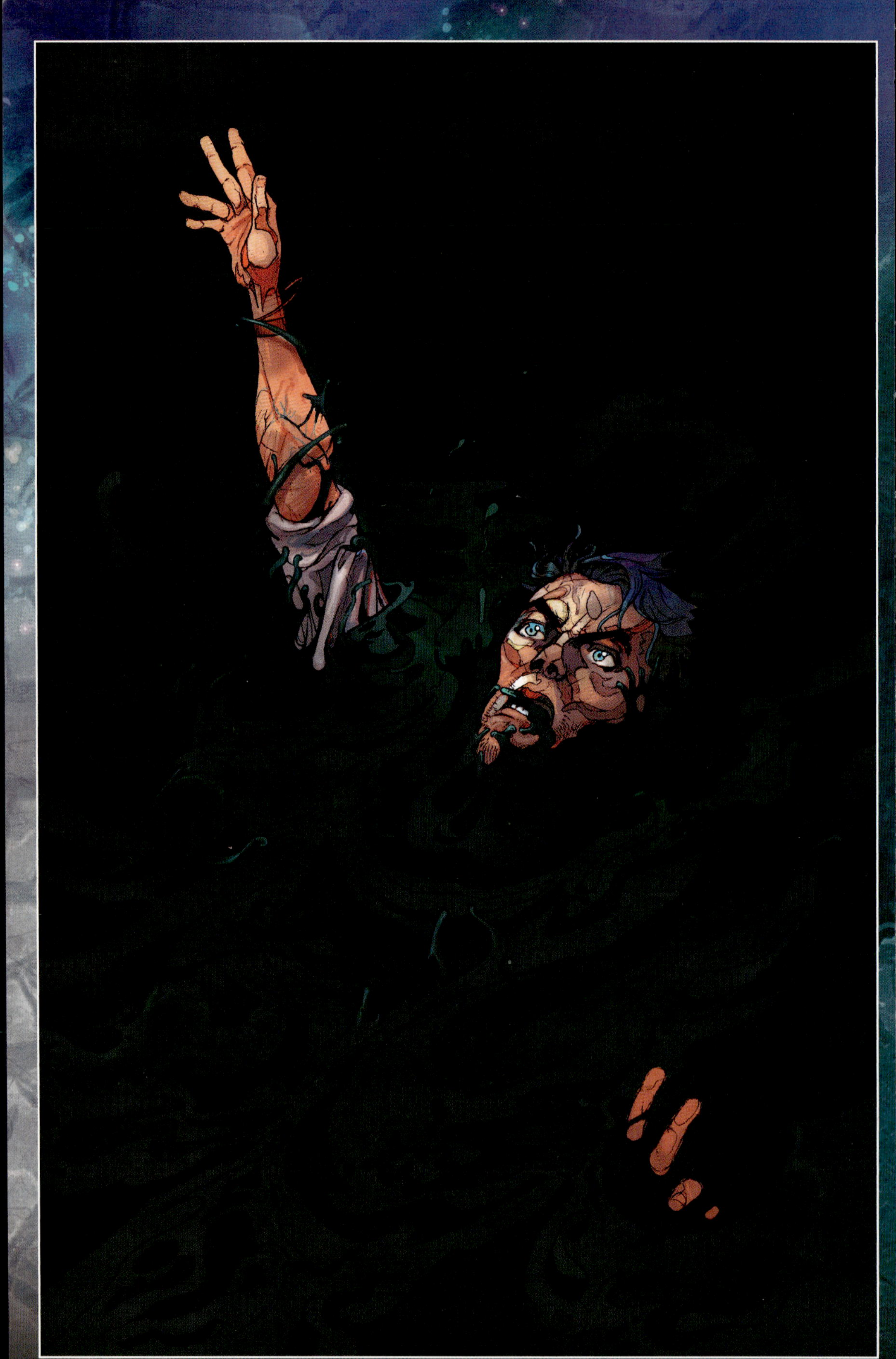

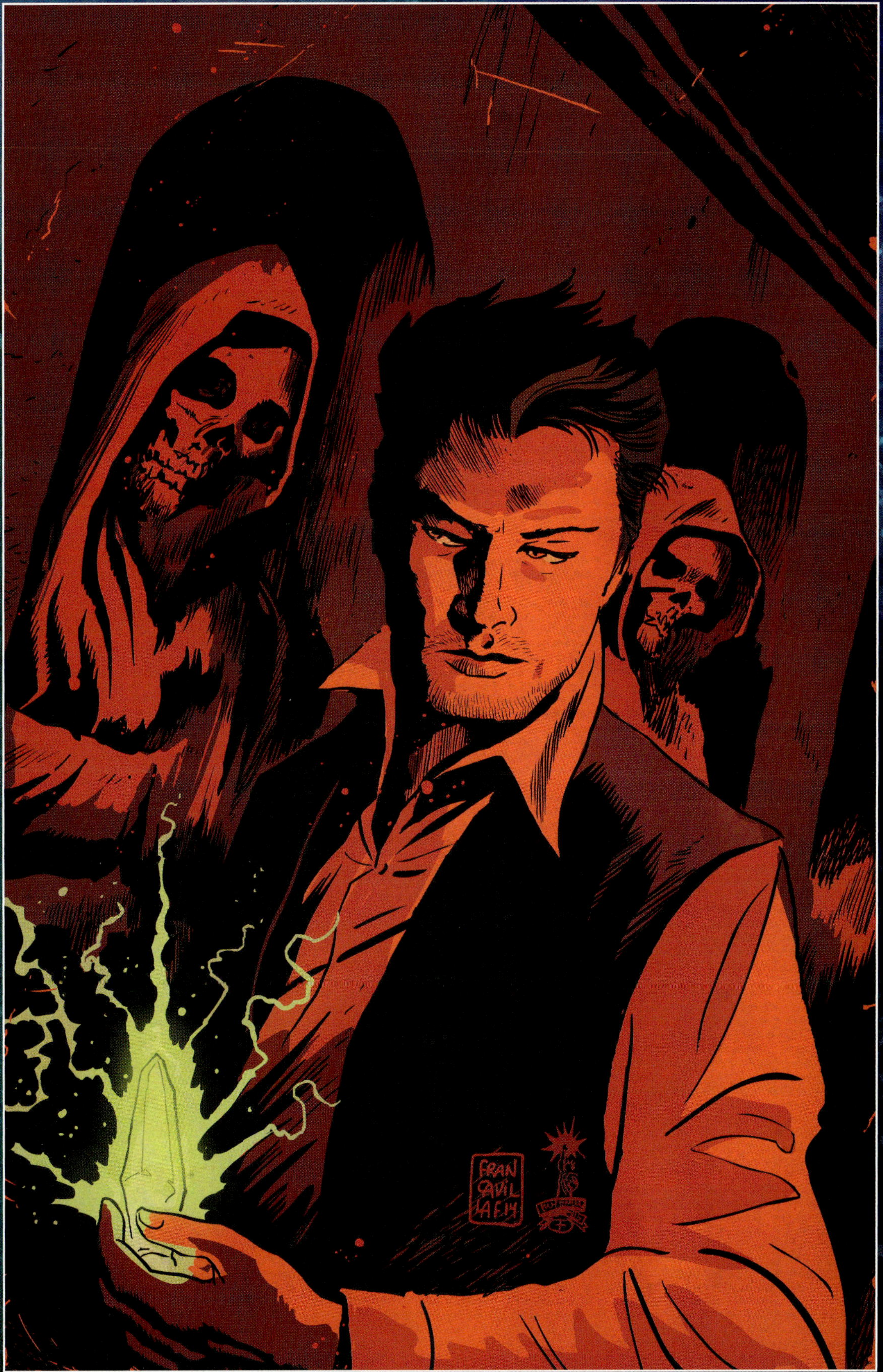
FRAN
CAVIL
LA F.14

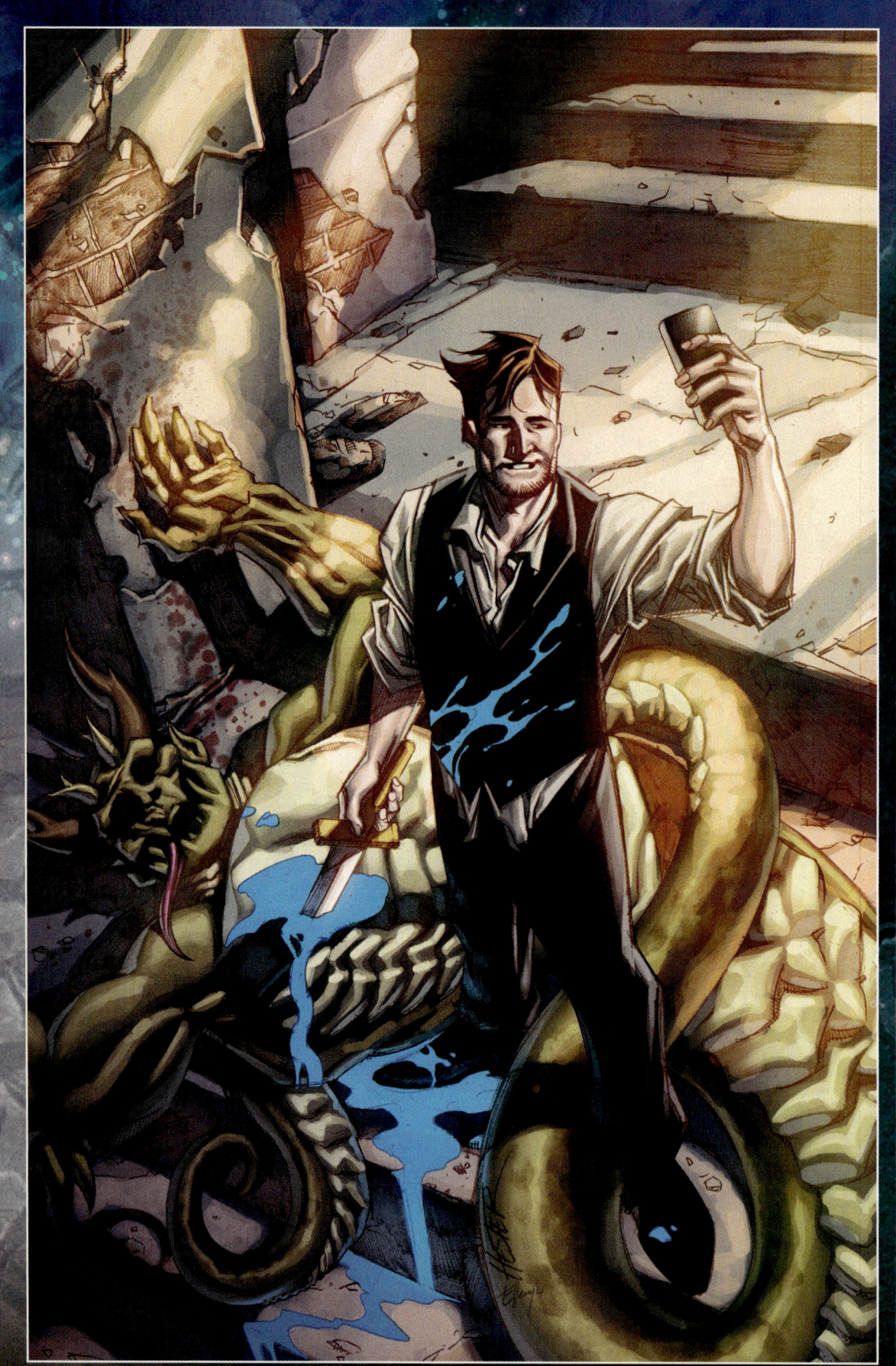

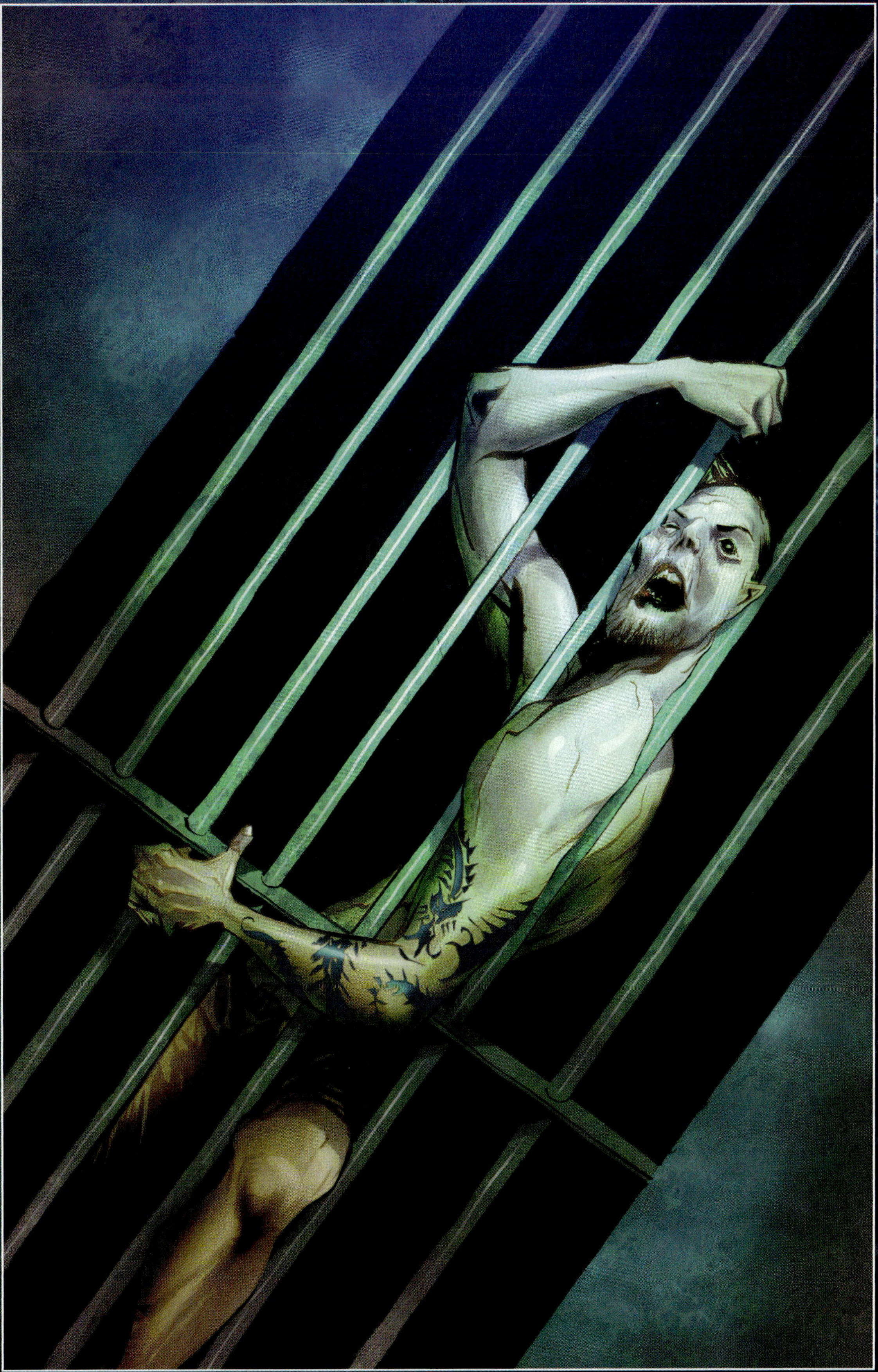

issue #3 cover by JAE LEE
colors by JUNE CHUNG

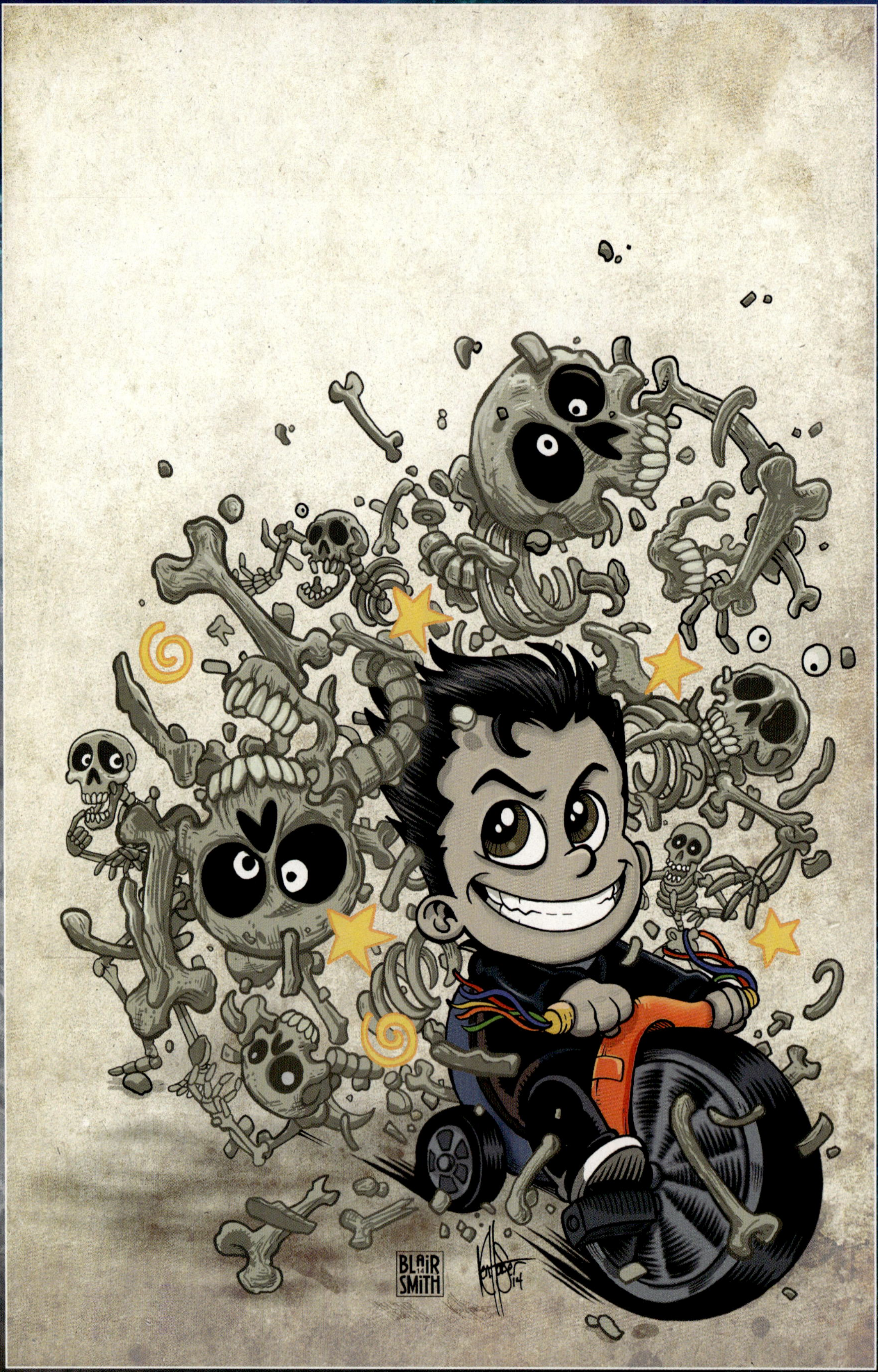
BLAIR SMITH

issue #3 cover by KEN HAESER
colors by BLAIR SMITH

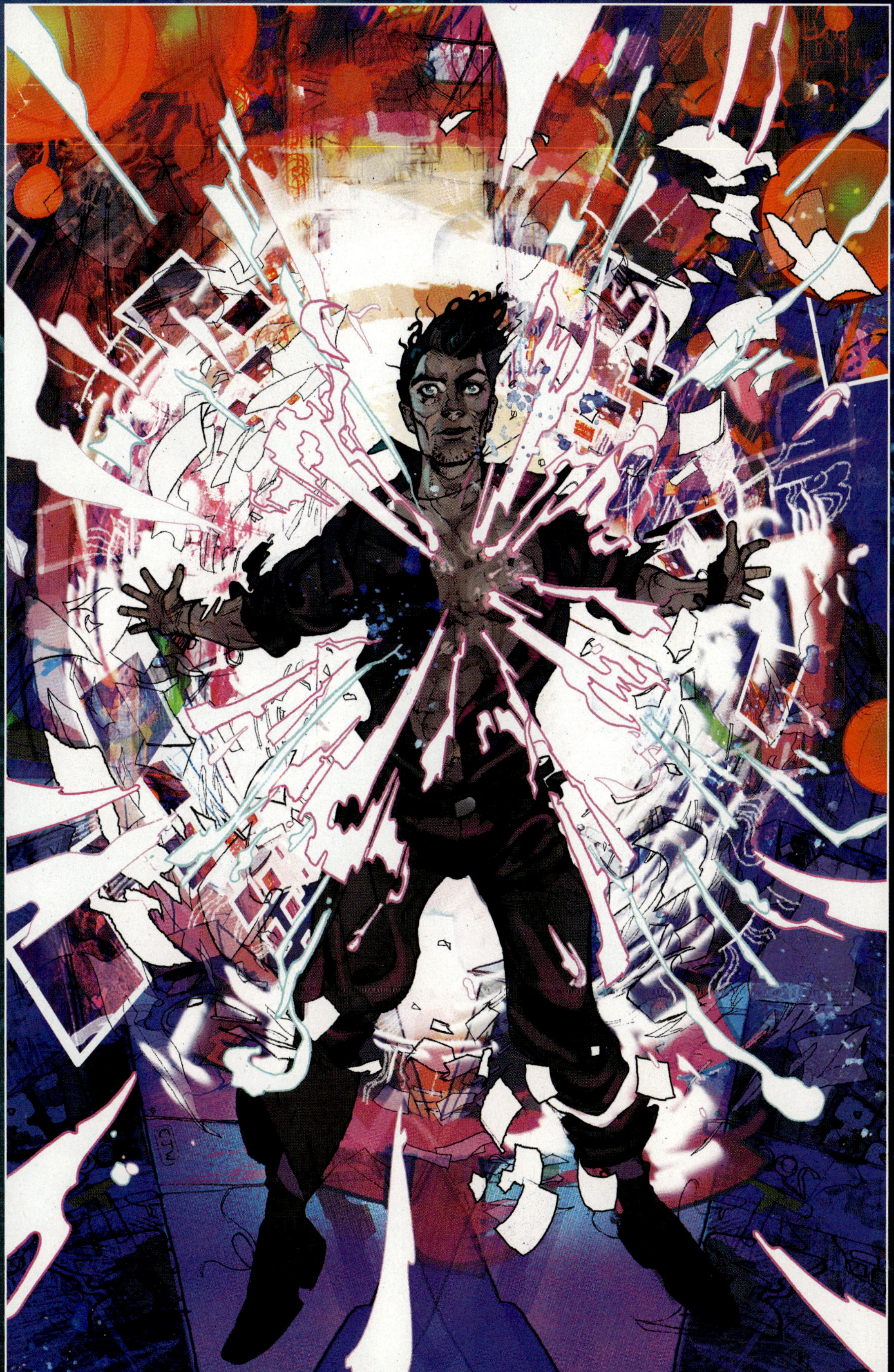

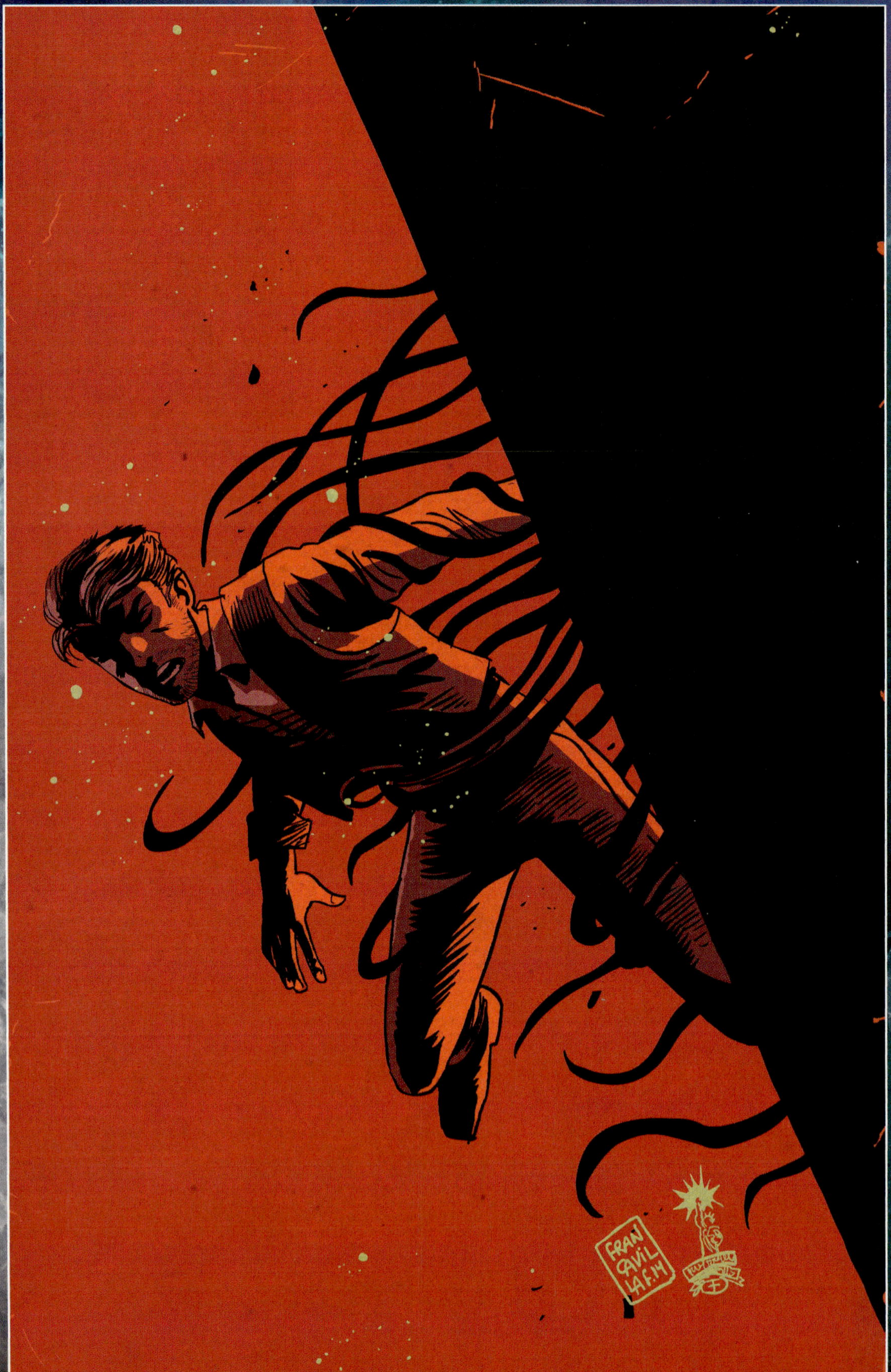

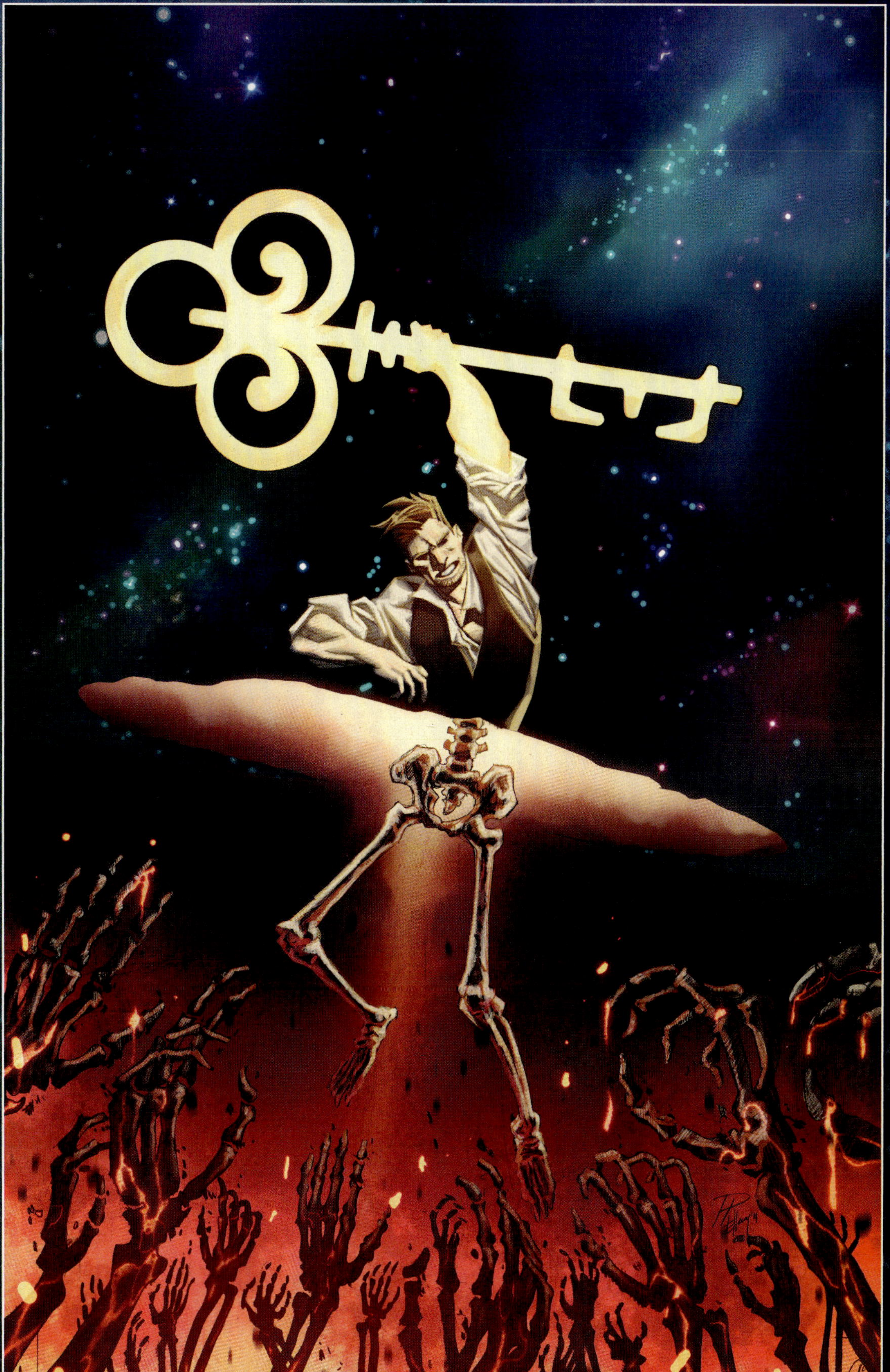

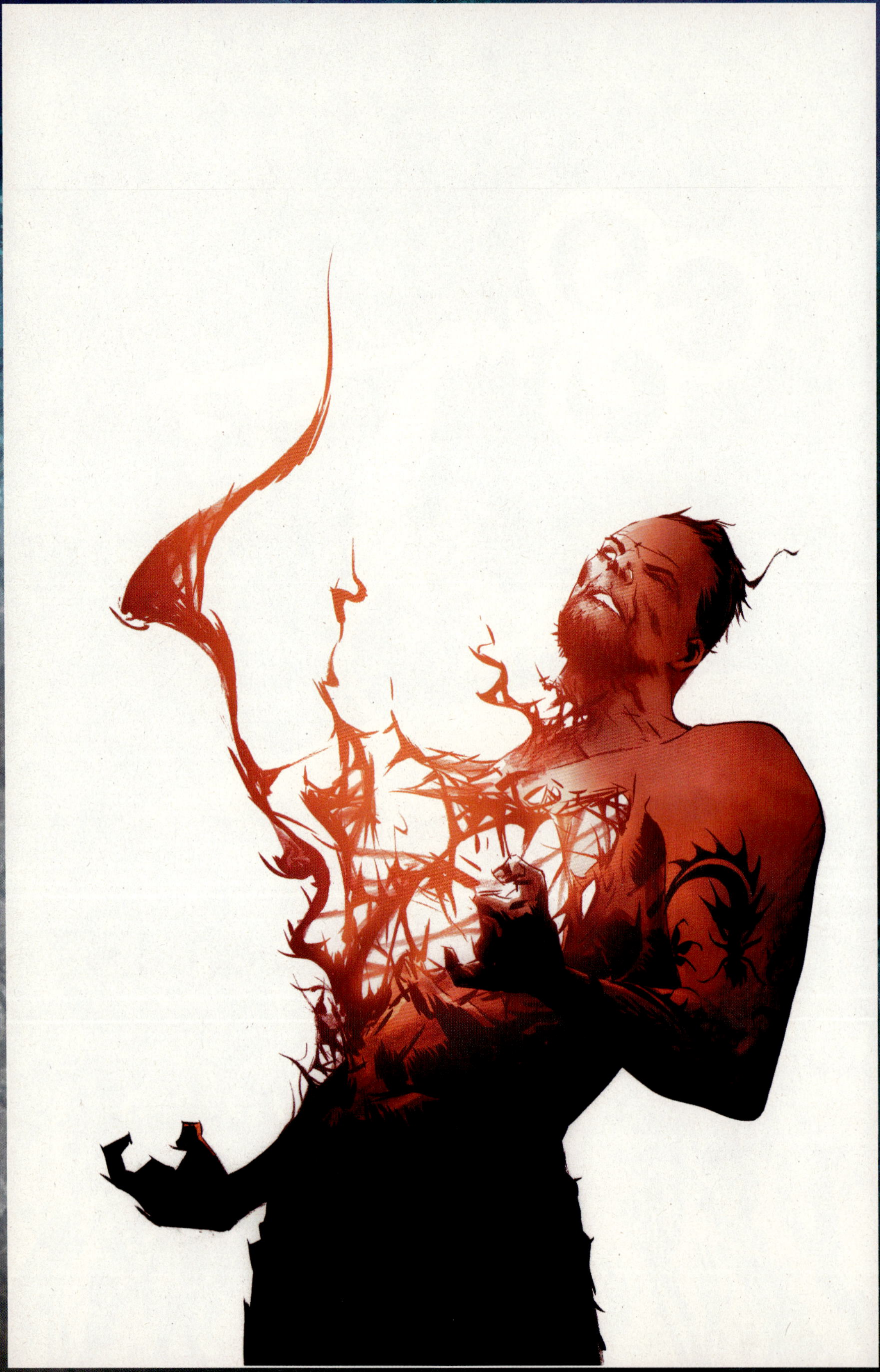

issue #4 cover by JAE LEE
colors by JUNE CHUNG

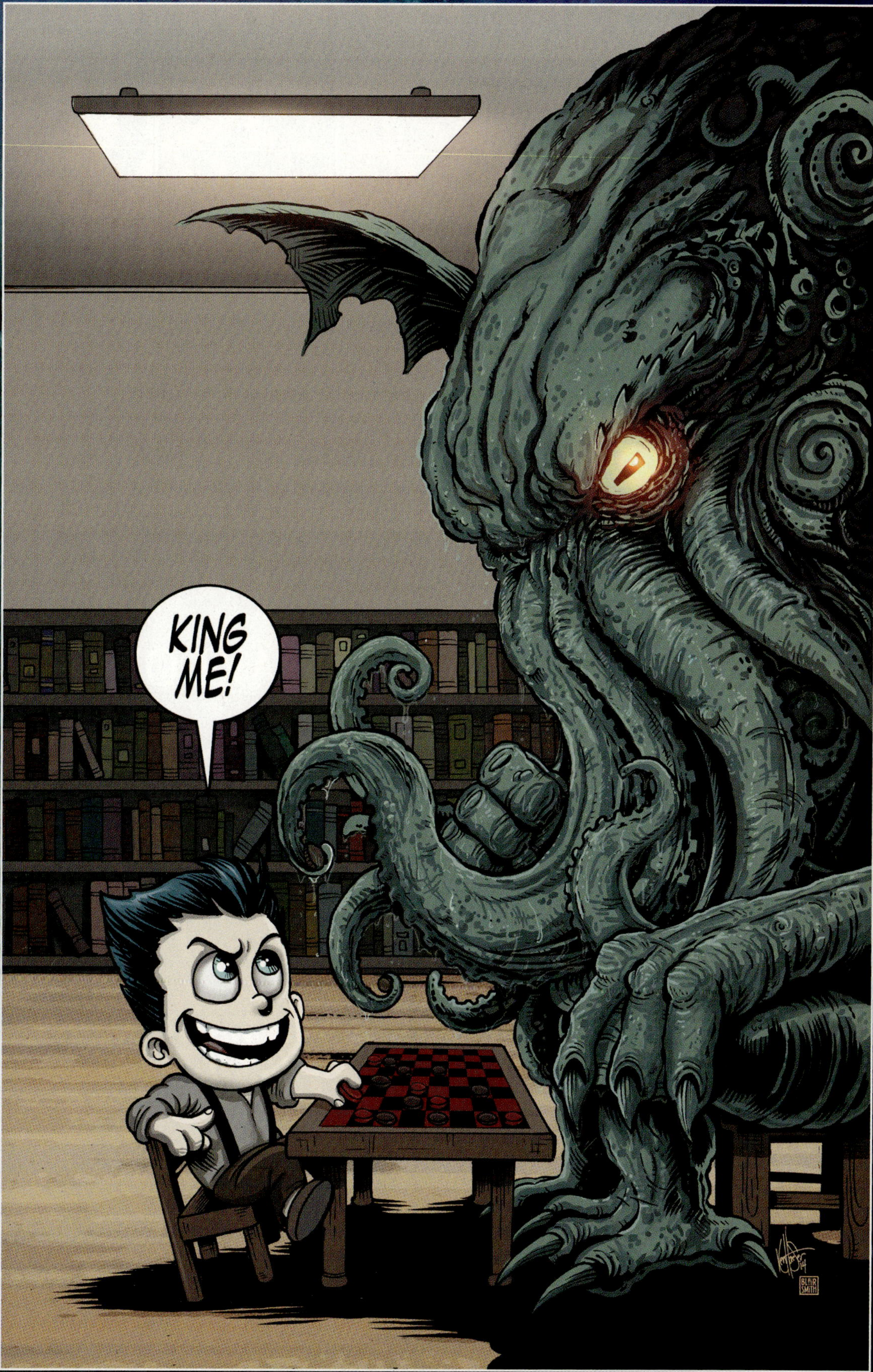
KING ME!

issue #4 cover by KEN HAESER
colors by BLAIR SMITH

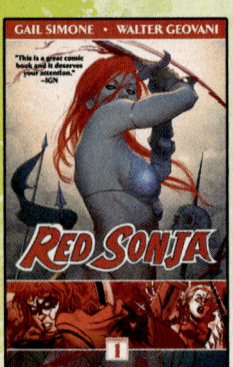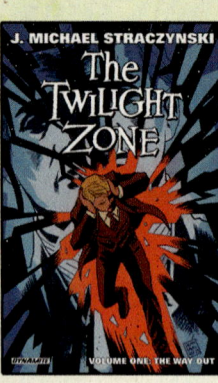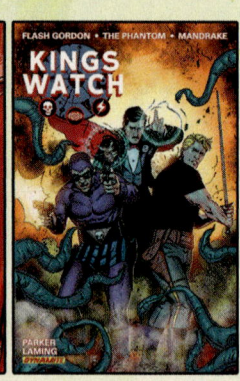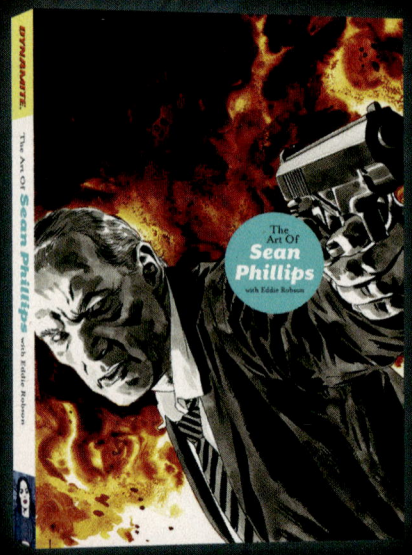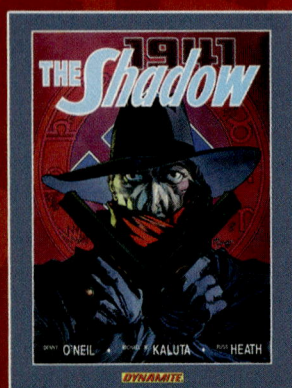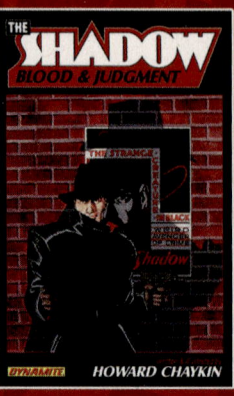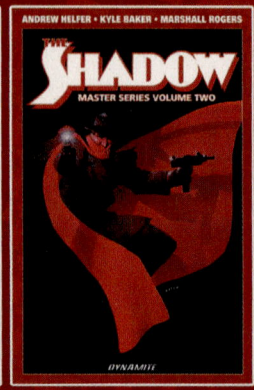